The GearMaker's Locket

by Shannon L Reagan

May your Gears
turn ever smoothly!

www.shannonlreagan.com

Dedicated to:

A friend and her snazzy locket.

Chapter 1

A big blob of oil dripped from the car suspended above me in the double bay garage. It splatted onto my arm, trickling around it, then plopped to the cement floor. I groaned and pushed a curl of red hair out of my face with the back of my hand. It was possible I was the grimiest girl in town, but that would be my life if I remained a mechanic.

I glanced at my watch. It was already an hour past closing—again. Why was I forced to do every last-minute repair? Constant gunk under my nails, overworked, a house filled with belongings to sort through... Gramma's belongings. A week off would help. But my boss hadn't relented yet and I wasn't getting my hopes up.

A forceful twist of the wrench settled the stubborn nut into place. I wiped my hands on the cloth hanging from my pocket.

"Surely there are cleaner machines out there," I mumbled. "And kinder bosses." Quitting my job was the most logical course of action. Gramma had wanted me to return to my studies when she was gone. A pang of sorrow dropped into my stomach. Would quitting be a mistake? I needed money. I already had this job and a place to live—Gramma's now lonely house.

I stepped out from under the car and lowered it, glancing out the bay doors. People were strolling down the road going about their evening, but no more vehicles had pulled in.

"Good. I can deal with Duke and go home." I sighed.

At the sink at the back of the garage I scrubbed and scrubbed until the skin of my arms stung. Still black stains lingered. I removed my coveralls, glancing regularly at the parking lot. I walked into the lobby, determination swelling in me.

My boss, Duke, was sitting behind the counter. "Copper Rose. Is that sedan fixed yet?" His flabby bulk spilled over the sides of his stool. I buried a cringe. He was always at the garage, looming over his worker bees, hardly ever lifting so much as an oil cap, yet filth coated his sweaty flesh.

"Yes. It's in bay one." I hesitated. "Duke? About that week off..."

Duke narrowed his eyes at me, his fat cheeks drooping. He tapped a pen on the counter nearly as fast as my heart was beating. "I can't do without ya."

"I'll work late the whole month after. I just have so much to do now that Gramma..."

"You'll work late anyway," he growled.

I steeled myself. Losing my temper would *not* help. "I have to pack up her things. Then—then I won't miss work anymore." I cringed internally. When had I been reduced to begging in order to keep that lousy job?

"Fine." Duke spat. "But only one week. I don't wanna lose business just 'cause yer grandma kicked the bucket."

I clenched my teeth. *It's your smell that will drive off business, you uncouth...* I bit back the sharp retort. I had to keep this job until I knew what to do next, until I decided... "Thank you."

The bell on the lobby door jingled and someone entered.

"Miss Locke, I was headed home from work and noticed the garage door was still open. Could you…" a woman from the other side of town said.

I grabbed my bag and coat from under the counter before the woman could finish what she was saying.

"Not so fast, Copper Rose." Duke's stool squealed as he leaned forward. "Yer takin' this one."

My nostrils flared. "I…" *Count… breathe… stay calm…* I had to stay in control. My skills were valuable to other people. I just needed time to mourn… I needed to be ready.

He grunted. "And I'm rethinkin' that time off." Spit flew from his mouth as he shook his finger at me.

I glanced at the woman paused at the door, concern painting her face. I turned slowly, grinding my teeth back and forth. Duke glared at me, his arms folded tightly over his chest.

No more. I smiled. "No problem, Duke. I quit!"

His jowls quivered. "You can't do that. No one else will hire you."

"What do you care? Forget the week off. I'm going back to college." I felt a mix of relief and fear palpating in my chest. Was deciding really this easy? Maybe living in the city wouldn't be so awful this time… since no one needed me at home.

"You? Why would they take back a trumped up drop-out like you? You'll come crawlin' back here in no time."

I flung my purse over my shoulder and strode to the door. The woman held it open, gaping at me as I stormed out. Duke threw scathing words at me. Words I refused to believe. I could make machines from scratch and fix anything made of metal. I hurried past on-lookers who'd paused to watch the action.

Their gazes followed my long strides down the several town blocks and out into rolling farm country.

My anger drained away as I passed the spring green of the country. Aging asphalt slipped under me. Maybe quitting was a bad idea, but it was too late to change that now. The only thing I could think to do was go back to school. Hopefully the Dean would keep his word to hold my scholarship. But what would I live on? Maybe I had enough to get by until I found a job at school. If I packed up the house quickly I could even make it to the coming semester. I kicked a rock. It skipped along the dirt and settled in the grass on the shoulder of the road. I had the beginnings of a plan.

What could I do with the family farm? How can a person even have a family farm without a family? I would never wake to the smell of Gramma's homemade pancakes again. No one would check on me and cheer me up on a tough day.

A hawk swooped over a field startling two horses. They thundered across the field throwing their heads. Shadows trembled as a slight wind drifted through the large maples along the road. A fragile quiet settled over me. I slowed my pace as the farmhouse came into view.

Birds flitted through the yard and butterflies kissed blossoms sprouting from the rich, though crowded flowerbeds. But the house seemed lifeless. The porch swing rocked in the breeze. I could almost see Gramma sitting there knitting, her frail wrinkled hand raising above her head to wave at me. I would miss her smile of pure delight when she saw me approaching.

Hesitating, I unlocked the door and entered. Cool air lay still in the hall. A slight mustiness tickled my nose. Gramma

4

had been gone for only a week but the house seemed to have died with her.

A creak came from the living room. "Gramma?" I sometimes expected her to be rocking in her chair, knitting needles furiously clicking. I stepped around the corner, glancing at the empty chair. Gramma's basket of yarn sat next to it, vaguely gray with dust. I grabbed the door-frame, leaning my forehead against the wood.

Will I ever get used to her being gone? I pounded a fist on the frame. Losing my only family? I wanted to scream and yell— *Unfair!*—but all I got was a pathetic, dull thud. I fought the tears burning up from the hole in my chest, and mumbled, "Oh, Gramma. I miss you."

A beam of late New England sunlight touched my arm, warming, comforting.

Framed needle point samplers of dainty flowers hung on the wall beside sepia-toned photos. The sturdy fireplace lay cold, medication bottles trailing across the mantel. Hand-crafted shelves and cabinets lined the walls, holding the belongings of a woman who no longer needed them. Several empty boxes waited by the couch. I'd intended to fill them with Gramma's belongings, but now I would gather up the pieces of my life as well.

I pulled down a picture of my mother to gaze at her green eyes and coppery red hair. It was like looking in a mirror. "You left me too," I said pulling one springy curl out of my face. When had I quit waiting for her to come back? I couldn't remember, but I knew it had been a long time ago. My Gramma would never tell me anything about her son, my father. Eventually I gave up asking.

I sniffled, putting down the photo. Dwelling on the past wouldn't help. There were too many ghosts there, shadows of those who were no longer with me.

Bam, bam, bam.

I jumped at the noise from the front door. I hurried to answer it.

"Oh, Reverend Patterson. Good afternoon." I sighed in relief at the sight of a man I knew well. He'd never stopped visiting Gramma during her illness. I invited him in. He wore jeans and a black shirt with a little white collar. His casual style put the local farmers at ease.

"I wanted to see if there is anything I can do for you," the reverend said. "I heard about your job. Sorry. Small town rumors move fast."

I chuckled. "Thank you. There might be something you could do." My mind was racing with ideas and plans.

He moved into the dim hall. "I'm very sorry for your loss. I can hardly believe she's gone."

I rubbed one eye, hoping it was dust. I followed him to the living room where he stopped and turned to me.

The reverend slowly looked around the room, his eyes falling on the boxes. "You're packing? I assume you will be leaving us."

"I was going to box up anything of Gramma's that I didn't need, but now I've decided to go back to MIT."

He nodded, a smile touching his mouth.

I waved for him to take a seat. "But I'm worried about the farm. The back forty is being used for hay by our neighbor, but there aren't any animals anymore. I don't want it to sit uncared for." I busied myself pulling open the checkered curtains.

"What about Leatha—I mean, your mother?"

Glancing at my mother's photo, I shrugged.

Reverend Patterson shifted in his seat. "Oh, sorry. I thought she might have at least let you know where she is."

I shook my head. "No."

He shifted his feet against the old brown carpet. "MIT is a good idea. You can do better than being a car mechanic. Your grandmother always said you were doing rather well. She talked about your talent for robotics and engineering. A true prodigy, she called you."

I sat on the edge of a wooden chair near the cold fireplace. "Reverend—I'm not a prodigy. I'm just good at what I do." I looked down at my worn sneakers. College felt a world away after spending a year caring for my ailing grandmother.

"You could rent out the farm until you're ready to settle down. There's nothing wrong with getting away from here. Even your grandmother left this town to explore the world for a while. Though what she did, other than marry and have a son, still remains a mystery. Did she ever tell you where she traveled to?" He smiled and rubbed a hand on one knee.

"No, but she said she never intended to return here. You know how she loved big trees?" I asked.

"Yes. The bigger the better."

"She told me she loved them because my grandfather lived where the trees were bigger than skyscrapers. Of course she was exaggerating, but it made her happy to remember it that way," I said. A pang of sadness hit me right in my chest. "It's hard to believe she's gone."

"Of course." He stood, glancing around again. He was quiet while I wiped tears from the corners of my eyes. The sudden silence permeated the room.

I stood up, ideas coming to me. "Uh, renting out the farm is a good idea. I could use the money to get by while I'm at school. But the furniture, I won't need most of the stuff in the house." Yes. I would put my belongings in the barn and find a renter. "I don't have time to sell the all of it. I wouldn't get much money anyway. Does anyone in the church need anything?"

"Maybe you could give me a quick tour and point out the items you intend to get rid of," the reverend said, pulling his cellphone from his pocket.

"Yes." I grabbed a box near Gramma's chair then showed him to the kitchen. "The table and chairs, as well as the hutch, can go."

He typed on the phone. "Lovely."

I took Reverend Patterson through each room as he entered the list into his phone. He watched me place unusual mechanical tools and devices into my box next to books and photos that meant something to me.

In the laundry room, a grease-stained coverall was draped over the washing machine for a third time through. I tossed it into the garbage with a smile. I grabbed another one of my inventions from a shelf as I walked out.

"What exactly are those?" he asked.

"Oh." I handed him a tea strainer that looked like a long legged bird. "This would pull the tea strainer out of the water when the tea had steeped long enough. I made it for Gramma

8

before I moved back home. Most of my inventions were meant to help her as she got weaker."

"Fascinating. They look old fashioned yet they're functional and unique." He tapped the tea strainer and it bobbed up and down, reaching for the cup it was meant to dip into. He placed it into my box.

I placed another machine in next to the tea strainer. "I used whatever I could find most of the time."

We climbed the stairs. I set the full box inside my room and grabbed another empty one. The house didn't seem so lonely with the reverend there to keep the conversation light. The idea of leaving was settling deeper into me. I didn't have to know what I would do after college. There was time to figure that out later. I stepped up to the hallway wall, decorated with framed photos.

"Quite a lot of things on my list. You're sure about all this?" he asked, tapping his finger on his chin. I looked at him from the hall where I was pulling a photo of my great-grandmother from the yellowed wallpaper.

"Yes. I won't use the old furniture." I pulled down an image of great uncle Henry and a distant cousin named Bertha, all long buried in the old graves next to Gramma's freshly churned resting place. "There's not much more. Only the beds in those three rooms and the dressers."

He smiled, and peeked into the room across from mine.

"Sure." I went back to pulling down photos. A creak came from the end of the hall.

Reverend Patterson was climbing the stairs to the attic. "What's up here?"

I took two quick steps toward him and reached for his arm. "Oh, up there? It's mostly broken junk, but I'll pile anything of value on the porch for you. There are some family archives and a box of text books that I'll need."

He stepped back down.

I'd been holding my breath. Filling my lungs, I looked up at the closed door at the top of the stairs. As a child I'd thought treasure would be hidden in the attic's cobwebby nooks and crannies, but there wasn't actually anything special. I shook off the protective feeling.

"This seems to be a comprehensive list here." The reverend tapped the side of his phone. "Some men can come by with trucks over the next few days, if that's all right with you."

"I might be in and out, but you know where the key is." I put a picture into the box then led the way back downstairs and out the front door.

"She really was an incredible woman, always thinking of everyone else." He looked out at the large maple in the center of the front yard.

I should say something, I thought, but no words came. New leaves peeked from the winter-weary branches. I gazed to the spot where I used to lie, looking up at the branches swaying like a giant's arms over me.

"You take care of yourself, young lady. If you need anything else let us know." He put a hand on my shoulder. The pang returned.

"Thank you," I replied. He smiled gently and turned away. I watched him leave down the long, gravel driveway.

Behind me, the silence in the house felt like a weight

pulling me down. Maybe I was making a mistake. I didn't know how to fit into the big city. But I was never going back to Duke's Garage. I backed into the entry, resisting the need to shut the door, hating the oppression of enclosed space. Latching it, I dashed up the stairs, avoiding the living room and the empty rocker. I leaned my head against the worn attic stair rail and breathed deeply.

Looking up at the attic door, a shiver ran through me. "It's just an attic." But I put my foot on the first step. *I might as well get to it. The quicker the sorting is done, the sooner I can move on.* The old door creaked as I opened it. Musty air swooped over me, tickling my nose.

Cardboard boxes guarded the edges of the room and sat on sheet-covered furniture. A fancy bird-cage, curtained in cobwebs, decorated a tilting dresser near the octagonal window. "Oh, Gram. Did you keep everything?" I moaned. I grabbed a box and pulled it open. Aged photos looked up through films of haze. *No books here.* Still the photos drew me in and I carefully wiped the dust off each one as I reminisced. Faces familiar and friendly passed through my hands. Familiar and friendly, but gone.

I remembered sorting through these photos in my early teens searching for some sign of my father, my grandfather, anyone that might still be alive. But there was nothing.

The light was fading quickly and the small, dim bulb swinging from the ceiling cast eerie shadows. I looked around, wanting to find my books before daylight left entirely.

Tick, tick, tick…

I paused, straining to find the source of the ticking. Stepping past a box that bore my childhood scrawl on its side and then the near the window, I searched. The sound grew louder. It was coming from a leather steamer trunk jutting out from under an old desk.

Groaning at the solid weight of it, I heaved it into the walkway. I had never seen it before. It was beautiful. Even the tarnished latch was ornate. I opened it and a thrill shivered through me. The rusty hinges squealed. The ticking seemed to speed up as if excited by this game of hot and cold.

On the very top was a black and white photo of a young Gramma. She embraced a light haired man. Smiles of such joy and togetherness covered their faces. Had he died or left her? Why didn't she go back? I squinted at the aged photo. They stood in front of a very large tree trunk. Or it appeared to be a tree. It would have to be bigger than even the sequoias. Where were they? It had to be a trick of the light.

Pulling out several lacy Victorian dresses, I looked gently through pieces of jewelry, photos and strange trinkets below them. Why had I never seen these things before? I had been in this attic constantly as a child, but never found such obvious reminders of a time and place Gramma wouldn't talk about. Gramma's missing life; the trunk was full of treasure.

A small photo slipped from the stack in my hand and landed on the floor by my knee. A baby looked back at me with deep, dark, soulful eyes—like Gramma's. The face was round, the cheeks pudgy. Flipping it, I found the initials D. S. written in elegant script.

Hairs on my arm stood on end and my heart skipped a beat. Could it be Gramma's baby? Could it be my father? There was something about the image that left me curious.

Sifting through Gramma's lost life I felt like she was there beside me. It eased the ache a little.

As the last light of day sliced through the dingy attic window, something glimmered at the bottom of the trunk. The noise was so clear this had to be the source. I scooped up a large pendant on an intricate chain. It dangled through my fingers, the links strong yet elegant. The pendant was round with filigree etching framing a window of glass. A series of small gears turned in rhythmic harmony, clink, clink, clinking inside. How could it be running after all this time? It didn't have watch hands, but it did have a small clasp. *A locket?*

Such a work of mechanical genius intrigued me. My palm warmed as the turning gears seemed to beat in tandem with my heartbeat. The faint clink, clink, clink filled my ears. The filigree carvings seemed to glow. I flipped it over again and rubbed the surface, trying to figure it out. It wasn't a watch so why did it have gears, and what source of power kept it running? Clack, clack, clack—Clunk, Clunk, Clunk… The volume ascended as I reached for the clasp and carefully flipped it open.

Inside, the teeth of little metal gears interlaced and glistened—turning, turning, turning in perfect rhythm. Awed, I looked closer… Clunk, clunk, clunk. Light dazzled my eyes, sparkling and shimmering. Wind whooshed around me, spinning hair into my face. The turning gears pounding, pounding, pounding. My stomach roller-coaster dropped as my hair blew about. Still the gears turned, clack, clack, clacking with the beat of my heart.

I plunged into darkness, my breath coming in gasps. Cold sweat covered my palms. The clunk and clack of the gears reverberated in my head. Eyes closed, I spun, lost in the vortex.

Chapter 2

Clunk, Clunk, Clunk…

I landed on my feet, light surrounding me. A person collided into me. I flipped my hair from my eyes and looked around attempting to regain my footing. *What?* A crowd of strangely dressed men and women swept past me in two directions. My jaw dropped and hands shook. *Where am…?* Someone bumped roughly against me again.

"Hey. Get back to the UnderCity where your type belong," a man yelled. He scowled back at me as he walked away.

Metal skyscrapers rose above me, higher and higher. High enough to dwarf the Empire State Building. A huge clock regally displayed exposed brass gears. It clacked away, beats resounding from above. I was surrounded by a whole city of impossibly tall buildings, their sharp angles reaching to touch the sun. Ornate metals and colored glass decorated their walls like spots on a giraffe. I looked from the locket in my hand to the enormous clock. The locket quietly ticked like nothing had changed. *Where am I?* My mind screamed.

I spun around, looking this way and that. I was on a wide causeway spanning the chasm between the buildings. The crowd wore a strange amalgam of fashion, like elegant Victorian styling and the leather and metal of a rock band thrown into the blender. Lace, chains and sophistication.

"Wha..." I gasped looking around at the edgy wonderland. Everything felt real, but how could it be?

The flow of people increased, pushing me against a solitary steel railing. Puffy clouds drifted lazily under me as I grabbed the thin rod and froze, one foot nearly off the edge. Air burst from my lungs in short gasps and cold sweat trickled down my cheek as I froze, one foot nearly off the edge. I was so far up that the abyss grew dark five—no ten stories down. My eyes got lost in the depths. A walkway suspended in the air between buildings? How far up was I?

My throat constricted. I pushed my way back to the edge of one of the buildings and flat against its metal wall. People shoved past me. They traveled over the bridge with no apparent regard for the dizzying void below. The chilly wall sucked heat from my back while the locket flared warm in my clenched fist.

My breath came in ragged gasps. Where was I? What had happened? Everything looked real, but it had to be a dream. Closing my eyes, I breathed deep, focusing. *Wake up.* The noise of people and the clack of the tower clock above still rang in my ears. *This is a dream. Copper Rose! Wake up!*

I opened my eyes and still the people came down the wide walk. A man swung his fancy cane and it smacked against my leg. Pain throbbed up it. *No—how can this be real? Why can't I wake up?*

The locket! The gears were quietly ticking inside the cover. Something was strange about the metal jewelry—something lifelike in its tiny gears that seemed to pay attention when I looked at them. It altered slightly to match the beat of my heart. Had the locket brought me here?

"Ok—Home," I whispered and flipped open the locket.

Nothing.

"Take me home," I begged, flipping it open again. Still nothing happened. People hustled along heedless of others. A woman's handbag hit me. She glared and sniffed before moving on. A group of chortling young men shoved one of their buddies into me. The crowd continued on through the narrow walk. I pushed away from the sky bridge until I found a dead end passageway enclosed inside one of the buildings. I dashed into the dim space, gasping. I slid down the cold metal wall, immersed in the shadows of the empty hall.

"Take me home—please," I begged, flipping the cover of the locket one last time. Nothing.

My hands lay dejectedly in my lap. "No! I'm stuck."

"Excuse me?"

I looked up with a start to find a young man leaning into the alley. His eyes were dark, but lively. He adjusted the asymmetrical lapels of his red-brown leather coat as he stepped toward me. A chain, stretching from his pocket to his belt, jingled against his grey suede pants. His charcoal-black hair spiked almost comically.

"Sorry?" I said.

He stepped closer and pointed at the locket. "That's lovely." He gestured to the walkway. "I—I couldn't help but notice as I walked past you."

I eyed him. "Oh—thank you." I said. I bowed my head, but he took another step toward me. A crooked smile split his boyish face. I pushed an unruly curl off my cheek and his eyes flickered up.

"You have really beautiful hair." He scratched his chin. "It

16

looks like copper."

When would I wake up? I didn't even know if this—this place I was in—was safe. This man could be a thief or mugger. Though the smirk on his face and the mischievous tilt of his head made him look more like a curious puppy, eager to please.

"What's your name?" he asked. He grinned, so close now he towered over me. I closed my hand around the locket, standing quickly. He backed off.

"Bold, aren't you," I said, eyeing him carefully. What did he want? The locket warmed suddenly. I put the chain around my neck and slipped the device into my shirt, away from his prying gaze. He stared at my hair again as it bounced back into place.

"Well—Father always says I'm prone to speaking my mind —to a detriment at times." He looked me up and down, a slight scowl on his face.

"What now?" I said. I put my fists onto my hips and scowled at him. "What do you want?"

He put a finger to his mouth and scrutinized my clothes. The range of expressions that crossed his face left me baffled as to what his interest in me meant. I squirmed, pulling my dirty t-shirt hem down over the top of my grungy jeans.

The young man brightened and extended an open hand to me. "My name is Gad—and you are?"

I stepped back and pursed my lips in thought. He seemed more curious about me than surprised by my odd clothes and behavior. How would I act if I found someone dressed like him sitting in an alley crying over a piece of jewelry? *May as well play along until I wake up. Or until the locket takes me back.*

I cautiously took his palm in mine and shook. His grip was

strong and warm. When I tried to pull my hand back he held it and tilted his head again. He cleared his throat.

"My name?" I hedged.

Light danced in his eyes as he waited. "Mmm hmmm?"

Ugh, what will satisfy this overly friendly man? He's like a puppy that won't drop a ball. If he left me alone I can try the locket again.

"I'm—um, well Rose actually," I stuttered.

His eyes narrowed and the corner of his mouth curled upward. "Really? Only Rose?"

"Yes—um—can I have my hand back?" I asked, tugging slightly. He looked at our hands, then let go.

"Oh. Yes, of course. So sorry. Rose. That's a really pretty name. Are you from out of town?" he asked.

"Yes. You could say that." I shrugged. From out of town? Try from out of the world—out of the dimension—out of the universe—out of my mind! I still didn't even know where I was.

"Not meaning to offend, but you kind of stand out—in those clothes," he said. His eyes scrunched up.

I shook my head. "What does it matter to you? If you wouldn't mind letting me go... I need to get home," I said, and took a step.

"Please don't go," he said, putting an arm out to block me then dropping it. "I can help you get home."

"I'll be fine. Besides you don't even know where I live." I stepped past him, striding quickly to the end of the passageway. Why would he assume he knows where I live? There was no way he could.

I didn't want to get swept away again. I could handle many things, but that air bridge... I stared at the bridge just yards

18

away from me. Sweat beaded on my brow. I could see the darkness of the depths. I pulled myself up straight, eyed the crowd and dashed into the current of people heading away from the crazy bridge over nothing. I let myself flow with the crowd instead of ricocheting off them. I crossed my arms. My clothes were filthy and out of place, but people ignored me as long as I didn't run into them. I sighed. This city seemed endless. Where would I find a place to hide until I could wake myself up?

"This city isn't safe," Gad said appearing beside me.

I stopped, causing people to veer away from us. "Can you appear out of nowhere?"

"I'm sneaky that way." He grinned, then wrapped his leather coat over my shoulders. "Someone is bound to notice you." He pushed me forward as I still gawked at him.

I tried to push the coat off. "Look, I appreciate your concern, but I am better off by myself. As you can see no one is the least bit interested in me other than you."

"You're wrong about that." He continued leading me along, an air of false ease about him. "Someone has to keep you from getting hurt."

I turned on him.

His dark eyes locked on me, his brows tense. "Please. Don't go. This isn't a safe city. Please let me help you."

I looked at him carefully. He certainly couldn't know where my home was, but joining him was an option until I woke up. Or maybe I needed to figure out how to make the locket take me back. I could always lose him later. I looked down at my pants, stained and worn. "My clothes. You could help me find something more appropriate?" I shoved my arms into the leather sleeves of his coat.

"Yes. It would be my pleasure." He grinned. He took my hand and sped down the walk, pulling me behind.

"I can follow you just fine." I growled and yanked my hand out of his.

"Of course," he said, and looked at my hair again. His brow furrowed. He opened his mouth about to speak, but he shook his head.

I followed him. We wound our way into the crowd until we no longer had to fight the current of people busying themselves in the other direction. An occasional wide shouldered man in a hurry or a woman wearing a swaying bustle buffeted me from side to side. Gad reached back when once again I fell behind. He grabbed the too-long sleeve of the coat and pulled me to him. He grimaced when I flipped another curl out of my face.

"Your hair. Can you keep it covered—somehow?" he asked and pulled the collar up around my curls. Another copper curl sproinged out and he scowled, but continued to lead me. I shook my head. In real life people admired my hair. *Maybe red is offensive in this dream world. Figures.*

We traveled for probably ten minutes, along the elevated paths between, and even through, buildings. With a skip and jump of my heart, the sky bridges always reminded me how high up we were. Yet the whole scene appeared like a normal ground-level city the rest of the time.

Crowds of oddly dressed people came and went. Most wore fancier clothes than Gad, though some clearly were rugged-looking like him. We crossed over another bridge. Looking down, my heart raced. An opening in the clouds showed other walkways along the same building, stories down, but still no sign of the ground. My breath sharpened. *So very high. Too high. A city like this can't exist.*

Gad went around a corner into a large sunny opening surrounded by massive windows and store fronts. My engineer's eye told me the tops of many adjacent buildings had been converted into a garden-like shopping park. The taller surrounding buildings crept upward around it to form a valley in the sky—a SkyPlaza proclaimed a sign arching over the entrance. A fountain gurgled in the center of the stone and metal promenade. The familiar pulse of clock gears vibrated in my feet and chest. Above a row of stores, on the face of a nearby building, hung another exposed gear clock. My steps slowed as I watched the hands ticking away the time. The clock accounted for fifteen hours instead of twelve. My mind reeled. Gad pulled me over to his other side putting me between him and the building. His palm was warm and damp. A breeze wafted into my face cooling me. Could a dream ever be this vivid?

Around the SkyPlaza, people sat on curled iron benches and milled about, carrying bags bulging with wares. I tried to look around Gad's broad shoulders to take in the details of this fantasy land. Gad sighed and blocked my view again. The store windows contained moving mannequins dressed in what seemed to be the standard garb of the city. Other window displays were dominated by metal and mechanics mixed with lace. Items, strange and foreign, adorned every turn.

"Let's get you dressed into something... more fitting," Gad said. He looked around him pursed lips. "Hmmm. Where to take you? Ah hah! This should do it." He smiled and pointed to an ornate storefront. He took my hand to lead me to the door.

The inside of the shop was similar to any clothing store, though different at the same time. Racks lined wide aisles. When we approached the racks moved slowly displaying garishly outlandish frocks. The clothes were so strange. I couldn't even imagine ever finding a costume party that would account for such extreme garb, much less wearing such things daily. Gad tried to block me from the view of the other people in the store as he led me over to a curtained dressing area.

"You go in here and I'll bring you some things to wear." He looked me up and down again, appraising my size perhaps. "Stay inside please," he said. His face bore no trace of his earlier light mood.

I slipped in. "Okay." Inside the curtained area one wall was a mirror bordered by opulent copper designs. A subtle floral scent perfumed the air. A velvet padded settee rested along the opposite wall. I hung the leather coat on a hook. Then I dropped down onto the settee and rubbed at a smudge of dirt on my arm.

"Oh no," I gasped when I noticed myself in the mirror. No wonder people here looked at me with such disdain. My T-shirt, stained with auto-grease, was covered in dust and dirt from digging through the dirty attic. Bits of lint and even some cobwebs decorated my curls. I ran my fingers franticly through my hair to dislodge the debris. It explained why Gad kept attempting to hide me.

"Put these on." Several hangers swung from his grip, draped in folds and ruffles of fabric.

"I'll try," I said, wrinkling my nose at the strange garments. "Maybe I'll wake up." I grunted as I lifted the corseted bodice in front of me and grimaced.

Glancing into the mirror again, I sighed. I was truly filthy. What did I have to lose? I pulled off my dirty clothes and slipped into the cream and green striped ensemble. Pearl buttons slipped on my rough skin as I carefully fastened them up the front. A series of skirts from a petticoat to a flounced, solid green velvet overlay were next. The velvet opened in front like curtains to reveal the striped underskirt that extended just below the knee. A dark green bodice was last. Never in my life had I worn anything so fancy. Ribbons and beads were carefully stitched into the dark green, giving the whole outfit the look of a decorated cupcake. A sweet scent wafted from the fabric.

"Whoa," I gasped at my image in the mirror.

"Let me see," Gad said. He sounded like a kid awaiting a surprise. The metal rings chimed along the curtain bar as I revealed myself.

"Oh. Perfect," he said.

I blushed. I still looked a bit silly bare legged with messy hair.

"Can you—do you know how to…?" He frowned.

"What? Spit it out," I snapped.

Gad leaned close. "Can you braid your hair up or something?"

"Fine. But I need shoes to match this get-up," I sighed.

"Don't worry, Copper Rose," he said, and dashed out of view. I let the curtain swing back across the opening and my shocked face. I never told him my full name. We were certainly not at the point in our relationship for nicknames, if that was where he got the "Copper" from. He acted like a kid pampering a stray animal. *What's he going to do next? Take me home and ask his mommy if he can keep me?*

I shrugged and started working with my hair. Once I got it free of the lint and dirt, I plaited it, starting in front and winding it around behind my head. Satisfied, I turned to clean the smudges of dirt from my arms with spit and my thumb.

"Use this," Gad said, appearing in the small room. He handed me a damp handkerchief.

"Thank you," I said as he slipped out. The handkerchief worked much better, and I felt cleaner. The clothing was ridiculous, but clearly I would blend in better now.

Gad returned, handing me thick white stockings embroidered with vine-like embroidery. He handed me feminine boots and fingerless lace gloves in the same green as the dress.

"I feel stupid," I mumbled, looking at the fancy apparel.

"You look stunning," he said.

I shooed him out and pulled on the stockings. The boots were actually quite comfortable once I navigated the maze of lacings. Last of all I pulled on the gloves and cringed. They itched.

Giving myself one last check in the mirror, I tucked the locket inside the blouse, leaving only the chain evident, and stepped out of the dressing room.

Gad smiled. "That'll do perfectly."

I ducked back in to snag his leather jacket from the hook and my grubby clothes. He shrugged into the jacket, grabbed my clothes and tucked them into the satchel strapped across

24

his chest. Gad walked back through the store. He kept checking to make sure I followed.

"Oh, how charming you look, miss. What a perfect color on you," a store lady cooed.

"And such hair," another swooned, reaching out to bounce one of my stray curls across my forehead.

"Thank you," I said and stepped back. Gad's eyes narrowed at the woman.

The first woman grinned, pulling a headpiece from a mannequin. "One last bit o' flare and you'll be fit for a visit to Bromin Shere's palace." Without even asking she fitted the piece into my hair. The other girl whipped out a mirror. Before I knew it an array of matching feathers and ribbons adorned my head. It actually did complete the look wonderfully even if my head was covered in fluff.

"Beautiful," I said. I reached to my hip then realized with a rush of warmth that I had no way to pay them. "Oh—I—I don't have money."

"Your brother paid for everything else and this is on us," the woman squealed. She batted her eyes at Gad, who nodded at their work with approval. I smiled at their obvious pleasure. Gad pulled one edge of lace over my ear, concealing several longer escaping curls. Looking back and forth across my head, he nodded in approval.

"Thank you." I followed Gad out the door. "But how am I going to repay you?"

Gad smiled. "You don't need to."

"Yes I do."

He sighed. "There are more important things than repaying

me for some simple clothes." He took my hand and led me into the middle of the SkyPlaza.

Looking down at the frills, I couldn't see how these were simple clothes. I felt so ridiculous and everything was completely foreign. I wanted to shrink and hide, but I needed to blend in until I could get home... *Home? Home means a world without Gramma. Is that really home? But here? What kind of life is this?* For all I knew I was actually asleep on the dusty attic floor. But if I wasn't then I needed to give myself time to figure out where I was.

A buzzing hum erupted from above. Suddenly, I was covered in shadow. I stopped dead in my tracks. A massive dirigible loomed overhead, like some ancient, ocean going ship moved by a blimp instead of sails. The vessel crossed over the courtyard drenching it in a silhouette of darkness, then slipped past the far buildings and out of sight. Other than me, no one gave the ship a second look.

"Your—your mouth." Gad chuckled. Realizing I was gaping, I clamped my mouth shut.

"What—what..." My heart leapt. Where had this crazy locket taken me?

"Don't worry, Copper Rose. You'll get used to everything." Gad hooked his arm in mine and gentlemanly sauntered into the massive courtyard.

"Why do you call me that?" I said, scrutinizing him as he walked.

"Well—you know." He glanced at me then moved forward. "Your hair is copper." He chuckled dryly. "You're a copper Rose." He didn't notice my scowl.

I kept my breathing regular though my mind sprinted with

the possibilities. Could he really know my name or was it a lucky play on my hair color and the name I'd told him? Who was he?

Chapter 3

Gad kept himself between me and the majority of the crowd as we skimmed through the large SkyPlaza. The clock tower rose up above a squat building housing a massive, dark opening. The word AirDock spread over the tunnel in elegant script. People streamed in and out carrying shopping bags and luggage.

"What is the AirDock? That big ship—it went over the top of those buildings. Does the tunnel have something to do with it?" I asked.

Gad's eyes darted around as he responded. "The tunnel leads to the docks for ships leaving the city. That's actually where we're headed. This is the highest set of buildings in the city so the ships can come and go without as much trouble."

The highest point? The plaza was deceptively spread out atop the buildings as if it was on solid ground. My head was spinning. I couldn't wrap my reality around such a place. "We *are* still up really high aren't we?"

He looked at me and smirked. "Yes. We never left the upper levels of the city."

Gad pulled me along.

"Why do we have to leave? What if I don't want to?" I slowed down. He turned to look at me, his eyebrows drawing together.

"This city isn't safe for you."

I snorted.

Gad looked up at a curl across my brow. "Really not safe. It's best if we find a good ship that could... take us on a tour of sorts. Maybe see stuff outside the capitol city?"

I scrutinized Gad. His eyes darted around the SkyPlaza as if he expected something to jump out at us. I only saw people going about their business. If this was a dream, what did it matter if I left the city? It seemed important to Gad.

"What's the name of this city?" I said as we approached the tunnel.

Gad fell in beside me and smiled. "This is Rubaya, the capitol city of the Merald Province. I'm from out of town myself. We should go visit my home. It's wonderful," Gad said.

We had made our way halfway to the tunnel. Large potted trees and benches circled the SkyPlaza's large center fountain, a tower of dish-like levels in varying shades of metal. Water burst upward several feet from the top before cascading from dish to dish to land in a large pool of colorful stone bricks.

"Perhaps," I said. I looked over at the pool below. Would the bottom be gleaming with pennies, like fountains on Earth? I thought I saw a glint, but we were moving too quickly to tell.

"What brings you to the capitol city?" Gad asked. I looked at him and he grinned.

"Oh—well," I stuttered, then sadness hit me. My steps became ponderous and I stared down at the textured stone tiles.

Gad slowed his pace to match mine. "You look sad."

29

"Sorry," I replied.

"You can tell me. It's clear things aren't going as you planned," Gad said.

I sighed. I was walked onward. I came to Capitol City because of the locket. And I came to the locket because...

"In a roundabout way I'm here because my grandmother died," I said, still scrutinizing the angular designs in the floor tiles.

Gad stopped. I looked up as he turned to face me, his eyes large and sad. "Died? She—my sympathies." Gad bowed his head.

"Gad? Gad? Are you all right?" I asked. When he didn't look up, I lightly touched his shoulder.

"Apologies. I'm fine. I..." Gad replied. He looked at me. I was sure there was a tear in his eye. As I leaned closer to confirm that suspicion, his gaze flicked over my shoulder and his eyes enlarged.

"Gad?"

His voice dropped to a whisper. "Rose? Act—act normal and look at me—please." He put an arm around my waist as he tried to slip us around a group of people who had stopped to chat by the fountain.

"What?" I asked. A commotion came from across the SkyPlaza, but when I turned to look, Gad pulled me onward.

"Please, Copper Rose. Please," Gad said.

I shook my head in frustration. There it was again. It couldn't be a slip up this time. How did he know my real name?

"Don't look. Keep walking to the tunnel," he continued, a slight but unmistakable tremor in his voice.

30

I didn't know why, but I believed him. Something was wrong. People turned, admiration on their faces. They too, were looking behind me across the SkyPlaza. I tried to focus on the AirDock tunnel. The gossipy voices of several women reached my ears. They pointed behind us, covering their mouths with fans. A man said something unclear in breathy awe. Whoever was coming from the far side of the plaza parted the crowd with their very presence. We were swept away from the tunnel. I wanted to look, but Gad kept himself between me and the commotion.

People ahead of us smiled like fools and pointed. Gad led me through the ever thickening crowd. He hurried me along with his hand pressed on the small of my back. What was he so afraid of?

When the crowd thickened ahead of us, Gad huffed in frustration. He pulled me to a stop behind a potted tree, turning his back to the crowd. "Keep looking at me. We have to wait until they leave," Gad whispered.

"What's going on?" I asked. Out of the corner of my eye I saw an entourage surrounded by guards dressed in deep blue making their way to the AirDock. They passed close enough for me to see an odd crest on the chest of their uniforms. An S laced around gears. Fancy women walked alongside a uniformed man in the middle with brass epaulettes resting on each shoulder.

"A lovely day, full of lovely things," the man said. His tenor voice had a distinct tremolo to it. I looked over Gad's shoulder. The man at the center looked directly at me and stopped in his tracks. His intense eyes held me riveted. His long, thin nose separated sharp cheek bones overlaid in strangely pale skin. A chill ran through me and I tried to look away.

"No. Look at me," Gad whispered.

I looked back at Gad, too late. The man walked toward us, winding around the benches and the large potted tree. His entourage followed hesitantly, while his guards marched steadily to encircle us. I couldn't help but look up again. Dashes of color glowed in his oily black eyes. He was tall and slender in his well-fitted royal blue and silver uniform. Metal epaulettes adorned each shoulder. His shirt bore the same crest, sewn neatly as a patch where a pocket would be. His hair was an aged steel grey, though he otherwise looked no more than thirty years old or so. Gad kept his eyes averted from the stranger, his hand on my arm.

"Greetings," the man said, his voice vibrating.

"Hello," I found myself saying. I pushed an escaped curl back under the headpiece.

"Such radiant—such unique hair you have, miss," he said. His eyes ran over my face and head like a snake sizing up a rodent. I knew my copper curls were escaping the way they always did, as if they had a mind of their own.

"Uh—Thank you," I replied and pulled another curl over my ear to get it out of sight.

"Bromin Shere, Ruler of Grediaya," he said, bowing deeply. He swung out of the bow with a flourish, looking directly at Gad. My palms grew sweaty. I was happy to have his eyes off me, but the look he gave Gad...

"If it isn't Gad of the GearMakers. Come out of hiding have you? Little risky don't you think?"

The crowd stared. Three women near us gasps, their gloved

32

hands hiding their mouths. The crowd grew quiet and backed away.

Gad looked around and shifted his weight, nearly bouncing on his toes. "Bromin. I go where I please, as you know. Never seems to be a problem. Why? Are you suggesting the Capitol City isn't safe anymore?" Gad replied.

"Safe? This city is always safe for those who seek the good of all. Now—how rude of us. You haven't introduced me to your companion." Bromin looked at me. His smile made the hair on the back of my neck stand up. His gaze was intense. Dangerous. I kept my breath even and tried to smile normally as he extended his hand in greeting. Gad tensed from head to toe. Bromin scooped up the hand I offered. His nearly translucent skin was cool and felt like thick rubber gloves. He brought my hand to his chilly lips sending a shiver up my arm. Bromin looked up at me and smiled, those eyes. Gad's face purpled, his jaw and fists clenched.

"And you are?" Bromin inquired.

Gad looped his arm through my free one. He tugged me slightly away from Bromin, but the man still didn't release my hand.

"We just met. She's visiting. Her name is Izrraya. She's from Diadia Outer Province," Gad said. Tension clenched around Gad's eyes when Bromin continued to hold my hand. His tight grip was starting to sting.

"Really, Izrraya? Outer Province? You almost have the coloring of one from... from TreeCountry of GearMaker Territory," Bromin said. "Wouldn't you agree Gad Steele?"

Gad blanched.

"No. My entire family line descends from Outer Province," I said, attempting to sound convincing. This man made my skin crawl. I tried to pull my hand back subtly, but he tightened his grip.

"Izrraya? You really must come visit my palace. A jewel like you would fit in perfectly. Come now. I will give you the accommodations of a queen while you visit our great city. I assure you I can keep the riffraff away from you there." Bromin looked pointedly at Gad. He pulled one of my curls out and wound it around his finger. I shuddered and Bromin pulled me closer. Gad held on to my other arm and stared down Bromin.

"Oh, I think I'm all right. Maybe I can come by some other time," I replied, my voice cracking.

"Izrraya, such a blooming copper rose. You must come to the palace. I insist," Bromin said.

Warm, queasiness swelled up inside me. Copper Rose? Not him, too. How could everyone know my unusual name? I tugged at my hand struggling to get free, my breath keeping pace with my speeding heart. Bromin grinned and yanked. He spun me around into his arms, my back to his hard chest. Gad stumbled as my arm was wrenched from his. He leapt at Bromin, but fell to the ground as a guard snagged his boot.

Gad flipped off the ground like a gymnast. He grabbed my arm, but Bromin shoved him into the surrounding guards, knocking several down. They yelled and tried to grab Gad. He flailed as they pulled at his limbs.

I struggled to get away, to help him, but Bromin pinned both of my arms tightly.

"Hey. Let go of me." I squirmed to get loose and kicked my

foot back. Bromin lifted me, my feet dangling. My kicks hit only air. Bromin's grip hurt. My ribs ached. Gad rolled off the fallen guards, then vaulted over the standing ones, using the edge of the tree pot to push himself into the air. The guards reached for him then looked around baffled as Gad vanished into the crowd. Where had he gone?

"Find Gad. Don't let him escape," Bromin yelled. "Kill him if you have to."

Half the guards took off into the crowds.

My stomach lurched. "No."

And Bromin chuckled. "You are better off with me than that no good..."

Bromin put his mouth close to my ear. "Copper Rose. So long I have anticipated meeting you. You cannot reject an invitation to my palace. Not now. Not ever," Bromin whispered harshly, peppering oily spittle on my face.

He pulled me around the large pot, my heels dragging. Putting his foot on a metal bench, Bromin kicked it with inhuman strength. It fell and skittered across the ground knocking into a woman and her small child. People screamed, moving quickly away. Even the women who had accompanied Bromin vanished into the throng.

Thrashing in Bromin's grip, I screamed. "Let me go." He clamped a hand over my mouth, maintaining the vice-like grip of his other arm. He strode into the AirDock tunnel. The ticking of the massive clock overhead broke through the noise of Bromin and his small army. Or was it the locket's tick growing strong? People nearby gasped and dashed away as Bromin swept into the shadowy darkness of the tunnel below

35

the clock tower. A woman and her friend bumped into us. Bromin shoved her aside, releasing my mouth. She crunched against the wall, crumpled and lay still. I gasped. Her companion screamed and ran in the direction of a well-lit room on the other side of the tunnel.

"To the palace," Bromin commanded and clamped his hand over my mouth again. I stopped struggling. No sense hurting myself. The man's grip was iron.

The guards ahead of us turned left, away from the bright room, through an arch with the stacked-gear crest hanging over it. A shiver ran through my restrained body as the details of the design gained clarity. Three gears, one each of silver, brass and copper were interlocked up the middle of the shield. Laced between the gears was a snake shaped like an S.

Bromin hauled me under the crest and into the darker tunnel, without any apparent strain. My arms felt like they would break as Bromin held me tight around the rib cage. My breath came in short bursts.

I was carried through a maze of empty passageways. A line of gears decorated the walls at waist level, realistic looking snakes curling around and over the gears. Guards stood at regular intervals like frozen sentinels. The floor rose steadily as we passed through metal doors that slammed closed behind us. My limbs shook and my eyes flicked about. Where was I? Only hours before my life was my own and now—now I was being kidnapped by some madman.

Gad was right to think I wasn't safe. Everyone seemed to know me as Copper Rose. This nightmare felt so real it couldn't be a dream. If only I could pinch myself and wake up. If only...

Chapter 4

My arms were numb from Bromin's steel-strong grip binding them to my aching ribs. Light appeared ahead, hurting my eyes. My limbs shook despite not having walked a bit of the trek. Time seemed to skew and twist in those tunnels. Bromin strode forward, not appearing at all tired from having carried me such a long way. What was he? No one could be this tireless.

We entered a huge room with tall windows and a vast open floor. Bromin's crest, in massive form, dominated the wall in front of me. The room appeared to be a palace courtroom decorated with gently-turning sprockets. The interlacing of copper, brass and silver shimmered in cold, mechanical beauty. What would have been flounces and filigree elsewhere were sharp angles and metal. I shuddered.

"Welcome to my delightful home, Copper Rose. So nice of you to accept my invitation," Bromin sneered, releasing me with a push. I fell forward, my knees screaming painfully. I picked myself up from the metal floor. The guards filed in along the wall. A steel door creaked shut over the tunnel, blocking the only visible escape.

"What do you want from me?" I demanded, rubbing my wrists to get the circulation running freely again. Welts bloomed on my arms.

"Only to share with you the glory and splendor of my

empire," Bromin said with elation.

I glared at him. "I don't require your hospitality." I stepped toward the closed tunnel door.

He waved a finger at me. "Ah, ah, ah! No running away. There is nowhere to go from here. My palace floats in the clouds." His silky, venomous tone made me shudder. He strode to a window and looked out. My evening was definitely not going as planned. I would have been fine packing boxes, having a late dinner of grilled cheese and maybe end it by drowning my sorrows in a good book.

"Now my little GearMaker, I will show you my regal abode," Bromin said, and motioned me toward him.

"I'd rather go back to the city," I replied, holding my ground. What in the world was a GearMaker?

"Dear Copper Rose, you can accept your fate or be miserable. You are a guest here and there is no need to restrain you—if you cooperate. Now please follow," Bromin said, staring at me, his brow arching.

"Guests are usually free to come and go as they please." I stared him down. I was sure this was a case of mistaken identity, though how many curly red heads could be called Copper Rose? Maybe if I played along I could find my escape. I needed to open the locket again, or wake up. My mind raced, trying to land on one reality instead of being stuck in this revolving door of possibilities.

Unwavering, Bromin matched my gaze. His eyes were black ringing black. The flashes of light had gone. Something dark dwelled in those eyes, something dangerous.

I looked away. "I'll cooperate."

"Wonderful. Come." Bromin clapped his hands.

He strode over to a set of large metal doors opposite where we had entered. I followed, careful to stay out of his reach. I glanced back at the closed doors, feeling my hope dwindle. A guard pushed a button on the wall. Hidden gears clacked and the door opened. Two guards fell into place behind us.

Bromin led me to a massive twisting staircase rising up several stories. The banisters were works of art made from twined copper, brass and silver strands as supports. Textiles of woven metallic fibers and ornate lace decorated the cushioned couches and chairs smattered throughout alcoves and open rooms that we passed. Wide halls were decorated like galleries. Despite my efforts to avoid him, Bromin kept touching my shoulder. He pushed me slightly one way or another. Avoiding his unnaturally cool skin kept me on edge.

Going down yet another hall, Bromin stopped. He smiled. "You should see this." He pulled open a curtain to reveal a broad wrought-iron railed balcony. Bromin walked to the rail.

I looked out. A large flat plateau of elaborate gardens dropped off into blue sky. To the left of the palace across miles of empty space was the city. Many of the buildings reached up into the clouds like the palace. They were every shape, octagons, hexagons and less commonly squares. People skittered across the distant bridges between the close-set structures. Machines large and small hummed about doing tasks and transporting people to and fro.

I'd been making a big assumption that this was a planet like Earth and not a series of floating islands out of some fantasy. It seemed to be true that this palace was in the clouds of a foreign planet. But we had come here through a tunnel of stone, so it must have connected to the main city somehow. Then again, the city buildings were so tall I'd never seen the ground they rested on. Maybe if I understood the land I could figure out how to escape.

A yellow moon peeked over the horizon fighting the fading sunlight, but a red moon also hung full over the landscape—and a blue moon further away, only a small ornament in the sky. Three moons? I gasped.

Bromin looked at me and grinned. "Yes. A beautiful sight."

I looked back at him through narrowed eyes. Light dazzled in his irises before they went dark again. A chill ran through me and my breath quickened. I needed to understand more than the lay of the land. I needed to know if these people were even human.

Bromin turned from the balcony, clearing his throat. I followed behind him as he descended a curling staircase.

If I did get away, I didn't think I could ever find my way out of this labyrinth of a palace. After traveling a circuitous route that had my sense of direction entirely up in the air, Bromin led me to a double door and stopped.

"Time to show you your room." Bromin pulled the doors open, smiling coldly as he did. His tall lead guard stood beside me in a similar outfit as Bromin's. The blackened steel epaulettes and metal findings gave him a menacing air. Behind us the half a dozen other guards in brown uniforms blocked my retreat.

Bromin grabbed my hand, pulling me forward, but stopped when I resisted. "Day is coming to a close. Sleep now. I will introduce you to your task in the morning," he said.

"Task?" I stood in the hall, staring at this man. A task? What was this all about?

"Rustin." Bromin motioned to the lead guard. "Maybe she could use some help entering."

Rustin chuckled as I stepped back in fear. He grabbed my elbow painfully. Bromin walked away, his hands clenched behind his back. I looked back at Rustin. His lanky hair fell over his eyes as he leered. Which could be worse? Bromin's sadistic manners or Rustin, with whatever he had in mind?

He shoved me in and slammed the door. The lock clicked. My heart raced, and a sob rose from deep within me. My breath came in rapid gasps, my eyes darting to take in my contradictory surroundings. Was this a palace or a prison?

At least I was alone. What harm could come to me locked in a room?

A canopied bed sat in the middle of the room. Copper curtains, nearly the same shade as my hair, draped the sides. Lush carpets softened my footsteps while wall coverings muted the sounds. Two other doors led from the room. One hid a long closet thick with lace and frills. The other led to a gorgeous bathroom including an enormous claw-foot tub next to an ornate window. A dressing table adorned another corner of the room. The cabinet behind the door contained soaps, sponges, towels and a variety of perfumes. I found nothing that would help me jimmy the door or climb out the window and down. *Ha!* I went to the clear glass and looked out onto an endless drop. My hope sank.

I sat on the edge of the bed, my skirts piled up around me. I was trapped and alone. I pulled the locket off and rubbed the designs. Even if the locket worked and took me back to my simple, safer world, I would still be by myself. Gramma would still be gone. But I would be safe.

"I have to try," I whispered. Being Bromin's *guest* was worse than being alone in my benign world. I took a deep breath and looked into the little window to watch the gears. I became aware of my breathing—in—out—in—out. Hand shaking, I reached a finger down and lifted the clasp. The gears moving in rhythm with my heartbeats mesmerized me, but nothing more happened.

Exhaustion washed over me and, my stomach grumbled. I'd left the dusk light of Earth for midday in this nightmare. Different time zone? Hah! I had also traded my monotonous task of packing up an old house for a day more terrifying than I could have ever imagined. I wanted to be home in my bed worrying about my life, not in a palace of metal fearing for my life. I crawled onto the bed, pulled up my feet and lay there. Tears ran down my face, the locket clasped in my hand. It may have failed to take me home, but I had to avoid losing it, so I pulled it on then tucked it into my blouse.

I sniffled, still unable to stop the tears. This was entirely a nightmare. I would wake up in my childhood bed. Maybe when I did, Gramma would be there, too.

***

Light tickled my eyelids. The crust of dried tears made my eyes stick. The healing warmth of the sun fell across me. My mind worked slowly and I felt fuzzy all over. Gramma gone—a strange scary world—no, a nightmare—neither could be real. My vision focused on a tall arched window. Arched? Wait—two windows. My bedroom had only one! And a canopy bed?

My body was covered in a strange, wrinkled vintage-like

42

dress. The curtained bed rested next to metal textured walls. "No," I groaned. The nightmare wasn't gone. As my eyes cleared, the reality sank in. This whole thing was looking real despite how impossible it was.

The double doors to the room swooped open. I jumped to my feet, completely alert, heart pounding. A small woman came in, bowing. She was followed by two other women pushing a food cart. None of them made eye contact. They went about the room like it was some kind of hotel. One laid breakfast out on a small table. The other went into the closet. She pulled several pieces of very pink clothing out and put them onto a hook on the outside of the closet door. The small woman vanished into the bathroom. I heard the creak of a cupboard and the sound of running water. Steam billowed from the bathroom door while a heavenly smell rose from the table. My stomach growled as the aromas reached my nose.

The smaller woman came out of the bathroom and bowed deeply. She walked over to the closet door and looked me straight in the eye, raising a severe brow. She pointed to the dress and then to me before leading the other two women out.

"Can't speak huh?" I sassed to the closed door. I walked over to the outfit chosen for me. Light to dark pink hues, coated every ruffle, lace cuff and pearly button. *Pink? With my hair?* "I don't think so," I muttered. What could Bromin do to me if I disobeyed?

I sat down and stared at the food, unsure of myself. I lifted a pastry, but a foreboding came over me so I stopped. Could Bromin have poisoned or drugged the food? I didn't know what he wanted from me and he had proved himself to be evil. My stomach growled again. If Bromin wanted to kill me, wouldn't he have done that by now? It was take the risk or starve. I looked around the room and sighed. I would have to eat to have the energy to escape, so I bit into the pastry.

Oh, it was worth it! Warm juices trickled down my chin. Savory sausage, onion and seasonings spilled out of the flaky crust into my mouth. My courage and strength being replenished with each bite. I sipped the bitter tea down then dusted the crumbs from my gown.

The pink atrocity on the closet door glared at me, but I didn't care. I wasn't going to wear *that*. At least the green frock came from a friendlier source. I shook the wrinkles from the skirts and pressed my hand over the bodice to straighten it back to pre-sleep status.

Steam still billowed from the other room. I stepped into the bathroom and took a moment in front of the mirror to reset my head piece and curls. I looked at the path of the copper pipes from the large metal tub down into the ground. At least this place was civilized enough for running water. The tub steamed, bubbles spilling over the edges to trickle through a drain. I glanced at the still mildly wrinkled gown. Oh, to sink into that warm water and soak away the filth and fear. Hmmm. Or not. I really didn't want to be caught unaware while bathing.

With the locket tucked safely in my blouse, I left the bathroom. Cautiously, I grasped the curved handle of the outer door. It opened! The hall was long and empty, so I took it at a brisk pace, checking behind me at regular intervals. Maybe I could find a way to escape.

My memory of the day before was a blur of fear. How could I possibly retrace my steps to the gardens or the tunnel to the city? I dashed down a long curving staircase into another hall. I searched both ways in the new hall. A guard was walking away from me, so I hurried forward to the next turn and collided into someone.

"Oh, forgive me," a rich, gentle voice said. I jumped back panicked, from a young man in a button down shirt, a snug vest, and a simple cravat. A pocket watch dangled from a gold chain at his waist. His face was kind, masculine. It was topped with bronze-highlighted hair. His silver eyes sparkled in the morning light falling from a nearby skylight.

"I—I wasn't looking. Sorry." I blushed.

"Do I know you?" he asked. The corners of his eyes crinkled, as if from frequent smiling, distracting me from his words. He put out a hand.

"No." I gazed into his striking features and took his hand. He shook mine, but held on, his warmth seeping up my arm and all through me. Those silver eyes, the lock of bronze hair falling over his brow. My breath caught.

"Forgive my clumsiness. I didn't intend to run into you," he said. He bowed slightly then straightened his vest.

"Thank you—I'm fine, but if you would please excuse me. I —I need to be going," I stammered.

He stepped back releasing my hand. "Don't let me keep you, m'lady."

I continued down the hall. Glancing back, I found him watching me. My cheeks burned. I went around the next corner, but turned to look back. He was walking away as if nothing had happened. I watched until he was gone.

What in the world was wrong with me? The bronze-haired man was in Bromin's castle. He was one of the madman's minions, not some heartthrob to lose my head over. Yet, I wanted to turn around and go back, find out who he was, what he was doing in the palace. Why did his eyes brighten when he looked at me?

I huffed and rubbed both hands on my hot cheeks. "Pull yourself together," I whispered. A large sigh escaped me. I needed to find a way out.

Ahead of me was a door that was rather small compared to the other ridiculously tall ones I'd found. It was surrounded by windows to the outside so I tried it. *Locked!*

I rattled the handle, but then chuckled. Carefully I pulled a hair pin from my stacked curls. I bent over, conscious of the way the dress pouffed out in back. I'd never picked a lock for anything but fun, but most locks used the same techniques. I jiggled the pin in the mechanism. Maybe this world had similar locks to earth. I could hope...

Clink.

"Yes!"

And out I fled into a palatial garden. I looked back with a quick thought of the mysterious man. Maybe there would be some way down to the city. If I could get to that edge in the distance and see what was really there beyond.

No guards seemed to be patrolling. Bromin must have felt invincible to leave such a large area unguarded in a world of airships like the one I'd seen the day before.

Red rock paths intersected around dozens of planters, large and small. I dashed down one path, giving hardly a glance to the flower beds. Dead end. I back tracked to a long stretch that led to a tall hedge of trees and bushes that shimmered in the sunlight.

46

I traveled around the outer paths to a break in the hedge-line. Sneaking up to it, I found a fence obviously designed to keep people from falling.

My heart and hopes sank. A sheer cliff dove straight down for miles into hazy darkness. All along the garden edge the same drop extended past my vision. The city was a couple miles from the palace. It was as impossible as everything else in this crazy world. An amazing place, but not a single one of those insane bridges reached to the palace garden.

Chapter 5

"Impossible," I mumbled in disappointed awe as I leaned over the rail to see, at last, what the palace sat on. The ground, if it existed, was so far down I found no hope of scaling the smooth cliff-like face, much less jumping. I would need wings to escape. My lip quivered, tears forming at the corners of my eyes. Even if I could get back to the city, I wouldn't know where to go or who to trust other than Gad. How would I even find him? What could I do?

"Enjoying my garden?" Bromin said from behind me. I spun around. "I told you there is no escape from my hospitality." Bromin said. His smile seemed wrong, not exactly natural.

I hid my frustration and steeled my nerves. "This place is not exactly locked down," I said. "If you have any enemies, they are bound to figure out an easy way to attack you in this cloud-high nest of yours." I tried to mask the angry sarcasm boiling up in me.

Bromin looked me up and down. "As lovely today as yesterday, I see."

My skin crawled. I adjusted the waistline of my slightly wrinkled gown and held back a sassy retort.

"So little GearMaker, what do you think of my home?"

48

Bromin asked, stepping next to me. He set a heavy hand on my shoulder. I pulled back, but his gripped was as inescapable as yesterday.

"I don't know what you want from me or why you keep calling me a GearMaker. I just want to go home." Tears pricked my eyes.

"All in good time, my little GearMaker. All in good time. Though why you would want to go back to those dreadful tree houses I would not venture to guess. So organic. And all that dirt." He brushed his hands together as if to dust them off.

I looked around, confused. Here we stood in a garden of trees and flowers, yet he spoke of rural land with abhorrence. A bed of flowers near us bore pristine petals and not a single browned leaf. The dirt below sparkled. I leaned closer and touched a leaf. It was smooth, cold and fake. The dirt wasn't real either. Shards of black steel and dark copper flakes glinted in the morning light. Every petal and strip of bark across the entire garden was made of metal. But it looked so real. The leaves rustled in the breeze. Moisture effused air that seemed to come from the plant life, only it couldn't be alive.

Bromin smiled like a proud father. "Beautiful, you must agree. This is the largest collection of living metal plants in the whole of Grediaya." Bromin said.

"Living metal?" How could that be? This world... this place...

Looking out across the garden, my frustration rose. A vast expanse of colored sky canopied the grounds. Puffy white clouds drifted lazily past. The colors of the rising sunlight reflected off the palace's metal and glass creating a kaleidoscope of dazzling, dancing light. Were it not for the cold pit of fear in my stomach, I would have been in complete awe.

"Come," Bromin said, putting his arm out. I hesitantly stepped forward, but avoided his offered arm. "It is time to show you the task I have for you. You look like a sturdy girl who thrives on work."

I looked down at the grease ingrained around my fingernails. "Um—well," I stuttered as he led the way up the main path to the palace. What could he possibly want from me? So many horrible possibilities had piled up in my head, but not slave labor. *Patience,* I told myself. Somehow I would convince him of the mistake he had made. I would find a way back to Earth.

We walked inside.

Bromin didn't look at me as we went up the stairs, but his guards followed behind me, slinking, large men that kept me following their leader. Everything about this man showed a confidence and cruelty that left me in constant fear. A leash of fear? Is that how Bromin stayed in the good graces of the city people? In the SkyPlaza they had adored him.

"This palace is mostly for show, but it is more secure than you know." He stopped at the top and turned, glaring down at me. "I don't keep my greatest prizes and tools here. I have a better place for that—as you will learn soon enough."

Bromin continued down a hall on the second level. We passed the doors to the bedroom, but he continued. He stopped before a set of metal doors a little further down. "I know who you are," he said.

"I'm Izrraya from Outer Province. I told you," I replied. "I don't know this. Copper—person."

50

"Oh, what you claim not to know," Bromin said, shaking his head. He pushed open the door, motioning me in. Smells of sulfur and metal crinkled my nose. We stood in the entry of a massive room. I scanned the supplies and devices on row upon row of long metal tables. Deep cabinets containing tubs of springs, screws and strange metal parts lined the walls. A shiver of excitement ran through me. The things I could do in this workshop!

A man stood near the door, partially hidden by a cabinet.

"Alum. I wish for you to meet your new work partner, Copper Rose." Bromin gestured grandly.

The man stepped into full view. The bronze hair... The silver eyes... There he was, the man from the hallway. He locked eyes with me and a trace of a smile crossed his lips. Alum—his name was Alum.

"Wonderful to meet you, Copper Rose," Alum said, stepping closer to me. He looked down at me, his eyes drawing mine to his. Bromin cleared his throat and Alum backed away, the smile dropping from his face. Fear rose up in me again.

"This workshop is at your disposal until the work is complete," Bromin said to me.

"What work?" I asked. What was he talking about? It was bad enough that he knew who I was, but now he believed I knew what was going on.

"Come, come now. No more pretense. I know who you are. You know what I want. If you will not obey there are ways of making you," Bromin said, his voice growing deeper with unnatural resonance.

"Bromin, stop," Alum said.

Bromin scowled and stepped toward me. "Do not test my patience, Alum. She *is* a GearMaker. You have failed me all these years, but I know there is power in this one. I can *feel* it. She will be the one to give me a GearMade."

Alum kept his eyes down and cradled his left arm wincing.

"Please," I said stepping away from Bromin. "I don't know what you're talking about. I don't even know what a GearMaker is. I really don't know what you want from me."

Bromin brows shaded his face. Rainbow lights flared in his eyes, then went black. A smile tickled the corners of his mouth. "You honestly don't know? Do not toy with me," he said in a low, vibrating voice.

I watched his eyes scintillating dimly under his brows. Standing straighter, I glared at him. "I don't know who you are or where I am. I don't even know if I'm on Earth anymore," I snapped. He scrutinized me. "I was at my Gramma's house, then somehow I was here in this city."

A full smile spread over Bromin's face revealing his perfect, white teeth. "Ho-ho! How very clever of Daren. Your human Grandmother? How divine. That is where you have been all these years. They hid you in a different world! Left you clueless about who you are! This is fantastic." Bromin rubbed his hands together.

Alum was looking from Bromin to me in terror.

Bromin stepped closer, clasping his hands. "You are now mine to mold, and shape, and teach. They left you unprotected. Now, I will create my very own GearMaker to do my great work unhindered by GearMaker delusions."

The same terror I saw on Alum's face sank like a rock into

my gut. Bromin grabbed my shoulders in one swift move and looked gleefully into my face.

I pulled against his tight grip, trying to keep my feet under me as he shook me.

"Copper Rose. You are a gift from the fallen gods," Bromin said, a glisten in his eyes. "You are what I have sought for centuries. I will reward you beyond your greatest imaginings when you make a living GearMade being for me. I need an army of GearMades, like me. You will be the mother of an entire people."

"GearMade? I—I can make machines, but…" I said. I bowed my head, dread filling me. Bromin wasn't even a real flesh and blood being? Living machines. A large part of me felt a thrill of interest. "That—that is impossible."

"Not impossible. Your people brought my entire race into being. I am proof that GearMades can live and be more powerful than even the gods that created us. You! You can be the last great mother of new, GearMade beings," he said. His face was close to mine, smiling cruelly. I cringed.

"I don't know how. I really don't," I said. What would he do to me when he realized I couldn't do this impossible task?

"Yes, you do… And you *will*. You, my lovely Copper Rose, will bring to life a new race of GearMades. I know this is something you are capable of," Bromin said. He let go of me and stepped back to the door. "Alum. Your task is to teach her what it really means to be a GearMaker." He paused and smiled. "As I taught you." He watched Alum retreat, a look of horror on his face. Bromin smiled, his eyes twinkling vivid red as he closed the doors.

Rewards beyond my greatest imaginings? More like fears I never imagined could exist. I tried to catch my breath, to stop the shaking in my limbs. My feet were failing me. I grabbed a tall stool. Alum reached for me, but seemed to freeze. His face clenched. He stood straight, and avoided eye contact. I lifted myself up on the stool, the skirt of my dress hanging oddly over the seat. I leaned against the table, my heart rate slowly returning to normal.

Alum pulled a stool a few feet away from me on the other side of the table.

"Is—is—is he really—not real?" I asked.

He cleared his throat. "Not real? He is completely *real*."

I shook my head sending curls bouncing. "How can that be?"

Alum shrugged. "GearMades are not born. They are created. They are made of mostly machine parts. But yes—they are, without a doubt, alive." His voice quaked and his silver eyes sparkled. He cleared his throat again. "You are from that other world? The place Bio's come from?"

"I'm from Earth. I'm human," I said, furrowing my brow.

"Human? You a measly bio? I don't know how they get here or why, but I do know that you are not a human. Not if you are *the* Copper Rose."

I squinted at him suspiciously. "Why does everyone know my name?"

Alum stared at me.

I leaned my chin into my hand. "Would you at least tell me what a GearMaker is?" A range of emotions crossed Alum's face; none of them clear to me.

54

"We are the people who originally ruled all of Seranova, including Grediaya," he said.

"We?" I asked.

He nodded. "Yes. My family and I are GearMakers. So are you and yours."

"No, I'm not."

Alum sighed heavily, rubbing his neck. "We were the first in this land. But we were lonely, so we used our great skills to create a race of living machines to breathe and eat and work beside us."

"The GearMades?"

Alum looked at me as he spoke, his expression nearly blank and his words like he was reading from a textbook. "Yes. A race completely constructed from inanimate materials and yet fully alive." He looked at his arm and tugged the cuff down.

"And I'm supposed to make one of these things?"

Alum nodded.

"Because I'm *the* Copper Rose, a GearMaker?"

Again he nodded.

I shook my head and scowled. "What makes me so special? Why haven't you just built him a *friend*?"

"Me?" He rubbed his chin. "Uh—I'm a Tinelle. Not a Locke. And besides..." He gestured to my hair.

"Oh, sheesh." I threw my hands in the air. "My hair has nothing to do with my talents."

He said nothing. I wanted to wipe that "Yeah, right," expression off his face.

"If I'm not human what am I? Are GearMakers machines too?"

55

"No," Alum said. "We are like bios, but we live much longer. Our features are metallic colors without being metal, and we can create living machines."

"This is ridiculous. This whole thing is all out crazy," I mumbled and slipped off the stool. Even Alum, with his enticing eyes and handsome visage, was bonkers. Me a GearMaker? Able to give life to machines? Hah. Not likely. I walked away from him.

I was in awe of the mechanical nature of this world. Even in the workshop the blinds were controlled by a crank and a series of elaborate gears the length of the tall window. The closed cupboards called to me, tickling my desire to create. I wandered over to a cabinet and opened it. I poked through a tub of strange, clear spaghetti-like things. Next to that stood a stack of books. I grabbed one and flipped through the pages. Sketches and schematics flashed past. Even the simplest machines drew full attention to the aesthetics. Techniques for coloring metals, how to etch surfaces into life-like textures... The list went on. I set that book down and searched through another and then another.

No noise came from the rest of the room. I turned with the last book in my hand. Alum was still sitting on the stool, as if he too might be a machine on pause. His silver eyes sparkled despite his expression of sorrow. I walked over and laid the book out in front of him.

I pointed to a vague diagram of a human figure surrounded by schematics for wiring and joint construction. "Is this what Bromin is talking about? Is this how to make a GearMade warrior or soldier?"

Alum sat up straighter and reached out to the book. He slid

it closer to him. "I have tried more than once to follow these instructions," he said in a low voice.

"And?"

He shifted in his seat and avoided my eyes. "It never worked. Not even when I was little and Bromin believed that GearMaker children were more likely to be able to bring life to machines."

"Little? How long have you worked for him?" I asked, my voice rising an octave.

"No, no," Alum said waving his hands, palms out in protest. "He took me—he took me from my family when I was six. I have no choice but to do what he tells me."

If Alum had been Bromin's prisoner since he was a child, what did that mean for me? I rubbed the locket through the fabric of my dress. If only I knew how the locket worked, I could escape. Maybe I could take Alum with me, too, and free him from a monster.

I looked him over, a man more mysterious than when I stumbled into him. Alum had tried to stand up to Bromin in my defense and yet had never successfully escaped the man's—machine's power. Alum seemed so confidant and sophisticated at first, and now looked hopeless and dejected.

"What *can* you do?" I asked.

Alum fixed his gaze on a tall, old cabinet. He walked over to it, his steps gaining length. I followed. He pulled open the metal doors and I gazed at the shelves of machines. They were intricate and complicated. The beauty astounded me.

I carefully pulled one out, an insect-like mechanism, and set it on my palm. Its round body was cool and its spindly legs stuck out at sharp angles, pressing softly against my palm. It hummed at my touch as if it pulled energy from me to start its small motor whirring. Like a spider, it bobbed up and down as if waiting.

"Don't put it down or it will take off. It has tuned itself to you and will now retrieve any small item you tell it to," Alum explained. His voice had returned to a normal tone. He was standing taller and the corner of his mouth was rising up. It wasn't a smile, but it was an improvement.

"Anything?"

Alum tipped his head back and forth. "Within reason." He shrugged. "Actually I have had little opportunity to test its abilities." He reached over and picked up the retrieving spider between his thumb and forefinger.

"I see. Hmmm..." I gathered up another machine. Lovely curled wires, like vines, wrapped around an oblong shaped body. I couldn't guess its function other than beauty.

A small smile touched Alum's mouth. "A listening device. Well, for recording. It can record visual and auditory data." He pointed to the small holes in each side of the machine. The vines curled as his finger touched it, undulating over its body and back to its sides. I laughed as it tickled my hand.

"The hard part is getting it to crawl to the location you want. It seems to hit the mark though," Alum said.

"It looks like an octopus."

"A what?" he asked.

I raised my brows, amused. "A creature that lives in the ocean. Do you have oceans?"

"Ocean completely surrounds our world." He raised a brow.

I set the octopus machine back on the shelf, scanning the rest. Dozens of insect and animal-like machines sat on the shelves. Each had such different traits and colors. They were works of art.

"They're amazing. Really," I said.

Alum smiled. Bright red flushed his cheeks and neck. He fumbled to put down the spidery retrieval machine. It skittered toward the shelf edge, but he scooped it up and pressed a small button on the backside. It whirred to a stop and rested its body on the shelf.

Alum pointed at a shelf of machines. "These on the top shelf are for data and diagnostic collection for my work. Those are good for shaping metals, and the bottom shelf is machines that are less functional. I guess you could call them toys. I made them before I was ten years of age."

All the little machines were impressive, even the toys. That he could do such intricate work so young amazed me. I thought I alone possessed these prodigy-like skills. Was this what being a GearMaker meant? Would I be surrounded by people mechanically inclined if I was surrounded by GearMakers?

The machines twinkled. I stared, fascinated. I wanted to create. I wanted to learn everything those books contained. Part of me even wanted to make a living machine, if such a feat was as possible as Alum and Bromin claimed. I was torn. My breath escaped me in a big sigh. How did living machines gain life instead of only having life-like qualities? How could I even explore this if it meant doing the bidding of such a malevolent being like Bromin?

"How?" I said.

Alum looked at me, his eyes curious. "How, what?" he asked.

I hadn't even realized I'd spoken aloud. I shook my head. Life would have been a lot simpler if I'd never known such things were possible.

"I don't understand how a machine can become alive," I said. "Are you sure they aren't just robots? Really sophisticated, really smart robots?"

"We have robots," Alum replied. "The GearMades are actually alive. They breathe, eat, heal from injury and even grow in intelligence like any of the other races."

"Will they starve if they don't eat?" I grinned. "So if we locked Bromin in a deep, dark dungeon and threw away the key, would he die?"

Alum chuckled. "No, but without food GearMades will go into a state of dormancy until some kind of fuel is put in them. They don't have to eat like we do, but they do need fuel for their brains and muscle systems. I have known some who consume liquid fuels and others who are connoisseurs of fine food made for bios or GearMakers."

"But—how?" I mumbled and looked off across the room.

Alum chuckled again. "You keep asking that."

"I'm glad I amuse you." I moved back to the tables. The skirt of my dress caught on a leg bolt. I growled and I pushed the fabric back into place. Nothing felt right. Nothing was right. "How in the world do I make a living machine? How many of you GearMakers can even do it?"

Alum walked over, his voice low. "No GearMaker has brought a GearMade being to life in nearly a thousand years."

I huffed. "You're kidding. Then why does Bromin think I

60

can do this?"

He looked at the ground and swirled his foot against the tiles.

"Alum?"

Breathing deeply, he looked up at me. "You made a living machine when you were a child. No one had brought anything more than a metal plant to life for centuries before that. So Bromin believes you could bring a GearMade person to life as well. He has hunted for you since word of your butterfly creature reached him."

Air escaped me as I threw my hands up in the air. "No! I can't do this. I can't make this stupid army of his. I never made any butterfly robots!"

"No, you never made any butterfly robots. You made a living metal butterfly."

Shaking my head, I grabbed for the stool next to me and somehow managed to pull myself onto it. "No. No, this can't be true. I can't make living machines. I have never been to this crazy world before. I don't belong here. I just want to wake up —or go home—or get out of here, whatever it takes. When would I have ever made a living machine?"

"When you were three or four, I think. Before you and your mother supposedly vanished from GearMaker Country."

I stared at him. I'd been about five when my mom took me to Gramma's house. I still couldn't remember anything from before then.

A sunbeam streaming through the tall windows of the workshop hit the creations in Alum's cabinet. They twinkled like Christmas lights and reminded me so much of the machines I'd made for Gramma.

Alum leaned close, putting his hand on my arm. "Copper Rose," Alum said in a quiet voice. "You may not believe me, but you are the only GearMaker that has the potential to make this army he wants. Bromin won't stop with threats."

"Just because I supposedly can doesn't mean I should. What'll he do to me if I can't make a living machine?" I asked.

He turned away.

I backed away from him. No matter how I got to this world, I had to get back out of it. Being the slave of a machine was not for me. If the locket wasn't going to help me, then I would simply have to do something about it myself.

I dashed to the door and peeked out. The guard at the end of the hall had his back to us.

"What are you doing?" Alum whispered from behind me.

I headed out the door. A siren blasted shaking the building.

Chapter 6

I froze. An alarm? Was it because of me?

Alum ran over to me. "Don't worry. I'll go see what is happening. Stay here. You are safest not getting in the way of Bromin's guards." I frowned at him. He watched me a moment then slipped into the hall. I looked out, clamping a hand over one ear. Alum moved quickly to the guard.

"Where are you going?" the guard yelled over the wee-ooo-wee-ooo of the alarm.

"Oh—I am looking into the problem. If the alarm system is malfunctioning they will need me," Alum said. The guard scrutinized Alum, fingering the weapon on his hip and scowling.

"Fine. Move on." The guard resumed his position. Alum disappeared around the corner.

I closed the door and leaned my forehead against it. The alarm was less severe inside the room, but still made my ears ring. How could I escape? I tugged at the locket inside my blouse. Would it work this time? I mustered all my will, pulled it out and opened the lid. *Useless thing*. Nothing happened.

The sounds of a large group of guards passed by. I shuffled away from the door, my eyes searching the room for another way out. The bedroom exited through the same hall and even

63

nearer to the guard.

The door behind me opened. "Still here? Good," Rustin said, holding up a key. "Don't leave these rooms." He left and the lock clicked.

"Now what?" I mumbled.

The doors on the left wall had to lead to the bedroom. On the other side of the room was a metal door that blended into the metal lining of a welding area.

I pushed the welding torch out of the way. There didn't seem to be a handle. I ran my hand over the metal. The ridges of a hidden handle bit into my palm. I pushed my hand into the metal flap and grabbed the handle edge. I pulled, but it only creaked.

"Please open," I whispered and tugged.
Click.

I sighed in relief. I went into the dark room and closed the door behind me. The siren was muffled, but still pulsed across the palace. A dim light saturated part of the room in a soft haze of light, enough to see it had a high ceiling. It was as large as the workshop if not larger. The tall windows were curtained blocking all the sunlight. The light was coming from a machine the size of a mini-fridge on a metal table not far from me. It was a transmitter reminiscent of an art deco radio. The gauges rose then fell emitting a gentle hum. An old style phone ear piece hung from a hook on the side. I could tell how it worked at a glance, but who would I contact? I didn't care. The speaker was palm sized. I twisted the dial, static fuzzing the sound. "Hello? Is anyone there? I'm being held prisoner. Help me." The lights on the transmitter suddenly went black and the scratchy sound ceased.

"Rose."

I looked up, but no one was there. Maybe my ears were only ringing. Who would have whispered my name? A door opened on the far end of the room. An elongated rectangle of white light stretched all the way to my feet like a road through the otherwise dark room. The silhouette of a person inside the room passed the door opening back into the darkness.

"Who's there?" I dashed over to the door.

"Go," the voice whispered, low and harsh from the deepest shadows.

"But who are you?"

I heard an intake of breath.

"Go, quickly." The voice was high, feminine. "Find the floor marked with a triangle over a crescent. Go."

I stepped slowly into the empty hall, looking back as I did. "Come with me? I need help getting out." Such desperation permeated the voice. "Are you a prisoner too?"

There was only silence. I sighed then inched down the hall. A sob came from the darkened room, but the door slammed shut before I could return. I grabbed the handle, turning and yanking. It was locked.

Shaking my head, I dashed down the hall, the smack of my boots echoing. The walls and floor were sheets of metal. A sheen sparkled where the light hit. A long blue carpet ran down the middle of the hall, leading to a staircase curling downward. The siren made me want to run, but guards' footsteps in the distance checked my speed.

I slipped down the unadorned, spiral staircase into shadows and dim light. Perhaps Bromin thought servants didn't need to see to do their jobs. Down, down they went. I passed two levels, but kept going. Would this take me to the tunnel back to the city?

The stairs ended in a foyer. To one side was a vacant laundry room and to the other an empty kitchen through swinging doors. I entered the kitchen and snuck along the utensil littered steel counters. Decorative metal shapes besprinkled the large wall on the other end of the room. Was there some kind of pattern? Was that how I could find the triangle over a crescent? If they were code to the locations in the palace I had no way to decipher it.

A tantalizing smell reached my nose from yet another kitchen. The well-lit room was visible through a set of windowed doors. I headed to a small door that led out the other direction. Somehow I had to wind my way through the palace undetected and into the court room with the hidden tunnel to the city. I heaved a sigh. Was the triangle over a crescent floor where it was?

"Stop where you are." A guard stood in the door I'd entered through, his bronze gun pointed at me.

My heart raced. "I'm—I need something to eat."

He narrowed his eyes.

"Really. I need food."

The guard dropped the gun to his side, but kept it in his hand. "Bromin said you were to keep to the workshops."

"But what about keeping up my strength?"

The guard approached me. "I will take you to get a tray of nutrition then return you to the workshop wing. You can't be roaming under the current situation."

"I think *not*." I hurled a large pot at the guard, smashing it into him.

Dashing into the other kitchen, I tipped a metal shelf across the doorway. The female cook screamed, over powering the siren for a moment. Out the opposite swinging door I ran smack into another guard. He was so startled I was able to run past him.

"Men, this way," the second guard yelled as I dashed down a dark thin hallway. *Oh goody, a whole crowd to join the fray.*

"Out, out… I need a way out," I muttered, gasping for breath. I ducked through another door. This place was a maze and I seemed to be getting deeper. Every plain door I tried was locked or led to windowless storage.

Around a corner a strip of yellow light ribboned the floor ahead of me. "Sunlight!" It was a staircase. I started up the steps, then down one of the wide ornate halls lit by sky lights. I tried opening doors as I went. Things couldn't get worse— could they?

"Stop!" It was Rustin entering the other end of the hall behind a figure that was headed right at me.

My mind raced. I turned back to the stairs only to find soldiers coming up it. I leaned my back against a door, my mind sprinting. Where could I go?

"Rose!" the person running from Rustin exclaimed.

I jumped back "Gad!"

He collided into the door, Grabbing the handle. "Open, open, open." He smiled at me as he yanked. "Thank goodness I found you."

I started pushing on the door. "They're nearly here."

"Open, you ridiculous…"

The door flew back on its hinges, throwing me forward. I stumbled against a settee, my arms and legs tangled in a mess of ruffled skirts. Gad slammed the door shut and flipped a latch.

Someone grabbed my arms, pulling me up; someone taller than Gad, with a spicy metallic smell to him.

"Let go!" I struggled against strong arms.

He released me and backed off. "Rose. It's me."

I stood, untangling myself from the stupid dress until I was upright and standing. Alum was there near me. I sighed in relief.

Alum glanced from me to Gad, who busied himself wedging a heavy metal and upholstered chair under the handles. Something thudded against the door. Gad shoved a small end table against the door as well.

Boom!

"Is there a way out of here?" Gad yelled over his shoulder. Another boom came from behind the door, followed by heavy pounding.

Alum pulled a couch toward the door. I hurried around the room checking the windows

Crack!

A thin black line formed down the door's length.

"Yes. Not that way, Rose," Alum said.

Thump. Boom. Crrrack!

"That won't keep them out long," I mumbled. "We could get out through the court room where the tunnel to the city is."

Alum walked to the fireplace. "That won't work either." He

68

pulled the grate of charred wood aside. "Come this way."

"Open up," Rustin yelled through the door. "You can't get away so give up."

"Push on the back." Alum motioned us forward.

Gad ducked in and pushed with his feet. The back of the fireplace shifted to reveal a short tunnel sloping downward. Gad disappeared down the polished stone slide. I put my feet in and slid. The passage grew dark then my feet hit the ground. I ducked out of the tunnel into a small room. Tools and bits of metal cluttered crude shelves. A simple table sat by a small window at eye level through which Bromin's metal garden still glimmered, peaceful and beautiful as before.

I looked up the ramp. "Alum?"

"I have to reset the grate. I'm coming." His voice was muffled up the tunnel. A crash came from upstairs. I held my breath. One second... Two... Where was Alum? Nothing other than the distant sound of the siren reached my ears. Did they capture Alum?

The grating sound of metal on stone reverberated down the tunnel. Alum appeared, jumping deftly to his feet. I blew out.

"They can't hear us down here," Alum said. His eyes sparkled. My cheeks burned red. He was so handsome, but something wasn't right.

Gad turned, narrowing his eyes at Alum. "What took so long?"

Alum's brow puckered. "You're one of the Steele's. That GearMaker spy and trouble maker, aren't you?"

Gad glanced at the window, then back and Alum, his eyes going wide. "You're that missing GearMaker boy from Pyria, aren't you? No one else was reputed to have such silver eyes. Everyone thought you were dead. This where you been all these years?" Gad asked.

"Yes," Alum replied.

"You're colluding with Bromin Sleaze?" Gad looped his thumbs in his belt, still glaring.

Alum leaned forward, scowling. "Not by choice."

"Then what is it?" Gad said, stepping forward aggressively. "You were up there a long time after that door broke."

Arms crossed, Alum glowered. "Are you implying something?"

I spread my hands between the men. "Stop you two. This is ridiculous," I hissed. "We have to get out of here. If Alum is trying to capture us wouldn't he have led Rustin down here?"

"Can you get Copper Rose away from the palace?" Alum asked.

"Of course I can. We need a way outside. My ship is hovering at the edge of that infernal garden. It has some kind of protection stopping me from landing there," Gad replied.

"If I get you to the garden, can you get her away from here?" Alum asked.

"Yes, but we have to hurry so guards don't find my ship. I need a better way to get back to it." Gad jabbed his thumb over his shoulder at the room above. "Since I can't go the way I came."

Alum gave Gad a calculating look, then resignation crossed his features. "Fine. I'll get you out of here. But you have to promise to keep her safe."

"So—how do we get out of here?" Gad complained from

70

the other side of the room.

"The window has a catch," Alum said. "It shouldn't be hard for you to slip through. It comes out on the side of the garden farthest from the main doors."

Gad leapt onto the table. "Perfect." The window hinge creaked as Gad glanced out. "Will the gardens be crawling with more of Bromin's minions?" Gad looked directly at Alum, his eyes narrowed and brow raised.

Alum leaned forward, his fists on his hips. "Minions? What are you insinuating?"

"Nothing." Gad turned back to the window.

I listened for the guards from upstairs. Only birdsong from the garden reached me. "Alum, you have to come with us."

Alum cleared his throat. His silver gaze bore into me. "I can't." He looked away. "You haven't been here long enough— for him to make you stay." He sighed heavily. "If I hurry they will see me elsewhere in the palace and never suspect me of any wrongdoing. I will be safe."

I climbed onto the table and grabbed the sill to hoist myself up. Suddenly large hands were around my waist lifting me. Alum was beside me, a wan smile on his face.

Wriggling my way out, the swarf that made up the garden dirt bit into my skin. Gad was edging along the building, looking back for me. Alum waved me toward him.

"Now—let's go!" Gad whispered.

"Alum," I said, crouching down to the window. "Come with me. You could be free," I pleaded.

"Oh, Copper Rose," Alum said. "I am bound here, and there is no time to explain. It is more important that you are safe."

Sadness filled his eyes.

"Please," I begged. His warm hand brushed down my cheek. My blood raced.

A commotion came from around the corner of the building, some twenty yards away.

"Over here," a man called out, his voice echoing around the garden. A guard had appeared from around the corner. "Right where he said she would be!"

I gasped and jumped up. "How did they find me? So you are helping them?" I asked, my heart sinking.

Alum looked away from me, his lips pinched together. He ducked back inside. The window at my feet clicked shut. How could he pretend to save me? I dashed through the brush along the building, running to the cliff edge. The leaves of the high bushes tinkled as they moved.

"We found her," a gruff voice yelled from behind me. "She's with the intruder!"

I looked back and saw guards running after me, their armor clunking menacingly.

I ran, my limbs pumping, my muscles burning. Could I make it in time? Gad sped ahead of me, closer and closer to the edge. He stopped, cupping his hands around his mouth. His foot slipped sending him toppling over the edge.

"Gad!" I screamed. He was gone. What would I do? There was nowhere to go. All I could do was jump and hope the locket would save me before I smashed into pieces on the bottom of the abyss.

"Copper Rose. Gad is dead. Stop and I will be merciful," Bromin said, his voice unnaturally loud for the distance.

I looked over my shoulder along the palace wall. Bromin appeared from behind his guards, shoving several into the bushes in his haste. His eyes flared with light. I sped forward, my boots sinking in the metallic dirt. Adrenaline pushed me faster and faster, the edge looming closer. Bromin and the guards bore down on me. Bromin's eyes flashed red then went black again.

"Copper Rose," Bromin said. "You know there is no escape."

I jumped.

Chapter 7

I fell. Hair whipped across my eyes, blinding me. My stomach flip-flopped and I felt weightless. Frantic, I reached for the locket.

Thump!

Arms were around me and I wasn't falling. I tossed hair from my eyes. Gad let go of me and returned the controls of a little boat.

"You're here," I gasped, adrenaline racing.

Bromin appear at the cliff edge. "Nets, men. Get the nets out."

"It's not over yet," Gad said.

I looked up, still close enough to see Bromin scowl.

"Get the air-skimmers. They'll not escape," Bromin said.

Gad dove for the controls and I grabbed the side. The boat moved smoothly away from the palace. The guards reached the edge and flung something over. A massive net spread out, falling gracefully toward us. Gad yanked the rudder, but one edge of the net snagged on the boat's keel. I fell to my knees. The small boat pitched downward on one side.

"*The net*," Gad yelled.

I tugged at it.

"Get it off," Gad said, struggling to control the ship.

"I can't—it—it won't give," I screamed. My hands were burning from the rope friction.

Gad pulled a knife out of a sheath at his hip. "Catch."

"I can't," I squealed, but he tossed it anyway. I threw out my hand as the blade glinted and spun. I cringed and grabbed. "Wow." The knife had landed perfectly in my hand.

I hacked at the weave. In seconds the net fell limply into the chasm below us. A ruckus came from the cliff, but we were far enough that I make out the words. Another net flew at us.

"Duck," Gad yelled, sharply turning the boat the other direction. I caught myself just in time.

The net drifted past.

"It missed us," I said.

Bromin cursed in frustration from above.

"Hold on." Gad jerked the other way.

"How are we going to escape?" I asked crouching down on the deck and holding tight to the rail. The city approached as we flew further from the palace. The buildings towered over us by stories.

"Keep holding tight. We're goin' down," Gad laughed and leaned hard on the rudder.

We dropped like a sub in water. A buzzing came from the distance.

"What about the air-skimmers Bromin called for?"

"Air-skimmers can't maneuver like I can. They're too bulky and cumbersome compared to a swift vessel like my baby here," he said as the airboat dropped downward. I watched behind us for any more nets or the air-skimmers, but the buzz of the unseen pursuit diminished.

"But where can we go?" I asked.

"Copper Rose, you needn't worry. I'll take care of you," Gad said.

"You can't drag me through this ridiculous world without telling me what's going on." I scowled, but he returned a smile.

"Yes, I can. Now watch this," Gad said. We drew near the endlessly tall buildings. He aimed between a pair of wide skyscrapers. The boat slipped into the shadows, leaving all signs of the palace behind. Gad switched on a dome-shaped brass light attached to the front.

A sharp-scented fog thickened around us. It stung my nostrils. This part of the city was quiet and cool. No bridges of bustling people crossed our path nor did any ornate windows adorn the facades. Those shops and fancy people had to be a mile or more above us in the very same buildings we skimmed past. Instead coarse constructions functioned as scaffolding and passage between buildings. The destitute skulked along, their faces covered and coats pulled close.

"Where are we?"

"This is the UnderCity," Gad said. "Only the elite live on the upper levels. The working people and poor live down here. Even Bromin's men don't come here without a reason."

"But—but won't catching us be a big enough reason for them to come here?"

"Well, yes. But I have a plan." Gad smirked.

I cocked an eyebrow. So far Gad had come through. Slick buildings passed by through the mist. In the calm of the shadows, my speeding pulse slowed. Why would Alum lead us out only to somehow notify Bromin of my location? I remembered the feel of Alum's hand on my face, the look in his eyes... His touch right before he left me to Bromin's men. The crack in my heart left by my grandmother widened. I shook my head, resisting the urge to cry.

The UnderCity was a different world from the sun-infused glory of the city's upper reaches. Gad guided the little boat between the sooty metal walls. The infrequent, gritty windows were nearly opaque. No adornments or fancy clocks decorated these walls. The smog drifted and curled around us as we traveled, burning my throat and stinging my eyes. I felt like everything was closing in on me. Time seemed to slow as we glided along.

Looking over the edge and around our boat, I found no propeller or balloon to lift it. No motor and no logic could account for how we were staying afloat.

Gad chuckled. "We're not going to fall."

I scowled at him and glanced out into the mist, my anxiety increasing as the murk grew heavier. "What is going on here?"

When Gad remained silent, I looked over at him. He shrugged.

My fists clenched and unclenched on the ruffles of my gown. "You showed up in an alley and act like you know me, like some kind of long lost cousin. I have been dragged all over this city, kidnapped. Some crazy machine thinks I'm not human." Pressure increased behind my eyes. "And Alum probably told Bromin where we were after making me think he was a victim."

Gad looked at me, his eyes wide. "Forget about Alum. I'm going to get you out of this awful city and away from that mad man. Stick with me a little longer, ok?" he said.

Gad seemed to be striving to keep me safe but I felt my life speeding out of control. "Fine," I snapped and folded my arms in front of me. I knew Gad didn't deserve my ire. But even more so I knew I shouldn't be upset by Alum. I could pretend it was only because no one deserved to be Bromin's prisoner, but that would not have been the truth.

The silence of the UnderCity was deafening. Moisture clung to my skin, chilling me. I relaxed my shoulders, attempting to throw off my conflicting emotions.

Gad's brows remained furrowed as he steered through the thick mist. Several buildings appeared ahead looking like dressed down versions of the upper stories. Gad veered as if anticipating what was to come. The haze parted around rudimentary bridges and ramps yards in front of us. Gad swung the boat between and through the rustic frameworks. A huddled figure ducked as we whipped over him. Like a roller coaster ride, Gad traversed the maze with expert skill, leaning into each turn. My knuckles whitened as I gripped the side.

The boat leveled out into an expanse of empty mist. A large building loomed up out of the fog. Long, dark bridges going nowhere were sticking out from the building like stiff arms.

I sat back, my eyes wide. "What...?" The haze thinned as we approached.

"Only a safe place we can land—and a faster means to get away from this dreaded city. We can catch a large airship on the other side," Gad said as he gently guided the boat.

The narrow bridges became clear as we got near. Boats similar to ours were tied up along the spidery, floating...

"Docks?" I asked.

Gad nodded. The boat bumped up against a dock. He held a finger to his mouth, hushing me. Leaping out, Gad nestled the vessel against the protruding wood and metal platform. Ships and air-skimmers bobbed in the air, their ropes dangling between their hulls and the docks as if they were actually in water. I had no time for more than a moment of continued amazement at this phenomenon. Nothing had helped me understand the technology. Gad reached out his hand and helped me onto the dock.

"Let's get going," Gad whispered. He entered the building, not letting my hand go. We hurried through the grubby, unadorned ticket station. It was littered with garbage, boarded-up ticket booths and rustic dwellings like a homeless camp. People skirted around us, avoiding eye contact and hurrying away.

A tall, broad shouldered man stepped out of the shadows behind a dilapidated ticket kiosk. Gad strode over, waving for me to follow. I hurried after him and glanced into the dim interior of the kiosk. Cobwebs hung across one corner of the cracked glass and crumpled papers littered the counter. I followed Gad into the shadows, where the tall man waited.

"Gad. You escaped. We feared the worst." He patted Gad on the back. I stood at a distance, the drear of the place sinking into me.

"No worries, Laurent," Gad said. "Is Frent here?"

"Come along." Laurent pointed to a dark hallway a few yards away.

Gad stepped past him and Laurent's eyes fell on me. He

gave me a slow once over and offered his arm. "Such a beauty in this dismal place? I could whisk you away to somewhere more fitting." He raised a brow and winked.

Really? I scowled at him. After all I had been through I was certain I looked anything but beautiful.

"Back off Laur. This one is not for you," Gad growled, stepping between us.

"No harm done, Gad. I meant nothin' by it." Laurent backed off, hands up in surrender. "Let's get ye to Frent." He ran a hand through his blonde hair and walked across the chipped tile floor into the hallway. Gad put a gentle hand on my back and we followed.

A door opened, and a dark-skinned man in leather stepped out.

"Decided to drag yourself back here?" The new man's voice rumbled.

"Frent," Gad chuckled and gave the man a hug, slapping him on the back heartily. Frent grinned, holding the younger man out at arm's length. He was several inches shorter than Gad, yet he managed a commanding presence. His black hair greyed at the temples and his hands looked rough.

He opened the door all the way. "Please, come in here so we can speak. Laurent—you will take care of things?"

Laurent waved and continued past the door down the hall. "Sure thing, Frent." He winked at me and stepped into the dark. Gad growled something under his breath then ushered me into the room. It was a small, unadorned room. A stack of crates occupied one corner, a crooked table took the other and plenty of cobwebs laced over it all.

"Gad. Your father won't be pleased about your misadventures." Frent gave him a stern look.

"I think he'll forgive me this time." Gad nodded at me.

"Do you?" Frent squinted at me. "That information you were after was too important for you to be sidetracked no matter what the distraction. You know that."

Gad stood straighter. "Frent," Gad replied, sternness in his voice.

Frent leaned against the table, crossing his arms. "Did you manage to accomplish your mission in any respect? Or was it all about the sideshow?"

My irritation flared. I came up beside them, glaring. "I'm not a sideshow," I snapped. An unruly curl fell across one of my eyes. Frent stared me down. His eyes flicked to my hair and his eyes grew wide. There it was: the shock that crossed faces— good, evil or unknown—starting with Gad in that alley. Each time, anyone saw my copper curls, they acted like they'd seen a ghost. Frent stood straight, his eyes never leaving my face or hair.

"See. And Bromin knows she's here," Gad said.

Frent took his eyes off me to look at Gad. "I see—You did the best thing. We can find another way to get what we needed." Frent looked back and forth from Gad to me then stared. He sputtered. "But I really should... We should inquire..."

I huffed and crossed my arms over my chest. "Either tell me what's going on or quit looking at me."

"Ha. *Yes* m'lady," Frent said. The crinkles by his eyes deepened.

"Copper Rose, you're better off not knowing everything until we have you away from Bromin." Gad looked over his shoulder at the door. "We have to get you out of the city."

Frent leaned toward Gad. "How did Bromin know? Could he still be attempting to succeed at making more?" Frent said.

Gad gave me a guarded look. "What did he want from you, Copper? I wasn't at the palace long enough to figure that out."

Shock spread over Frent's face. "You were in the palace?"

"I sent you word that I had to rescue her. Where did you think I was going?" Gad rolled his eyes. "Ends up she'd gotten herself half way out of there before I even found her."

"He wanted me to make a living machine and insisted I knew how." My voice cracked. "When I convinced him that I had no clue what he was talking about he became giddy with excitement. He assigned Alum the task of teaching me."

"Alum? As in *the* Alum?" Frent gasped.

"Yes," Gad said. "I saw him with my own eyes."

Frent leaned closer to Gad. "He isn't dead?"

Gad nodded, his lips tight.

"This is serious," Frent said to Gad.

Gad looked at the door and back. "Yes, I think Bromin *Sneer* will tear the city apart to find her, Frent. I need to get her out of here tonight."

"I don't think we are at that much risk if she stays here a little while," Frent replied. "Surely there is much to be gained. She has been in Bromin's lair. I would be irresponsible not to…"

My heart leapt. "Bromin's a lunatic. A frightening and serious lunatic. I would prefer to get as far away from this crazy city and Bromin as possible, if you don't mind." Maybe home was not as lousy a place as I used to think. No one ever hunted me there.

"Frent. Please, can we stop this interrogation and get out of here," Gad pleaded. I saw the concern on his face.

Pounding steps came from the hall. Laurent burst in and stood gasping in the doorway. "They're in the UnderCity. You have to go now. Bromin's men are coming."

Frent looked at Laurent in shock. Fear welled up in me. I didn't want to go back and find out how cruel Bromin Shere could be.

"This quickly?" Frent looked over at me as if I had sprouted antlers.

"Gad?" I stepped back, an urgency filling me. Gad grabbed my arm and pulled me past Laurent into the dark hall.

"Where are we going?" I asked.

Frent hurried up beside us as we reached the ticket station again. "One of our trade vessels is scheduled to depart in the next day. I guess they'll be leaving ahead of schedule. If Bromin's soldiers don't stop outgoing flights, you'll be able to slip on as they're leaving. The ship is listed as going to Merou District so Bromin won't be able to trace you," Frent explained in a hushed voice.

"And false leads?" Gad asked, peeking quickly at me.

Frent leaned closer to Gad. "Jilliea and Theily."

Gad nodded somberly. "They'll do. This is quite a risk to take."

Laurent leaned down and kissed me on the cheek. I pulled back and Gad stepped in front of me, scowling.

Laurent's brow creased. "Keep her safe," he said and stepped back into the shadows. Gad's severe expression softened and he saluted to the darkness.

"Tell him we're grateful for his help, and thank you, Frent." Gad put a hand on the shorter man's shoulder and leaned closer. "I'm not sure when I can make it back here, but I will relay everything to my father."

Frent nodded and slipped a canvas pouch into Gad's hand.

"Hurry," Frent said, vanishing into the dark hall.

Gad led me through the station, winding around people and kiosks. He took me down a tunnel to the left. I shivered. It was not that much different from another tunnel I'd been down only the day before. It ended quickly at a half-circle platform in the open air. Large docks stuck out like sun rays. Massive ships rested lazily against the docks. Hints of the dirigible balloons peeked out atop the massive hulls. Gad pulled me down one stretch, searching the sides of each ship as we went. It was eerie dashing along the dock in the fog. Ships rose up through the mist like ghosts. Some clamored with activity while others were silent. At the very end of the dock was a large airship adorned by dark green sail and one large dirigible balloon. Gad yanked on a dangling rope hanging from the upper rail.

"Who ye?" a voice echoed from above us.

"No one of consequence out for a stroll," Gad replied cryptically. A rope ladder fell at us. I yelped in surprise. The ship rail towered above us at least twenty feet. I knew what was coming next.

"You've got to be kidding," I grumbled looking down at the frilly skirts still hanging from my waist.

"Do I ever kid?" Gad smirked and gestured to the rope and bowed.

"Not so far."

Gad frowned. "It's the only way."

The only way? My last two days had long passed ridiculous. An evil dictator, floating boats, jumping off cliffs and now I had to climb a rope ladder that high? What was wrong with using ramps and stairs?

"If there was any other way up we would take it," Gad pleaded, steadying the ladder for me.

"Fine. But if I fall and die it's your fault."

"Perfectly reasonable. I'll be right behind you," he beamed. I hiked up the skirts, grabbed the sides of the ladder and cautiously put my foot onto a sagging rung. As I suspected the whole thing shifted and torqued with my every move. Progress was slow. The rope lurched as Gad joined the climb following close enough to unnerve me even more.

"Try to go faster," he whispered up to me.

"Yeah, right," I mumbled adrenaline coursing through me. "Don't look up."

"Hah. Like I can see anything through all those ruffles. Don't worry, Rose. Keep moving."

Each rung required concentration and painstaking effort for me to lift my foot, move it up another rung and fight the resulting twists and shifts it caused. The wretched skirt snagged and pulled at me. The mist was so tight around I could no longer see the dock and our destination was mostly shrouded as well. I was half way up when a sound echoed from the distant building, still invisible in the murkiness. Marching footsteps sounded from somewhere nearby.

"Oh, no," Gad moaned.

"Hey, you gonna get up here or not," the man called harshly from above us.

"Just go," Gad called back. "We'll make it up soon."

"As you say."

A hushed flurry of action sprang up on the ship. I continued climbing, now shaking. Bromin's men were on their way, and here I was dangling from a ship that looked more apt for a nineteenth century ocean, than the air.

The ladder swung away from the hull, nearly throwing me off.

"Hey," Gad yelped.

"Get the air-skimmers," a voice called out from the dock.

"Stop your ship," another voice said. "Bring it to port or you will be detained."

I looked down to see Gad kicking at two men in brown uniforms. The closest guard grabbed Gad's foot, pulling it from the rope rung. The second one lost his grip and leapt back to the dock just as the ship jerked away. Gad held on with one hand.

"Gad," I screamed, hugging the ladder so tight it bit into my arms and hands. Gad pulled himself back up and drove his heel down. Blood spread across the soldier's face sending splatters into the breeze. A growl erupted from the man.

Gad bent and swung his hand at the rope cutting one side with a small knife. The ladder shifted to the left. Gad's feet swung helplessly in the open air, one hand holding the ladder.

"No. Gad." I tried to reach him, but latched back on to the

86

ladder as my own hold shifted. Gad hitched his legs up catching his feet on the bottom intact rung. Yelps and growls flew at us from the guard hanging from the broken rope. Gad was again leaning back precariously. Like a monkey he contorted until he could hack away at the swinging rope.

"You won't escape," the man yelled.

The rope gave way and the soldier fell, screaming. He vanished into the fading haze.

Chapter 8

Low clouds slipped past us as we rose up, sending chills through me. I knew that soldier was gone, but I was sure I could still hear his screams echoing in my ears. The man above called down from the ship rail. "Goodness. You two gonna hang there the whole trip?"

The cold air added to my shivering.

"Uh—I think we need some help. Could you reel us in?" Gad replied.

"*No*," I snapped. "Give—me a minute."

Gad put his hand on my ankle, warm and comforting. My clenched fists relaxed and I found myself climbing up another rung. Then another, and another. The weathered faces of two airmen appeared over the now visible rail. One reached out his hand to me. I swatted it away and continued to the last rung. Grabbing the rail, I threw my legs over onto the solid wood of the deck. My knees buckled as they let go, and I fell to the surface of the wood deck. My head swam, my breath coming in gasps.

Thu-dump. "Thank you men," Gad said from on the deck behind me.

"What did ya do? This is cut clean off half way down."

"We had an unwanted stowaway." Gad chuckled as if it was

actually funny. I rested my forehead on the deck not willing to take any limb from the solid deck quite yet.

"But you took care of it, I see. Good for you," the second man replied.

Gad cleared his voice above me. "Planning to get up anytime soon?"

I looked up to see him standing over me. "Uh—this seemed like a good place to stay for now."

Gad's amusement was plain across his face. And the other men, also grinned like idiots. My ears burned, no doubt red enough to camouflage themselves in my hair. Gad smirked and laughed, joined by the others.

"What are you laughing at?" I sneered directly at Gad, feeling the heat suffuse the rest of my face.

"Oh, Copper Rose," Gad said. "You have nothing to be upset about. You're doing fine."

"Don't patronize me." I pushed myself up, tangling in the ruffles and nearly ending up on my backside. "I suppose most people have a crazed minion along for the ride too? Was he one of those GearMades? Is that why he was so kamikaze?"

"I dealt with it. You've nothing to worry about." Gad shrugged.

"Nothing to worry about you say?" A low growl trembled my voice. "Look at me! I'm on a floating boat in the middle of a world run by a lunatic who wants me as his prisoner because he thinks I'm some miracle worker. And you tell me not to worry?"

Gad shrugged again. The other men conveniently found business elsewhere on the deck.

I stepped closer to Gad, my fists on my hips. "Why are you dragging me all over the known universe? I have only known you for two days. Two days in which I have nearly been killed half a dozen times. Which part are you implying I don't need to worry about?" I crossed my arms and glared. Most of the men chuckled again, and Gad approached me. He reached for my arm, but I pulled away. I huffed, finding better control over the shaking. He gave me an exasperated look then glanced around, his back straight and eyes flashing. At the wave of his hand, the men scuttled away like lemmings.

"Who are you?"

He bit his lip, raising an eyebrow. "Good question." Gad scrutinized me. "Do you feel that I think less of you for freezing up on that ladder? It was far from ideal circumstances."

"Far from ideal?" My voice squeaked. "You really know how to downplay the extreme. But why would I care what you think? You seem like a playful, innocent boy one minute and then issue commands like no one would question the Great Gad. Worst of all, they do what you say. Then it's back to innocent troublemaker. Who are you?" I suppose magnifying his inconsistencies made sense. But what really bothered me was that he seemed to have known me from the minute he first saw me, like Bromin and Frent had. Who was I, was the better question. What did they know about me that they wouldn't tell me?

"I know what you're thinking," he said.

"No. You really don't."

"You'd be surprised. Things aren't as random as you think," he replied then walked past me. He stopped to look back at my stubborn stance. "It's rude not to announce your presence to

90

the captain when boarding an airship. We can get back to this later—when I find a better way to tell you... Well. When I figure out what to tell you."

"Fine. But I'll hold you to it." I followed him, pulling my arm away when he tried to take it. A slice of sunlight hit the deck, yanking my attention to the world around me. The fog was gone, and the ship was skimming over a green, lush valley. The reds and golds of evening sunlight spread over the land. The metal city was nowhere to be seen. The day had dashed past me.

I fell into a stony silence as Gad walked up to one of the men. He wore a close cut beard of silver-streaked blonde. His loose shirt was blue and covered in a well-worn leather vest.

Gad put out his hand to the man. "Captain. Thank you for making a change in your plans for us."

The captain shook Gad's hand. "Captain Aktil. Welcome aboard the Sapphire Lily. I'm here to serve you however you need Gad." He nodded toward the rail where we climbed aboard. "Only too pleased that little stunt didn't go any worse for you and your friend."

Gad pulled the captain aside and exchanged a few hushed words. The captain nodded. Gad slipped the little package from Frent into the expectant hand of the captain.

Captain Aktil walked over to me and bowed slightly. "I can guarantee you a quick and untraceable journey."

"Uh, thank you." I said, watching him stride over the deck to call out instructions to his men. The captain looked much like the people he commanded, though the set of his shoulders and the look in his eye made it clear he was in charge. I watched as he pitched in to pull a rope. Gad also jumped in to help, leaving me feeling alone and useless.

"Enough of this," I grumbled. If Gad could help, so could I. Besides, if the Sapphire Lily was my ticket away from Bromin, I was definitely going to do everything I could to make sure nothing more went wrong.

I glanced up at the sails and dirigible. Airmen danced about among them, seemingly oblivious to the dizzying heights, loosening a line here, tightening one there. The puzzle floated in my mind, nothing but a chaotic jumble of ropes, until suddenly it wasn't. The picture snapped into focus.

I strode over to a line dangling loosely down from a metal spar high above me. The rope was thick, but my two hands together were a match for it. I leaned my whole weight, pulling it tight and fastening it to a nearby hitch.

"Oy, girlie!" an airman shouted from above. "What d'ye think yer doing?" He swung down from his perch with the liquid grace of long practice, and dropped to the deck beside me. Gad ran over, his face all alarm.

"What?" I said. "Isn't that right?"

The airman examined the line and tested my knot. "Er, yes, miss. 'Tis, actually. Sorry, miss. It's only with the way ye come aboard, I took ye fer—somethin' else."

"That's all right," I said. "This is my first time on an airship."

"Then—how…" he stammered.

Gad's worried look broke with a laugh. "She's a proper GearMaker, mate. That's how!" He clapped the airman on the shoulder. The man gave a quick bow and swung himself back into the riggings.

When the lines were all secured and the men seemed to trickle away to simpler tasks I walked over to the rail to watch the ship move through the clouds. The adrenaline of our escape left my system, draining my energy away. I looked down at my shaking hands, and my thoughts turned to Gramma and Alum. I couldn't guess why the hurt from Alum's possible betrayal hurt nearly as much as losing Gramma. I had only known Alum for a day. I shook my head trying to get his alluring silver eyes out of my head. He had seemed a good person trapped by a mad man, but I'd been wrong.

"Look," Gad said, startling me out of my thoughts. We had passed beyond the valley and over a snow speckled mountain range. In the distance I saw the green of what could be another valley. Fluffy clouds whisked past. The airship moved along like a skater on smooth ice.

"It won't take long to get where we're going. The Sapphire Lily is one of the fastest airships I know," Gad grinned, putting his hands on the rail. He relaxed and gazed out at the horizon with me, nearly shoulder to shoulder. I couldn't make sense of this reckless man with a smile in his eyes. I didn't mind the companionship though. It took my mind off everything I'd left behind. I was on the biggest roller coaster of my life, and yet here he was keeping me steady. I fingered the locket through my blouse. It was still there hiding. On cue as I thought about it, it warmed against my breastbone. I sighed. Gad glanced at me then back to the passing terrain.

**

As darkness fell, the captain led Gad and I down into the hull. He pushed open a small door and pointed at another one

93

a few steps away. "These two berths should be adequate for your needs. I suspect it will only take two days to arrive in TreeCountry."

Gad motioned for me to enter. "Thank you Captain. We don't require anything fancy."

The captain grunted and narrowed his eyes. "As you say, sir. Is there anything else you need?"

Gad shrugged. "No, I think this will be enough."

"Uh…" I stepped closer to the captain.

"Yes?" he replied. He and Gad waited.

"I—I would like more comfortable clothes." I glanced at Gad's shocked face. "Not that this dress isn't nice, but… I really am more comfortable in…"

Gad cut me off. "We can solve this Captain Aktil. I know you need to instruct the night crew."

Captain Aktil grunted and plodded back up the tight stairs.

"I don't know that pants are a good idea."

"And why not?" I stepped right up to him.

He hemmed. "Not all of the people who work this region understand…"

A thought occurred to me. Why did I need to hunt out better clothes? All I needed was cleaner clothes. I reached quickly into the satchel hanging loosely over his arm. The rough texture of denim hit my fingers and I pulled my jeans and t-shirt out.

I grinned holding them out in front of me. "This will do."

"No really it won't." His hand flew at the pants, but I pulled them out of reach.

"You told the captain we could work this out and we just

have." I went back to my door and swung it open, a grin plastered on my face.

"Fine. Go on in." Gad rolled his eyes. "I'll be right next door."

I stopped, dread turning my insides cold. "Are you sure Bromin can't trace this ship?"

Gad pursed his lips and scowled downward. "He shouldn't be able to. Once we cross over into GearMaker lands tomorrow, we should be safe. There's a whole protection net that can only be crossed by ships equipped with a transponder."

I scrutinized his expression. "Well—it will have to do then." I sighed and stepped into the cramped room. The door squeaked as I closed it. The bunk was already pulled down from the wall and covered in sheets. A small sink and cabinet hung beside it. The opposite wall had a pull-down table that would only fit when the bed was up. The small closet next to it was just the size for a toilet. I knew I shouldn't expect more from a sailing vessel. I looked down at my torn, filthy dress then up into the mirror above the sink. Who was that in the glass? I recognized the copper hair and the eyes were the right color, but I couldn't be that exhausted person standing there.

I twisted the handle on the sink and tepid water poured out. I rubbed water over my face and the back of my neck. The prick of tears forming in my eyes made me grab the questionable hand towel from a rung on the cabinet. I rubbed at my face till it stung.

"Ok," I whispered to myself. I pulled open the cabinet and found a carefully folded night gown on a shelf. I sighed then changed out of the dress. The nightgown was soft and rather

Victorian, but I didn't care.

I held up the different pieces of clothing to see what might last another day. I could wash my jeans and make them work until something better was available. The shirt? I had doubts. There was a tear in the sleeve and grease so deeply imbedded in the cloth that there was little life left in it. I threw it into a waste bin under the sink. The green skirts sat in a pile on the floor. I kicked them to the wall and assessed the blouse. It was a sturdy material though fancy. Somehow I could come up with an acceptable outfit from all that.

With a bit of soap and more energy draining effort I scrubbed the jeans clean in the small sink. I left them, rhythmically dripping, over the back of the chair.

I flipped off the old fashioned electric light that hung from the ceiling, then curled up on the mattress. I was asleep within minutes.

**

In the morning I dressed in the slightly damp jeans, the blouse and the green bodice. The boots fit perfectly under the hems. I tucked the blouse into the pants, placing the vest-like bodice over it. Perfectly feminine in my opinion. When I got to the deck, I felt more like the real Copper Rose.

Airmen's heads turned as I crossed the deck smirking. I joined Gad and the captain. They turned to me when the crew grew silent. The captain's jaw dropped, but Gad suppressed a laugh.

"I need to see where we're going—and if anyone is following." I put my fists on my hips, but smiled.

Gad chuckled. "I see you resolved your discomforts."

"If you don't mind, Captain Aktil?" I tossed my hair over my shoulder.

Gad elbowed the captain.

"Forgive me, m'lady," Captain Aktil said. "Breeches on a woman are not unheard of. I simply assumed that a graceful woman from the city would never…"

"I'm a country girl. I've lived my whole life on a farm, so this is perfectly good by my standards." I adjusted the bottom of the bodice. "So could I please know if there is any chance we're being followed?"

"No, miss. We seem to be clear all the way to the borders of TreeCountry. We will need to stop at several guard posts in order to pass through the ElectraShield." The captain gave a pained look. "There is no faster way, but anyone pursuing us cannot get through."

Sighing, I shook my head and walked away from the men. It felt so good to be back in pants. I stood at the rail, letting the fresh wind blow my curls free from the hair clips.

The airmen were nice to me, but they were reticent to talk. Rather, they seemed to serve me as quickly as possible, bow awkwardly, then resume their duties.

The dirigible floating above us needed lots of care. The sails obviously helped to steer us, but I couldn't get anyone to explain how the ship worked, so I explored to figure it out for myself.

We passed over a tall range of mountains and a valley spotted with villages and farms. The first several guard posts were simple structures on the ground. They sent a dinghy up, checked the ship's ID and inspected the cargo before deactivating a hole in the shielding. Until the hole appeared I couldn't see anything. The yellowish hue of the shield domed over each area, overlapping to cover the land into the distance.

Other than being on a flying boat things couldn't look more normal. That land could have easily been part of Earth's past. It still wasn't home though. Nowhere was, anymore. Had the reverend come to collect the furniture we had discussed? *What will he think?* My belongings were still scattered around the old farm house in boxes and even still sitting out in the open. *Police might be scouring the woods. Or have they given up?* Time was different here, but how different?

"Gad..." I cut myself off. How could I ask about the differences in our worlds when he probably didn't even know about earth? Gad watched me, waiting. I shook my head and he turned back to the landscape.

I looked behind us. The sun shone from high in the sky, but still no other ships appeared.

"He won't find us. He wouldn't dare come here," Gad said, coming up beside me. The wind mussed his hair even more than usual.

"How do you know?"

"Because..."

Gad gestured to the trees. A thick forest of varied greens spread across the horizon. He raised an eyebrow at me and grinned, so I looked closer. The hills scooped down into a tree heavy valley. The trees looked strange and out of proportion to the farms leading up to the forest edge. The branches were wide like beaver tails, sprouting upright smaller branches into mini forests. I squinted. Buildings stood on one of the branches

—on most of the branches.

"No way," I gasped. Yes, it was a forest of trees, but the trees were as tall and thick as the city buildings far behind us; towering behemoths. We descended closer. Sure enough, the trees were big enough to have villages dotted throughout the branches.

"Hahaha!" Gad guffawed. "You should see your face."

"Are those trees real? How can they even exist? They're huge and the branches—Do they naturally grow like that?" Massive birds dove in and out of the upper branches. I pointed a finger at them, still gaping.

"Birds? What kind of birds get that big?" I asked. I could only hope they weren't meat eaters. Gad laughed again, his eyes twinkling.

"Those are skywings, not birds. People wear the wings to harvest the fruits and fungus from the trees. TreeCountry is the biggest source of food in all the land and—and it's home," he said.

I was amazed. "Really? You grew up here? Your family is here—in this—this—forest?"

"Yes. We're going to my father's home" Gad looked at me strangely. "I really want you to meet him. I know he'll like you. A lot."

"Ok." I was not so sure about that, but Gad had yet to let me down.

The final check point, guarding the beginning of the forest of massive trees, was more like a fortress. The structure rose up high enough that the ship could pull next to it for inspection. This time one of the uniformed men walked over to Gad and I.

He patted Gad on the back. "Gad. Some new intel for us?"

"Perhaps, Jayeth," Gad replied.

The guard's eyes narrowed on me. "And you are?"

Gad stepped in front of me. "She's with me."

"But..."

"She must be allowed entrance." Gad looked down on Jayeth in the commanding way he had.

The other guards were filing off the ship. Jayeth shuffled his feet then smiled. "Go ahead. It's not like we're at war. Not sure what all the new safeguards are for anyway." He waved at me and hurried over to the gangplank.

The sailors pulled the ramp over to the fort and the ship moved forward into the trees.

I looked over the rail. Furry creatures leaped among the top-most branches. Some were striped with tails like monkeys, while others had flaps of skin between limbs like built-in parachutes. From above, the trees seemed close together, but I looked down and saw that the trunks were football fields apart from each other. A wide dirt road wound between the trees and the village life that seemed to exist on the floor of TreeCountry. We dropped low enough to navigate below the forest canopy.

On the road horned striped beasts of burden, larger than any horses from Earth, were pulling carts brimming with large melons, fruits, and crinkled mushrooms big enough to sit on. Children on the wide branches dashed from one smaller upright branch to another, playing games and hiding behind massive leaves. The flat branches midway up the trees were so wide across in places that whole neighborhoods of cottages and gardens fit with room to spare. Botanical fragrances and the tang of wood smoke monopolized the air. It was too unreal. Too amazing and beautiful.

The captain came up behind us. "Gad, sir. A dinghy can take you to the Center tree. We must hurry to Merou District to allay suspicion of where we've been," the captain said coming up behind us. Gad nodded.

"Yes, Captain Aktil. We're grateful for the risk you've taken." Gad clapped him on the back and gestured for me to follow. Thankfully the dinghy was on the deck and was easy to climb into. The man sitting next to Gad grabbed a lever, pulled it, and turned the rudder. The dinghy sputtered, rose above the rail and out into open air. I leaned closer to the lever, but still couldn't see anything to make the technology understandable to me. Yet another technical challenge I was drawn to, but had no time to explore. Somehow I had to figure it out before I left this world.

The dinghy was fast and agile. It dodged in and out of the tighter branches toward a tree that was wider than those around it.

Gad pointed. "Drop us off at the tree three to the left of the Center Tree."

The man grunted. We turned sharply, forcing me to catch myself from falling.

The dinghy landed on a wide flat branch set up like a runway. Gad leapt out. I followed. The dinghy rose up again and buzzed out of sight.

The wood underfoot was smooth. It was a tree. It should feel unsteady. But it was as solid as the ground. The edges of the branches were yards away on either side, and the entire surface we stood on was flat. I looked up at Gad who was grinning.

"Quit laughing at me." I walked away from him.

"I'm not laughing," he snickered, coming up beside me.

"Please tell me there are no rope ladders here."

"There are no rope ladders here." Gad was now chuckling, ready to burst. "Come. I want you to meet someone." He hurried along.

The trunk was as thick around as a high-rise building. It even had a door big enough for several people to pass through. The oddities seemed endless. We entered and started up a spiral staircase carved so naturally from the wood that it looked grown. Light reflected from a series of mirrors throughout the curling passage, a warm glow blanketing the stairs.

Gad led me past half a dozen open doorways to other branches. Eventually we exited through one that was wider and more ornate than any of the others.

A whole world existed on that branch. A path led through a tidy garden to the door of a two story cottage. Outbuildings and more gardens dotted the radiating branches as well. A large windmill spun in the breeze, turning a series of gears attached to the side of the house.

"Wow," I exclaimed.

Gad walked ahead of me, waving me onward.

"Father. Father," he yelled out like a kid. He turned back to me. "I want you to meet my father, Daren Steele. He's most likely to be in his rose garden. Come along."

This place was so rich in colors and smells. Shrubs lined the path. Massive flowers hung from the tree branches that reached upward from the one we walked on.

Gad led me around the house and out onto a smaller, though still significant, flat limb. We passed under a bower of small branches, each rising from the edge of the path and expertly twisted into an arch. I stopped inside, grabbing a woody branch. Before me was an amazing, lush garden of rose bushes in full bloom. Their heady scent filled my nose. Most of the roses were as copper as the brightest new penny.

A middle-aged man, with a touch of grey in his dark hair, looked up from the garden of roses. He stood slowly, leaning on a rake, brushing his other hand on the thighs of his dark green pants. The sage shirt that fell loosely over his shoulders had come free from a wide suede belt. His eyes lit up as he saw Gad, and he hurried over.

"When the rumors reached me... You had me worried, Gad. I'm glad to see you in one piece and so soon." He enclosed his son in an open hug, the rake bumping Gad on the back.

"Father, I had to hurry home. I had to..."

The man looked past Gad to me, still standing in the archway. He froze, eyes wide. "Leatha?"

My heart jumped as I stepped forward. "No. Leatha was my mother's name."

"It can't be," he gasped, walking slowly to me. The rake dropped to the wooden ground as his strong arms wrapped around me, pulling me tightly to him. His large hand smoothed my hair as if I was a child. He buried his head in my curls, mumbling. I wanted to pull away. Who was this man to hold me so tightly?

"Oh, my Rose, my Copper Rose. You have come home to me."

I pulled away and looked at him. I put my hands up to give myself space. "I'm sorry, sir. I've never met you before."

"Father. She doesn't know," Gad said in a soft voice. Gad's father backed up. His cheeks were damp.

"Oh, my dear forgive me. I have waited so long. I was losing hope of ever seeing you again," he said. His dark-brown eyes glinted.

"I'm sorry, but I don't know you," I said, stepping from his reach. This had to be another trick or mistake.

"It's no wonder you don't remember me. You left when you were only five-years-old. I would never forget those copper curls, though. And you look like your mother."

"You knew my mother?" I said, my suspicion growing.

"Oh, yes. She was the most beautiful woman I ever knew, and so intelligent, too." He touched a hand to his heart, a hint of tears in his eyes.

"Who are you? How could you possibly know me or my mother?"

Gad's father looked straight into my eyes and caressed my cheek with his large palm. "Dearest Copper Rose. I'm your father."

Chapter 9

"No, no, no." I backed away. "This can't be. You can't be." The same dark, rich eyes as my Gramma's looked at me. "You? You're Gramma's son? But— But—" I stammered. He reached for me, then let his hands fall to his sides. If this was my father...

"My name is Daren. Did she never speak of me? Surely your mother told you something," he said. His brows lifted.

"My mom? She…" If this man was my father then I wasn't alone anymore. But I couldn't believe him just because of a resemblance to Gramma. Or could I? The baby picture in the trunk in the attic. The initials on the back were D. S.—Daren Steele. It *was* my father in that photo.

Daren walked over to the closest rose bush. He caressed a large rose like he had my cheek. "I created these roses for your mother. When you were born with hair to match their brilliance, your mother insisted you be called Copper Rose," he explained. "I thought you were forever lost to us. Every day I have tended my roses, hoping for the return of my wife and daughter—my precious little Copper Rose."

A tear ran down his cheek as he looked up at me. This man was my father? He loved my mother and— Wait.

"But that means…" I whipped around to find Gad standing

only a few feet behind me sheepishly gazing at us.

"Yes." Daren came up beside me. "Gad is your older brother."

Gad looked up and flashed a grinned at me. He shrugged, while I stammered for words.

"How did you know, Gad?" I asked. Mischief sparkled back at me from his eyes. "When you saw me in the city, how did you know who I was? I didn't even know I had a brother."

"The locket," Gad said and pointed at my neck. Daren looked at Gad and back to me, his eyes wide. "Well, that and your hair. No one has copper hair like that other than Mum and my lost little sister."

"The locket? Really? That's where it went." Daren looked at me in shock.

I stepped away from both of them, grabbing the locket through the fabric of my shirt as if it would protect me. "What about the locket? All this time you didn't even bother to tell me that you're my brother. Clearly this crazy locket has something to do with all of this since it brought me here. I still don't know where I am or how I got here or even if you are who you say you are. I want to believe you, but..." I was trying to wrap my brain around these new ideas, but a buzzing in my head kept me unfocused. This was too much, too fast. I had thought I was alone. Through a whole year of sickness, Gramma didn't even tell me I might have a brother and father.

"If it is *the* locket...," Daren said and leaned closer to me.

"It is," Gad said to Daren. "She appeared out of nothing only yards in front of me. The locket was in her hand, like in the drawing in the house. Uncle Brehan once told me the

106

locket could take someone where they needed to be. I guess you needed to be with me."

I looked at the two of them, father and son. The resemblance was obvious. Not only did they look like each other, but they also looked like Gramma. What more evidence did I need? I stepped back and sank down onto a stone bench. Gramma didn't just go to another town or country. Gramma came here, to this crazy place. Somehow she was transported to this very world I stood in. Her love of large trees suddenly made all the sense in the world. So why didn't she tell me? Why did she leave me so alone?

"Gramma's locket. It brought her here, didn't it?" I asked. Daren nodded. "She was your mother. She never even told me your name. Why would everyone leave me in the dark? I have a right to know who I am."

Daren looked pained. "She must have been protecting you. Our world was no longer safe for you. None of the GearMakers are really sure where the locket came from. It has been around so long. I don't even know how it got to Earth to bring my mother here."

"GearMaker? Bromin kept saying that I'm a GearMaker."

Daren stepped closer to me, his brows arched. "Bromin? You know that evil GearMade?"

"Father. She's fine. Please," Gad said, putting a hand on his shoulder.

"No," Daren said. A scowl formed on his face and his fists clenched. "What does any of this have to do with Bromin Shere?"

"He captured her before I could get her out of the city. He

caught a glimpse of her hair in the crowd. It was all I could do to get away myself, and rescue her later."

Daren stumbled backward as if struck. He sat down onto the other end of the stone bench. Daren looked up at us. His children. "How will we protect her now?" Gad shook his head, but was silent, looking downward.

I looked back and forth between father and son, my father and brother. "Please. You tell me you're my family. I didn't even know this place existed a couple days ago. Now I find that everyone in this crazy world knows who I am and yet I don't? Please," I said.

I no longer had to wonder at Gad's motives. He took care of me because he believed I was his sister. Now I, myself, was starting to believe it.

"Copper Rose. I know all this is hard to take in. My own mind is reeling, so I can't imagine what yours is doing," Daren said.

Daren's expression was unreadably complex. He rubbed a hand across his eyes. "How could this have happened? The locket dropped you right into Bromin's territory. If only it had brought you to TreeCountry."

I looked at Gad. "Alum and Bromin both thought I was one of these—these GearMakers. Am I even human?" This was all unimaginable. If I wasn't human then was I a GearMaker? But what in this world did that actually mean?

Daren heaved a huge sigh. "Dearest Copper Rose, you are part human. Your Gramma is from Earth, but you were born here."

"That would explain—that would be why I was considered

a mechanical prodigy at home. I'm really a GearMaker." I looked at my hands. Alum's skill, the mechanical nature of the city and the amazing modes of transport. All from a race of people like me. A race of people I belonged to. I looked up at the two men. My family—my heritage.

I fingered the locket again. "But how do they all get here? The humans? Is it these lockets?"

"There is only one locket," Daren said, his hand on the bench between us. "Humans from Earth ended up here other ways we aren't sure about. Most don't even know Earth, since it was their ancestors who came here originally."

I nodded. "And GearMades? GearMakers made them using their... their magical abilities?"

"Hah," Gad laughed and leaned against an upright tree limb. "Magical? I guess it would seem like magic. At least we used to have that ability."

"Bromin is one of the oldest of the GearMades. He is perhaps a thousand years old if the rumors and ancient histories are true. GearMakers are like humans with longer lifespans." Daren motioned me closer.

I slipped a little ways down the bench. "What kind of longer lifespan?" I asked. What would all this mean for my life? Everything was changing so fast I couldn't even fathom what my life could be anymore.

"Grandfather is what, reaching two hundred and thirty years, Father? He lives in the Shaley region," Gad said, leaves rustling as he shifted his stance against the branch.

"He's two hundred and thirty nine right now."

I gasped. "Really? You aren't immortal are you?"

Gad chuckled.

Daren ran a finger over the stone of the bench. "No, not immortal though some would like to think they are. There are histories that say some have lived to a thousand years old, but these days five centuries or so is about as old as we get. Your grandfather lives in Tianiu, where he was born. When my mother returned to Earth it broke his heart. Being home helped him be at peace."

Gramma had been so devoted to me. How could she break the man's heart? How could she leave her own child? "Why? Why would she leave if she loved him?" I asked.

Daren sighed. "I wish I knew. She only said that she felt she had to return to Earth for a while and we never saw her again."

"Oh no," I looked up at Gad.

"What is it?" Daren asked.

"Gramma. She—she died last week. I found the locket when I was going through her things to…" I couldn't stand it.

Daren buried his head in his hands. "I hoped she would return despite how long it had been." He looked at me, a tear running down his cheek. "I see now it was just a dream."

Gad sat next to him and patted Daren's knee.

I felt like an outsider even though I was wanted to believe I wasn't. I was deprived of a decade and a half of life with my own family. If the loss of his mother was hard, what would telling him my mom had disappeared do to him? I couldn't stand it. Here Daren was overjoyed at my return and all I could do was bear him bad news.

I stood suddenly and strode out into the rose garden. I had to be alone to think. The roses brushed against me, their petals soft to the touch though uncharacteristically cold. Thorns hid below the gently serrated leaves. I touched the stem of one flower and felt the hum of metal, the spark of life. Were these living machines? Impossible, but there they were before me, their living essence distracting me from the moment. *We are a race gifted with technological abilities beyond that of Earth.* What did that mean exactly? Growing up, people called me a mechanical genius. But this rose was something even more. It was metal, yet alive.

I jumped when a hand touched my arm.

"Forgive me," Daren said. His eyes were clear and his expression gentle.

"I'm sorry." I bowed my head. "I feel like a harbinger. I have to be the one to tell you that your own mother is dead. I also have to tell you that my mom is gone, too."

His eyes grew wide and he held his breath.

I put a hand on his arm. "She's not dead. Or at least not that I know of. She disappeared when I was about eight years old." His sadness eased, but his shoulders slumped.

"I don't know what to say," he replied.

Gad came up behind him, putting his arm around Daren. "We will get to the bottom of all these mysteries."

Daren touched his son's arm and stood straighter. "I know, Gad. But Rose, having you here makes all the difference in the world. You have to believe that. I can only hope my mother had a good life after she left. If she raised you, then at least she wasn't alone. Father and I always knew she wouldn't live as long as us, but we both hoped to get her back. That is not to be." He gave me a wan smile. "If Leatha is alive then eventually we *will* find her."

I reached out to the flower again. The dying sun cast sharp angles of light over the garden. The copper petals sparkled like prisms.

The past few days were a whirlwind, but prior to the revelations of this afternoon I had believed I was alone in life. Now I had a family. For the first time since I was eight, I wanted to find my mother and find out why she left.

"The day is coming to a close soon, my dears." Daren straightened himself up. He pulled me close. "If you're feeling anything like I am then you've had too much new information for one day. Let's get you settled in. There will be time for more talk tomorrow. I want to get to know my daughter."

Gad grinned. We walked back down the garden trail to the cottage, Daren's arm around me and Gad ahead of us. The setting sun showered brilliant, colored light across the branch homestead and filled me with hope.

***

I slept in my childhood room. It was simply furnished, but several small metal toys lay in a corner and an aged, colorful quilt hugged the bed. Morning light woke me. I found a pair of soft leather breeches and a flowered blouse on my dressing table. We had all talked, well into the night, of simple things. Stories of Gad and I growing up, of TreeCountry and of my grandfather. Gad said he would take me to meet him someday. I felt more at home than I had since—well—since Gramma died. I tried to retrieve memories from the five years I lived in TreeCountry, but could only remember Gramma and a few memories of Mom before she vanished.

"Thank goodness for the comfortable clothes," I said as I came down the stairs.

"We scrounged through Mother's old things," Gad said. He looked at me up and down. "I thought those would fit you. There are more you can go through later."

"Anything to stay out of that dress." I groaned, and Gad laughed.

"What should we do today, sis?" Gad asked.

"I don't think I can take any more life-changing information like yesterday, so can you show me the rest of the buildings here?" I sat across from Gad and looked over at the spread of luscious smelling foods. Daren walked up behind me. I looked up and saw the warm eyes of my father.

"Good morning, Copper Rose. Did you sleep well in our little tree house?"

"Yes, I did, Daren. Is that what I call you, or do I use Father?"

He came around to sit by me. "Father is perfect, or Daren if you wish. Having you here means more than you can imagine, so I don't care what you call me." He scooped a heaping spoon of an egg-like dish onto my plate and another to his own. I grabbed some toast while Gad poured an iridescent pinkish-orange juice into three glasses.

We ate and conversed. They talked more about TreeCountry and the current harvest of pila fruits. I poured another glass of the delicious juice as I listened. The tingly fruit smell wafted through my nose. Sunlight angled across the table and through the glass, casting jewel-like tones. I held up the glass and looked through, tinting the view outside the window.

Something huge flew past my distorted vision.

"Wha…" I jumped, spilling a little of the juice as I put it down.

"The skywings are here. Time for work." Daren stood and placed his dish in the metal sink. Gad returned the remaining food to a chest-like refrigerator unit sitting on metal vine legs that curled up the sides.

Outside a dozen or more adults were descending into the yard. They wore large, Da Vinci looking wings on their backs. Big leather bags strapped around their waists hung like saggy tubes.

"Reporting for today's assignments, Daren," a brusque grey-haired woman said. She walked forward gracefully, folding her wings back like a bird. She glanced quickly at me, then looked at Daren.

"We need to harvest the western quadrant this week. I will be here or at the tree roots helping at the silos," Daren said.

"Will Gad be joining us, sir?" a flaxen haired young man asked.

Gad shook his head. "Sorry, not today Hyran."

"Good gathering. Off with you," Daren called out, followed by the hoots of delight and the rustle of wings spreading for flight.

"They're harvesting pila fruits?" I went over to Gad as we watched the crowd take turns leaping into the sky.

"Yes," Gad said. "That was pila juice you were so fascinated by at breakfast. The season is almost over. Then we have a couple months of quiet before the harvest of thryat fungus which grows at the top of the trees. I wish I could join in this year, but..." Gad turned to Daren who gave him a stern look.

"We don't know what will happen this year." Daren looked at me. "Gad is needed elsewhere since Bromin is stepping up his efforts to take over." He grimaced and pushed a hand through his hair.

"What do you mean?" I shifted my feet.

Gad hooked his thumbs in his waistband. "We weren't sure how Bromin was going to succeed at his goals. But after what happened to you and discovering that he has Alum... You need to tell Father everything you know about Bromin."

I huffed. I didn't want to relive that. One thing kept nagging at me. "I don't understand how machines can be alive," I said.

"I can't really tell you how it works. Sadly, the skills to create GearMades have been lost. There are few GearMakers older than eight hundred years." Daren looked thoughtful. "From what is happening to Bromin it's probably a good thing. I suspect that time has driven him mad."

I rubbed the locket through my shirt. "Bromin wanted me to make a living being. That's what Alum has been trying to do for him all these years. Bromin insisted I can do it," I said, feeling a rush of fear for Alum. If the skills were lost how could Alum ever succeed?

"So he's still trying to create a GearMade?"

I shrugged. "I guess."

"For several hundred years—before he became this strong —Bromin asked the GearMakers to create more GearMade beings," Daren said. "But we refused, and eventually he gave up. We don't know what changed over a decade ago to make

Bromin steal GearMaker children. We suspected he was attempting a different way to get what he wants. Alum was one of those children." Daren shook his head. "An army of GearMades—without the compassion, humanity and intelligence GearMaker's of old put into them? Well, let's say I don't want to see our world after that kind of takeover."

I knew Alum had been unable to succeed, which was hopeful, but then maybe that would make Bromin more determined to get me. I stepped away from them. I didn't want to go back to that man. That machine. I felt safe standing in the middle of this paradise of trees, but fear crept back in like a pernicious weed, rooting wherever it could take hold.

I pushed my hands through my hair. "Is there any way to convince Bromin he's wrong? I'm no more capable of making living machines than any of you."

Gad pursed his lips. "Well..."

"What?" I scowled at my brother. "What makes it likely I can do this ridiculous task?"

"You're a Steele," Daren said as if this explained it all. "And a Locke. The Steele and Locke family lines were the most powerful. We're from the family lines that created and gave life to the first GearMades, three thousand years ago. Before that only lesser beings—animals, plants and such—were created by any of the families. Bromin knows who you are because not only are you a Steele and a Locke, but as a child you had skills no one had seen for generations."

"The butterfly," I said, feeling uneasy.

"Yes," Daren said. "You created it when you were only three. No one knows how you did it. It sat lifeless in your hand, you chattering on about how you made it. Suddenly it lifted into the air, buzzed around your head and dashed off into the trees. No one believed us. Why would they? No one had given that level of life to any of their machines for so long. But Bromin must have found out. " He sighed. "I woke up one morning to find that the locket and the two of you were gone."

If he was my father why would he lie to me? But it was hard to believe that I was this person they spoke of. I wanted to remember something so amazing as giving a machine life. I scowled at the ground. Why couldn't the locket have dropped me here in my real home instead of where Bromin could find me? A shiver of cold fear ran through me. I didn't want to go back, but would Bromin ever give up chasing me?

"Father, you're scaring her," Gad insisted. "Let me give her a tour of the workshops and the rest of the tree. There'll be plenty of time for answers later."

"Of course." Daren put his arm around my shoulder and looked down at me. "My dear Copper Rose, don't worry." He squeezed me close. "We'll protect you. Bromin hasn't ever succeeded at an incursion into TreeCountry. I doubt he can do anything while we continue to protect this land."

Daren's words and Gad's smile warmed me. I wanted to feel safe. I felt a little better, but not enough. Too much of what they'd said, too much of what I'd seen, told me Bromin wouldn't give up that easily.

Chapter 10

Gad gave me a full tour of the place where I was born. Storage spaces were carved right out of the upright branches of the tree. The flat branches were wide enough for entire homesteads. Normal trees even rose up from the soil that accumulated across the limbs. Shelves of bottled pila juice filled one storage cubby. Others were full of bin after bin of metal parts from old machines. The other buildings on our branch were overflowing with gardening seeds and supplies, canning and equipment repair.

On the farthest edge of the homestead where the branch thinned, a field of squash bathed in sunlight. Just beyond rested a small one-story building. Moss covered its roof and vines trailed up the sides. If not for the clear cobble walkway I would have believed it was abandoned to the elements. "What's that?"

Gad looked. "Ahhh... I was saving the best for last, but I might as well take you now."

He led me to a path of worn stone pavers, each a different hue. Wildflowers grew beside them. We reached the building. Though it was chipped and starting to fade in spots, the door was cheerful and painted a beautiful emerald green.

Gad stepped aside and waved me toward the doorknob. "Go ahead." He grinned.

I grasped the copper handle and entered the large, sunlit room. Gad followed. Workbenches and cabinets lined the walls. Machines large and small sat haphazardly under benches and hung from the ceiling on thin wires over the thick wood table in the middle.

"Wow," I whispered.

He laughed. "You should see your face! This is the workshop that used to be yours, but I took it over. You can have it back of course," Gad said. He stepped into the room and around the large table. "Take a look."

"Mine? I thought little girls had playhouses. It's so wonderful," I said in awe. My brain raced through all the things I could create in that cozy workshop. I ran a finger along the table edge. In the center was a large machine already in progress. I touched it gingerly.

Gad came up beside me. "It's a weed puller. Father is always working so hard when I'm away. I thought I'd make something to help. As you can see it's still a long way from finished," he said. "I haven't been home much the past few years."

I ran my finger over the workings. "Hmmm..." I could see what he was trying to do, but an idea popped into my head. "If you put an additional set of gears here to work the side blade, you may find that it'll cut more." I pointed at the lower mechanism.

Gad leaned over to see where I was pointing. His brow wrinkled, a finger tapping his lips. He reached into a box under the table and pulled out a gear. He held the gear in place, looking at me for approval.

"That should do it." I smiled.

He set the gear down next to the machine. "I didn't even think of that. I can weld in a framework for the gears and it should do what I want."

I stepped back and walked around the table to another machine that looked more like something meant for the kitchen. "You would have."

"No, I wouldn't," Gad said. "I may be a Steele and a Locke, but I got more of the watered down human side of things from Gramma. Nothing I make is ever very good compared to pure blood GearMakers, but since I have a lot of life to go I figured I should try."

I tilted my head and looked at him. "I know enough about you to say that you have plenty of skills to boast of without needing some magical mechanical skills. Besides…"

"Besides what?" he insisted.

"You have Gramma's eyes and her compassion. Obviously you got her adventurous spirit too," I said as a tear formed in my eye.

"I wish I could've known her." His baby finger traced the wood grain.

"She would have loved you."

We spent an hour looking through the workshop. Gad showed me tools I'd never seen before and taught me how they were used. There also seemed to be plenty of screwdrivers, hammers and pliers. Apparently some tools are universal across worlds.

As I looked through everything, I wondered what was the magic tool or element that made living machines possible. If I, in my childhood, created a living creature from a machine then

I should have some hint of memory to remind me what I did. No matter how hard I thought, I couldn't remember anything. My curiosity was only putting me at greater risk. But I wanted to know the secret lost to my people. *My people. What a thing to say. Me, having people.*

"Copper Rose?" Gad said waving a hand in front of me.

I looked up and realized he had been speaking while I was lost in thought. "Oh. Sorry."

Gad pointed at the door. "I hear Dad calling us."

"Oh!" I set down a tool and a gear, and glanced over the tables of parts begging to be put together. "Let's go."

Gad led the way out of the workshop. Dad was still hiking toward us through the rows of squash when we reached the end of the colored stone trail.

Dad stopped walking. "A member of the Council of Elders wants to discuss what you found out." His eyes dashed around before landing on me. "And he wishes to meet you, Copper Rose."

"Is he coming here?" I asked.

Dad stepped closer to me. "Gad told me you might be having a little elevation trouble."

"Oh, sheesh." I threw my hands up in the air, glaring at Gad who was openly laughing. "I'm dealing with it."

Dad chuckled.

"Really. I'll be fine."

Dad walked down the path and I followed quickly, shaking my head at Gad.

"Gad," Dad said. "Yuthin is waiting to take us."

We descended the staircase in the main trunk of the tree,

then exited onto the limb I originally arrived on.

"How do we get there? We—we're so high up," I asked. Gad's chuckle was practically sinister. I stepped away from him, my hands out in front of me. "No. No rope ladders. I refuse. And none of those skywing things either. I want something solid under me."

"Aw, you're no fun," Gad replied, patting me on the back. I gave him a scowl.

Dad pointed down the open runway. A small air-skimmer was waiting for us near the end. The pilot nodded and watched as we got into the seats. His gold hair shimmered in the sunlight, and his features had a timeless youthfulness about them. The long straight nose and sharp cheek bones gave a severity to the gentle look in his dark eyes.

"You all right in a dinghy? I know it's not solid ground, but you seemed fine before," Gad asked, smirking.

I glared at him. "Did I have a choice the other day? My life hasn't exactly been under my control since I landed on that sky bridge in the city."

"No. I guess it hasn't." He shrugged. Gad leaned back lazily. "We're ready, Yuthin."

The dinghy rose soundlessly off the landing branch. Like other small boats, there wasn't a sail, motor or propeller of any kind.

I leaned out as far as I could to look for any exhaust or mechanisms below. Nothing was obvious. I leaned the other way, but my heart fluttered as I perceived the ground so far below. Still I didn't find what made the boat float. I sat upright in my seat, breathing deep to steady my nerves.

Yuthin gave me a strange look and turned back to the rudder.

I threw my hands in the air. "How in the world do these things float?"

Gad burst out laughing and Yuthin's lips curled up into a small smile.

My cheeks felt hot. "I'm glad I amuse you."

Gad shook with laughter.

Yuthin shook his head and steadied the boat. "Gad, Sir. If you please. You may topple the ship."

"Oh sorry, Yuthin. I couldn't contain myself. Rose. The look on your face. I can't help it."

I scowled at him. "Why would I know any of this when I grew up in another world? A world that *doesn't* have floating ships."

He blushed.

"I'm sorry." Gad reached out to take my hand, but I pulled it away. He tilted his head and frowned. "I really do apologize. I take these things for granted. It's hard to remember that you haven't lived in our world for most of your life."

Yuthin leaned close to me. "Miss Copper Rose, if I may. It involves an element called Iridium. The uncanny nature of the element allows it to float when it is in a solid form."

Yuthin was soft-spoken, but something was odd about him. I couldn't place it. He looked like other GearMakers, but there was something else about his movements and his smokey eyes that I couldn't identify.

Gad patted me on the knee and wiped a tear of laughter from his now calm face. "Yuthin works in the building yards.

Perhaps we could go visit. I can get someone to teach you how Iridium works."

"It would be an honor, Miss Locke." Yuthin tilted the rudder sharply and the dinghy descended the final few yards to the branch of yet another sky-scraper of a tree. I held tightly to the edge of the little ship.

Gad leapt out as we landed. Yuthin put out an arm to help me balance as I climbed out of the little airboat which was hovering a foot above ground. His skin was cool and unnatural like...

I jumped away, rubbing my arms and staring at Yuthin. He smiled back with a coldness that did not match the kindness in his eyes.

Gad turned back. "Copper Rose?"

"He's like Bromin," I gasped, my heart racing. Yuthin's expression fell and sadness filled his eyes.

Gad looked between us. "Oh. Yuthin is a GearMade. But don't worry. He's perfectly safe."

Yuthin stepped out of the dinghy and approached me with his hand outstretched. I moved back further. What was a GearMade doing here?

"No need to fear, Miss. I greet you," Yuthin said bowing.

"But you're..."

"Rose. Most GearMades aren't like Bromin," Dad said, putting an arm around me. He pulled me forward a little till I planted my feet.

"No. I could never be like he, Miss Locke. I live and serve amongst my creators, side by side. Please do not fear me," he said, his eyes gentle. The stiffness of his mouth was maybe a

124

trait of being a machine, but the eyes said it all. The eyes were as alive as can be. Lights dazzled softly in the grey irises. I softened and put my hand out nervously. Yuthin carefully took it and kissed the back of my hand. I blushed and pulled away.

He gave me a look of understanding. "I will wait to take you back home."

"Thank you," Gad said.

Dad led me to the cottage at the trunk of the tree limb. It was smaller and more rustic than ours and appeared to be part of the tree.

A withered old man dressed in a simple tunic and pants stepped out the front door and waved. His hair was silver white around his deeply wrinkled face. His eyes were a piercing, rich blue.

When we got to the cottage he stepped forward and grabbed Dad's hand. "Thank you for coming. I know you have much to concern yourself with, but I would like to help." He took my hand. "Copper Rose. My name is Tenze. I serve on the Council of Elders with your father. You are as beautiful as your mother. It is an honor to meet you."

My mother? People here knew her. I rubbed a hand over my face. I never got to know my mother and probably never would.

Tenze led us inside to an earth toned sitting room with nubby upholstered furniture. He carried a tray to the small table and poured an amber liquid into cups.

Once we were all seated Tenze turned to me. "We have been working on a plan to keep you safe from Bromin. Most of the council doesn't believe there is any reason to worry so it is not going to be easy." He handed me a cup of steaming liquid.

Gad huffed.

"They mean well," Dad said. "Many of the council have never left TreeCountry. They don't understand how dangerous our world has become. If we do nothing while we wait for them to see the truth, I fear it will be too late."

Gad sat on the edge of his seat and put his cup down a little too aggressively, causing it to spill. "They better catch on soon. Bromin is serious. He'll come here once he figures out this is where Copper Rose is."

"We know that." Dad put a hand on Gad's knee. Gad leaned back in his seat and folded his arms.

"I don't want to put anyone at risk." I gripped my cup tightly, my stomach churning. "What can I do? I don't want to go, but I will if it means keeping people safe."

"No," Gad snapped. "You're my sister. You have as much right to the protections of the GearMakers as anyone else."

Tenze smiled. "Remain calm. We are all in agreement here in this room. We want you to look at the shield matrix. Perhaps you will see improvements we have not thought of. We are working on protections that won't be noticed, but this will take more time."

"Yuthin already invited us to the shipyards so Rose can see the fridium," Gad said.

"Good. Find an opportunity to get to the top of the tree."

I gulped. "Will Bromin really attack? He may be strong at his own palace, but here, too?"

Dad shook his head. "Yes he would attack if it meant achieving his goals. I wish you didn't have to be involved in all this mess, but you need to be aware of what is going on. We don't know all of Bromin's plans."

Gad rolled his eyes. "Some people actually revere Bromin. But I can't see how they can be so blind unless they are pretending to support him because they want to survive. Reports already tell of GearMakers disappearing. Airships traveling between provinces vanish as well."

"Factions within the Council of Elders will not accept the intelligence Gad and others have been bringing to us," Tenze said. "They believe we are strong enough to repel any attacks."

Tension creased my brow. "No one saw this coming?"

"Some of us did, but it hasn't made a difference here at home," Gad said. "I suspect Bromin intends to rule the entire world—after wiping out GearMaker kind. He wants it all and for some reason he hates us."

"He's proven himself a mad man," Dad said and stood. He walked over to a window then back to us. "The technology that has been showing up is progressively more violent."

"The Council refuses to enact greater protections for a solitary person." Tenze drummed his fingers on the chair arm. "I proposed an increase in power output from the shield matrix to keep Bromin out for now. That won't require any great efforts."

"Will the Council allow that?" I asked. My ears were ringing. I never thought I would need protection, but now I was being hunted by someone more dangerous than I could have imagined.

Tenze scowled and looked out the window. "I am waiting to find out."

"We have to keep you away from Bromin. That's all there is

to it," Gad said. "A GearMaker working for Bromin would be devastating. He'd bring his hatred to our lands and would stand a good chance of defeating us. This is why he can't have you."

"I would never help him."

Gad leaned toward me. "He could force you. We couldn't explain GearMaker level weaponry and technology coming from Bromin, but maybe now we know where it's coming from."

The room was silent. Gad tapped a tooth with his fingernail. "We're not a violent people so any GearMaker creating this stuff for him would have to be forced or as mad as Bromin."

"You suspect Alum?" I replied. Obviously something was off about Alum no matter how entrancing his silver eyes were. The momentary attraction I'd felt was not enough to refute his betrayal when he pretended to help us.

"The machines Alum made were nowhere near the advancement you speak of," I said. "If Bromin has one GearMaker captive then why not more?"

"Other children were kidnapped when Alum was, but we know Bromin no longer has them," Gad said, avoiding my eyes. Dad looked down and stayed silent.

I shuddered. "How do you know?"

Gad shook his head.

"They were found—all of them, except Alum," Tenze said. "They were found in different places over the following years."

Sadness cloaked the three men.

I looked back and forth between them. "Were they dead? Dead or..." I didn't continue. Even if there are worse things than dead it was obvious Bromin was dangerous enough to kill children. "So why didn't people think Alum was in Bromin's custody?"

Tenze shrugged. "It was assumed he was dead like the others. His family has been notified that he is still alive. They want to speak to you, but they live in an outer province. It may take them time to get here. Since we don't know how to get him free of Bromin..."

"Or if he wants to be free of him. They'd be better off still believing he's dead." Gad gave me a sidelong glance.

I shook my head at him. "I understand how serious things are. Anyone who doesn't attempt to escape or fight that—that man, has to be in league with him. But what *is* being done to stop Bromin?"

Gad scrunched up his lips and let out a big sigh. "Well, we are really only gathering intel and adding protection to the cities and lands still outside Bromin's control. We aren't sure what he's doing, or rather, we weren't sure. After what happened to you we now know he wants to increase the GearMade population to create an army. I don't know what to do if he achieves that goal."

Dad sighed. Gad hung his head.

I smiled at them. "I will help any way I can."

Outside Yuthin's voice increased. Someone was arguing with him. Tenze headed to the door, but it burst open, slamming against the wall. A tall man with thick dark eyebrows and a black beard strode into the room. "Tenze? I came to discuss your proposal to increase the power of the shield matrix. No one will agree to this level of defense in a time of peace."

"We believe Copper Rose will only be safe under greater protections and it will not harm anyone to increase our defenses," Tenze said calmly.

"Safe? Why wouldn't she be safe in TreeCountry?"

Tenze walked to the man, who towered over him. "Bromin has already kidnapped her once. If he discovers she is here then he may attack."

Kilain scowled. "Daren, are you still on about this nonsense that Bromin wants to take over the world?"

Dad hurried over, his arms spread out. "My daughter has the right to know she's safe in GearMaker lands."

"That outsider?" he spat, glaring over at me. "If you believe that he will attack to get her back then hand her over to him and be done with it."

Gad leapt up, but I grabbed his arm. He pulled against me then stayed. My hands shook. Was this really happening?

"Kilain. There is no need for this." Tenze put a hand on Kilain's arms. "The long lost are not outsiders. It is not the way of our people to shun anyone. You know this. What is the harm in a little more protection as a precaution?"

Kilain yanked his arm away. "You will keep manipulating the Council for your own purposes all to protect us from the monster Bromin, but in truth you're plotting to take over the Council and rule our people. You are the danger."

"Kilain, exhibit some control," Tenze said. "We are not plotting against the council's wishes. We only want to work in cooperation with the council to keep GearMakers safe."

"The council has spoken. These are unnecessary measures

for a risk that is fictitious." Kilain pulled away from Tenze and leaned over, a single finger pointing at Dad. "I am warning you Steele. You and your rebel boy will not rule our people. If you make so much as one move in defiance of the council I will see your entire family banished from GearMaker lands." He gave a sweeping scowl and stormed out, leaving the door sitting open to the evening air.

Chapter 11

I went to bed that night worried. I completely agreed with the plan to keep me away from Bromin, but Kilain scared me. Would he really banish Gad and Dad all because of me? Gad told me, "That grouchy elder is only bluffing." I wasn't convinced.

The next day Gad dragged me out of bed. The staircase inside the trunk took us round and round, all the way to the ground. The trek across TreeCountry took me through a place full of the amazing and unusual plant life. People watched us as we passed, smiling and waving at Gad. We arrived in the field surrounding the ShipYard tree as the sun broke over the tree line to bathe the massive forest in it's warmth.

Looking up from the hardened ground, there seemed no end to it's height. I looked up and up and up from half a mile away. The gloriously green canopy spread across the sky like a giant's umbrella. The tree before me was bigger than any I had yet seen.

I gasped. "This tree could be its own country. It could have its own hemisphere!"

"This is the ShipYard tree." Gad lifted a hand across the vista, morning light spilling through the thin mist. He pointed at the row of large vessels spread in front of the trunk on the hard packed soil. "Ships are built on the ground or the first three branches. Higher up are the dock branches where new crafts are launched from and the levels above that are the docks for our active fleets. Our WarShips berth on the last few levels—though I don't believe they leave dock enough these days."

The wide, flat limbs near the bottom of the tree were bare of smaller, leaf bearing branches. Hundreds of ships floated next to dozens of dock limbs that spiraled around the trunk. Vessels of every kind and shape hung from dirigibles or floated like a cloud. On the ground the skeletal beginnings of ships sat in cradles awaiting their skins and trappings. My head felt light.

At the end of the building yard was something different—something that drew my attention away from the awesome tree. A ship sparkled in the distance. "The metal…" I started walking to the unusual creation on the ground, but Yuthin approached. I regarded the craft. Sighing, I walked back.

"Are you ready for answers?" Gad said. He winked at me.

"Yes." I came up beside my brother. "I have so many questions. And I hope I can help with ideas to defend TreeCountry."

"We will do our best to answer them." Yuthin waved for us to follow. He walked to the closest ship. "These on the ground will join our fleet of passenger and cargo ships."

Shipbuilders paused in their work as we approached. A stocky man leapt down from the future deck rail. His wide feet hit the earth with a thud, his knees bending to cushion his landing. He rose from the crouch and strode over to Yuthin.

"Is there an issue?" the man said in a gruff voice.

Yuthin turned to him. "No." He gestured to the man. "This is Geren Meredan. He is our lead designer. I am giving a tour of our ships to Miss Locke."

"And—the shield matrix?" I asked leaning toward Gad.

Geren's expression went from momentary awe to narrowed eyes and tilted brows. His glance swept across my face, then to Gad standing next to me, and then settled on my hair. Yuthin's gaze bore into me before he nodded slightly. I sighed. Maybe this was one of the people who didn't believe Bromin was a threat.

I smiled at Geren. Still, I had questions and the lead designer would be a good person to answer them. Maybe I could win him over. "I heard the shield matrix is an impressive piece of technology. What I really want is to know how your ships fly. Everything else about them makes sense, but for something to float without a propeller, wings or a balloon... I cannot figure it out."

He continued to look at me. Was he assessing my intent? But then a smile creased his craggy features. "Yes, Miss Locke. We would be honored to show you our techniques and designs. But the shield matrix is off limits to... Well. It is for our technicians only."

"That will be wonderful. I understand," I said "Would all of you call me Rose—or Copper Rose." They said nothing. "Please?"

"Yes—Copper Rose. I will make sure your request is honored," Geren said.

Bowing slightly, Geren led us over to the vessel he had leapt from. "This is a CarrierShip. The freight capacity will be enough to haul an entire month of pila fruit to the outer villages. We will have it completed before the Pila season is over. While we take the time to do the job right, my workers build fast. Most have decades of experience."

I nodded and then leaned back to catch a glimpse of the sun lit metal hull still glittering in the distance. "What's the metal framed thing at the end?"

Geren and Yuthin sighed.

"Ah. The WarShip," Yuthin said and shook his head.

"It's not one of our successes, Miss—Uh, Copper Rose." Geren reached for my arm, but pulled his hand back and waved me toward the trunk of the tree. "I would rather take you to the upper levels. Please. Over here if you will."

Geren and Yuthin led us to a box at the trunk of the tree.

"Has Kilain gotten to everybody?" I whispered to Gad.

He grimaced and shrugged. "I don't believe so, but I know he's skeptical about our claims. It really is beyond any of our control. Word of your return spread fast so people will form their own opinions about you. For years they've seen the little creature you made flying around TreeCountry. You are a bit of a legend. I hate to see GearMakers become so divided, but we have to act against Bromin soon."

"I want my copper hair to be just a hair color, not a sign for people to be in awe or afraid of me. I've done nothing to deserve it. I don't know how I made that bug thing live. I couldn't duplicate it if I tried."

Gad scrutinized my face. "You might be more capable than you know."

I scowled.

"Well—we can at least satisfy your curiosity about our ships." He grinned. "And I'll make sure you get a look at that shield matrix," he added in a quiet voice.

Ahead of us was a strange contraption. To call it an elevator or a window-washer bucket wouldn't do it justice. The boxy structure contained benches and even a small table like a sitting room. The curled iron bars were shaped like leaves and vines making a cage around it.

Yuthin pulled open the door, which resembled a garden gate. As I stepped in the floor felt solid, but my hands shook a little and went cold anyway. The whole structure was attached to a rail traveling the height of the trunk. Connected to the top four corners were ornate chains that reached into the canopy of the tree.

I sat next to Gad on a bench at the back wall of the elevator with Yuthin across from us. Geren secured the gate and flipped a switch on a control panel. Up we went. The sides vibrated and the gears squeaked ever so slightly. I found myself holding my breath and gripping the seat. My knuckles turned white. I rubbed my hands together and tried to force myself to stay calm.

We stopped, with barely a sound, at the first level of branches. Geren stepped out and across a metal bridge to another building yard. The vessels were wood and had masts for future sails and to attach the gas filled balloons.

"PassengerShips are made to carry a small amount of freight as well." Geren spread his arms out at the beautiful creations. "We keep these transports simple, but decorated for the enjoyment of the passengers. I hear you came in on the Sapphire Lilly. Fine ship that one. Oversaw its construction myself a good thirty years back."

Men were installing a wide paddled propeller into the

closest craft.

I stepped closer. "What is that for?"

Gad walked over and gave the ship a look of appraisal. "Fine workmanship."

Geren smiled and stood a little taller. "That propeller is for the electrical generation system. It rests low in the ship's storage area."

I drew closer and watched the workers lace the insulated wires through the hole. The large battery they installed looked different than I expected, but the system was logical. I could even tell what they were going to do next. Gad continued down the row of ships, greeting men who called out to him. Geren continued the tour. Half way down the BranchDock I was getting restless to see something new. Nothing about these ships was a mystery to me other than why they made them look like boats that would go on water.

We made it back to the elevator and continued upward. We got off at each level where more ships were in various stages of construction.

I scooted over to Gad as we traveled to the next level. "There are very few WarShips in the building levels. Why?"

Gad smiled. "Be patient. There aren't many, but when you do see them you will be impressed."

I settled back in my seat, avoiding the suspicious look Geren gave us.

At the fourth and fifth levels we reached the docks for active ships. Geren explained the docking control system for bringing vessels in or launching them safely. The ships were astounding. Many older ones were still running at peak efficiency so I could observe the progression of their technology over the years. At level eight were the WarShips.

Their exteriors were metal reinforced and yet they still could fly. Protecting the dirigible from an attack would pose problems. So how did they plan to solve it? I peppered Geren with questions until he seemed flustered.

"The small ones are called BattleBoats," Yuthin said as we approached a row of smaller ships. These were the ones that floated without any obvious source of lift. They were rigged with collapsable propellers to increase speed.

Geren patted the hull of one small BattleBoat that looked more like an in-air submarine. "These small beauties give us the agility and stealth the dirigible vessels cannot."

I was antsy to know more. Geren seemed to want to show me every single ship, but had completely avoided any of the defense systems for the ships or TreeCountry.

"Gad," I said when we were a few yards from Yuthin and Geren. "What about the shield matrix? Where's that?"

He looked at the upper branches. The cable system disappeared among the leaves. Gad hurried forward and I followed, glancing back at Yuthin and Geren. They were distracted by the installation of a large propeller on one of the ships. Yuthin nodded at us. We got in the lift.

"Hold on." Gad punched a button and the lift rose. We were nearly to the next level when Geren started running toward the lift cable.

I sat firmly in my seat, grabbing the edge as the lift accelerated.

"Come back here," Geren yelled at us. Gad cupped a hand

around his ear and shook his head, the corner of his mouth lifting. He pretended to poke at the buttons in exaggerated motions then shrugged down at Geren. We sped past several more dock branches then into the tree top.

Smaller branches passed rapidly. The lift hit one. Leaves ripped off and blew about the floor. My stomach roiled. "Does —does—he have another way—to the top?"

The lift slowed. Gad grimaced. "Sorry, Rose." The lift suddenly jolted to a stop. "Oh no you don't," Gad said punching a button on the control pad. The lift moved upward again at a normal speed. The trunk became slimmer and slimmer the higher we got. "We're almost there. It should take Geren about ten minutes to get around the trunk to the other lift."

"Other lift?"

"There's one on the other side of the trunk, but of course only this lift goes to the top. Geren will have to take the stairs the rest of the way." Gad smiled into the ever-thickening branches. "Here we are."

The lift slowed then settled against a platform that circled the remaining trunk like a deck. It was cut off a story above us, but a tall metal spire rose out of the wood into the sky.

Gad stepped onto the platform. He disappeared around the trunk.

"Gad?"

He peeked around the trunk. "Come quick. It won't take Geren long to get here."

Around the other side a staircase stopped next to a door in the bark-covered trunk. Gad looked down the stairs and huffed. He led me through the door into a large round room. The metal spire rose from the middle. I could hear the buzz of electricity as gears turned large horizontal wheels around the spire.

The control board caught my attention. Power indicators, buttons, dials and readouts were spread over the panel on the spire. "This is an astounding level of power output. What does this thing do?"

Gad pointed. "See here? The wind turbines on the tops of the surrounding trees route power here. There's an invisible, low level power field which domes over most of TreeCountry from this point. When a ship passes through without a pre-approved code, the system signals to the guard posts and the SkyTeam. They deploy smaller ships to intercept." He watched my face as I ran my fingers gently over the controls. "Any thoughts?"

"I don't know yet." A dome of power? Maybe the system could do more than warn. Maybe it could repel.

Thud, thud, thud, thud. Someone was coming up the stairs.

Gad dashed to the door and looked out. "He'll be here soon. About five minutes."

I wanted to know more. How did it work? "Hmmm..." I typed a few commands into the console. A small red light started pulsing franticly in the corner of the screen. "Uh-oh."

Gad hurried over and looked. He shook his head and pushed a black button. The red light went away. "Better hurry out of here."

"Kilain did not want them near the Shield Matrix," Geren said from somewhere below.

Gad and I dashed out the door.

I could hear the heavy breathing of someone climbing the stairs. "I'm sure this is an honest mistake, Geren." Yuthin's voice sounded nearby.

Gad pulled me around the trunk. "Quick. Back to the lift."

We were nearly at the metal gate when Geren came puffing around the trunk behind us. "What have you done, Gad Steele?"

Chapter 12

Gad turned to Geren, a look of confusion on his face. "What do you mean? I tried to stop the lift, but it kept going."

"I will not fall for lies, young man." Geren's face was suffused in red, his temples throbbing. "Just because the rest of TreeCountry adores you does not mean you can do whatever you wish. I will be reporting this grievous breach of security to..."

"I'm sorry sir," I said. All eyes turned on me. "I wanted to try the controls on the lift and did something wrong. Gad was able to stop it here, but I was a bit afraid to get back into the lift. I had to get my anxiety under control—heights, you know. I don't do very well."

Geren watched me through narrowed eyes. "Really?"

"Yes," Gad replied. "She thought she could handle it, but..."

Yuthin came up behind Geren. Would Geren fall for my confession? I kept my breath slow and regular, though my heart pounded.

"Little strange for a GearMaker of TreeCountry to be afraid of heights don't you think, Miss Locke?" Geren frowned.

"Well—yes it is, but I was raised in a different place—where we always lived on the ground." I looked over at the lift, sighed then smiled at the man.

Geren's face relaxed. "You'll get over it soon. We must get this lift back to the ship levels. Do you think you can get back in now? I will keep the speed reasonable."

I stepped into the lift. "I think I can manage."

"Settle yourself while I check something," Geren said, then went back around the trunk.

"Miss Rose, it is time to show you the Iridium," Yuthin said, following Gad onto the lift.

Geren rattled the doorknob.

Yuthin winked at me. "Geren is a gifted designer. He takes his work very seriously."

"That's why he doesn't like me much," Gad whispered, sitting next to me.

Yuthin shook his head at Gad. "You do tend to take life less —seriously."

"Just say it," I said grinning. "Gad is trouble. I knew that as soon as I met him."

Geren appeared around the trunk, a satisfied curl to his lips. He entered and closed the gate.

"Rose was agreeing how much trouble I cause." Gad leaned back with his hands behind his head. Geren grunted and turned to the controls. The descent was slow. I wanted to get over my fear of heights, but this world always had a new scary moment for me.

We exited onto one of the branches that we had skipped earlier. The flat tree branch was covered with warehouses and a scattering of smaller buildings. Geren led us to the largest of the structures. It was made of wood and metal. Three walls had large doors that could be rolled up into the high ceiling. A dozen small vessels bobbed from chains tethered near the door. Beyond were larger ships though still significantly smaller than the WarShips with dirigibles at the dock branches. The ships were at various stages of completion like puzzles with part of the picture still unclear. One looked like it was all wood, but the metal frame still gleamed through a few slats.

Yuthin led us across the warehouse. Windows stretched the full height of the walls. Offices and meeting rooms were stacked three stories high at the back of the building. Geren led us through a swinging double door then up a staircase leading to the upper stories. I glanced back into the warehouse at every window we passed. The ships bobbed lazily in the air while people worked on them. *Amazing!* I wanted to play with some of this floating metal.

"This will be good. Trust me," Gad said. We followed Geren and Yuthin into a large conference room. The walls had large diagrams pinned up all over. I started reading the notes on one, my fingers tracing the lines of the design. A lot of the information made sense. The word Iridium was repeated throughout.

I turned to the three men. "I want to know more about this floating metal."

Yuthin sat on a padded chair and smiled. "Iridium is an alloy that is lighter than air."

"Yes. You told me that yesterday."

"Well we turn it into an alloy," Gad said. "It starts as a base metal, an element all its own."

I looked over at Gad. "That's impossible."

He nodded and pulled out a chair for me. I scooted the chair forward so I could look at the drawings and design plans spread all over the table. My brain was racing. So much new technology and so many ideas were spinning around my brain, but I still wanted more. It was like having blinders removed. "How can metal float?"

Geren spun in his chair to face me. "The fridium element is mined underground. When treated with an acid and blended into silver the fridium develops the ability to float like it was a gas instead of a solid. Based on the amount of fridium to silver, the metal will float up to different elevations before leveling out. For this reason we work with it in warehouses after mining it."

I tapped a schematic with my fingernail. "You make your ship frames out of it and then they—they float? But how do they land? And how does it keep floating after you put all that wood or other metal on it? Wouldn't that weigh it down?"

Gad chuckled. "Slow down Copper Rose. One question at a time. Let poor Geren catch up."

Geren scowled at Gad.

Yuthin pulled a paper from a disheveled stack and handed it to me. "Each frame is rigged with a low electrical current and electrical storage device. The wire touches the metal and when activated the alloy sinks lower. The higher the current, the lower the ship goes."

"Wow," I said. It was hard to contain my awe. So many new possibilities opened up to me.

Gad tapped a diagram of a smaller boat on the table. "We have to make the ships smaller, too. Which is why it's perfect for fast little dinghies and such."

"Yes. Iridium has its limits." Geren scratched his brow. "We cannot seem to conquer the problems caused by the weight of the other building materials. We have augmented the frames of larger, dirigible powered vessels with Iridium to aid in the lift, but it is never enough on its own to lift something such as a full WarShip."

Gad leaned forward in his seat. "We need to hope Bromin doesn't figure that out first. I found out that he obtained a supply of Iridium even though the source is in GearMaker lands."

Yuthin shook his head. "That source of Iridium may be part of the advancements he has been making, but the progress is too quick for anyone other than a GearMaker."

Geren huffed. "I would like to know how he is doing these things. We have the best engineers in all Seranova, yet he seems to surpass us."

I looked down at the table top, not seeing the designs under my spread out hands. Bronze hair and silver eyes filled my mind and I sighed heavily. Alum. What did he have to do with those advancements? I pinched my lips together. A swell of cold ran through me. What were Alum and Bromin capable of?

Gad put a finger on my hand. "Alum was also too young when he was taken to know the location of Iridium mines. If he was helping make the things we have been seeing in the border lands, he would not have been in the palace. Bromin would never keep his greatest assets so exposed." He smirked. Could he read my mind? "You saw how easy it was for me to get in."

I raised my brows and tried to slow my breathing. "He was

keeping me there."

"He would not have kept you there long," Yuthin said.

Geren was eyeing all of us carefully. Something about the conversation seemed new to him.

I looked at Yuthin. His eyes were soft and warm as he looked at me. "Gad was wise to move so quickly to infiltrate the palace. Bromin is all about show. He may be rethinking the security of his palace now that our Gad has shown him how exposed it really is."

The chair creaked as Gad leaned back, smirking. "All in the service of our people."

Geren stood up and shuffled some papers into a stack. If Bromin's weapons and technology were getting better quicker than the GearMakers, then he could become an even bigger threat to them—and to me.

Afternoon sun stretched across the table from an outer window. My stomach grumbled. "Learning all this new technology will take some time. I would like permission to visit and observe the work going on here. I'll be sure to stay out of the way." My stomach growled again and my cheeks warmed.

"You are welcome in the shipyards anytime, Miss Locke." Geren glared at Gad, then smiled at me. "But the shield matrix is too sensitive for people unfamiliar with the technology. You understand."

If Kilain found out about our little jaunt up the tree, Geren might not even let me into the shipyards. I nodded in agreement. I would tell my idea to Yuthin and Tenze. Even Father and Gad would know if we could make the shield repel intruders.

147

Yuthin stood. "In the meantime we should all be getting on with our day. We've obviously kept the two of you past the midday meal. Your father will be wondering where you are."

"We will escort you to the base of the tree." Geren smiled then exited the room. Gad and I followed. Yuthin took up the rear.

We walked back through the warehouse of floating creations. I eyed the metal, wanting to touch it. "I would love to get a chance to play with some fridium," I mumbled to Gad.

He veered away from me, bumped against a table of tools and crates and walked back. I watched with curiosity. Gad pulled his hand out of his coat pocket. A stick of silver floated up an inch before he grabbed it again. He pushed it into my palm and leaned closer. "Don't lose it." He chuckled and walked on ahead. I ran my fingers across the smooth metal. It was so light in my hand. I suppressed a grin and tucked it deep in my pocket.

As the elevator clicked its way down the trunk I yawned even though my mind raced. We'd spent the better part of the day touring the dock branches and the building yards.

We were nearly to the ground when a glint caught my eye at the end of the row of partially built ships on the ground. The silver framed ship was calling to me. I wanted to see it. Was it made from fridium? It looked too big based on what they'd told me, but maybe that is why the project failed. I watched it in the distance until the elevator slipped too low for me to see it anymore.

Geren pushed the gate open and I skipped forward, glad to be back on the ground. I walked backwards. The three men were stepping out of the elevator. "I want to go look at one more thing. That silver ship on the end."

Geren hesitated, but I ignored him and walked purposefully down the row of vessels. I had passed several before Geren came up next to me.

"Really, there is nothing significant about that ship. It is somewhat of an—an embarrassment actually." Geren rubbed his roughened knuckles.

"How so?"

"What do you mean?" Geren said.

I looked the short man in the face. "How is a ship with such a beautiful frame an embarrassment?"

Geren didn't respond. He spluttered a little, so I continued my brisk walk away from him. Gad chuckled behind me. Breaking into a jog, I passed the last wooden hull. My breath caught in my throat as the bare ship appeared. The metal ship was tucked behind the others and was farthest from the most active areas of the ShipYard tree surrounded by brush and weeds. It didn't look like a failure. Nothing was wrong with it other than being incomplete. In my head I sifted through the design specs of the many other boat blueprints I'd seen earlier. It was bigger and sturdier than any Iridium ship I'd seen so far. Was that the failure? It wouldn't float right?

Breathing a little heavily, Gad came up beside me. His eyes sparkled. "I'm supposed to be the troublemaker."

"Humph..."

He walked over and patted a beam of the ship. "What do you think?"

I pulled a mossy ladder from the long grass growing under the floating hull and climbed into the partially finished boat.

Dry leaves were piled against one wall and enough dirt had gathered between the Iridium ribs for small wild flowers to grow. A tangy smell of moss, dirt and metal effused my senses. The ribs rose above me like pillars to heaven. They had left it like it was dead yet it bobbed slightly as Gad hoisted himself up the rickety ladder.

Gad chuckled. "I have never seen Geren hyperventilate before."

"Oh, he isn't coming to drag me away from here, is he?"

"Not at all. Yuthin is reasoning with him—to maybe give you some time to look around without interruption. Maybe this will make him forget our trip to the top of the tree."

"I doubt it." Balancing along the wide spine, I walked the length of the sleek ship and turned back to Gad, who leaned casually against a beam. "I see nothing embarrassing about it—other than the neglected state it's in. What about it made it unsuccessful?"

"Geren is being ridiculous. GearMaker's can't seem to accept that some technologies may still be beyond them. This was their attempt at a Iridium framed WarShip. Someone got ambitious and tried even though we haven't solved the weight to lift ratio problem. That's what happened to this poor girl." He patted the beam. "She was started before her time. She's tried to float away a time or two during particularly strong storms. This old lady wants to fly."

"I think she's beautiful." I walked back over to Gad. I sat on the beam next to the ladder and judged the distance to the ground. As if accommodating me, the ship lowered a yard allowing me to jump the remaining few feet. I looked at Gad. "You coming?"

150

Wide eyed with mouth gaping Gad, stared at me. "How'd you get it to do that?"

"Don't be ridiculous. I took advantage of a little wind pulling it down."

He closed his mouth and scrutinized me. "There was no wind."

"Quit being silly and get down here."

He leapt, bending his knees to cushion himself as he landed. I started back out of the shadow of the nearly completed CarrierShip blocking the Iridium vessel. Yuthin and Geren were now surrounded by half a dozen workers several ships away.

I looked back at the Iridium frame chained to the ground like a trapped animal. The wheels of my brain turned, gaining speed. Parts from different ships and blueprints spun around the picture of the pretty vessel in my mind. Things were fitting together like a well-placed puzzle. The Iridium alloy formula jumped up in front and started rearranging faster than I could understand why. When I looked at it again it was different— better. Another glance at the real ship and I knew what I could do. I knew what I wanted to do.

"I keep hoping someone will figure out how to make her fly." Gad's eyes sparkled as he watched me concentrate.

I grinned and nodded. "That would be nice." I looked back one more time, but instead of seeing what was actually there, I envisioned the completed creation. "If someone actually took the time—That would be very nice."

Chapter 13

Days later Dad was making breakfast and I was sitting at the table drinking a glass of pila juice. I fiddled with the locket, smoothing the chain in my fingers.

It had been nearly a week of paradise in the massive trees, falling asleep to soft breezes humming against the walls, food that always left me full and satisfied, and no more frilly nineteenth century dresses.

As I sat there, an old farm house drifted into my thoughts. Was it coated in dust or was the time difference severely skewed so I could walk right back into my old life? I had a family now where my mechanical skills were normal. Did MIT have anything to offer that this world didn't? I couldn't imagine going back to any Earth city or even the small trees of the family farm.

Looking up at my father I realized I had no desire to go back to Earth. Only when my thoughts strayed to Gramma and Alum did I feel anything other than peace and happiness. I also tried to ignore the reminders of Bromin. Maybe I was safe.

Dad set a bowl of something similar to oatmeal on the table, followed by a plate of sliced fruit. He sat down across from me and propped his chin on his laced together fingers.

"You still keep it on?" he asked, nodding at the locket.

"Just in case." The locket warmed up. "This strange piece of jewelry brought me here and is clearly a huge part of our family's lives."

He nodded. "It sure is. Do you mind if I see it?"

I hesitated, then pulled the chain over my head. Dad took it. He turned it around, and looked into the little window at the gears.

Dad rubbed his finger over the filigree etchings. "It always fascinated me."

"I want to know more about it." I fiddled with a fork and watched my father. "I want to be able to control it and understand why it does what it does. Maybe it could help us find Mom."

Dad sighed and nodded.

Gad hopped down the stairs. "Another morning. Another day and no sign of Bromin anywhere." I flinched at the name, but smiled at my brother. He flashed his infectious grin at me and patted my shoulder. Gad sat and filled his plate with food. He shoveled several mouthfuls into his maw.

"What are both of you planning to fill your day with?" Dad asked, still fingering the locket.

"Wor-thop," he garbled.

"Workshop, Father," I corrected. Gad swallowed loudly.

"Sorry. Yes. Rose and I are going to do some new things now that she finished your weeder," Gad said, then crammed his mouth with food again.

I scowled at my brother. "You finished. I only made a suggestion."

"It's working wonderfully to save my aging back. Hah! What

do you think you'll build now?" Dad asked, looking at me.

I glanced at my hands. So little grease lingered there now. What mess did get on me didn't bother me like it had on Earth. I didn't care what I made. "I don't know."

Dad watched me pensively.

"What were you two discussing in such hushed tones?" Gad asked lifting a piece of fruit to his mouth. "The possible upgrades for the shield matrix?"

Dad stood. "The idea of making the shield matrix repel intruders is worth exploring, but Kilain has made it impossible for us to do anything more right now." Dad cuffed his son on the shoulder and walked to the stove for a steaming pan of fried tubers. "But no. We were talking about the locket. And no hushed tones were used."

"I'm curious about the locket," I said.

"I wish I knew more," Dad said. "It's as old as the first GearMades, I believe. Perhaps older. It even exists in folklore. The GearMaker's Locket. No one knows where it came from or why it does what it does. It's a thing of awe and beauty though, isn't it?"

"Well..." Gad drawled, still chewing.

"Yes?" I said and glared at him.

He took a swig of juice and put down his fork. "We might be able to get more information about the locket from Brehan," Gad said. "I don't know where he is though. He kind of—disappeared a few years back."

Dad shook his head. "There is no way to search for him now. It's best to stay here to increase our defenses. There will be time when things are safe again." Dad put the locket back into my hand and closed my fingers around it. "Keeping you safe is the most important thing. Come now. We have a busy day."

"You had an idea for skywings capable of more maneuverability didn't you, Copper?" Gad asked.

I smirked getting up from my seat. "Yes. We could give it a try as long as I don't have to test drive the thing."

Dad chuckled.

"Can you blame me?" I smiled and gave Dad a kiss on the cheek.

Crack!

Something crashed outside the cottage. We all ran out of the house. Yuthin was crumbled in a heap of shattered skywings. Dad reached down to help Yuthin extricate himself. The GearMade fell back to the ground in a heap and reached up to Daren.

"Run. Bromin's coming," Yuthin gasped and collapsed, a wide slice on his forehead trickling silvery black blood.

"Quick, get him inside," Dad yelled, pulling the rest of the skywing harness off Yuthin. We lifted him. I strained under the weight of his mechanical body.

Yuthin stirred.

"Be still, Yuthin. We have you," Gad soothed. Once inside, we put him on the sofa. I turned to get a wet cloth, but stopped short.

Yuthin was holding my wrist painfully tight. "Don't delay. You need to be safe. Please run. Please go. Do not let the Copper Rose become prisoner." He fell back to the cushions and released my arm. A distant explosion shook the cottage.

The buzz of BattleBoats filled the air. We looked at each other, our eyes wide.

"Go," Dad whispered, looking from me to Gad.

"No. We can't leave you," Gad insisted.

Dad grabbed his tall son by the shoulders and shook him lightly. He looked down at Yuthin then up again. "You must. He wants Rose and you can keep her safe. Please. Go now." He leaned back down to Yuthin and waved for us to leave.

A whistle followed by another explosion echoed through the forest. Sirens screamed over the buzz of approaching vessels.

Gad turned to take my hand, but I ran past him, grabbing a leather coat off a hook by the door and reaching to my neck to ensure the locket was there. We ran to the trunk stairs and leapt downward two or three steps at a time. Gad paused at the door to the landing strip and held it shut. Outside the muffled sounds of attack swelled.

"Copper, I know you don't want to, but—skywings?"

My already speeding heart rate increased and the shaking in my hands amplified. I looked at my palms as another explosion went off. "Just go." I gave him a shove. We ran down the landing strip. My eyes darted across the skies looking for the enemy. We got to the shed at the end of the landing strip and threw it open. Inside hung a dozen or more skywings. I shook my head and squeezed my eyes shut.

"Wish we had the new ones you thought of," Gad mumbled. Opening my eyes, I grabbed a pair of skywings. I fumbled with a set of snaps and buckles, the skywings falling from my back. Gad tugged one of my straps into place. He deftly finished fastening it on me. Acrid smoke stung my nose as another explosion echoed from the ground not far below our tree.

"Ready for this?"

"Yeah, right," I mumbled in response. A buzzing sound came from behind the tree. It wasn't the familiar sound of GearMaker ships.

Gad reached over and pulled a pair of goggles over my head. I snugged them over my eyes. "Now or never I guess," I said in a strangled voice. My hands shook, cold sweat making them slick. I looked over the edge of the branch. What choice did I have?

Gad looked back at me. "Come on."

My breathing raced, but my legs were frozen in place. I started backing up, panic rising in me. The sounds of fighting grew muffled as I watched the ledge.

"Copper? You have to jump. We have to go now." Gad pushed his face close to mine. "Look at me. We have to go. You'll be fine." I shook my head forcefully.

Gad stepped away. "You leave me no choice." The edge loomed before me. I couldn't do it.

Boom!

I flinched. Flames leapt from a distant tree. Gad gave me a shove, pushing me off the branch. I screamed as the skywings listed, but they grabbed the breeze, hoisting me upward. A branch appeared only yards from me. Yanking at the lever straps that were meant for steering I tried to turn, but still went the wrong way.

"Like this," Gad yelled from above me. A quick glance and I

157

was able to replicate his movement in time to miss getting to know the leafy branch better. Another branch rose up in my path. I veered, but not far enough. Leaves fell as the bark scrapped my leg.

A large air-skimmer brimming with men in the blue and brass uniforms of Bromin's army appeared around the tree ahead of me. I let the skywings drop low to avoid the next branch and the air-skimmer.

"I see the copper head girl," an airman yelled.

"Get 'er." Three men hoisted a net over the edge of the air-skimmer and tossed it at me. My skywings dipped lower and lower, the net falling gracefully toward me. My mind spun, frantic. I watched as if in slow motion at the net lazily falling. The jeers of the men told me that my chances weren't good. What could I do? I'd never flown skywings before, but I had poured over every design for them I could find. The net was getting closer and so was the ground. Thinking through the schematics, I reached over to the opposite steering strap and yanked. The skywings banked hard and sped me forward. I grabbed a branch and used it to catapult away from the air-skimmer.

The wings lifted up. I was gliding! I pulled the straps and smoothly flew past several large trees and out of sight from Bromin's soldiers.

"This way," Gad quipped, appearing from nowhere. "You're a natural."

My limbs quaked like leaves and my heart leapt. "Hah."

We flew past the large trees. Small limbs grew wildly across the wide branches and houses or gardens no longer dotted

158

their bark surfaces. We passed over the hard packed dirt road through TreeCountry and left the sounds of battle behind us. My chest tightened. Was Dad still safe?

"If we stick to the high branches to the edge of TreeCountry we might avoid the air-skimmers," Gad said. I slowly followed Gad upward, successfully dodging all but the smallest of branches, which scratched across my skin and clothes.

A great shadow slipped over us. "Sir. Here on the starboard side. I saw something." The voice was coming from a massive warship with cannons poking out like cactus prickles. The ship skimmed quietly over the trees.

"Oh no. We're not safe yet." Gad gulped and veered toward me as a ball of fire fell at him. He dodged and the flaming mass plunged to the forest floor.

An updraft of wind helped us slip into some branches under the ship. I followed Gad's lead and collapsed my wings as we grabbed onto the branches. We clung onto opposite sides of the trunk which was as thick around as a telephone pole. We linked arms to keep each other from falling.

"Gad, your wing." A thin white trail of smoke trickled up from his left wing. Gad swatted at the end of the wing, wincing as the embers slowly died. Another ball of fire fell through the trees.

Spheres of flame dropped all around us, sizzling as they crashed through the branches. Aboard the not-too-distant ship, voices rose.

"He wants her alive, you idiots," a man yelled. We froze. "Does anyone see her?" The ship inched along, slowly moving in an arc. It flew over us twice.

"I thought I saw something coppery red," the first man replied, a tremor in his voice.

"You thought? I don't see a thing. Move to the next sector."

A man yelped then the ship moved on. The large, overlapping leaves above us rustled in the breeze.

My hands were aching. I leaned close to Gad. "What can we do? Sooner or later they'll find us."

"We're going to have to make a dash for it and hope they don't," Gad whispered. "If we go through Edder's Pass we should be able to stay away from them. Keep your eyes and ears open for more ships."

"I can't hold still any longer or this waiting will make me crazy," I replied.

Gad chuckled and spread his skywings. "I knew flying would grow on you." He leapt into the air like a raptor. I followed, dropping quickly before leveling out.

Skimming from tree to tree, stopping occasionally to check for ships, we were able to leave the sounds of fighting behind. Each explosion and distant scream coming from the center of TreeCountry ripped into my heart. Dad was back there in the smoke and flames. If anything happened to him it would be because of me. I'd only just met him and if I lost him now... The raw wound of Gramma's death still ached. I couldn't add to it.

Night fell like a lazy blanket over the trees. Stars twinkled and a yellow half moon rose below the larger red one to paint the landscape in eerie light. We were skimming through trees much shorter than the ones in TreeCountry. They were almost as small as trees on Earth. The air changed, growing crisp and biting. Gad pointed at a small clearing and glided to the

160

ground.

I landed softly behind him, then stood there, my arms and legs shaking. Gad hoisted his wings off. He unlatched the front of my harness, slipped the straps over my shoulders and let it drop to the ground.

Weary, I walked into the shadows of a nearby tree. I stretched aching muscles and rubbed the pain out of my neck.

"Now what?" I asked, leaning against a tree trunk. The adrenaline of fleeing was drained away leaving me despondent. Worry crept into my mind and a dread for the unknown.

"Father is safe," Gad said quietly. I looked at my brother and shivered. Gad sidled up beside me. The comforting smell of his leather jacket filled my nostrils.

"What are we going to do?" I mumbled. He patted my back.

"First we need to eat. After some sleep we can start out in early morning. We'll hike over Edder's Pass."

"Hike? Why not keep going on the skywings? I've gotten pretty good at flying and we go much faster using them." I stepped over to my wings and tried to untangle the straps.

"We can hide better on the ground. Only a few people know about Edder's Pass. The ice season isn't here yet so we should be able to move quickly and get to BoulderBeam City."

Gad pulled his backpack from the pile of skywings.

"BoulderBeam?" I asked.

He opened the pack and rifled through it. A wrapper rustled and he handed something to me. The smell of jerky reached my nose. I grabbed the handful of dried meat and started ripping pieces off with my teeth. I hadn't realized how hungry I was.

"Yes. We can get a ship in BoulderBeam. Figure out where to go from there." Gad spoke with a garbled voice as he, too, chewed a strip of meat. He handed me several more pieces and lowered himself onto a nearby log, his head hanging. He started thumping the log with his fingers and rubbed his other hand over his face.

I sat on the other end of the log. "Dad is safe." The thumping continued. "Right?" I hunched over and shivered. The cold was more obvious as my body cooled down. "Are you ok?"

Gad's hand stopped. A scowl darkened his face as another shiver ran through me. "Of course he is. He'll contact us as soon as he can. If only Kilain hadn't stopped us from upgrading the shield matrix..." Gad scooted over to me and put his arm around my shoulders. He rubbed his hand up and down my arm fast. "You're cold. I wish we had better accommodations for the night."

"Don't worry," I mumbled.

"No, I hate being unprepared. I do have a blanket we could share." He pointed into the forest. "The thick group of trees over there should block any wind and give us some cover."

He patted my arm and reached over to his pack. Gad handed me another strip of jerky. "Eat up. Then we sleep."

I frowned. "Fun."

Gad got up and pulled the blanket from the pack. He wrapped it around my shoulders then walked over to the trees. Moonlight came and went as grey clouds skimmed past.

What had become of my life? Was I never to have any peace? The attack shouldn't have been possible. Even without the upgrades the shield matrix should have given more warning than it did. Someone very talented had to be helping Bromin defeat GearMaker technology. How else would his ships have gotten through TreeCountry's perimeter defenses?

A big yawn caught me off guard. What could I possibly do in a cold clearing in the middle of nowhere? I walked over to Gad, swaying.

I sat against the biggest tree and pulled the blanket over my legs. My back fit perfectly into the curves of the wood. My eyes drooped, but flew open again. I sighed and forced my eyes closed. The rustle of dried leaves reached my fuzzy brain, and Gad pulled the blanket over me better.

"Thanks," I mumbled.

He sat next to me. "Get some sleep, little sis. We'll be safe for the night."

His shoulder warmed mine. Safe? Was anywhere safe? I wanted to believe him, but in this crazy world it seemed anything could happen.

Chapter 14

"Copper? Wake up."

I opened my eyes to Gad leaning over me. I pulled my stiff body away from the tree trunk, my clothes damp with morning moisture. Groggy, I tried to straighten myself into a standing position. Fog drifted lazily through the forest. It felt ominous and my mood fell. We were safe, but what about my father? What had happened in TreeCountry after we escaped?

Gad folded up the blanket and shoved it into the pack. "We need to get moving before the sun burns off the fog. We'll be more exposed once it clears."

I looked around. "Where are the skywings?"

"I buried them." He pointed further into the trees. "They're too cumbersome where we're going. And if we leave them lying around someone would know we were here."

I crossed my arms to warm myself against the chill. "Let's get going then."

Gad tossed a piece of jerky at me and chuckled as I fumbled to catch it. I growled at him. He raised an eyebrow and a big smile spread over his features. "Think you can keep up?"

"Yes, I can keep up. Why are we going to—BoulderBeam?"

Another piece of jerky came flying toward me. I caught it easily that time. Gad pulled the pack onto his back and waved for me to follow. "It's the best place to get a fast little ship this side of TreeCountry. I'm not sure where we can hide you, but even the ability to keep moving would help." A look of chagrin crossed his features. I suspected running and hiding were not within his natural instincts.

"Anything to get away from Bromin," I muttered and started walking.

The woods were thick with brambles and underbrush. Hours of trudging brought us to a forest that was open and light, but the terrain was getting steeper with every step. Sharp inclines kept my legs burning from the strain, distracting me from the heartache I felt—the unknown fate of my father and the people of TreeCountry. I needed to believe that Dad was safe.

Rocks and gravel slipped underfoot on the grueling switchbacks. Twigs tugged at my clothes and skin leaving hatch-mark scratches beaded with blood. I grew surly from fatigue and worry. I wanted to rest and be with my newly found family. I wanted to be in the workshop building the new skywings. Flying a pair had brought me new insights into how they worked. I should be sitting at the breakfast table with Dad drinking pila juice. Why would Bromin want to destroy these people? They appeared to be peaceful farmers to me, peaceful farmers with a knack for technology. Surely there was no harm in that.

"Is there nothing that can stop a GearMade?" I mumbled under my breath as we went up another switchback.

Gad looked back at me. "What do you mean?"

I stopped in my tracks. "Is there no way to destroy this crazy, homicidal machine person?"

165

"Well—I don't actually know." Gad adjusted his pack. "They aren't immortal, but even if they are machines, GearMades are still alive." He paused on the path, his back turned to me. "It's hard to kill someone." Gad turned, his face serious.

Kill? Could I? Would I? I wasn't sure I meant that I myself would do it, but yes it meant killing. How else do you stop someone evil, be they man or machine?

Screeeeeeeeee…

A squeal pierced through the air breaking me from my thoughts and into a panic. Gad looked up franticly. Something zinged by and landed at my feet. I looked down at the metal pod sticking out of the dirt. A blinking, red light glared at me.

"Pick it up, Rose," Gad said.

"But—what is it?" I reached down, but flinched back.

"It's a thither. It won't hurt you."

I reached out and touched the cool metal casing. The blinking stopped and it hissed open. Inside was a rolled piece of paper. I pulled it out, glancing at Gad, then unfurled the paper to find elegant script.

"It's from Dad."

Gad leaned closer. "What does it say?"

I pulled open the paper and read out loud. "It says: *Safe.*" I breathed deep and smiled. "*Keep going. Communications no longer secure.*" I looked up at Gad. "What does that mean?"

"Great. There's no way to respond." Gad sighed heavily and shook his head.

I rolled the silvery long pod in my hand. "What is this thither thing?"

He bounced on his toes. "A thither locks onto the blood

166

programmed into it and goes to that person."

"Really?" I tucked the thither in my coat pocket. "Interesting." The paper crinkled in my other hand. Dad was safe, but the danger wasn't gone. I sighed.

"We're lucky this found us," Gad said. "I wonder what he locked onto. We need to move faster. I need to get you somewhere safer than this." Gad bowed his head and trudged up the next steep incline. I looked around, confused, exhausted. I wanted to curl up under a bush and sleep.

Gad skillfully led me through the best paths, covering our trail as we went. We did reach the mountain pass by mid-day.

"Rose, get up here," Gad said. He held out a hand to pull me up the last steep steps. He took me a few more yards to where the brush thinned and the cliff walls spread out.

The view was magnificent. The mountains were more beautiful than any I'd ever seen. The mountain walls rose from above us. Green leaves poked out from weathered bushes and trees fighting for the sunlight that suffused the sky. Purple, blue and tinges of red stone mixed and spread under sprinklings of soft snow. The tang of cold tingled in my nose.

"FarReach Valley is below the pass. BoulderBeam is not far from there."

"I hope so cause I think my leg fell off back there. I'm all into a brisk hike, but this—this is mountain climbing." I reached down to rub my aching knees.

Gad made a sour face. "Really? This is one of the easiest passes to cross on foot. It's too narrow for vehicles which is why it's not traveled much."

I heard a strange, low buzz. I looked around frantically, but saw nothing dangerous. "What's that noise?"

His eyebrows tightened around his eyes. "What?"

I leaned close to a branch and the elusive sound increased. "Don't you hear the buzzing?" It wasn't the hum of a insect wings, but like many little machines. "What in the world," I said under my breath. It left me uneasy.

"I don't hear anything," Gad said and started walking down the rock strewn path.

The buzzing flared up then lowered to a constant hum. On a tall bush crawled a small beetle, clicking its brass wings at me. The eyes sparkled with light. Looking past the beetle I also saw the bush branches shimmer the same way Dad's roses and Bromin's garden plants had. I gasped in awe. "It's all machines." I looked at Gad. "All these plants and bugs are GearMade?"

Gad barked out a laugh. "Of course. Edder was a well-known GearMaker. He loved to experiment with mechanical life to see how it could evolve and exist on it's own. Dad learned a lot from him."

"Wow." I looked back down to the beetle as Gad continued down the trail around a large bush.

"Rose, run."

I turned and gasped. Gad was running back to me when two filthy men grabbed him and pinned his arms behind him. Two more ran up behind me and grabbed me before I could get away.

"Let me go!" I kicked backwards and one man chuckled near my ear. His stench filled my nostrils. They dragged me forward until we were close to Gad.

Another man was sauntering down the trail as three additional men surrounded us. The man's clothes were torn and so dirty the color was unclear.

"What 'ave we here?" He said. "Anythin' ta say fer yerself, Gad?" His rotting teeth flashed in a wicked smile. I shuddered.

"Hello, Huist. Been awhile," Gad greeted in a dejected tone. The man cackled.

The buzzing sound swelled again. My temples throbbed lightly as the sound eased off.

"Let us go," I snapped, kicking the shins of a man holding me. He grunted, but held on tight.

Huist smiled again, pointing at me. "Hmmm—there's a bounty on a girl such as you. The notice didn't say there was spunk as well as the attractive curls. Copper. An unusual color ain't it?" Huist sneered as he pulled on one of my curls. I yanked against the arms of his minions. "Hold her tighter. Can't 'ave her escapin'."

I glared, dark anger pouring from me. "You don't know what you've gotten yourself into." They couldn't know how much I trembled inside. My breath rasped against my clenched teeth.

Huist turned to his men who chuckled wickedly. "Ooo, the sassy girl thinks she be scary."

Gad gave me a warning look. "You know how this goes, Huist. You capture me. We threaten each other. I get the better of you every time and then we go our separate ways."

"Not this time ye don't," Huist growled and grabbed me away from the men holding me. He clenched my arm painfully as he pulled me close. My lip curled as his unwashed smell

169

curdled my nostrils. He ran a filthy finger down my arm. "Maybe we can 'ave a little fun 'afore we deliver this little lady to his greatness."

"No," Gad yelled out. One of the men slugged him in the gut. Gad doubled over and they hauled him back to his feet.

Chill swept through me. The men and plants blurred in my vision as a rage like never before saturated me. "No one is touching me." The buzz of the insects amplified to a low roar. Several of the men looked around confused. I yanked my arms away from Huist. He grabbed me around the waist and hoisted me off my feet. A metal beetle flew right into his face. From the trees and bushes around us more insects attacked.

Gad vanished in the flurry of men batting at the swarm. The air grew dark and thick, the din nearly deafening. I elbowed Huist in the belly, sending him to the ground. He pulled at me, sending me toppling over him. Metallic bugs crawled over him, biting and skittering, but not one touched me. Huist yelled and screamed. I stood up and stomped on the back of his knee sending him all the way to the down.

"Gad," I screamed and ran through the thick cloud of pests to find him. Shiny insects followed me, swarming around anyone who tried to stop me. Three men ran away down the pass swatting at the attackers that followed them. The other men fell away from Gad, writhing and screaming. Bugs skittered down the mouth of a man near me. He gagged, flailed and fell to the ground not moving. A trickle of blood ran down from his mouth.

My stomach dropped, both my hands clamped over my open mouth. Gad looked from the insect covered men to me, his mouth open and eyes wide. Pain lanced through my head, pulsing from the buzz of the swarm.

"Stop you crazy bugs!" I turned away. Huist lay moaning where I'd left him, several bugs still crawling over his welt covered arms. I swayed, dizzy and nauseous. "Just stop," I screamed, falling to my knees. The buzz roared past my ears. I cradled my throbbing head in my hands unwilling to look at the groaning men.

Someone took my arm. I swung a fist.

"Rose," Gad said.

I leapt to my feet and wrapped my arms around him, sobbing into his shoulder. What had I done?

My brother gently pulled me away to look into my face. "Copper Rose. Look at me. We need to get out of here." He led me down the trail, quickly passing the unconscious and injured men.

The swarm had dissipated completely. Gad led me through the pass into a forest. I stumbled along at his rapid pace, trying to shake the horrified feeling inside. Were some of those men dead?

Gad kept looking at me as we traveled.

I shook my head, stumbling over another tree root. "Did I do that?"

"I don't know." Gad's voice was monotone. He kept walking, but looked over at me. "If you did, you saved us. Huist may be incompetent, but he's still dangerous."

Eventually the trail grew nearly solid with tall thin trees and started back down the mountain to a large valley below. A deep blue river sliced through it like a snake ending in a massive lake where the valley looked like the bowl of a spoon.

Checked stretches of farm land dotted the river edge. We continued onward as dusk approached, my legs aching. When I felt I couldn't take another step, the steep incline flattened and the forest thinned showing the sparkling lake in the distance.

The craggy mountain walls curved away from us to the city. Massive boulders pushed up from the valley floor like giant fingers thrusting out of the soil. The largest boulders surrounding the city melded into the cliff wall. A huge fortress was carved directly out of the stone overlooking the land. Roads and web-like paths laced downward. A substantial wall, also constructed from stone, hugged the city.

"You don't do anything small do you?" I said.

"Small? Who needs small in Seranova?" Gad quipped putting an arm around my shoulder. I sighed and shook my head. Gad wouldn't like Earth. He would be bored within a day.

"Are you sure Bromin's men won't find us here?" I asked, turning to look up at him. He shrugged and we started walking across the grassy valley in the moonlight.

"I don't know what places are safe anymore, but we'll be subtle and only about an hour." Gad sighed. "Let's get going."

We hurried between the shadows cast by bushes and trees. The first two of the moons had only risen a quarter of the way across the sky, each a sliver of gold or red light.

When we reached the city gate the blue moon was rising above the tree-line, leaving enough light spilling over the city to cause eerie shadows to stretch across the roads.

Gad motioned me to follow. He led me around the corner. Gad leaned close to my ear. "We have to get to the other side of town. I know an airship merchant who would never betray us.

He might have a small, stealth ship in his yard, but we can only reach him from the trail that goes by the fortress." Nodding, I looked up at the cliff and gulped. Gad continued leading.

Awnings stuck out from doorways allowing us to keep to the shadows. We skimmed along the streets past sleeping buildings, keeping away from the ones doused in noise, the light spilling from windows and doors. We ignored people we passed in the hopes they would do the same.

The city fortress loomed over us, and a crawling sensation went up my spine. I paused. Across the street a man, nearly invisible in the black shadows of a store front, was looking right at us. His eyes glowed inhumanly. I froze, fear trickling through my senses. The man seemed tensed, ready to leap into action. What could we do if he attacked? That glow to the eyes... Was this a GearMade?

Gad quietly grabbed my arm not noticing my distraction. He pulled me forward again, around a corner, away from the watchful eye of the shadowed man. Soon we were through the gates to the fortress, winding our way through a neighborhood. A road twisted around the castle base to an outcropping of stone jutting out like a runway. Ships nestled into cradles and caves in the cliff. A small light flickered in the window of the building at the beginning of the runway.

"Almost there," Gad whispered.

A prickle went up my spine again. Something wasn't right. Without realizing it, I had gripped the locket in my fist, holding it tight against my beating heart. Gad clasped my other hand, his eyes scanning the terrain franticly.

"I missed something. What?" he whispered harshly, pulling me into the shadows of a willowy tree. We looked out through the long trailing branches as if through a curtain. The misty moonlight played tricks on my eyes. Shadows seemed to move, but when I looked closer, nothing was there. My hand in Gad's throbbed from his tight grip. I wiggled my fingers. He let go and mouthed an apology, then was back to scanning the landscape.

"There." Gad leaned in close to me and pointed to a building at the end of the lane. It was the man with the glowing eyes. He creeped forward sticking to the cover of shadows. He made a motion and a dozen more figures appeared, all cloaked and slipping soundlessly forward along the path toward us. I gulped. If we left the shadow of the tree they would see us.

"What can we do?" I whispered. Gad looked all around, a helplessness clear on his face. A whirr buzzed in my hand. Gad's head whipped around, his finger to his lips hushing me, but he stopped and looked closely at the locket as I opened my fingers. Click, click… whirrrrr… Little sparks flashed inside the spinning gears.

"What is it doing?" he asked. "Can't you stop it?"

"I…"

Gad stepped back in surprise as the locket increased in volume. I reached for him.

Click, click, clack, clack…

"No—no, no, no." I didn't want to go back. I had a family I wanted to keep. I had a brother I liked. I had too much to learn —so much technology to—Maybe if I didn't open it. All I could see was the locket, the gears whirling wildly—and the cover popping open on its own. I reached for Gad again and caught a handful of fabric. My vision filled with the locket, then darkness and spinning.

My breath wheezed out of me as I was dropped onto hard ground. Pulling myself up, I rubbed my eyes as my vision cleared. I looked at the locket. What could I do if I understood the silly thing better? I remembered getting a hold of Gad's sleeve before the locket opened itself.

"Gad?" I spun around, frantic. I was surrounded by thin, tall trees. The ground was carpeted in short brush and grasses. Daylight covered the sky. No hills or mountain ranges broke up the landscape. No one was there—anywhere.

"Gad," I screamed out into the echoing silence. I looked at the locket again and angrily shoved it into my shirt. What purpose was there in dropping me into the middle of nowhere, all alone? "Gad. Where are you?" I spun around. Sure enough, he wasn't there. Morning light was spreading over the sky above me. The brighter it got the further I could see. Nothing. Nothing, but tall spread out trees poked into the sky like a forest of pencils.

A shadow drifted over me and I looked up expecting clouds. The hum of an airship reached me as did a wave of fear. There was nowhere to hide. Another ship appeared not far behind the first massive ship, and then another, and another. At least fifty ships filled the sky. Blue banners hung from their sides bearing the snake winding around three gears. It could only be Bromin's armada.

"Stupid locket," I grumbled under my breath and scooted up against a trunk, hoping the sparse branches high up would afford me some kind of camouflage. The ground started shaking rhythmically. Earthquake?

"You've got to be kidding."

On the ground, between the distant trees, columns of

175

soldiers appeared headed straight at me.

I ran. I ran as fast as I could knowing it was hopeless, but hoping a miracle would surface again. I grabbed the locket.

"Take me back to Gad. Take me back, please take me back," I pleaded. The sound of air-skimmers erupted from the ships.

"Oy. Get 'er."

My legs burned, but I kept going, begging the locket to save me. What had it been thinking putting me right in the path of Bromin's army? As it had when I first arrived in Grediaya, the locket quietly clicked inside it's shell.

A net came flying down over me. Hoots echoed around me as I tripped on the ropes and rolled over the forest floor, the net wrapping tightly around me.

Trapped.

"Can't be," a man said as he approached. Half a dozen men appeared in my restricted vision.

"It's the GearMaker brat, Bromin's been lookin' for. We got her." Another man hoisted me up, cocooned in the net.

"Captain says bring her aboard. We must leave the armada and get her to CapitolCity immediately," the first man insisted. I writhed in my prison with no success.

"Better leave her in that till we get her on the ship. Quite the fiery wildcat," a third man said and grabbed my feet. It was over. I was alone. No one knew where I was. No one could save me.

Chapter 15

Bromin Shere.

He stood before me, malevolent. Triumph glowed in his eyes as he walked over to where I was trussed up on his palace floor. He flipped a hand toward my feet and a guard came over to quickly untie them. Twinges of pain spread down my limbs as the blood rushed back into my feet. Awkwardly, I pushed myself up onto my knees, slipping on the metal tile floor. The trembling from inside me left it hard to breathe.

"Sweet Copper Rose, how I have missed your company," Bromin sneered. A heartless look filled his eye. He walked around behind me. Pulling me up by my hair, Bromin held me against his shoulder. Tears sprang to my eyes from the pain. Acrid metallic breath brushed my skin. "You left so quickly last time. I simply insist you stay longer. A lot longer."

Fear welled in me like a tsunami, but I squashed it. I knew so much more than I had before. He wouldn't kill me. Bromin needed me.

"Must I? I really have other places to be so if you don't mind letting me go…"

"You GearMaker whelp." Bromin yanked back on my hair again and I squealed inadvertently.

I breathed in deeply, steadying myself. "What makes you

think I'll do anything you say? You don't really know who I am." My voice still trembled slightly.

"I will find a way to make you do my will," Bromin growled.

An involuntary chuckle rose from me.

He tightened his hold. "You think this is amusing? Maybe it is you who does not know who you are dealing with."

I smiled despite the way he had my head bent backward. "Perhaps. Or maybe I know exactly who I'm dealing with." He threw me forward with such force I fell to my knees with a crack of pain. My tied hands barely stopped me from landing on my face. After a moment, the pain in my knees subsided to a throb. There would be bruises but nothing felt broken.

I looked over my shoulder at Bromin. The white of his face was spectral. Maybe machine faces didn't flush when emotionally charged.

"Copper Rose. This does not have to be painful. Your stay could be pleasant, enjoyable even," he said.

Back to the sweet talk? Did he really think he could charm me into obedience? I pushed myself up to my knees ignoring the pain. "Enjoyable? Can't imagine how that could be." Twisting my wrists in the tight rope, I tried to ease the sting.

Bromin leaned down close to my ear. "Whatever they taught you on your little trip home was lies."

"They didn't teach me much. More than anything they reminded me who—I—am. And *that* is what you need to be worried about," I said and knew it to be true. The locket could not disappoint me by denying me passage to Earth any longer. Home was in Seranova. Home was TreeCountry. And my purpose in life was no longer a wandering path. I knew what I would do in my life and Bromin Shere should be afraid. I would do anything in my power to fight for my family and the land we called home even if that meant destroying Bromin.

The machine man looked at me, the edges of his mouth creeping upward. I could only hope he noticed my determination. He broke eye contact and turned his straight back to me.

"You will create an army for me. You will give life to GearMades like myself. If you do not, I will destroy everything you love," Bromin whispered, menace curdling his voice. "How about we start by fixing that sassy mouth of yours." He turned and looked at me, his arms behind his back, his face steady and confident.

He grinned at me. "Take her to the *music* suite."

My breath caught. What kind of music? Maybe I was afraid.

***

Sound... endless sound in discordant tones, reverberated in my every cell. Light flashed in my vision like small fireworks. Cognitive moments came and went. Was I drugged? My mouth felt dry and tasted nasty, but the noise wouldn't stop and sleep never came for long. Had it been three days or a month? The cool metal slab I lay on was unforgiving and a bitter mist tickled the edges of the room. Aches spread through every joint and muscle. When I could stand, my feet slipped on the slick metal floor. I ran my hands over every wall, but couldn't find a way out. I was in a metal cage. The constant whining noise coupled with a squeal echoed, echoed—reverberated in the cell, in my brain. Tepid water and tasteless food appeared at random intervals. I would eat then forget hours, the haze in my brain growing thicker. I was starting to wonder who I even was… What was I doing?

Standing in the middle of the room, my head bowed, I swayed, exhausted, nearly every bit of sanity spent. The floor looked nice, comfortable. Maybe those were silvery sheets, a mattress of fluff? No—it was hard or was it? A rattle reached my ears, but it echoed into the cacophony. I glanced up barely able to hold my eyes open. Gad was standing in front of me! No. It was Gramma. Wait—were they even real?

A figure stood in a doorway holding out a hand to usher me out. The noise stopped, but I could still hear it ringing, ringing in my head. I tried to focus my vision, teetering in place. The figure put a hand on my arm.

I pulled away, falling back onto the metal bench. "Don' toush me." My voice slurred in my cottony mouth. Closing my eyes, I tried to make sense of anything. The sharp corners of the room were becoming clearer. A black rectangle gaped at me where the door had been.

And there before me was Bromin.

"Alum seems to think you can be turned to my way of thinking. For this reason I will allow you a breath of fresh air. Would you care to follow me to more friendly accommodations? Trust that no one will find it as easy to pull you from my grasp again." Bromin smiled as if his statement was that of a gracious host. I eyed him suspiciously. I didn't want to give in. But I needed sleep soon or I wouldn't be clear minded enough to fight back.

"Okay," I said, following him as he exited. I had to use the door frames and walls to occasionally steady myself. The guards stayed at a distance surrounding Bromin and me. My vision blurred and I tripped, catching myself on the wall. I pressed my face into it. My fingers traveled along the cool metal bumps, helping me focus. I couldn't keep going. The only thing I was sure of was the wall holding me up, the ridges of each gold flecked design... the spinning... spinning...

"Carry her," a voice said from behind me. The wall left my touch and I fell into oblivion.

***

Cool... Soft... Something swept my brow as I stirred. Every joint screamed in agony if I moved. Was that me screaming, too? A hand, warm—soothing, caressed my arm. I calmed, slipping back into sleep.

Light trickled through my eyelids, shadows passing... A warm touch on my forehead reaching my senses before the darkness of sleep came over me again.

My next awareness; light streaming in a window. My eyes were open. Sitting up, I looked around at the room I stayed in during my first, brief time with Bromin. The windows now sported shiny bars.

I sighed. "Great." I dragged myself out of the bed, catching a whiff of body odor. How long had I been in that metal cell? How long had I been asleep since getting out? My leather coat was draped over a chair by the resplendent dressing table. I walked over to the window, wishing Gad would show up again, like the bad penny he was to Bromin. I wanted him to whisk me away like a good big brother. Wrapping my fingers around the metal bars, I shook them, but they didn't give at all.

My life on Earth may have been lonely, but there I was strong and smart. Somehow I had ended up a helpless prisoner, incapable of doing what her captor wanted. I hung my head, the warmth of a foreign sun bathing my skin and hair.

Bromin didn't have to know how helpless I was. Right before he'd thrown me in the 'music suite', I'd had a moment of clarity. I warmed at the memory. Nothing would take my family away. This was my world now and I would fight for it. Even constrained in the palace, I could focus on resisting Bromin.

"Don't think that bars are my only upgrade to your security."

My heart sped up, but I knew who it was speaking. I turned around, steeling myself for the battle. Bromin stood in the open double doors.

"You already have creepy down. Do you really have to keep sneaking up on me?" I said.

Bromin chortled, humorlessly. Was he capable of any proper emotion?

"Are you ready to start your task? If it gives you comfort, you may be the only GearMaker capable of this. You will be honored for your success. Or you will pay dearly for your resistance."

I glowered. "How kind of you. Maybe I can figure out how to make a GearMade by taking you apart." I put my fists on my hips and stared him down.

Bromin chuckled again. "Such wit."

A soldier pushed a cart into the room, covered with silver domes gushing steam. An incredible smell reached my nose, inspiring my stomach to growl loudly.

"Consider this your chance to start over." He waved a hand over the cart. "Nourishment—free of mind altering agents." Then he gestured to the large closet, it's door askew allowing me to see the frills. "Garments I consider appropriate for a woman under my hospitality." He smiled when I grimaced. "Only my hardened soldiers will be attending to your needs. Trust that they are immune to any wiles you might use on them." Bromin shooed the soldier out.

I stumbled toward the food, hoping this was the end of our verbal sparring for the moment. "No problem. Do I get to eat and maybe dress before I start this slave labor?" My hands shook from weakness.

"Of course. What do you take me for?" Bromin grinned, his eyes narrowed.

"Do you really want me to answer that?" I quipped.

Bromin turned from the room chuckling. "I will return soon." The door slammed shut and a series of clicks sounded as locks were pushed into place. How had he entered so silently?

Bromin's assurance that the food wasn't drugged didn't comfort me. I had no ability to resist the food my hunger was so deep. I dived in, eating only slow enough to not choke. How long had it been since I'd eaten?

When my stomach couldn't hold any more, I looked down at myself. The smell emanating from my clothes was enough to inspire me to check in the closet.

I groaned. "You've got to be kidding." Lace, ruffles, satin… It looked like a costume closet for musical theatre. What kind of rebellion would it be to stay in what I was wearing? Could a GearMade smell anything? One thing was for sure, I could smell myself. I decided to swallow my pride. The closet offered me only a few choices I was willing to put on, none of them without a skirt, so I settled on the least frilly gown available.

Bromin could come back anytime and the bathroom door had no lock, so I chose to sponge myself down rather than fill the large, inviting tub. I pulled on a soft, sky-blue gown. It had more bows than anyone ever needed, but the color didn't clash with my hair. I needed to be able to move and feel comfortable. That dress was the best option.

I was surprised to find the thither and Dad's note still in my coat pocket. Even the locket was still around my neck as if Bromin knew nothing about it. Why would he take the risk of letting me keep it? Maybe he didn't know what it could do.

The locket stayed around my neck, hidden in the bodice, but I tucked the thither and note between mattress and blankets at the head of the bed. I took time to wash my suede pants and cream blouse in the sink and hang them out to dry so I could wear them later. Bromin couldn't force me to be a fancy lady and have me building machines. Soap bubbled up between my fingers as I rubbed the fabric against the sink. Dirt swirled down the drain with the rinse water. I draped the clothes over an ornate wood chair in the corner. Maybe they would still be there when I got back. I could only hope.

The soldiers returned as I finished cleaning myself up. One rolled the cart away. Several other soldiers surrounded me and led me out a single door near the windows into a sitting room. A posh couch, cushioned chairs and ornate metal side tables encircled a plush rug. The double doors on the opposite wall stood open revealing the familiar workshop on the other side. Bromin was standing there.

The soldiers peeled away from me and marched over to Bromin, standing at attention behind him.

"Your sleeping quarters are connected to the workshop so

you will have no need to ever leave here," Bromin said as if this was a treat. "There is also the sitting room for your pleasure. But I trust you will not be entertaining guests or have need for extended sitting. The entire wing is secure. Work hard, work long and we will get along. I will check on you in a day to see your progress." He walked past me, continuing to smile like a cordial employer, granting me such privileges. "And know that I can *sneak up* anytime I wish."

I sneered, but bit back any retort. If nothing else I believed him capable of making my life very hard. I had to make him believe I was doing what he wanted until I could find a way out —a way back to my father and Gad, if they were both still safe and alive. A sinking hopelessness tapped at my resolve. How did he manage to appear out of nowhere? Could there be cameras? Or listening devices? Would he know everything I did?

The door thudded shut. The lock clicked its song of finality and the room grew quiet. My breathing was labored. Even mustering all my willpower, the fear that lunatic of a machine-man inspired was more than I could take. The shaking took over my body and I slumped to a stool, resting a hand on a metal table-top. The visible shaking matched the jelly feeling in my innards. Weakness from being tortured was probably compounding the problem.

How was I going to get out this time? Locks, bars, soldiers breathing down my neck. Maybe Bromin was invincible?

Warmth around my neck eased the shaking. The locket was still there, still aware. I pulled it out of my collar. Why hadn't Bromin taken it? I was so out of it for days he could have searched me. If he knew what it was, he would have. For such an ornery piece of metal it seemed like it might be my only defense against Bromin—or perhaps my worst enemy. If I could only get the locket to do what I wanted.

I looked at the clicking gears, following the motion with my eyes. "Home. Take me home. I have a home now so please— please take me there." My eyes blurred. The residual warmth of the burnished metal seeped into my cold fingers. The gears clicked away and I matched my breath to their rhythm.

The gears beat in sync with my heart. I flipped the casing open and, like so many times before, nothing happened. Who was the master? Me? Or the locket?

"Stupid fickle thing. Just work," I snapped at the locket.

"Maybe it only works when it feels like it. Or perhaps it knows more than we do and we only need to accept it's will," a rich tenor voice said. I looked up.

Alum. He was still here. He was still gorgeous and made my heart flutter by his very presence. But he was still not to be trusted.

Chapter 16

Alum smiled sadly. "So you decided to come back to me." He stayed several yards away, his arms hanging by his sides. He looked forlorn.

"Coming here was not exactly my choice." Anger seeped into my words replacing the bone-quaking fear.

"Gad should have kept you safe," Alum muttered, shaking his head.

I dropped the locket into my blouse. "It wasn't Gad's fault. Bromin attacked TreeCountry. Gad and I kept running, but Bromin is rather persistent. I'm not even sure if my father is safe right now or if Gad is even..." I looked down. "Or even if he's alive," I whispered.

Alum nodded, his shoulders drooping. "Sorry. I don't mean to fault Gad or your father. I'm sure they did everything they could to protect you. I would do the same for my sister—if I even have one." Alum sat down in a nearby chair, his shoulders hunched over.

"Your family knows you're alive."

His head snapped up, his eyes intense. "They—they do?" Alum turned away and paused. His breathing slowed and he looked back at me with his expression harder, sadder. "I am not the child they knew anymore. That person is dead. They would have been better off not knowing."

I eyed him standing there dejected. "Sorry. We thought your family deserved the truth," I said calmly, though I felt a need for caution and distance. I had to consider Alum a danger to me in more ways than one. His resignation and sadness annoyed me. Why had he stayed with Bromin all these years? Alum had complete freedom of the palace and was brilliant. If Gad could break in, Alum could have found a way out. "Maybe you don't believe in truth. Maybe Bromin has corrupted you enough that they're better off believing you're dead."

Alum looked at me, a silent plea in his expression. "No. I would fight him if I knew how. Only—there is no escaping him."

"Humph." I narrowed my eyes and stared until he turned away. "How did you get in here anyway? Sneaking around like Bromin does?"

Alum shrugged and pointed at a fancy door next to the welding area. "Wasn't that…?" During my last visit that room had been dark with a transmitter and a woman. The door had now been remodeled to look like the other doors.

"It's gone. The communicator. It's not there." Alum grimaced. "Bromin insisted I reside close to the workshop as well. He sealed the outer doors to that room. Now I'm a prisoner like you." He gazed at me, a hardness to his features.

I fiddled with the locket through the blouse. I couldn't figure out Alum. "Don't blame me. You're the one who told Bromin where to find us when Gad and I were escaping off the cliff. I don't want to be locked up with you."

"That wasn't me. You must believe me. I would never

188

intentionally betray you." His face grew crimson as he turned away. "He tracked me. He…"

"I don't have to believe anything you say. You're one of Bromin's lackeys." I had work to do. I had to at least pretend to make a GearMade until I found a way to escape.

Alum sighed, keeping his back to me. Clearly I was alone in my goals. I scanned the ceiling and corners of the room, but nothing looked like a monitoring device. That didn't mean they weren't there though.

I walked the length of a table to a closed cabinet. Throwing open the doors, I started examining the items inside. Everything looked the same as my previous visit; strange supplies I'd never seen before and tools similar to those from Earth filled every shelf. Before me were racks of tools and supplies, and table after table of space to spread out on. Metal sheeting coated the walls in one corner, adorned with old fashioned welding tools. Beside that unit was a long, wide steel sink. Ahh, the possibilities. So much I could make with all this equipment.

If my ancestors made machines live and if I had when I was a child, then the potential was in me, but I had no clue how to do it. My head throbbed momentarily. Why couldn't I remember doing this miraculous thing? I wanted to know how as badly as I wanted to keep the technology from Bromin.

"Where to start?" I walked over to a drafting table in the corner and pulled out a clean sheet of drafting paper. A small drawer under the angled top held a variety of pencil-like writing sticks and drafting tools like those you would find in the 1800's on Earth. The ones that were completely unusual to me, I simply set aside.

I knew I had to start small. If I could get a butterfly machine to live then making something a bit bigger seemed reasonable. Making something as big as a man...? I wasn't sure I could do any of it, but at least I needed a chance of success. The pencil in my grip skimmed over the paper, a joint here, a tail there. Something that looked like a large eared cat or lemur appeared on the page. Ideas flowed through my brain as I drew and put notes along the sides. The shape changed to accommodate abilities for stealth and agility. The limbs became more flexible in appearance and the layers of mechanics more complicated.

Overhead lights switched on and someone entered pushing a cart. The smell of hot food wafted over to me, but I continued to work.

Alum looked over my shoulder. I chose to ignore him and flipped the page to begin the designs for the main computer components to run the robotics. I knew time was passing as I puzzled through problems. I was completely wrapped up in the process. It made me feel alive. My mind was clear. I could visualize the creature coming together in my head.

"You could use filament nerves from the brain chip instead of those more rudimentary wires," Alum said close to my ear.

I looked at him over my shoulder and my heart jumped at his closeness and the rich smell of him.

"What?" I tried to focus. "Filament nerves?"

Alum walked to a cabinet and rifled around inside. He returned with a roll of paper and a box of clear-looking spaghetti. I scooted my stool back a little as he set the tube of papers on my drawings. My fingers tingled as I reached out to unfurl it. Technology years, maybe centuries ahead of what I knew lay before me. I leaned over and traced the diagrams using my finger, reading the text and looking at the schematics.

"I saw this in one of the books," I said. The process of using the filament made so much sense. A smile curled the corners of my mouth. Oh, the applications this electrical system could be used for!

"This is a basic wiring for a simple machine brain," Alum said pointing to one corner of the directions. "I think it would be more complicated to be applied to living machines." He placed one of the filaments in my hand. It was like gossamer thread.

"Wow."

Alum smiled slightly. "I am sure you can figure out how to use these."

"So." I hesitated. "These—these filament nerves—they are what you use even in simple machines?"

Alum stepped back and sat on a stool. "They're the closest thing to the nerve functions of flesh and blood beings. I have used the metal wiring, but never had the smooth action or reaction time as the filaments allow for. I don't even think you need to practice using them." He chuckled and his eyes twinkled. "I can see you're absorbing all of this. I bet you'll get it right on the first time." He seemed pleased, like he was proud of me without me having even succeeded yet.

I know I was blushing. "Uh, thank you, I guess." I handed the filament example back to Alum without looking at him and went back to the schematics for the nervous system of my creature. Nervous system? On Earth it would be the electrical system. Despite the horrors of this world, I couldn't help but be excited by all the wondrous technology.

Hours passed. Alum occasionally advised me on the plans that seemed to magically appear under my pencil tip. He brought me food that I ate without tasting it. Something in me was growing, changing. The ideas flowed from me, filling the pages with designs I had never dreamed possible. I felt more complete and whole than ever before.

It was very late at night when I stepped away from the drafting table with the stack of design pages in hand. I placed the pages out on the long metal tables so I could look down the line of them and make sure everything was in order. Elation lifted me to see the creature, layer upon layer across the table. But then my mood dropped like a stone falling through water.

"What is it? Is there a mistake?" Alum asked from across the room.

I shook my head. "I don't know how to do it."

Alum stepped toward me then stopped, his eyes widening fearfully.

Bromin cleared his throat behind me. "Why do you insist on this belief—this lie that you do not possess the skill to bring machines to life?"

Steeling myself, I turned to face down Bromin. "You cannot even fathom a world like the one I come from. Machines are merely tools. They don't have a heart. They have no mind and no willpower."

He stepped closer, his hands behind his back. "I know you were the one to give life to a machine that was only a child's toy."

"When I was three, I am told." I glared. "I don't remember

doing it."

Bromin stepped closer. "You will create my army. You will give life to machines."

I put a fist on my hip. This was a dangerous game, but I didn't know any other way to play it.

He strolled past me to view the designs. Alum moved away from Bromin as if they were magnets facing the wrong way. Bromin glanced down critically.

"What is this?" He fixed me with his sharp gaze.

"Designs for a test run." I raised my brow, tempting him to challenge my choices.

"A bat eared pet?" he sneered.

Alum approached, a hand raised. "It is best to start small. I have been monitoring her…" Bromin moved like a blur. *Smack!* His hand pulled away from Alum's face slowly. I cringed. Alum wiped a trickle of blood from the corner of his mouth and winced.

"The girl will explain her reasoning," Bromin said, his voice still cool as he looked back at me. "Well?"

"How many machines have you created?" I waited. Bromin looked at me. "If you want to question me then maybe you should find someone who can do things your way—oh, but wait. You have had people doing things your way all these years. How did that work out for you?"

Bromin grabbed Alum and drove him to his knees. Suddenly there was a brass gun in Bromin's hand, pointed directly at Alum's head. "You will do what I say or I will kill Alum." Somehow I managed to maintain a straight face. Sweat trickled down my back. *Breathe normal—breathe normal.* I felt a tick, tick, tick in my head as the moment seemed to slow and race all at once.

"Go ahead."

"What?" Bromin said, surprise in his voice.

I started pulling the pages of my design into a pile ignoring the tremor in my hands. "Go for it. Shoot him. Only take it out of here. It would be a bit messy don't you think?" While inside I was rejoicing at the look on Bromin's face, I didn't miss the look of hurt and betrayal on Alum's.

"You want me to kill the boy?" Bromin said returning to a venomous voice as he shoved the nose of the gun into Alum's hair. Alum froze, the look of anguish etched deeply in his face.

"I didn't say that's what I want. I'm only saying that it's your choice if you want to kill him." I stopped what I was doing and looked straight at Bromin. "I may be some great GearMaker who can give life, but my experience is that of a three year old child I can't even remember being, so go for it. I'll muddle through."

Bromin looked from me to Alum and back again. His eyes narrowed. I smiled, ignoring Alum's gaping mouth. I looked back to my designs, trying to feign indifference. Walking over to the table I picked up a page and headed to a cabinet that I believed would have some of the things I needed to start the robot. The paper crinkled as I laid it out on the nearest table. I pulled open the doors with a creak that cut through the silent room. Out of the corner of my eye I could see Bromin watching at me, still holding the weapon to Alum's head.

I started pulling tools and supplies from the drawers and put them on a metal tray. Occasionally I stopped to check something on the designs. Ignoring the situation behind me and the racing of my heart, I stepped to the next cabinet, opened it and froze. All Alum's beautiful little machines were in front of me. My hand wrapped around the spindly little retrieval device. I looked up the tall wall to the high ceiling. Air was blowing gently from a ventilation grate. I'd seen a similar grate in the bathroom.

Alum had told me the viny legged machine was a listening device. The small size and agile legs might allow it to crawl and climb to locations hidden and small—like under a piece of furniture or the ventilation shafts! *Hmmm…*

"We will do it your way," Bromin said. "For now." I closed my fists around the machine as I spun to face Bromin.

He stared, his eyes glittering with flecks of angry red, as he shoved Alum to the ground then strode out the door.

Alum pushed himself to his knees stiffly and watched the door click shut. Relief flooded through me like a gush of air. Alum rubbed his hands, gently touching his lip where blood beaded. I bent behind the table, and with a wave of guilt tucked the little machine into the deep hem of the blue skirt. I closed the cabinet and went back to my work. I cared if Bromin killed Alum, but I didn't care if Alum went away and left me alone. His presence left me conflicted. I'd told Gad I didn't care for him, but I was wrong. Being near him I felt the smoldering attraction like the first time I saw him. Then logic would leap in to scatter my desires. Alum was working for Bromin. Alum was not to be trusted.

"Why do you talk to him like that?" Alum's voice wavered as he came up beside me. "He won't put up with it for long."

"See this?" I lifted a curly strand of hair up to him. "This is red. Where I come from that means a certain amount of sass and fire so get used to it. This is who I am."

He bowed nearer to me. "It's not red. It's copper. Here that means a certain amount of power. Power far greater than any sass or fire, as you put it."

I pushed past him holding the tray and paper and set them on a table by the windows. The moonlight streaming through was my only connection to the outside. Alum followed me.

"Don't you have something else you could be doing?" I snapped, quelling the flutter that ran through my chest when he was near. I glared at him then picked up a tool and several sheets of metal. My hands remained steady. The affects of the torture were decreasing, but I would need sleep again soon. I closed my eyes and tried to push all thoughts of Bromin from my mind—and all thoughts of Alum. I thought instead of the little machine hidden in the folds of the annoying skirt and breathed deep. Then I started working.

Alum stood close for hours looking at me as I formed a basic housing for the computer parts. I had to make several adjustments to allow for the filaments. I knew there had to be some way to protect the fine nerves. I looked closely at the space and scowled. I still couldn't see how they would survive the movement of the machine when I was done.

"There are casings that can be tacked in that allow unrestricted and safe running of the filaments," Alum said, as if reading my mind.

I frowned up at him. "Fine. Where are they?" His presence was grating on my nerves. The corner of his lip twitched upward and his eyes twinkled. Alum walked over to a cabinet I had yet to look in. He brought over a large box of casings. I

196

remembered seeing something like that on the filament diagram. Alum watched me, sphinx-like.

"I can figure this out myself." I picked up a second piece of metal to start forming the body frame.

"I don't understand," Alum said. "What is your problem with me?"

"You decided to stay here when you could have escaped with Gad and I. Even if you didn't betray our location to Bromin, you act like you prefer to be here," I said.

"I don't."

I slammed the soldering iron onto the metal table top, harder than I intended.

Alum flinched.

"I understand that you've been his prisoner since you were a little boy, and you say you're not working for him, but you could have escaped. You could have come with us. So sorry if I question your allegiance." I stared at him, fatigue suddenly weighing me down.

Alum fingered the buttoned cuff of his white shirt. "Yes, when I was little I was so afraid I did everything he wanted me to." He stood still, but there was torment in his expression. "But then I got older and began to resist him."

I paced away along the bank of tall windows and crossed my arms. "All I see is you, still here under his thumb." A hand came down on my shoulder, warm and strong. I pulled away and twisted around to face him, my jaw clenched. He was quiet and handsome yet he lived imprisoned showing no free will.

Alum gazed steadily at me. "We are very much alike. I don't choose this. He has ways to control me. The only thing I can do is try to keep what little of myself he allows."

I wanted to scream at him, but instead spoke in a low growl. "We are nothing like each other. Don't even compare yourself to me. I could never accept such a fate without fighting. You don't care about anyone but yourself." I walked back to my work and picked up a piece of metal. I scanned the pile of tools and parts, unable to think which piece should go where.

"He tracks me," Alum replied, his voice a soft whisper.

I stopped and turned quickly to glare at him. "What?"

"He tracks me. Bromin knows everywhere I go and everything I do. When I leaned out the window he... That is how Bromin found you. If I had escaped with you and Gad, he would have found you again immediately." Alum pursed his lips, his brows furrowed in inner turmoil. "Bromin can't give life to machines, but he does have ways of creating sophisticated machines, horrific ones."

"Tracks you? But how?" My eyes narrowed.

Alum held out one arm, sighed and unbuttoned the cuff of his shirt. Slowly he rolled the fabric upward revealing spider-like dark lines under the skin.

Bile rose in my throat. Sweat beading on my forehead.

"What is that?" I covered my mouth as a sour taste spread through it.

"He imbedded a machine in me when I was little. He used it to track me and to—to send electrical shocks through me. Over the years it spread throughout half of my body. Bromin can connect to it—remotely." Alum pulled the sleeve back down, covering the marks. "When I was younger he shocked me for entertainment it seemed. I would be doing something, then suddenly I would be writhing on the floor sobbing and calling for my mother. The more I obeyed him and quit asking for my family, the less he did it." He kept talking as if there was no emotion attached to the words, but I could see it was true. "It started small, only a few threads winding through my wrist. In more recent years the strands have traveled much further. My left side is..." He took a deep breath. "It's almost like the strands are alive."

I turned away, unable to deal with the forlorn, resigned desperation in his face. He put his hand on my shoulder again. I let him rest it there.

"I'm sorry," I said through my hand, still covering my mouth.

"I know," Alum replied, the life and warmth back in his tone.

If Bromin was capable of this, how far would he go to get what he wanted? Alum—what he had suffered. There was no way he was working for Bromin willingly—no way.

Chapter 17

Early morning sunlight caressed the metal framework. My hands could barely hold the tools as I finished attaching the last filament nerve casing. Metal clattered against metal; my head shot up. The soldering gun landed at my feet.

"Copper Rose," Alum said quietly, his voice slurred. "The three moons are setting. You still have not recovered from your time in—the 'music suite.'"

"Uh." I rubbed my eyes, too exhausted to make anymore progress. With a shaking hand, I picked up the soldering gun and placed it next to the creature's frame, so cold and lifeless. I took one glance at Alum, then shuffled off through the sitting room to the bedroom, the dress skirt swishing against the floor. I heard an echo when his bedroom door clicked shut on the other side of the workshop. If only the transmitter was still there. Or would Alum lie to me about that?

I wedged a chair under the sitting room door handles. Then I searched behind furniture, in the bed canopy and even along the molding, but nothing appeared to be a camera or microphone. There didn't seem to be anything so I carefully pulled the listening machine from my skirt. The little legs tangled in the lacy underskirt. "You silly spider, let go."

Out of my bra I pulled a small screwdriver and a few small tools. In my waist band I had stashed some wire and even a bit of the filament. With the parts laid out on the bed, I thought through my idea. The image of Bromin holding a strange gun to Alum's head came to mind and my stomach lurched. I couldn't get attached to a man who worked for Bromin. I just couldn't, but what if Alum really was attempting to fight him?

Searching the room had given me a second wind and the tremble was only in my legs. Sitting on the edge of the bed, I tinkered with the listening device until I had the machine figured out. It was a simple matter of pushing a series of small buttons on the belly of the machine to program it to travel around and return to its home base at set intervals. If everything worked right that spider machine would listen in on conversations throughout the palace. Maybe I could discover what protections were in place and find a way to escape. I set it for daily returns. Eventually the return time would need to be lengthened to record conversations from further away, but it wasn't like I was going anywhere—yet.

In the bathroom, I pulled off the ventilation grate, set the machine down and gave it a nudge. "Come back when you're done, little spider." It crawled away on its vine-like legs making hardly a sound on the metal tube.

I carefully hid the tools and remaining materials throughout the room, I pulled off the dress. A twinge of regret passed through me. Alum seemed sincere in his concern for me, but I felt like I shouldn't tell him what I was doing with his machines.

Suddenly I fell. I landed on my hands and knees, then sank to the floor, my breath racing. I rolled over to look at the textured metal ceiling. A tear trickled from my eye. How long had I been drugged and sleep deprived? Unease crept over me leaving a tightness in my chest. Sooner or later Bromin would realize that I couldn't do what he asked, then he might send me back to that awful room.

My fists clenched and I breathed in sharply. My limbs all shook, my head spinning. Pulling myself up, I noticed the corner of a rug folded over where I had tripped. I flipped it back into place then dragged my weary self into the closet.

A voluminous white sleeping gown hung next to the frilly dresses. I pulled it on, and crawled under the covers of the large bed, grabbing the locket in my fist. I wanted to go home to TreeCountry. Gad didn't even know where I was so how could he rescue me?

I jumped out of the bed and dashed to the window, colliding painfully into the window sill as I lost my footing again. What if they never found out where I was? What if they couldn't save me this time? I looked out into the still dim morning light, hoping, praying I would see my escape riding in on some Iridium ship. The hair on the back of my neck rose. Something pinkish coated the sky like a dome over the palace. The setting moons shimmered through it, but they were discolored and distorted by the ripples and glow of the dome. Blue light skittered over the pinkish lightning. A black winged creature, silhouetted by the moons, flew near the dome. It swerved, hitting the shield with a flash of red flame and the creature was gone.

Bromin wasn't exaggerating. Security had been increased and it looked like nothing would survive getting in or out of the palace now.

***

The next morning I dressed in my now dry blouse and

202

pants. I walked to the window, buttoning the leather vest. The pink tinge of the electrical field was gone, but an odd waver disturbed the air like heat waves. There was no sign of the listening spider in the bathroom vent so I went into the workshop and started working. About an hour later Alum entered the room.

My eyes ran from his handsome face to his left arm. How far had that torturous net of fibers traveled? I shivered and tried to mask it by grabbing a tool across the table.

"Are you feeling any healthier?" Alum asked.

I nodded.

He smiled, his eyes twinkling. "You've been asleep for an entire day and night."

I gaped at him. "A whole day?"

How could that be? I should have noticed the passage of that much time. But the shaky feeling inside was gone and my head was clear. I didn't like to lose track of time, yet sleep was what I had obviously needed.

"Bromin was not pleased, but I reminded him that you would do better work completely recovered from your ordeal."

"You said that to him?" It was hard to believe Alum could ever show that he had a spine around Bromin.

"Yes."

We looked at each other across the room. I was assessing him, wondering what his true motives were, while he was— well, maybe he was watching to see what I would do next.

Alum walked over to the table. "What can I do to help?"

I hesitated, my eyes again slipping to his left arm. "I—I need to weld some parts. Can you help me find all the equipment?" I gestured to the welding corner.

"Weld?" His eyes narrowed. "Yes? You mean the hot tacking tools. You will need protective eye covers first."

Alum reached into a short cabinet and pulled out two sets of dark lensed goggles. He handed one to me. I reached to take it and his hand brushed mine. The invasive strands under his skin left ridges. I pulled away.

My heart quickened and my neck felt hot. "Does—does it hurt all the time?"

Alum's face relaxed and he shook his head. "No, only when he activates it. The rest of the time he only tracks my location—if I haven't fooled the sensor."

I paused, fighting off the ache on his behalf. I had to stay distant.

Alum and I worked together, day after day, exchanging words only when needed and enduring Bromin's unpredictable visits. We steadily put together the cat sized creature.

The spider took three days to return the first time, to my great frustration. I pressed the button to replay the recordings. Casual mentions of the electrical shield regularly came from the disembodied voices. Some also mentioned *the asset* in hushed and frightened tones. I suspected the electrical shield might be similar to the shield matrix in TreeCountry, but the asset could be anything, including myself.

Every time the listening spider returned with more hints about the workings of the palace in the mix of banal conversations.

"'You shouldn't worry about your family, Brenth.'

'Why not? There've been disappearances in the city. I sent

204

my family away, but what if...'

'Shhh. Not so loud. No one will know if you just do your job.'"

I shook my head. The fear in the man's voice was clear. He wanted to protect his family, but did he know it was probably from the very man he worked for?

Soldiers and staff talked about meals, the weather and their personal lives. It was clear many were only doing their job without any desire to harm anyone. I pushed the button again to move to the next conversation hoping for more data to help me escape.

"'Bromin doesn't know.'" The voice was distant and quiet. "'The vents that come out low on the cliff are not consistently covered by the shield.'

'What? No. Bromin would be very... We have to fix it before he finds out.'

'But how?'

'Um. I don't know, but it's a priority.'"

I was ecstatic. Exposed vents? There might be a way out through them. Oh, but there was a drop of unknown depths. I turned my mind to that problem whenever I could.

Later that day I took another of Alum's machines when he was out of the room. I altered the octopus-like retrieval machine with pinchers to grab things larger than the little legs could. I altered the programming as well. I dubbed it The Octobot. I needed it to deliver something. It was unbearable believing that my family didn't know where I was.

Thithers were surprisingly simple machines. Using a drip of my own blood, I programmed the thither to hopefully go to

Gad or my father.

Picking up a scrap of paper, I'd taken from the workshop, I considered what I could write. If I was too vague, Gad wouldn't be able to figure out what I was saying, but if Bromin ended up obtaining the note it wouldn't matter. I honestly didn't believe Bromin would kill me, though I would be punished. Shrugging, I scrawled down the information about the electrical shield and the vents then paused.

Time is running out. Miss you both. See you soon?

I wanted to give them more, but the listening spider was bringing back less and less new information. The thither had to be sent soon so I could escape before I had to make my GearMade creature come alive. I paused and tapped my front tooth. Maybe a few more days of information would help.

My frustration was growing each passing day. I had fiddled with the creature as a way to stall the inevitable. I was adjusting the sensors in the ears one day when Bromin stepped up to the table. I tensed but kept working, my lips pressed together. He watched and Alum stood wide eyed across the room.

Bromin leaned closer to the GearMade creature, eyes narrowing. "What are you doing?"

"It needs to be able to hear."

"Yes." Bromin tapped the metal toes. "You will be giving this simple abilities?"

I nodded. I didn't need to mention the additional sensors in the nose or the increased hearing range I was working on.

Bromin stepped back, out of my vision. "This is practice for a more complicated being?"

I kept working, attempting not to hold my breath. "Yes."

Having Bromin right behind me was unnerving. I turned to face him. "Yes. I've learned a lot that will work for the GearMade you want from me, but there is more I have to figure out. Do you think this is a quick and easy process?"

Bromin's nostrils flared. "Does it have to be—cute?"

I shrugged and smiled.

"Hmmph." Bromin turned and strode out, looking back to glare at me before locking us in.

A tense giggle erupted from me as I looked back at the machine. I patted it's head. "You are a bit cuter than I planned, aren't you." The glassy eyes stared back, lifeless. I leaned closer and whispered. "Anything to irk the great Bromin."

Alum walked over and stopped across the table from me. He was shaking his head, but there was a gleam in his eyes and a slight smile on his lips.

That evening, over a month after starting my project, I sent the thither off down the ventilation shaft on the back of the Octo-bot. It was time to take the risk.

I laid out my suede pants and vest on a chair near the bed, washed my blouse then hung it in the bathroom. I glanced at the vent, then crawled into the big bed wearing one of the old fashioned night gowns that kept showing up clean in my closet. I rubbed the chain around my neck. It had become a habit to check the locket.

Sleep was slow coming that night. Constant threat hung in the air and my fear fought with my determination to beat Bromin. The excitement of releasing the thither into the vent had faded only to be replaced by an unidentified anxiety. Bromin wanted more than I could give and sooner or later his patience would give way.

I imagined sitting with Gad and my father in the rose garden back home. Peace settled over me and I slept.

***

A soothing hum filled my senses. I rolled over, enjoying the warmth of the blankets, hoping to sleep a little longer.

Someone cleared their throat and my eyes flew open. Bromin was sitting right next to the bed swinging the locket chain from his finger like the pendulum of a clock. I rubbed my hand across my neck, a shiver filling me.

"Interesting bauble. It has gears yet they never move." Bromin watched it go back and forth. "You wear it so faithfully and I cannot figure why. Did it belong to a long lost relative?" He smiled cruelly.

My stomach dropped and heart raced. What did he know? I leaned against the headboard, pulling the blanket up to my chin. When the chain swung my way, I grabbed for it.

Bromin clasped the locket in his palm and pulled it to him. "I can hear all the machines near me. Every mechanism, every gear—every tendril. They are like heartbeats to my senses. This locket has no heartbeat." He hung the locket in front of me, holding it tightly. Sure enough the gears were still. "If the machine inside doesn't work any longer, why not part with the useless carcass?"

"It's mine," I said.

"Ah. So it is." He picked something up from the ground and held it up like it was something nasty. "Is this also yours?" The Octo-bot dangled from his fingers twitching and struggling against his grasp, but the thither was gone. My eyes gaped and I

208

pulled the blanket up further, looking over the hem waiting for the consequences to rain down on me.

"Well. No need for words is there. I would appreciate it if you kept your focus on your work in the other room. I either want to see that beast moving about on it's own by the end of the week or the full designs for a proper GearMade man."

I nodded, fear dropping like ice into my gut. The creature was perhaps the most amazing machine I had ever made, but how could I bring it to life?

Bromin put the locket down on the night stand, but stood and picked up my pants and vest. "You can keep your useless jewelry, but I told you I prefer proper dress in female guests. I tried to be tolerant, but you still don't seem to show the proper respect for your—situation."

He walked away from me and I reached for the locket. Bromin turned back quickly and grabbed my hand in his vice like grip. "One week Ms. Locke."

I winced. He let go and exited the room. I snatched the locket from the side table and held it close. The click, click, click of the gears tickled my ears.

"You smart little thing, playing dead for the scary robot." I sighed, looking down at the red marks on my arm. Later that day Alum asked about the finger shaped bruises. Anger showed on his face, but I kept working. I needed a miracle and soon.

***

The morning I woke up to intricate designs of frost on the tall windows, I knew I was out of time. For days I'd hardly slept. I searched every book and diagram in the workshop to no avail. The week had come and gone with no word from

Bromin. Fear swelled in me like an instant storm. I couldn't make the GearMade creature live.

Late that afternoon Alum walked over to our creation. "We should give this little guy some skin or fur." Alum seemed to view the robot as alive. I still could see more robot than living, breathing creature though. I wanted to believe that it was alive. Maybe that would be part of what brought it to life. I had no clues so I was guessing and questioning everything.

"Even if I do get it to come alive, it still won't be able to grow fur or clean itself with a rubber tongue," I grumbled. The tension inside me was making me as tightly wound as the spring I was fitting into the leg. A spring might act as a ligament, but it was still a piece of metal. I shook my head in a way I did far too often.

Alum looked at me and raised his brow, his silver eyes dancing in the light from the windows. I suddenly realized how much I had come to rely on Alum. I felt a kinship with him, a bond formed through working together toward a mutual goal.

But what a goal it was.

"Alum?"

He stepped closer and reached a hand across the table to caress my cheek. My breath caught and warmth spread through my face. How gentle Alum was, how calm. He smiled a sad smile and sighed.

"I don't know how," I whispered. I shivered and pressed my face into his warm hand. His thumb rubbed across my cheek-bone.

"You will figure it out," Alum whispered. "I believe in you."

I glanced over at the creature. It looked at me with dead

glass eyes. Somehow I had to bring life to them. We couldn't tinker with details and cosmetics forever. I looked back up at Alum, smiling.

Alum's face contorted and he yanked his hand away. Sparks slithered up and down his left side. Spasms ravaged his limbs, knocking him to the floor. My hand shot up to my mouth and I gaped in horror. He kicked and thrashed against the table legs, a silent scream creasing his lips.

"Alum!" I ran to his side. He waved me back as more sparks trailed across his skin and stopped. He lay in a disfigured heap, panting and limp. His eyes turned to look at me fearfully then rolled back into his head and he was still.

"No, Alum," I cried and knelt beside him. I gently pressed my clammy fingers into his neck. A slight but regular pulsing dashed under my fingers. His chest barely rose with each slow breath. He was alive. My eyes pressed shut and a sigh of relief escaped me.

The main door opened and I leapt up, my heart still racing and prickles going up my neck.

Bromin came in, a grin on his face as his eyes flicked down to the unconscious Alum. "I have waited long enough, dear Copper Rose." He kept walking toward us.

I hurried around the table and blocked the way to Alum. "Don't touch him."

"I never do," he said almost cheerfully. Bromin held up a small round thing like a key fob for a car. His thumb hovered over the button on it. "Should we have some fun?"

"No!" I yelled and reached for Bromin's hand then froze. He was too strong for me to stop him. My only option was to distract him. Maybe he would lose interest in hurting Alum.

In one step Bromin was face to face with me, looking down from his greater height. "I am done waiting for you to find your power again. I know it is in you. I can sense it." He sniffed me. "I can smell it. Power."

Barely breathing, I stood still as he leaned closer. My skin crawled and I recoiled, but Bromin grabbed my arm and pulled me to his chest.

"No other of your kind looks me in the eye or fights me like this. You are unlike any GearMaker…" He ran the back of his hand over my cheek, his thumb still angled to push the button that would send electricity coursing through Alum. His touch was so cold and threatening compared to Alum's tender touch.

"The things you and I will be able to accomplish once you learn to tap into that power…"

"I can't do it," I said in barely a whisper of air.

Bromin's eyes flashed red and narrowed. "You persist in this stubborn lie?" He pushed me to arm's length.

I gulped and mustered my courage. "I don't know how to do it. Even in TreeCountry they say no one knows how it's done anymore. Please let us go. We're no threat to you."

My arm throbbed in pain as he clenched harder and pulled me back to him. His nose was almost touching mine and I groaned, pulling away. He wrapped his other arm around me and kept me close, against his hard chest.

"You will bring life to that obnoxious little beast you built. Then you will make me a GearMade General for my army of soldiers, all created by you. I will do whatever it takes to— inspire your ability."

He let me go, turning unnaturally fast. He strode away. At the doors he stopped, and leaned toward me. "If you do succeed I have a little package that will be arriving for you sometime tomorrow. If you fail—Hmmmm. Well—I wouldn't want to destroy the surprise!" He chuckled and slammed the doors shut.

Chapter 18

For a moment I stood, attempting not to slip to the floor in a puddle of fear. A shudder ran through me as I tried to get the feel of Bromin's touch out of my head. Anger replaced my fear and I shook my hand to get the blood flowing. "Uhhggg!"

I pulled the locket from my collar and flipped it open. "You. You stupid locket. You could save us. Yet you sit there, useless gears clicking away. What good are you?" It clacked, ignoring me.

Behind me a stool crashed against a table leg. I spun around. Alum was trying to stand.

"No. Stay down."

He pulled himself up before I could get to him. He was leaning on the table, his right side barely holding him up against the limp limbs on his left side. His clothing was ripped as if the electrical current burned away the fabric where the black lines were.

I put his useless left arm over my shoulder so he could use me to move. Alum grunted, looking to the sitting room door. I shoved stools and crates aside with my foot as I helped Alum maneuver the distance. He leaned heavily on me. Once in the sitting room I was barely able to keep his weight upright.

We reached the couch and Alum fell to the cushions. He

groaned as his head whacked the arm before sinking onto the cushions. I helped him roll to his side. Sweat was trickling down his face from the exertion. His silver eyes were dim, but followed my every move as I grabbed a fallen pillow and carefully wedged it under his head. He heaved a great sigh and went limp. A long rip in his left sleeve showed livid red welts all over his skin. I bit my lip and reached out to touch him. He was burning up.

"Not good," I muttered and dashed into the bathroom. Scooping up a wash cloth, I turned the cold water on full. I had soaked several cloths before realizing tears were streaming down my face uncontrollably.

A moan came from the other room and I ran back. The wet cloths dripped cold water behind me.

"Alum?" I put one on his forehead and another over the rip on his arm. He flinched, but then relaxed. "Alum? Can you hear me? Oh, please be okay." His breathing evened out and he seemed to be sleeping. A shudder of fear ran through me as I remembered Bromin's promise of a surprise. What did that mean? Could things possibly get worse?

I stared at Alum a long time hoping he would show some sign of waking up. I touched my cheek where he had caressed it so gently before Bromin showed up. I missed Alum's quiet stare and deep voiced advice that I had used, but not appreciated. These weeks of work had given me a great respect for him, but he didn't know. All my mistrust melted away as I watched Alum's shallow breathing. I had to free Alum of this prison. Through the open door our creation stared as if challenging me. I had to try to give it life.

Throughout the night I checked on Alum, changing out the

cold compresses when needed. I paced from the couch, through the doors to the workshop and across that long room. The creatures eyes seemed to follow me, but I knew it was only a reflection of light in the glass orbs.

The blue moon still doused the room with light, but early morning was close. I couldn't take the eerie gaze any longer.

I stopped next to the beast, staring at it. The memory of how I made that butterfly thing live was nowhere inside my head no matter how I searched for it. Dad told me I was holding it on my hand and then it flew off. My robot was a bit big to sit on my hand, so I leaned over and put my hand on it's head. Closing my eyes, I slowed my breathing and concentrated. The metal cooled my palm. I thought through the parts, carefully assembled... "Live," I whispered.

I opened my eyes and saw the creature staring back at me, as lifeless as before. I heaved a huge sigh and left the room. Alum was still sleeping and seemed to have cooled down some. I yearned to tell him I was sorry for doubting him. I ached for him to be well again. My head nodded as I sat in the chair across from Alum. Images of robots coming alive and little machines crawling out of ventilation shafts danced through my head. I needed sleep, but Alum needed me. Maybe I could just lay my head back and... Sleep sank over me and the dreams faded into mist.

***

I woke up groggy and stiff. Alum hadn't moved from the couch. His breathing was still shallow, but regular. Back in the workshop I pulled open every cabinet hoping some brilliant insight would leap into my head. I needed to get us out of the palace or make the robot creature live. Nothing jumped out at me. No spontaneous genius popped into my head.

The moment I dreaded arrived around noon. Bromin, grinning, entered the room. I was standing by the cabinet of books as he sauntered over to the robot on the other side of the room. He ran a finger over the back and down the nose then flicked it with a *twang*.

"This is not a living robot, my dear. This is a wasted hunk of metal."

I slammed the book in my hand down and spun to face him fully. "Is it that obvious?"

Bromin waved a finger back and forth at me. "Ah, ah. You should talk more respectfully to me. I did promise you a surprise today."

I was tired, frustrated and sick of being afraid.

"I am tired of waiting, sweet Copper Rose," Bromin said. "I don't believe you are taking me seriously so I have decided to give you some additional incentive." Rustin and two other guards hauled someone in through the doors. I strained to see amongst the tangle of grappling hands and arms. Rustin pulled back a fist and slugged the prisoner in the gut. The person groaned and doubled over. Rustin grabbed the peppered dark hair and pulled the man up.

My heartbeat pounded in my ears and pain lanced through my chest. "Father," I gasped, feeling weak like I took the blow to the stomach myself. I ran to my Dad, but Bromin cut me off, grabbing my arms behind me.

He leaned over to my ear and I snarled at him. Bromin chuckled. "Your dear father has decided to make a visit. The troublesome man left TreeCountry for a short jaunt and my men were there to invite him to stay with us."

"Rose?" Dad said, his voice cracking through swollen lips. His eyes were ringed with bruises and he winced every time the guards jostled him.

"Your father will be staying in the music suite until such a time as you succeed. Create a living machine for me and he will go free. Fail and he will die. Simple arrangement, don't you think?"

Rustin yanked my father backwards so he would trip and the three guards dragged Dad out backwards, his eyes boring into me. Bromin let me go so quickly I had to catch myself from falling face first into a metal table. With a flicker of satisfaction in his expression, Bromin exited, pulling the door locked behind him.

"Give me my father," I screamed. Running to the door, I pounded using all my strength. "Let me out. Don't hurt him." It was to no avail. I turned my back to the door, sinking to the ground. I buried my face against my knees and sobbed. All the fear and tension of weeks cascaded down onto me. How could I defeat such a beast as Bromin?

Desperation and resolve filled the hollow Bromin had left in me. There was no escape. I had to make that wretched robot come alive. I had to find a way.

"All right," I mumbled. "You want to live? Then I'll make you live." I strode back to the cabinets. Pulling books out, I skimmed each again searching for the secret. It had to be somewhere. Maybe it was right under my nose.

Book after book contained techniques and mechanics that would have amazed me any other day. How to make war ships

218

indestructible, ways of lighting a garden without wires, methods for coloring metal to look like skin. There was nothing about how to bring any machine to life. If it was some kind of magic power, then all knowledge of how to use the innate ability was lost in the strange history of this land. I screamed in frustration and hurdled a book across the room. It bounced off the windows, hit a table and fell face down on the floor.

Something had to be here that would help make this happen. I breathed deep and looked around the room again. If sheer willpower was all it took the creature would have been living within minutes after Bromin dragged Dad through the door.

I picked up the fallen book. It was open to a page about a water and electricity method for coloring metals. Alum was suggesting something about a proper skin for the little beast when Bromin rudely—cruelly, interrupted with a light display on Alum's skin.

Maybe if the beast looked more lifelike, it would be more lifelike. After scanning the process described in the book, I lifted the robot into my arms. It might have been the size of a small dog, but it felt as heavy as a big one!

I set it near the welding area and turned the faucets on. Water poured slowly creeping higher. I snatched electrical cables from the other side of the space and pulled them to the sink. Going down the list of chemicals and the colors possibilities, I selected a variety that would give swirls of colors almost like a coat of curly hair. At the last minute I grabbed an extra chemical. I suspected it would be good to cause a smooth look to the face if I applied it directly to the metal rather than by sprinkling it on the water surface like the other method I was using. The safety goggles were overly large and thick gloves made my fingers feel like sausages.

"Okay you creature," I said to it as I smeared the chemical over the snout and around the glass eyes. The surface of the water already shimmered with the curly, swirly chemicals. I slowly lowered the creature into the water as per the instructions. Once it was all the way in and the chemicals had coated the creature I flipped a switch which sent the electrical current dashing through the entire sink to fuse the coating to the metal. I stared at the beautiful colored lightning dancing across the water. It made the creature seem to move.

"Please, come to life," I said sadly. White hot heat burned my chest. "Ouch." I pulled out the locket. It was glowing and shaking. What could this be? Maybe—Just maybe...

I flipped the lid open and the electrical current leapt from the bath to the locket and back again. I jumped, squinting at the painfully bright light. My skin sizzled with the power in the air, or was it coming from me? Something deep inside me hummed and tingled as the process continued. The electricity to the tub buzzed down and shut off, the locket grew still and cool, resuming its endless clicking of gears. I gasped, blinking to clear my spotty vision. It seemed so dark in the room by comparison to moments before. Gingerly I closed the locket and placed it back in my shirt. The burned skin on my chest smarted. What had happened?

I grabbed the tongs and tried to get a grip on the creature to see if the coloring had worked, but it kept slipping out of my shaky grip. "Fine you beastie. I'll drain the sink and let you dry in here."

Crouching down with my fingers still trembling, I flipped

220

the lever at the outer bottom of the sink to remove the plug cover. The soothing gurgle of water reached my ears. I sat on a chair next to the wall and bowed my head down. I slowed my frantic breathing. What had I had to get a response from the locket? Had it really reacted to my desire to bring the creature to life?

Shreeeeek.

What? Metal scratching metal? I stood up to make sure the machine creature wasn't getting damaged. A little face lifted above the edge and peered over. Damp eyes blinked at me from the little face.

My jaw dropped. "You?" I shook my head and gasped. Bat like ears popped up to frame the eyes and black nose. A grey coloring like chinchilla fur covered the face metal which shifted and rippled like skin as the creature lifted itself to the edge then slipped back down.

"I—did it." My voice rasped. Elation coursed through me like the energy had moments before.

"Oh," I yelped as the creature emitted a squeak of protest. The final bits of water were circling the drain.

"Reeee. Keek, keek," it peeped to me, tipping its head.

"Let me help you out of there," I said and reached out. It backed away only to slip and fall face first into the draining water. It spluttered and gasped then shook from head to toe, spraying droplets on me. I got a grip on its midsection and lifted the now squirming machine—creature from the sink. It nuzzled into my shoulder and turned deep eyes at me. Blinking several times, it emitted a series of noises that I suddenly knew was some form of communication.

"I don't know what you're saying." I set it down on a table.

It stood on back legs and repeated the same noises again.

"You need to be dried? I thought you did a good job of that a moment ago." How could I understand the squeals and screeches? This was impossible.

"Reeeki. Grrr," the bat eared beastie said.

I ran to the bathroom, past the still unconscious form of Alum, grabbed a towel from a rack and ran back to the workshop.

"Okay, okay. I'll dry you." I wrapped a thick towel around it, wiping off the lifelike metal surfaces. It nuzzled into the fabric, rubbing as if to relieve an itch. I played with the big ears and patted the soft nose. The once stiff metal was now elastic like skin, but still tough.

"Amazing." I grinned despite myself. "You need a name."

"Keeeereeeky." The creature leapt off the table and dashed into the sitting room. I watched in awe. The ripple of muscle and ligament stretched under the skin as each limb moved. The tilt of the head... The gleam of its eyes... All so real. It was alive. Somehow I had done it—again. I could make living machines.

Chapter 19

I dashed after the squeaky beast, and ran right into Alum. He grabbed the door frame to steady himself.

"I did it." I felt breathless, like I could fly.

Alum winced, a look of sadness enveloping his face. He grabbed me by the shoulders. "You can't show it to Bromin. I can't let you."

The look in Alum's eyes was so severe I didn't know how to respond. My elation sank like a rock into the pit of my stomach.

"He'll kill my dad if I don't." I pulled away from Alum and picked up the creature that crouched next to us, who squeaked a question at me. I looked at it and tried to understand. "What?"

"Kreeeki shiiyk." It jumped from my arms and dashed to the sitting room window. It balanced on the window frame and peered out.

"You hear something? What?" I walked over and looked out. I couldn't see anything unusual.

"Rose. You have to escape. You have to get away," Alum said from the doorway.

I turned on him. "How can you say that? I have to free my father."

"You have to go. Now that you figured out the secret to

bringing machines to life Bromin will do anything to control you. He will even—try to..." He gingerly rubbed his left arm. "You have seen what he did to me. Bromin will never release your father no matter how much you do for him. You know this." Alum tried to step toward me, but sank to the floor, every limb trembling. I ran to him and kneeled at his feet.

"Are you all right? You should still be resting." I touched his knee.

His silver eyes pierced through me. "You did it." He whispered, his voice shaky. "I knew you could and look. You did it." He waved his other hand toward the window where the creature was still perched.

It looked at us and then back to the window, the ears twisting forward and back, picking up sound for possibly miles if my mechanics had worked right. "Kreeeki shiiyk. Kreeeki shiiyk."

I smiled. "He needs a name. I think he wants to be called Kricky." The little being jumped up and down repeating the name.

"Kricky it is," Alum said wearily. "Copper Rose. You have to listen to me. Bromin cannot get a hold of Kricky. You have to escape."

"There is no way and you know that. He can track you everywhere and he has turned the palace into a fortress. If Gad knows where I am, I doubt even he can do anything in time."

A smile creased Alum's face. "Don't be so sure."

I sighed and shook my head. Even if there was a way out, I wasn't leaving my father—or Alum.

"There is a way. He cannot track me everywhere. My secret

room. I developed a deflector. It—it deflects the signal to make it appear I am elsewhere, but only a short distance and for a short while. I—I did—I..." Alum hung his head and his arm dropped limply.

"Alum. Please let me help you to the couch. You must rest," I pleaded. He nodded and lifted his arm. I pulled him up and supported him to the couch. Alum sat and laid his head back, staring at the ceiling. His eyes seemed to have faded to an unhealthy grey.

"Give me—a day. Please wait a day to show him," he mumbled and closed his eyes.

I pulled a blanket over him. "I guess. But Alum, I have to try to save my father."

"Please wait...They—will come—soon."

"Who? What?" I sat next to him as his breathing slowed to the steady rhythm of sleep. The lines of his face relaxed.

I groaned. Alum was right, but I had no choices. Bromin could arrive any moment and Kricky would be right here for him to see.

"Shiirii?" Kricky said. He was sitting on the arm of the couch tilting his head at me. This creature was showing an intelligence I hadn't expected. Of course I hadn't expected to be able to bring it to life either.

I scooted closer to the arm and looked the creature in the eyes. "Kricky. Listen closely. No one else can see you. Only Alum and I can know you're here. Will you hide? Will you stay out of sight?"

"Vriiigt," Kricky chirped. Somehow I knew he was agreeing to do as I said. I heaved a deep sigh. Exhaustion came over me

225

and a tear trailed down my cheek. Somewhere Dad was being tortured. I had never felt so trapped in my life. I didn't want to show Kricky to Bromin, but if I didn't Dad would die. Maybe Bromin would at least let my father join me in the workshop if I kept working for him.

Alum's breathing was steady. I touched his brow and sighed in relief that his temperature was normal again.

I pulled myself up, fighting my weariness, and walked back into the workshop. It looked like a tornado had trailed through it. Reaching down, I picked up a fallen stool and pushed it under the table. Then I straightened the neighboring table and picked up more stools. As daylight faded, the workshop returned to normal.

Somehow I had to convince Bromin I was still doing what he wanted. Maybe he would give me my father if I switched to what he really wanted; a human-like robot, a true GearMade. Pulling supplies to a large work surface, I set to work without even making design drawings. Kricky was hiding in the other room, guarding the still sleeping Alum. Occasionally I could hear his little squeak and knew he was listening for anyone approaching.

Like every evening a food cart was pushed through the door with only a quick glance around the room by the soldier bringing it. After a momentary surge of panic that he would find out about Kricky, I looked back to my work and he left. I kept going on my task, ignoring the food.

Night slipped by. The new machine's framework developed in front of me as my hands picked up pieces and fit them together as if by instinct. The initial brain chip and filament system stretched across the table. This one was far more complicated than Kricky's. By the time pink light started to fill the morning sky, I was finished. I grabbed a sheet of metal and stared at it, sleep calling to me. I needed to start the structure plates for the human-like limbs. My body was running on pure adrenaline and willpower.

I set the metal down. It clunked on the table. I dragged myself to the sitting room. The distance seemed so much farther than before. Alum still slept, though now he was laying on the cushions instead of sitting up. Kricky was curled up next to him looking more like a cat than ever before.

"The bedroom's too far away." I laid down on the opposite couch.

He lifted his gray head and hummed at me before laying back down and closing his glass eyes again.

I would save my father—somehow.

***

Creeeek. Kaboom.

I jerked awake. Alum and Kricky were gone. The sound had been so close. Midday light snuck through the curtained windows. I ran to the workshop. The food tray I had ignored the previous day was gone. My work on the far table lay undisturbed.

"Alum?" I whispered.

He looked out from behind the welding area half wall, smoke drifting into the air behind him.

"Thrrriiiik?" A little nose, followed by familiar little eyes, peeked around as well.

"Kricky?"

The little machine creature skittered over to me.

227

"Sorry. Didn't mean to wake you." Flecks of metal speckled his hair. The right side of his face was scattered with small cuts. The sink lay in several large chunks amongst the smoking remains of the welding area. A massive dent torqued the cabinet door. Nuts and screws were melted into the now pock marked floor.

"What happened?" I demanded.

"How do you think we explain the lack of a lifeless bat eared machine?" He stepped back and sank onto a stool.

I kept looking to the double door, a quiver in my belly. "Someone is bound to come in here soon." I picked up the welding torch that was laying a few feet away and carried it over.

"We needed a good reason why it would be gone." Alum gave the slightly smoking rubble an appraising look, nodded stiffly. We stared at the debris, only the hiss of hot metal filling the air.

"This is a bit ridiculous you know," I said.

Arms came around me and the torch clunked to the ground. Alum turned in shock.

"Ridiculous seems an apt description," Rustin said, pushing me at Alum. Alum grabbed my arm. He pulled me up, his hand lingering.

Rustin scowled. "What seems to be going on here?"

"We had—an accident." I pulled myself straight and faced Bromin's head guard. What if he figured it out? My eyes widened with fear, but I tried to keep my voice steady.

Rustin looked at the mess. "Hmmm. And how did it happen?"

228

"Testing a theory," Alum replied, his expression blank.

"Where's that crazy creature thing?" Rustin stood with his fists clenched, glaring at us.

I pointed to the rubble.

Rustin looked at the heap. He grabbed my arm and pointed across the room to the layout of joints and nerve filament channels.

"What's that?" he demanded.

"A new one. One like a man. It's what Bromin wants isn't it?" I couldn't stop the challenging tone in my voice. Bromin scared me to death, but Rustin was a bully. "I figured some things out with the creature. I'm putting those ideas into a bigger machine."

Rustin squeezed my arm painfully and shoved me away. I caught myself on a stool. He walked over to the table and reached out to the new machine.

"I wouldn't touch that if I were you. It's at a critical stage," I yelled out to him.

"It had better be near a finished stage." Rustin sneered at me. "Though we are having a lot of fun with your dear father."

I gasped. Dad. I glanced around for Kricky again, ready to hand him over, but he was no where to be seen.

Rustin stormed out of the room, kicking the food cart as he went. It crashed against the wall, spilling food all over as the door slammed shut.

I leaned over, breathing deep. How many near misses could I tolerate? My nerves were raw. Bromin wanted a living robot and I wanted my father back. I had work to do. Making explosions to cover up my success at the very task that could save my father was not in my list of to-do's. Nor was playing chicken with someone like Rustin. Daylight was quickly fading. I had wasted a whole day sleeping.

"Kricky," I called out. Alum approached me and I glared at him. "I'm calling Rustin back."

"You can't," Alum exclaimed.

Kricky dashed to me from behind a cupboard. "Shrik kitity."

Alum stepped over to Kricky in two big strides and scooped up the robot creature. "Kricky," he said, his face close to the robot. "Hide. Hide and don't come out if *any* of Bromin's men or Bromin come here. Don't let anyone see you until I say it is safe again."

Kricky squeaked in reply, then leapt out of his arms. He stopped in the sitting room door, peeped at us and disappeared.

I ran after him. "Kricky, come back. Don't listen to Alum. Please. Kricky." I heard nothing, standing there in the dim light. A hand rested on my shoulder and I whirled around. "Why did you do that?"

Alum reached out to me and I slapped his hand down.

"I had to stop you from giving him to Bromin."

My jaw clenched. "You have no right to do that. Don't you care about anything? All I have is my father and my brother."

"So give them a chance to get you and your father out of here."

"I have been here for weeks and weeks. There hasn't been even a hint of evidence that anyone is coming. And you! Do you have some plan to get us out? What about this tracking

230

deflection you have come up with? Can't you find a way to get us out of that wretched energy shield?"

Alum's expression dropped, making me even angrier.

I looked up at his silver eyes. "You shouldn't have sent Kricky away from me."

He crossed his arms, a stubborn glint in his expression. I growled in frustration and left him standing there.

I retrieved the torch and put my anger into my work. Limb by limb slowly formed. It had taken nearly a month to make Kricky. This was a more complex robot and would take even longer, though I knew what I was doing now so maybe that would speed up the process. Could Dad last another few weeks? Would Bromin's patience last?

The room grew dark. I carefully fit pieces together then tinkered with them. I flipped on a small work lamp and kept going. Half way through a knee joint a brighter light clicked on. Alum's shadow spread over my work surface.

"Move," I said and glared at him.

"I know what you are doing." He shook his head.

I grabbed the long neck lamp near me and craned it over to cast light on my work again. "Good for you. You may not care about your family, but I care about mine so leave me alone." I went back to work, anger boiling inside me.

"You don't understand."

I stood up to face him. "Let's look at this. You were taken from your family when you were five. I was taken from my family when I was five. I will grant you that being tortured by a villain is going to be a bit different than being abandoned by your mother. And yes I did have one person left to love me, but

I found my family and I am not going to lose them now."

Alum pulled up a stool and sat. He grabbed the other knee joint and started tinkering using a small screwdriver. "You still don't understand."

"I am fed up, Alum. You tell me you can't escape and yet you can confuse Bromin's tracking device. Can you disable it or can't you? Do you want to escape or not? What is it you really want?" I looked him in the eye. I couldn't stand the back and forth anymore. Why did he never seem to tell me everything?

Alum sighed and looked back at me. Sorrow bent his brows and turned the corners of his mouth downward. "I want... All I want is..."

Anguish leaped up inside me, but I quickly squelched it. My eyes burned with tears. I hastily wiped one out of my vision.

"I don't have time for this. You don't want to answer my questions and I have to save my father." I grabbed the joint from his hands and turned to pick up the welding tool to finish the attachments for the leg. Alum grabbed my arm and stopped me.

"Let go of me." I pulled away, but couldn't get free of his firm grip. He pulled me into his arms.

Alum looked down at me, his bronze hair falling over his forehead. He bent down and pressed his lips against mine. His hands moved up to cradle my head and hold me there, his warm lips against mine until my lungs screamed for breath. I couldn't help myself as I pressed closer to him, kissing him back—losing myself in his touch. Warmth spread down my limbs and they quivered.

I pulled away. "No!" Tears poured down my face as I

stumbled back. Alum stepped toward me, but I pulled a stool in front of me blocking him. The metal joint in my hand clunked against the seat. "No."

He stared at me, sorrow filling his expression. Alum turned and walked into the darkness.

Chapter 20

Legs connect to knees. Arms lead to shoulders and attach to the spine—the metal hinged spine. Bit by bit the body, both machine and human in appearance, evolved under my hands. Since Kricky was hiding from me, I had to finish this humanoid machine. I had to show Bromin I could do what he wanted. But could I recreate the circumstances that brought Kricky to life? What the locket did could have been a reaction. Or was the locket the key to giving machine's life?

Deep down I knew Alum was right. Even if I did show Bromin I could bring machines to life, he would never let my father go—or me. The thither must not have made it out of the energy shield. If it had, I would have heard something—unless Gad couldn't figure out a way in anymore—unless it was hopeless.

I felt as torn up inside as the metal sink now cluttering the corner of the workshop. The locket was the only way I could think to escape and that was the very thing I couldn't get it to do. It was sitting against my skin, even more cold and lifeless than ever, as if the magical effort had drained it. Even the clicking of the gears had taken on a slower rhythm.

I tried to sleep, my head on a table using my arms as a pillow. I kept telling myself it was so I could keep working as soon as I woke. In truth it was so I could avoid Alum, who was asleep on the sitting room couch again. How do you avoid someone you're locked up with?

The last few days ran through my brain. My father, Bromin, Alum, Kricky and back to my father again. Dad was being tortured, beaten, only to give me incentive to keep working. Constant fear plagued me as I tried to think of a way out of this for both of us.

Then I remembered Alum—Alum's tender touch, Alum's confusing words. My face warmed at the thought—the kiss... I shook my head. No. A kiss was not an answer. If he didn't have the willpower to help me fight Bromin, I couldn't get wrapped up in the way he made my heart leap.

"Forget it," I mumbled and pulled myself up. Sleep was not going to happen. The only distraction was work so I walked slowly back to the robot man growing slowly on the table. The main bone structure of the humanoid was complete. One joint still stuck once in a while and the shoulders seemed imbalanced.

I started on the nerve filaments which quickly got tangled. They kept breaking, increasing my frustration. I took a deep breath and started over. The filaments down the arms eventually lay straight and smooth in the casings, but I lost a hold of one and it curled up again.

"Grrr." I stepped back, my eyes closed. I needed sleep or maybe a real meal.

A food cart sat forgotten by the door. Scanning the contents of the silver domes, I decided I wasn't that hungry. I grabbed an apple-like fruit from a bowl and walked back. My teeth sank into it. The juices raced down my chin before I wiped them away with the back of my hand. I focused all my thoughts on

235

the red fruit, the juices, the taste. An image flashed inside my head: my father, bruised and bloody, laying on that metal bed in the dungeon cell. My throat constricted. I chewed slowly, trying to stop the tears.

Drops poured unchecked as I stared down at the being I was creating. The filament nerves were a knotted mess down one side. It had been long enough since Bromin's last visit that I was jumping at every sound, expecting him to appear and wrench more of my soul apart. I knew he would return at some unexpected moment and he would see the mess. He would find Kricky. Nothing good would happen. I was dying inside.

I heard footsteps from the sitting room and looked over at the tall shadowed figure of Alum. I rubbed at my face and nose with my free hand, to hide my quiet sobbing.

Alum came into the light and stood looking at me, stoic and unreadable. From behind him a dark figure appeared.

"Don't cry, Sis." The dark spiky hair and smirking face were unmistakable in the dim light.

"Gad." I dropped the fruit and threw my arms around him. He'd done it. He'd found a way to get to me. The strength of his hug lifted the fear inside me and hope tingled out to my limbs.

"Oh, Gad. How did you get in?"

Gad let me go and looked over at Alum. "My buddy here got me in. Seems he's got a few interesting tricks up his sleeve."

Alum shrugged. I narrowed my eyes at him. Three men slipped from the dark. I yelped, but Gad covered my mouth.

"They're with us," he whispered and put a finger to his mouth to shush me before he let go.

"We have to get Dad out of here," I insisted.

Gad leaned near me. "No worries, little sis. There's already a team infiltrating Bromin's dungeon."

"They better have the layout of the palace or they will never get through," Alum said.

"Ah, give me some credit, Alum buddy. We're right on schedule for the fireworks to begin." Gad patted Alum on the shoulder and grinned. Alum grabbed Gad's shirt and pushed him against a metal table.

"Listen close. You may be slippery and lucky most the time, but you tend to underestimate Bromin. Don't make that mistake this time." Alum glared and let go of Gad.

"All right. I don't intend to screw up." Gad straightened his jacket and scowled at Alum.

Anger flared in Alum's eyes. "And this time, don't lose track of her."

Gad glared back.

"Knock it off, you two." I put myself between them, my hands raised. "Alum, it wasn't Gad's fault I got caught. How did you get through the electrical shield?"

"Followed your lead. We crawled in the vents that are below the shield. It took the better part of a day, but here we are." He put his arms out dramatically.

I shook my head. "I didn't think the ventilation shafts were that big. Can we get back out that way?"

Gad grimaced. Alum huffed and turned to the window.

"I have a plan. Only I'm not sure when it will happen," Gad said, narrowing his eyes as he watched Alum. He turned to me, his eyes growing even more narrow. I didn't like the disapproving look in his eyes. My cheeks warmed and I rubbed my hand across the back of my neck, avoiding my brother's gaze.

"*Karrreeeekkikiki*".

"Shhhh." Gad scanned the shadows of the workshop, eyes sharp.

"It's Kricky," Alum whispered and smiled. "Kricky. You can show yourself."

"Kriiik?" Kricky crawled out from under the table where the new being lay. He waggled his ears then sat to preen himself.

"What is *that*?" Gad gasped. Kricky tilted his head this way and that, studying my brother.

"That is why you have to get her out of here," Alum said glowering.

"What do you mean? Is that...?" Gad reached out and stroked the little nose. His eyes widened and a grin split his face. "You did it!" Kricky cocked his head at the excited whisper.

I lowered my eyes, fear swelling in my chest. Even Gad was excited by this, yet my success was the very reason all our lives were in danger.

"What is this fantastic plan of yours?" Alum said through clenched teeth. "Jumping off the edge into a boat is no longer an option."

Gad turned and stood in one fluid move. He stalked to the window, looking down. "Hmmm. Well. We have a way out, we only need a way down."

Alum's eyes bulged. "You don't have a clue how to get her out do you." Alum stepped over to me. "Copper Rose, I..." Alum glanced away momentarily.

Leaning close to Alum, I whispered. "Alum? How is it they haven't set off any alarms?" His spicy scent tickled my nose and my face burned again.

"This device." He showed me a small black box. He was holding a button down and a small blue light was blinking rhythmically. "It's a more sophisticated version of the deflector I have in my hidden room. As long as the people getting your father don't run into anybody physically, they will be invisible to Bromin's sensors. I have managed to keep my technology a step ahead of his sensors most of the time. Let's hope that's still the case."

Someone shuffled through the sitting room doors. I held my breath.

Gad strode over to the figures. "Sure enough. Drenth, Hend. You're right on time."

Two men came into the lamp light helping a third hunched figure between them. The tall, gangly man had dark skin and the other was short and stocky with blonde hair. The man in the middle had gray in his black hair. It was Dad!

I ran over. "Dad. Are you all right?" One swollen eye opened and looked at me.

"Rose?" he muttered disbelieving.

"Yes, it's me. I'm so sorry." I hugged him and he winced.

Dad reached for a metal stool. "Not your doing, darling."

"Wait." Gad peered out of the window. "I think it's about to start. Uh. Maybe we should get back some."

Gad pulled Dad's arm around his neck, but Dad sank, unable to support himself. "Hend, could you help?" The tall man came over and took Dad's other arm. They led him away

239

from the windows.

"What's happen…"

Blinding light seared my vision. A huge boom knocked me back. Like the gasp of air before a storm, everything seemed to slow then rush back into real time. I blinked rapidly to clear the spots in my vision. Chunks of flame started raining down on me, stinging as they skittered down my skin, a cacophony bombarding my senses. Alum pulled me to him, shielding me from the chunks raining down on us. Something small and metal latched onto my leg; Kricky.

"Father," I called out.

Alum was close to my ear. "Gad has him. He's safe." Alum's broad shoulders and arms were circled around me as my heart raced. What had happened?

"Bring her," Gad yelled over the din, a smirk on his face. He and the other men dashed past us, dodging debris as they carried Dad back to the windows. Chill night air surrounded me and I pushed away from Alum. The outer wall was now a gaping hole of rubble. Pink light from the electrical shield sizzled, buzzing like an ailing bee before it vanished. The siren was blaring across the palace. Shouts echoed.

"The guards are coming," Alum yelled to Gad, then took my arm and pulled me to the edge. Gad was looking out into the black of night. The three moons had yet to fill the sky with light. Flames were licking up the walls of the workshop consuming any flammable matter it could find.

"Oh my goodness," I gasped. All that remained was a crater coming nearly all the way to the palace. The garden lay in pieces. Sparks trailed over the ground, fizzling. The electrical shield was broken!

Two long black boats rose out of the darkness toward us. The prow of one long boat nudged up against the workshop floor, stone crumbling where it hit. The stocky man leapt into the boat then reached back to take Dad from Hend and Gad. They both jumped in as well.

Laser bolts started flying at us from the ground. The second boat dropped down into the crater and people aboard started firing back. Alum pulled me over to the boat, and helped me up. Gad grabbed my arm until I was in, then reached back for Alum. The boat sank a yard below the broken floor. Kricky soared through the air landing in the long boat with a squeak.

"Alum," I screamed. He looked back at the door and the flames in the room, then at me. He pursed his lips, rubbing his left arm.

"We can't wait," Gad yelled. Alum scowled then jumped. He collided with the prow. His arms were wrapped around it and the entire longboat leaned forward sharply.

"Too much weight," someone called out from behind me.

I held onto Alum's arm struggling to pull him aboard. Gad grabbed his other arm and pulled. Alum kicked his leg up, but the boat continued to sink. It touched down yards from the palace, flipping me out onto the ground next to Alum. I gasped, spreading a hand out on the solid ground beneath me. The boat immediately lifted into the air. I looked up and Kricky bounded over the edge, landing next to me with a thump.

I scrambled onto my feet. "Gad!"

My brother leaned over the edge, fear painting his features.

They dropped back away from the crater and the palace.

"Alum. Get her to the other boat." The boat listed dangerously close to the crater edge then lifted again. Gad stuck his head out, pointing toward the other side of the crater. The boat pitched forward throwing Gad half out. He clung on with one arm and leg in.

"Gad. No!" I tripped over a broken bench and Alum pulled me back.

Shipmen held onto Gad as he struggled. He looked back at me and used his loose hand to wave me toward the other boat. "Go, Rose. I'll see you at the main ship. Go—go now." The boat scrapped along the edge of the crater then into the darkness.

With an arm around me, Alum pulled me around chunks of broken cliff around the palace steps. Chime-like tinkling came from the confetti of metal plant parts. Kricky skipped in little leaps over and around obstacles. We ducked and dodged to avoid being seen by the guards firing into the night from the remaining palace windows. The other long boat lifted up from the dark crater and behind a gazebo leaning towards the abyss.

"Come on," Alum said, his eyes sparkling. I took a big breath and kept running. Alum matched my pace, stride for stride, keeping himself between me and the building.

"Down there," an amplified voice yelled out from above us. Laser fire showered down at us.

"Stop," a voice boomed. The laser bolts ended momentarily before resuming their attempts to hit the boats. Alum grabbed my sleeve and pulled me along so fast I could barely keep my footing. I glanced over my shoulder at the palace. Bromin appeared at the top of the stairs, his face lit eerily by firelight. Soldiers poured out the massive door behind him, then toward us.

We ducked behind the broken gazebo, its tilted roof acting as a shield.

A man from the boat waved us over. "Here. Hurry."

I stepped forward. My foot slipped and I slid down the craggy new cliff face.

"Rose," Alum yelped and pulled me back. He hugged me to him gasping.

A man from the ship held out a hand as the bow edged closer. "Quick. Help her in." The hull crunched against loose rock, pressing closer—as close as it could go. Alum held my hand while I could reach out with the other. Another man appeared from the ship. Together they hoisted me in. The wood edge of the boat dug into my ribs and I yelped. They set me on my feet on the deck. I rubbed my torso, wincing, then turned around, frantic.

Alum picked up Kricky who kicked and fought his grip. I reached out and Kricky calmed. Alum gently placed the beast into my arms.

I grabbed his hand before he could step back. "You have to come. You have to. Bromin saw you. Please."

Alum pulled his hand from mine and caressed my cheek. "Copper Rose. I'm not leaving you." He reached his hand up to the waiting men then jerked backward out of reach under the ailing gazebo roof. He fell to the ground and convulsed, electrical sparks dancing over him.

"Alum," I screamed and dropped Kricky to the ship deck. The onslaught of electricity eased and Alum lifted himself up onto his elbows. The stomp, stomp, stomp of approaching guards reached my ears. Alum looked behind him then waved

243

us on, mouthing, "Go".

The ship hummed to life and skimmed away from the cliff face. Another attack of electrical shock wracked Alum's body.

I could hardly breathe. "No. Go back for him." I leaned over the edge, reaching into the growing distance. The men pulled me back, though I kicked and screamed. "You can't leave him. Please—please go back." When the light from the palace disappeared from view, I sank to the deck and sobbed.

A bearded man leaned close and looked me in the eyes. "We had to leave him, Miss Copper Rose. He knew the risks."

"I don't care. Hasn't he been through enough?" I looked back into the dark night. The acrid smell of smoke and melted metal stung my nostrils and eyes.

"Aye, he has, but your safety is more important, especially if..." He didn't finish what he was saying. He watched as Kricky slinked over to me, ears drooping. The living machine crawled into my lap and clicked protectively.

The man's eyes were wide and his jaw slack. "Amazing." He shook his head. "I'm Temany. We'll all be here—if you need us. We're headed to the main ship. There you can meet up with your brother and father." He walked to the other end of the longboat.

I sat next to a pile of coiled rope. The wind froze sending a shiver through me. Kricky nuzzled against me, but his flexible metal skin only chilled me further. Silent tears occasionally escaped my eyes as we traveled through the black night. Numbness replaced the rush of adrenaline. What would happen to Alum? The smoke cleared and three sliver moons rose slowly above us, their colors faded to mere tinges.

A commotion across the boat caught my attention. We were approaching a large well-lit ship, its sails billowing in the night air. Dark scoring peppered the side of the longboat already docked with the ship. Moonlight painted everything with muted colors as men raced around carrying people on stretchers to the cabin. The hull of our ship bumped against the big ship. A man jumped onto our deck. He grabbed a rope and threw it back to the waiting crew. Airmen helped pull us up tight to the side.

They helped me over the rails and onto the broad deck. Kricky jumped up onto the rail and chittered irritably. The men jumped back and gasped then stepped closer, curious. Scolding them, Kricky leapt to my side.

"Copper Rose?"

I turned. Dad was limping toward me. His clothes were torn and singed. Across his face bruises from green to nearly black mottled his skin.

"Father, you should be resting."

"I had to know you made it back," he said, his voice scratchy. "I had to know you were safe." Sailors were dashing across the deck, pulling ropes and hoisting a last sail into place.

I pulled Dad's arm over my shoulder and turned him back toward the cabin. He leaned heavily against me, the weariness evident in his slack face. He glanced momentarily at Kricky as the creature walked beside us. Dad was too heavy for me. I lowered him onto a crate not far from the cabin door. He leaned against the stack of crates behind him, closing his eyes.

A rough-looking fellow hustled by.

"Gad? Where's Gad?" I asked.

The man looked back at me. "I haven't seen him."

I reached to my father and steadied him. "Dad, I'm going to get some help finding you a bed."

Dad nodded. I dashed back onto the open deck, scanning the men for my brother. I caught sight of one of the men who had infiltrated the palace to rescue my father.

"Hello," I said coming up to him. "You were with my father in the longboat?"

"Yes?" He hesitated and tried not to make eye contact.

"I need help moving my dad. Where's Gad?"

He looked at me and pursed his lips. "I am very sorry."

"What do you mean?" I asked.

He shuffled his feet. "Gad fell."

I backed away shaking my head. "What do you mean?"

Another man came up beside the first. "We tried. The longboat took so much damage. Then he fell. "

My heart skipped a beat. I could imagine his body, broken and bloody laying in the crater. I gasped for breath. "No. No. That can't be. He has to be here somewhere." I looked from face to face, all the expressions of pity.

"It's true," Temany said, coming up to me. "Gad is gone."

Chapter 21

"Dad?" I touched his shoulder, but he still didn't wake. Soon after I learned Gad was missing, Dad had fallen unconscious. We were rushed back to TreeCountry, which was still believed to be the safest area in all the GearMaker lands.

The attack on TreeCountry followed by the abduction of my father inspired The Council of Elders to allow upgrades to security. Once approved by the guards, every ship had to pass through a controlled arch. Anyone who tried to enter anywhere else was repelled by the shield matrix. They insisted on completely checking out our ship despite Dad's need for the advanced healers. Eventually we were allowed through.

The healers assured me that my father was going to recover. Three days in the HealingTree and all my father did was lie still. When his fever flared up he would thrash, calling out for me—and Gad. I was always there, waiting, hoping for him to open his eyes.

I didn't tell anyone what Kricky really was as he gamboled about. Some people looked at him suspiciously when they weren't being entertained by his antics. It was odd to gain comfort from a metal creature.

Not even Kricky could ease the ache deep in my gut though. Gad could be dead or a prisoner. I had no way to find out what happened after he fell. My brother—lying dead in a crater or being tortured by Bromin. Either thought left me fluctuating between anger and sorrow. It was a sorrow deeper than losing Gramma had caused me.

And Alum... I missed him. I missed his steady, quiet presence. I missed his tender touch. Kricky would occasionally gaze out the window and squeak sadly. Perhaps he missed Alum too. I sat there waiting, hoping and wishing for Gad and Alum to return to me.

Sleep slipped over me late in the third day as I was resting my arms on Dad's bed. Something brushed through my hair and I looked up, bleary eyed. His hands were clenching and his eyes fluttered.

"Dad?"

"Rose?" He blinked at me. "Where...?"

"You're in TreeCountry." Gently I placed a hand on his and gripped. I couldn't help the smile that broke across my face. The relief was like the cool mist of a waterfall.

He turned his head to take in the rest of the room. "Gad?"

Agony swelled in my chest. "He—Gad didn't get away. We don't know—where he is. We've sent thithers, but get no response. I..."

Dad's eyes pressed shut. Fat tears squeezed out and ran down his cheeks. "Is he—dead?"

"I don't know."

Several tense minutes passed in silence. Dad's breath slowed. How could I muster a dollop of hope?

A blue garbed woman came in and smiled. "Daren. You're awake. Your daughter would not leave your side and that silly creature she brought has been causing quite a fuss."

248

He squinted at her. "Creature?" His gaze fell on me.

"Shrrrreeeeki. Krick." The bat like ears rose over the footboard of the bed. Dad's glance shot to the black eyes and soft looking muzzle.

Gently I picked up Kricky and brought him close to Dad. "This is Kricky. He, um... Well. Kricky is my newest — friend."

Dad's mouth opened in an amazed 'oh' and the healer beside me gasped, her eyes wide. Regaining his calm, Dad asked, "Does Bromin know?"

"No. And we can't let him find out." I looked at the nurse and she nodded. Kricky jumped onto the bed, sinking into the bedding. He curled up at the end right below Dad's feet and chirped.

"Alum made Kricky hide. If he hadn't... Bromin said he would kill you." A tightness formed in my chest. Would I have really done it? Would I have served Bromin to make his army only to save my father or Gad? Or Alum?

The healer kept looking at me oddly. She checked Dad's bandages and vitals. He was watching me thoughtfully, with anguish rimming his eyes. I knew it was not only physical pain. Was Gad dead or alive? We had no way to know, no way to find out. Time was my enemy. Would it give us closure or answers?

Father healed quickly after he regained consciousness. A sprained wrist was the least of his problems. His broken ribs made breathing difficult. He was covered in cuts and contusions and the broken ankle might never heal right.

Once they let me take him home we were hardly ever alone. Guards were posted throughout our tree. The guards stayed outside the house though. Healers checked on him twice a day. In the morning I would help him to a padded chair near an open window so he could look out at the trees. Kricky often stayed with him like a faithful pet, hiding only when visitors came. The visitors were good at distracting Dad from his sorrow. I wasn't as lucky. I tried to stay in the background, fixing meals, tending the gardens and wishing for a miracle to bring Gad back.

Nightmares plagued my sleep. Images of Alum writhing, electricity slithering over his body and Gad laying in the metal cell covered in blood, his face unrecognizable.

I had hours of time to think, hours of time to miss Alum and Gad. Restless feelings were filling me as Dad's health improved. I caught him watching me, worry in his eyes. I was drowning in 'what ifs'. My mind kept racing through the night of our escape, wishing for a miracle to change the past.

One sunny morning, weeks later, I found my father cooking breakfast, his hands steady and only the slightest tinge of bruising left on his skin. He was standing without his cane, though it was leaning against the cabinet only a foot away from him.

"Breakfast?" He smiled.

"No," I replied.

He limped toward me. "You were calling out in your sleep. Nightmares?"

I looked out the window, avoiding his gaze. "I need to put my energy into some hard work. If you don't need me..."

"I will be fine," he said.

I sighed and went to the door. "I'll be in the workshop."

"Copper Rose? Please talk to me."

"I can't," I said and walked away.

I didn't stop until I reached the workshop. Kricky slipped through the door before I closed it. The room looked exactly how it had before the attack on TreeCountry. Was it weeks or months? I couldn't be sure anymore.

Leaning against the worktable, I fingered the pages of the new skywing designs Gad and I had worked on. The skywings appeared in my mind layer upon layer. As flaws became apparent, I imagined the mechanisms bending and stretching to solve the problems increasing agility and distance. My mind felt clearer than it had been since losing Gad. Nothing else made sense except this design.

I reached over to a pair of skywings sitting on the side table and started taking them apart. Moving like a machine, I put together the new framework, adding in the features I had envisioned.

I was aware of Dad standing in the doorway watching me at some point. I glanced at him and he waved me back to my work. He seemed to understand my need to lose myself for awhile.

Dad left food for me. Hours later I managed to choke it down cold, unable to notice the flavor. Then I returned to rebuilding the skywings. Kricky watched intently between stints of play. Eventually he curled up on the edge of the worktable, out of the way.

My father came and went, leaving food for me. Night turned to day and back into night. I completed the new skywings sometime in the early morning, before light painted the sky. I laid them out in front of me before my head sank onto my folded arms.

251

***

A week later Father was sitting across the breakfast table from me. "Those new skywings are really working out well, don't you think?" He pushed a bowl of oblong berries toward me.

"Yeah," I replied without looking up from my food. I popped a few berries into my mouth.

He continued watching me. "What are you working on now?"

What could I say? I couldn't stop building new things. I had to keep busy or the dreadful images and nightmares wracked my brain. I was doing the only thing I was good at: making machines.

"It's nice to have you eating here in the house again," Dad said over the clink of silverware against the plates.

I looked up. His dark eyes seemed so sad. I knew he was seeing the same sorrow in mine.

"I'm so sorry, Dad." I hesitated. "I—I need to keep going like this—for awhile longer."

"I understand, but please take care of yourself," he replied, and stood up to clear his plate.

He washed the dishes then the cookware and put everything back in its rightful place. If anyone could understand how I felt, it was my own father.

I scooted my plate away, then pulled it back. "Actually..."

He turned. "Yes?" he asked when I didn't continue.

I pushed the food around on my plate with the fork. I didn't want to make anymore mistakes, but my ideas wouldn't let me rest. "I—I kind of need to see the current security set up for TreeCountry."

He narrowed his eyes in thought, giving me an appraising look. "Really?"

"Yes. Do you think Kilain will have a problem still?"

He shrugged. "I doubt it will matter if he will. The council is largely in favor of increased protection now."

"I think I'll go to the ShipYard Tree. I have some ideas for the shield matrix—and some other things." I stood up and carried my plate to the sink, but stopped in front of my father's scrutinizing gaze.

He took the plate. "Ideas? Sure." He looked down at the dish in his hand, scrubbed it, rinsed it and put it on a drying rack.

"We need something—something to make TreeCountry impenetrable—something that gives us a chance against Bromin." I stood up and stepped toward Dad. "No one is taking my family from me again."

***

The next morning I tucked a large roll of drafting papers under my arm and walked in the direction of the ShipYard tree. No one knew I was coming. I didn't want Geren bothering me. I convinced Kricky to stay at the cottage to keep my father company. Only a few people knew what Kricky was and they were not talking about it, but in person it was obvious he wasn't made of flesh and blood.

I took a different route that kept me off the roads and let me enjoy the plants and animals that lived in the less traveled areas. Burnt patches of ground and charred scars on tree trunks increased in frequency as I got closer to the center of

TreeCountry. I sped up, ignoring the twinge of smokey smell that lingered near the burned spots.

Life was abundant despite the damage. Small trees were interspersed among the massive trees. Vines trailed, berry bushes grew wild and mosses climbed over rocks and fallen branches as big as Earth logs. It was almost like being back home and taking walks with Gramma.

By the time I reached the row of ships at the base of the ShipYard tree a weight had lifted from me. The silvery frame shone in the daylight. A smile tweaked the corners of my mouth. There it was: the Iridium skeleton of the abandoned warship.

'I keep hoping someone will figure out how to make her fly.' Gad had said to me so long ago. Now I intended to make that happen. A chill ran through me as my fingers ran over the closest Iridium beam.

"You'll be completed soon," I said to it. "You'll take to the skies like no other ship before you." My fingers still rested on the metal. Yes, my ship! I looked out at the men working on other ships. They were efficient and skilled. I needed a team of workers. I needed the best or else the ship would never succeed.

I strode to the entrance of the ShipYard Tree passing dozens of ships, and ignoring the people's gaze.

"Is that the copper girl?" a young man applying sealant to a large cargo ship said. I ignored him and kept going as an older man directed him back to his work. I came around the last ship by the tree's elevator and saw Yuthin standing with a group of men. When the men stopped speaking and looked my way, he too, turned his head.

A smile broke across his face. "Copper Rose." He walked over and held out a hand in greeting. "What an honor to see you again. How is your father? Recovering?"

I shook his hand. "I think he's on the mend at last."

The men were returning to the closest ship and looking at me over their shoulders. I fingered the edge of the designs still tucked under my arm.

Yuthin led me to the base of the tree. "Tenze told me about the creatures existence. I know it is not meant to be well known, but I wish to meet this GearMade being you have given life to."

I knew Yuthin had a better understanding of what Kricky was than anyone. I could tell from the quiver of excitement in his voice. "You can come by the cottage anytime to meet Kricky. He tends to stay close to Dad or me."

"Thank you," he said in a soft voice, his eyes twinkling with azure light. He looked at the ground and then straightened up. "What brings you to the ShipYard?"

The roll of papers rustled as I shifted them. "I have some ideas for the Shield Matrix. And some designs. I was hoping…" My confidence failed me. Who was I to demand a team of their best workers to help me build a ship they had given up on long ago?

Yuthin glanced at the papers. "Designs? Oh, by all means. I would like to see them—if I may."

I held them out. Yuthin carried them to a wood plank held up by sawhorses. He waved for me to follow. By the time I reached him, the roll of papers was spread out. He grabbed a chisel and placed it on a corner.

Yuthin scanned the page, his mouth falling open silently. He turned to the second page. Ten minutes passed as he slowly perused the designs.

He reached the final diagram and looked at me. "Is this really possible?"

"There's only one way to find out," I said. "I was hoping..." Once again I felt inadequate.

Laying the papers back into a stack, Yuthin scrutinized my face. "Yes?"

"I really want to turn that large Iridium ship frame on the end of this row into a functioning stealth ship. I think it may be the only way—the only way to get Gad back—if he is alive." I sighed and wrung my hands. And the only way to save Alum. If only I knew where either of them were.

"I see." He rolled up the designs and handed them back to me. "This is an innovative plan. I think you should have whatever you need."

Tucking the papers under my arm again, I smiled. "Really? It won't take away from the people you need to finish other ships?"

"No. You should have a full team of our best workers. I can take you up to the offices right now." Yuthin took my elbow momentarily to turn me toward the elevator. "We can get a scribe to start on replicas of the designs."

"You don't have any machines to copy things?" I asked.

"Interesting idea, but no we don't." He tapped his chin. "Maybe you could develop that idea sometime."

I nodded.

"The team rotations are in the Iridium offices. I can point

out which groups might be best suited to this—um—delicate work."

The ride to the fridium warehouse branch seemed much shorter this time. Yuthin hurried me through the building to the offices and into a long room on the bottom floor. It had windows to the outside and into the warehouse. A long table sat at one end surrounded by comfortable chairs. The other side of the room had smaller tables and a counter stacked with reams of large paper, drawing instruments and a row of books. Within half an hour Yuthin had several young men and women sitting around the large table copying my drawings by hand.

Walking around the room, I watched and checked their work, each step increasing my hope. More people came in as the first set of duplicates were completed. Yuthin introduced each of the team leaders for the work crews. We sat around a smaller table.

Trays of sandwiches, sliced fruit and pitchers of water were brought in and placed on the counter. We ate as we went over the drawings. I found the team leaders knowledgeable and astute. They made suggestions and explained unfamiliar technology. I had never collaborated with a team of people before. It was exhilarating.

"What is this?"

I looked up.

Geren was scowling from the doorway, his fists firmly planted on his hips. "What is the meaning of this—this chaos?"

My heart dropped into my stomach. What would Geren do? I didn't want to give up.

Yuthin hurried over. "Geren, you simply must see these

designs."

The man blustered, but followed Yuthin over to a table with the original designs laying in a stack. Yuthin slowly pulled the pages back one at a time, allowing Geren time to see. The expression on Geren's face went from anger to wonder. He glanced over at me. Everyone in the room seemed to be holding their breath.

"Hmmmm." Geren rubbed his head. "I—That ship is not going to ever fly. We tried. We really did."

Yuthin leaned closer to Geren. "If we allow our five best teams a few weeks to work on it, this design may change that."

Geren turned, his eyes ablaze. "Our five best teams? No. No. A project of this size would require workers from the other branches. This is not going to work, much as I wish it could" Geren leaned in close to the drawings, scrunching his face up. "What are these crazy things off the sides anyway?"

I stepped forward. "Wings."

"Wings? Like a bird?" He crossed his arms and glared at Yuthin. "Who ever heard of a ship with wings?"

"The wings add extra lift," I said. I jabbed my finger toward the drawing. "They can fold in to allow the ship to pass through smaller spaces and can give additional stealth by letting the ship glide. We can also give it sun powered propellers that will give it nearly silent propulsion. This *will* work."

The room was silent as Geren and I stared at each other, waging war without a single word. I held my breath in anticipation.

Geren was the first to break eye contact. "Two weeks. Ye can only have my best teams for two weeks. After that you have to accept that that beast of bones cannot fly."

I smiled, my eyes still maintaining their sharp gaze. "If it isn't flying in two weeks, I will take it apart myself!"

Chapter 22

My dream had come true. Six weeks of constant work and my ship was ready for its maiden voyage. The sparkling iridium frame was now covered in a light weight, yet durable skin. The retractable side-wings had been tested and retested. All the features I wanted had been perfected to make it a true stealth ship.

The last thing it needed was a name and a crew. A mix of GearMakers and GearMades volunteered. Geren quickly changed from ambivalent to supportive. He and Yuthin weeded through the volunteers to find the best people to pilot the ship.

I was too excited to sleep, but dawn came quickly anyway. Kricky chirped in greeting as I came downstairs.

"Hey, Kricky." I pulled my leather coat on against the morning chill. The tangy smell of hide brought Gad to mind.

"I will find you—soon," I whispered, wishing he could hear me. I would not believe he was dead.

"Rose, wait," Dad said from his doorway.

I walked over and gave him a big hug. "I've got to get going. Are you coming now?"

He leaned against the door frame. "If you give me a minute. One of our ships was having navigation trouble in the valley last night. I was up late on the wireless attempting to guide them to the shield arch." He smiled at me and put a hand on my shoulder.

"What's the problem?"

His face scrunched up and he shrugged. "I couldn't tell what was happening. Their communication wasn't clear then they cut out. The guard post informed me they let them in, but they were in trouble. Hopefully the ship will pull in soon so I can find out what the situation is." He yawned and shook his head.

I pulled his hand from my shoulder and squeezed it before walking out the door. "Let's get going then. I'll wait outside."

"Yes, dear girl." Dad walked back into his room and rustled around. I stepped out the front door and breathed in the crisp morning air. A delicate crust of frost covered the garden plants. The chill tingled in my nose. My ship wasn't alive like Kricky, but I was excited to see how it flew.

The morning sun was peeking through the trees to bathe the flying ship in yellow light. The hull curved fluidly like a boat built for water, but it was shallower, sleeker. The front had a domed shelter of clear, crack-proof glass, like the windshield of an Earth sports car. A series of gears stuck out of the bottom as part of the sail and free-flight mechanisms. Their metal sheen glinted in the early light.

The hull was a rich brown like the wood branches around us. Using a coloring technique I'd seen in Bromin's workshop, we'd created a paint that actually allowed the ship to shift colors like a chameleon. The hull could look like a dappled forest tree top, a mountain rock face or even puffy clouds.

My heart raced with excitement. The creation was all mine.

"It's magnificent," Dad said, coming up beside me.

"Let's hope it works," I said, stepping on the gang plank. I held tightly to the rail and lifted my head high. My crew cheered as I stepped to the deck.

"How does it feel?" Dad called out from the dock branch. I grinned back at him.

I turned back. "Are you heading back home? We'll be gone for a couple hours."

Dad looked around and back at me. "I plan on waiting until that ship from last night comes in. I haven't seen it yet. But I can't wait to hear how your maiden voyage goes. I'm—I'm really proud of you." He wiped at his eye then smiled again.

"Captain aboard," Hend, a young soldier called out. I couldn't help but smile. A middle-aged man walked over to me. His chin was dusted with a day of black beard growth. His hair was laced with silver and touched his muscled shoulders.

"Are you ready for our first mission, Venrick?" I shook his outstretched hand. "I hear you are the best second a person could want."

"I will serve you the best I can," he said. "This ship is destined for more than this jaunt."

"Well." I looked around at the men and women gathered around me when a loud explosion rocked the ship. I caught the rail and looked around franticly, when another blast occurred. A dirigible ship headed toward the dock branch was on fire. The dirigible was sagging as it lost gas.

Gasps came from my crew when the smoking ship leaned precariously. It slowly drifted to one of the radius dock branches across from us. Airmen from all the docked ships

262

jumped their rails to help. Several smaller ships came up alongside the damaged ship to help ease it into dock. Suddenly it jerked downward and careened at the branch.

"It's losing flight capability," someone yelled from behind me. One of the dinghies caught fire and fell, but the pilot pulled open a pair of skywings and leapt into the air. I clenched the rail. The burning ship collided into the dock. The entire tree rocked. The groan of wood and metal stress ripped through the air. My ship bounced away from the branch. I winced and tightened my grip. The gang plank slipped then fell spinning downward.

Dad ran toward the damaged vessel. "Quick, secure it. Secure the ship!"

People leapt aboard the dirigible ship pulling thick ropes and lashed it to the dock. Dad dodged dockworkers hauling buckets of water from the trunk. He slipped, but caught himself on the wet dock.

"Dad!" My stomach lurched.

Crews from other ships were throwing fire suppressant pods from their own ships onto the flames. People started pulling sailors from the wreckage. Once my ship was against the dock branch and steady, I leapt the short distance back to the dock branch. The crowds were thick with people running and injured being carried. Long hoses pulled down the length of the branch were being used to send arcs of high powered water over the ailing vessel. Frantic, I dodged people.

"Dad," I called out. Where was he?

"Rose. Over here. Quick," Dad yelled. He crouched down out of sight behind the throng. I hurried through the crowd, making way for groups of injured and their helpers.

"Father. Where are you?"

People were calling out orders, or moaning in pain. I yelled over the crowd again with no answer.

A man I knew from the building yards put his hand on my arm and pointed. "Your father is over there helping the injured."

Spying my father between the breaks in the crowd, I wound my way to him. People bumped into me, constantly sending me into someone else. But then I found him, kneeling next to an injured man.

"Father, do you need help?" I crouched down next to the man on the ground. The unmistakeable blonde hair framed a partially burnt face I recognized.

"Laurent," I gasped. Dad looked at me. "I met him and Frent in the under city—the second day I was in Seranova." He was far different from the flirty man I remembered. "Will he survive?"

Laurent twisted, trying to rise. Dad put a hand on his unburnt shoulder to lower him back down. "I've seen injuries like this before. I don't know. He might make it."

I leaned over to help Dad, carefully brushing the hair out of Laurent's face, away from the burns. "What happened? A ship doesn't explode like that." His eyes opened and focused on me. He seemed to silently mouth my name.

"Don't speak," Dad said. Laurent tried to sit up, but fell back down coughing. He grabbed my arm and pulled me close.

"Gad—he—he was captured," Laurent said, his voice raspy. "CliffSide Fortress—Bromin taking him to the—fortress."

Laurent went limp and his eyes closed.

"Laurent, Laurent. Wake up."

***

An hour later I dragged my tired body over to my ship. The chameleon skin was now dark grey across the front where smoke had billowed past. I walked over the new gangplank onto the deck, my gut roiling. Bromin had Gad, but I didn't know what the CliffSide Fortress was or where. What if Laurent never regained consciousness? Waiting to know more was grating on my nerves.

I strode back down the gangplank and entered the lift before I knew what I was doing. I was down several branches before I stopped. Maps. Where could I find maps? I started the lift again and stopped at the branch with the Fridium warehouse. Hardly anyone was there. Tools were laying around as if dropped unexpectedly.

The upper conference room was where they kept archives. No one was there when I arrived. I flipped through page after page of large papers, searching for the CliffSide Fortress. Nothing was listed that way. Where was this place? How could I save Gad if I couldn't even find it?

Someone cleared their throat behind me. I whipped around to find one of the young apprentices watching me.

"I need some maps of the land," I said, coming over to him quickly.

"Um—Miss Copper?"

I leaned closer. "Bromin's lands. I need a detailed map of the whole of Seranova. Are there any?"

The young man ran a hand through his curly brown hair.

He stepped over to the counter which normally held food and drinks. He pulled out several very old looking charts. The young man placed them on the table.

"I believe those are what you're looking for," he said, then left the room.

I carefully lifted the first page. The paper was old and hand-inked. The smell of age lingered. My eyes took in the landmasses and waterways of Seranova. Far to the Northwest was remote land dominated by drawings of cliffs and jagged mountains. In tidy scrawl at the heart of this land were the words CliffSide Fortress. It was aptly named. The Palace may have been on a cliff, but this other location of Bromin's appeared to be on a massive plateau rising well above the valley below. I ran my finger all the way to the opposite corner of the map where drawings indicated the huge trees of TreeCountry. Dread filled me. How could we possibly get Gad back if he was there?

Somewhere between Bromin's palace in Capitol City and this CliffSide Fortress was a ship transporting my brother. No ship in the GearMaker fleet could make the trip fast enough. It might take days, a week even. And all I had to go on was the mumblings of a now unconscious man.

There was only one hope. The maiden voyage of my ship would have to be a rescue mission.

***

That night Laurent was still sleeping in the HealerTree. Fifty three men and women were on board when Bromin's warship attacked them outside TreeCountry. While damaged, the ship made it into the shield matrix dome, but part of the electrical storage unit exploded when they neared the docks. A strange compound of oil had doused the ship causing it to burn long and hot. It was hard to remove, even from skin. Eight people never made it out of the ship. Another five died en-route. Now all everyone could do was wait and treat the wounded.

I sat on a hard chair next to Laurent's bed waiting for him to wake, hoping for something more to go on. I couldn't leave without a clue of where Gad was. "Laurent," I whispered. One of the healers had been by ten minutes prior. They didn't think he would wake for days. He would need months to heal, if he even survived the night. "Laurent, where can I find Gad?"

He stirred and moaned then lay quiet again. I sighed heavily. He hadn't told anyone on his ship what he'd discovered. I knew that because I had questioned every one of them that was alive and conscious. The healers had threatened to make me go away if I didn't leave their patients alone. So there I sat, quietly waiting for Laurent to tell me what only he knew.

Hours passed. Someone brought me warm tea, which I sipped until it went cold. I reached over to hold Laurent's hand so he would know someone was there. His hands were broad with thick fingers where they stuck out of the gauze wrappings. The burns were extensive. My nose tingled from the pungent ointment applied to the burns and my eyes drooped from fatigue.

In my dreams Gad called out to me, pleading with me. "Why did you leave me? Why won't you come save me?"

I tried to speak. I wanted to tell him that I was searching. I wanted to save him. He called to me again, his face turning angry, his words hurtful. Why couldn't he hear me? I tried to get his voice out of my head, his betrayed expression out of my vision. But it was no longer Gad. Alum was the one so angry and hateful. Vicious red lines disfigured his face, which was contorted in pain and agony. "You did this to me. You, Copper Rose, left me to die at his hand. You Miss. You—You should wake up. Please Miss Rose…"

"What?" I opened my eyes, confused.

A woman was leaning over me. I wiped a bit of drool from my chin. "Sorry. Was I…"

"You were mumbling darling. It's morning now. You should really go home and get some sleep." She patted my shoulder.

"Thank you. I'll—I'll consider it."

She left, looking back only once. I rubbed my face until it stung. The horrified feeling I'd felt during the nightmare had decreased to a smoldering nausea. Placing my hand on the one part of Laurent's arm that wasn't bandaged I spoke my fears. "I have to save Gad. You're the only person who can tell me where he is. Oh, Laurent. Why won't you wake up and tell me? Then I could leave you alone."

"Gad?" Laurent's blue eyes were boring into me. His skin was nearly as white as the bandages covering half his head. One strong cheekbone was coated thickly in ointment. He seemed to recognize me and a slight smile lifted the corner of his mouth.

"Yes." I smiled, my heart beating faster. "Gad. I need to go get him. Please—where is he?"

He licked his cracked lips. "TwigWood… North of Chase river…" His breath came in gasps as if the strain of speaking was too much, but he cleared his throat and continued in the gravely tone. "Ten days from full red moon. Bromin personal transport ship. Get him — back." Coughing wracked him and his body hunched upward. The healer woman dashed over and put an arm around him. I grabbed the glass of water from the small bedside table. As the coughing eased I held the glass to Laurent's mouth. He sipped cautiously, most of the water spilling down him. Shaking his head wearily, he lay back down with the woman's help.

"Thank you," she said and took the glass from me. "You go get some sleep."

I turned from Laurent and left the HealerTree quickly. Ten days from the full red moon? Calculations ran through my head based on my new understandings of this world. There was no time for sleep. I had three days to get across half of Seranova.

Chapter 23

Before going anywhere else I found Venrick. He was in the ShipYard tree helping clean up.

He saw me approaching and hurried over. "Do you have information?"

I nodded.

He smiled in reply. "Wonderful. I will call back the crew."

The blackened wood across the dock branch stood out in the mid morning light.

"Our ship is safe," Venrick said. "We did a thorough check of it as soon as we knew everyone was safe—everyone that could be saved, that is."

I looked at Venrick, my lips tight. "This can't keep happening. Who is going to stop this insane GearMade?"

He shrugged. "Let's start by getting your brother back. I'll gather the crew and additional supplies needed for an extraction."

"Thank you." I followed him as he walked to the ship. "I've decided on a name for this beauty. Hope's Wings."

He smiled, nodding reverently. "Fitting."

We both gazed at the ship for a moment. Then he turned to me. "You should prepare for a longer journey."

"Yes. Send word to me at home when everything is ready.

I'll be as quick as I can." I went back down the elevator. My feet couldn't move me fast enough through TreeCountry and up to our home branch.

Dad met me at the door holding a thick envelope.

"The ship is already prepared to take off? That was quick." I took the envelope.

"A council meeting has been called. You were requested."

I pulled the letter open and scanned the formal request for my presence at the meeting in only half an hour. A shiver ran through me. Kilain's sharp angled signature was at the bottom. "Why me?"

Dad pursed his lips. "We'll have to leave immediately."

"But what do they want?" I asked, a pit forming in my stomach. Kilain was on the council. He'd already threatened us. What would he do now?

"I suspect..." He pulled on his coat and opened the door to the cottage. "They want a vote on allowing you to rescue Gad."

I sighed. "Kilain."

He nodded. "We have to hurry. I'll convince them."

Dad flew the air-skimmer across TreeCountry. The day was dashing through the afternoon. I looked across the forest toward the Shipyard tree, wishing I was there, readying my ship to launch. If convincing the council was necessary, then I would be as persuasive as possible. I ran my fingers through unruly curls and tightened the lacings on my vest. Out of habit I grabbed the locket through my shirt.

The landing strip on the CouncilTree was already crowded with personal transportation devices; air-skimmers, small ships and even skywings that people were hanging up on racks near the ornate rounded structure built into the trunk. Spires rose up around it, reaching for the tree top. The surface was coated in a rainbow of metals, sparkling in the afternoon sunbeams.

Like a procession, people walked to the building, lining up before the large double doors to file in. We entered, being bumped and jostled by the crowd. Many turned and gaped at me before moving on through a second set of doors a few yards in. Once inside, Dad lead me away from the crowd down a long, curved hall. The walls were interspersed with paintings and carved wood doors.

Putting his hand on a copper doorknob, Dad said, "Wait here a moment." The door opened silently. It was a coat closet of sorts. Dad pulled a robe from a hook on the wall and slipped it over his shoulders, pushing his arms into the sleeves. The rich red velvet was lined with silver and ran all the way down to his ankles. He closed the door behind him then led me around to another door. Two men in uniforms of green and gold stood at attention on either side of the door. One of them nodded to my father, opening the door for him.

"I need to take my seat. They will summon you when they're ready. Rose, all you do is answer their questions. You have nothing to fear." He went into the council room and the guard closed the door behind him. I stood in the hallway, controlling my breathing, struggling to relax. Why did they want to talk to me? Time was short before my ship should leave. I needed to be preparing.

Conversation I could hear through the door subsided. Someone started talking in a loud voice, though it was too muffled to understand. My hands, damp with sweat, shook. I rubbed my palms on my breeches and tried to quit fidgeting.

A man in a silver tunic with a red band around the waist exited. "They will see you now."

The council room ceiling was a dome of carved wood and colored windows. The audience sat on benches before the raised dais where I had entered. Plush cushioned chairs lined the risers, which curved in a semi-circle, allowing the council the ability to look at each other or the audience. My father sat several rows up amongst the other members of the council also dressed in colored robes. The man in silver led me to a cleared area in the front of the half circle.

I clasped my hands together to keep them from shaking. Tenze, wearing blue and copper robes, stood up from the chair closest to me. His voice was amplified as he spoke, his grey beard swaying with his words.

"I call to order this meeting of the Council of Elders. Before us we have Copper Rose Locke, daughter of Daren Steele and Leatha Locke."

The crowd murmured, but went silent at his raised hand.

"Copper Rose, please tell us the plan for the rescue of Gad Steele."

Tenze waved at me to start. I attempted to clear my throat, but only squeaked. When I found my voice I told them what Laurent had said about the CliffSide Fortress and the transport of Gad to it. I emphasized the need for urgency. The faces of the fifty or so men and women seemed unchanged by my words. What would it take to convince them that my stealth ship had the best chance to rescue Gad?

A woman in the back of the council stood, her pale yellow and silver robes rustling against her seat. "How can we believe your information is accurate and complete?"

I tried to smile at her. "I met Laurent on a previous occasion. He is a colleague of Gad's and is reliable."

The woman's brows rose and she nodded slowly. A hush came over the gathered people.

Kilain stood, scowling at me. "Despite this information, the Council has already decided that a rescue attempt of one, even as useful as Gad Steele, is not in the best interest of our people. I propose this council be ended. Let the work of supporting our people be a priority."

My father hung his head.

"No!" I stepped forward, lifting my hands animatedly. "The only risk is to me and my ship. If my crew agrees to go with me, then what harm can it do?"

Tenze approached me. He put an arm out to silence Kilain. "You are of value to a great many of us. Your skills are irreplaceable." His words were quiet and deliberate then dropped to barely a sound. "Listen closely." He spoke up again. "Already you have shown great promise—and you clearly know how to reach goals thought impossible." He winked before turning back to the council.

Kilain stepped closer, bellowing. "The council has spoken. Let it be so."

Three others called out, "Aye."

The reverberating sound of a large gong shook the room, then people moved to the exits. My head rang long past the end of the sound. I felt like my heart was breaking. Dad came up to me and led me out the door. When we passed the large closet of robes, Dad slipped his off and held it out to a young man who stood in the doorway looking official.

People swarmed around me as they exited. More of them pointed than when we entered. A harsh whisper rose between them, with noticeable mentions of my name. The heat, the jostling and tripping... I just wanted out. How could I accept the decision of a council that less than a year before I'd known nothing about? They were abandoning Gad to be tortured and killed by Bromin. Why were my skills more important than his life? I needed to get out of that hall, out into fresh air—away from the noise and chatter. I pressed forward trying to escape.

My father took my hand, his face etched with sorrow. "Let's go home."

I sighed. Dad led me through the crowd and out to the air-skimmer.

Yuthin met us there, a grimace on his face. He put a hand on Dad's shoulder. "Daren. You should be allowed to save your son. Kilain is behind this. He will destroy our people before he will believe the threat from Bromin is real."

I grew frantic inside. "Is there no way to change the council's mind?"

He didn't respond.

My hands were clenched. "Please. I know I can do this."

"I laid out all the arguments in favor. This is not going to happen. We have to hope that he finds a way back to us on his own." His shoulders dropped as he sighed heavily. I looked back at the building. Kilain was standing at the door watching me, his features harsh. I hurried into the air-skimmer, feeling like I would crawl out of my skin. I couldn't accept such defeat or have faith that Gad would survive without help.

Dad didn't say another word as he flew us home. I fumed inside. Dark would soon fill the sky and it would be a whole night before I could try to change the council's mind.

Exhaustion battled with my need to save my brother. Kilain seemed to rule the council using threats, but I didn't want to get involved in the politics of TreeCountry. I only wanted to save my brother. Tenze was kind, but he too was stopping me from going. I looked out into the large trees.

Or was he? I thought back to Tenze's words. *'You clearly know how to reach goals thought impossible.'* Maybe he was trying to tell me something. I couldn't accept the decision of the council, but Kilain scared me. What might he do if I did defy the council?

We landed back at home as the dusk light started teasing the edges of my vision. After wishing my father a good night I went to my room.

My thoughts were all over while nothing coalesced into a useable idea. Restless, I paced. Still nothing made sense. Still nothing came to me. Still sleep evaded me.

So I paced back and forth—back and forth—back—and—forth.

Chapter 24

Kricky jumped through my open window onto my bed, landing with a fwump. Resting his head on his front paws, he watched me as I tread a path around the room. Night fell, but my brain still held me more awake than my tired body could fight. Only one thing was clear; I had to get Gad back. I could never leave him to suffer because of me. So many times he had saved me. Now I had to do the same for him—no matter what some old GearMakers said.

I grabbed my coat, gave Kricky a pat on the head with a command to stay with my father. I scribbled out a note on a scrap of paper, blotting the ink in my haste. Then I tiptoed down the stairs of the cottage into the darkened living space. It must have been later than I thought if Dad was asleep. Putting the note on the table, I slipped out the door, latching it behind me.

The fresh air filled my lungs, invigorating me. The light of the three moons dashed across the landscape of our family tree, painting it with colors. I descended the trunk stairs to the landing branch. What next though? I could only think of one place, my ship, Hope's Wings.

A pair of modified, stealth skywings were in the wing cabinet. I snugged the skywings straps across my torso and dove off the branch with hardly a flutter of anxiety. The wings allowed me to drift most of the way to the DockBranch and Hope's Wings. I was imagining taking off by myself, but that wasn't practical.

Small flameless lights ran along the main limb of the DockBranch. I landed, carefully running a few steps to keep myself from falling. All seemed quiet until I approached the berth of my ship. Hushed voices were drifting over the railing and flickers of light reflected through the cabin windows. Suddenly my senses were alive. The hair rose on the back of my neck as I inched closer to Hope's Wings.

"Copper Rose?"

"Ahhhh!" I leapt away from the dark figure that had come up behind me.

It was Hend. "Its only me."

I stepped closer, my heart still racing. "But what are you doing here?"

Another figure leapt from the deck to join us. The silvery gray hair was obvious. "Copper Rose. Your crew awaits you."

"Venrick, but how...?"

"There's a job to be done and a ship that needs a chance to prove itself." He winked.

"I can't ask all of you to defy the council." I hung my head, but then caught sight of the kaleidoscope of shadows cast by the moons. Looking up I found my companions watching me.

Venrick fixed me with his eye. "We are loyal to you. Everyone on this ship knows Gad. Bromin might have taken more extreme action against GearMakers sooner if Gad hadn't been there sabotaging his goals and bringing us intel in plenty of time for us to counteract Bromin's actions. We are with you."

My cheeks grew warm. "Thank you. How long before we can leave?"

"If you will step aboard we can be off immediately." Venrick took a step toward the ship and paused.

Black scars marred the wood branch were Laurent's ship had crashed. He was unlikely to survive his injuries. I couldn't let the council keep me from using the information he sacrificed himself to deliver.

"I see no reason to delay. We have to go a long way in a short period of time." I walked over the gangplank, Venrick close behind.

"Oh," I said. "We don't have…" I stepped on deck.

Venrick came up next to me. "What don't we have?"

"How can we attack a ship with only a crew of airship sailors?"

He chuckled. "Tenze predicted your need. Three of the best GearMaker soldiers are here as well as many others."

"Hah. Tenze." I smiled. "This is what he meant."

"He'll also have the shield matrix turned off long enough for us to get out," Venrick said.

I laughed out loud. "We should get going then!"

Venrick nodded his approval and strode off giving commands to the rushing crew. Steam billowed from the prow. Adrenalin surged as the stealth ship, my creation, edged away from the dock. Ropes were coiled into their place and the side wings unfurled partially. The ship raced upward into the night, floating like dandelion clock on the wind. Raising my head into the air, I grinned, energy coursing through me.

We slipped into the ship lane through the huge trees,

moving with greater speed and silence than I had thought it would.

Venrick came up beside me and smiled. "Quite a beauty you've created here. I've never left the dock more smoothly nor sped into the tree lane so fast."

I grinned in response. "At this speed we might actually intercept the transport hauling Gad." Looking around at the efficiency of the crew I knew they would not fail me. I sat down on a crate near the cabin watching as the ship veered into a less used fly path. We approached the edge of TreeCountry, our speed never waning, but I could hear the buzz of the shield matrix. My heart raced. I was about to run to Venrick to warn him. Suddenly the buzzing stopped and a haze in the air in front of us vanished. Tenze! I would have to thank him when we got back. Hope's Wings slipped through the air, out into the valley and the shield matrix reappeared behind us.

"Could you send the three soldiers to meet with me? We need to plan." I looked around, not sure where to go.

Venrick cleared his throat. "You meet with people in the captain's room. There's also a bed in there. Morning is a few hours off. Get some sleep and then you'll have time to plan."

The older man smiled and pointed across the deck.

"Oh—yes." I knew where the captain's room was. I had designed it after all. "But I was only meant to be captain for the test flight. You really should take over."

He pursed his lips, one eye narrowed slightly. "You will remain captain."

"Venrick. I'm an engineer, a designer. Not a..."

"There is more to you than that. I know you are capable of

this so I won't let you out of this commitment. Now go sleep, Captain Locke."

I opened my mouth to object, but he cut me off with a raised hand and pointed again at the captains room. It was mostly a conference room, but a small sleeping cubby was tucked against the space. With my biggest desire now in action fatigue was catching up with me. I shrugged and walked in the direction he pointed. There would be plenty of time for him to take over later.

I entered the captain's cabin through a carved wood door with metal inlay. Light flickered to life in the ceiling. Before me was a large wooden table laden with maps. I ran my hand over the newly copied representation of Seranova. They were nearly exact copies of the old originals I'd seen the day before, but it seemed someone had included the changes to Bromin's land and the clear boundary of where the GearMaker lands started.

Dark silhouettes of trees sped past the curved windows along a rounded wall. A large yawn stopped me and my eyes felt heavy. I couldn't recall when I'd last slept. A heavy burgundy curtain on the far side of the room was pulled back partially. Behind it in a small room sat a bed. A copper sink was on one wall and a built in cabinet on the other.

Looking back out the window, my stomach knotted. Dad would forgive me for leaving without waking him, but would the consequences fall on him, too? "Gad. I'm coming for you," I whispered then walked over to the bed, yanking the curtain closed.

I laid down. Exhaustion was hitting me so hard I didn't even slip off my boots as I pulled a blanket up over me. The deep whoosh of air on the side of the ship was soothing. My eyes closed and sleep crept over me. Glorious, dreamless sleep.

***

A door creaked in my half waking consciousness. I sat up to find daylight streaming from around the curtain. I jumped up, straightening my clothing and checking for the locket, then pushed the curtain to the side.

Two men and a woman were standing near the door.

"Hello," one of the men said. "Venrick sent us in."

I nodded and rubbed the sleep from my eyes. "Yes. Please come in." I recognized the men from Dad's rescue so I knew they were skilled. They smiled and nodded before pulling chairs over to the table.

"Captain," they greeted together. The woman nodded curtly. She seemed a no-nonsense kind of person. Would I be able to handle running a team of professional soldiers?

"I'm Hend and you know Drenth." He motioned toward the woman. "This is Senra."

Senra's bronze-tinged brown hair was cut short, but the way it curled against her scalp lent her a feminine air. She preferred breeches like me.

"So." I paused, biting my lip. They waited. Senra was scowling, her arms crossed over her chest. I fumbled with the maps until I found one of Twig Wood and the surrounding Chase river area. "So the ship—the ship we need to intercept will be here—somewhere."

A hand cupped over mine. Hend smiled at me. "We all want to find Gad. You're not alone in this."

"Yes." Drenth pulled the map toward him and tapped his finger on it. "This ravine would be a good place to mount an

282

ambush."

I sighed. "That could work. Can we assault one of Bromin's big warships?"

Drenth and Hend looked at each other and shrugged.

"We can try," Drenth said.

"No," Senra snapped. "This extraction has disaster written all over it. Gad was bound to end up in this situation with his reckless ways."

My heart fell. How could she say such things about my brother?

Drenth puffed out his chest. "Then why are you here?" he said.

"I was left no choice by my Uncle Tenze." Senra glared. "Even he saw the hopelessness of the situation, but didn't want this prized ship destroyed."

Hend's chair clattered to the floor as he stood. "This is uncalled for Senra. Gad takes risks no one else will to keep GearMakers safe. There's no need to besmirch his name. Copper Rose built a ship no one else could have. Our chances against Bromin are better now. You should be thanking her for..."

Senra laughed. "Thank her? An outsider? She isn't one of us."

Heat rushed up my neck. I leaned my hands on the table. "What's your problem with me and my family?"

"Nepotism. You would be nothing if you weren't the long lost child of a council..."

"Enough." Venrick said from behind us.

Everyone's heads turned toward the door. Venrick stood,

fists on hips, glowering at us. His greying hair made him appear to glow with power. Senra sat back down, her hands in her lap and head bowed. Venrick strode over and stood by the table. I sank to my seat and looked up, feeling like a child. He scowled at the team, but his features softened into a smile when he looked at me.

His large hand came down on my shoulder. "Copper Rose is your captain. A soldier does not question orders or defy the leader. That is treason." He looked around the group again. Drenth looked smug and glanced at the now humble Senra. "Gad deserves to be rescued no matter who he is." Drenth cringed and looked down at the table.

I sighed. If I couldn't control this group of headstrong people, how would we save Gad?

"Am I understood?" Venrick barked.

"Yes, Sir," the three replied.

"Now help Captain Locke figure out how to rescue her brother."

He turned and walked back out.

I rushed after him, pulling the door close behind me. "Venrick."

"Yes, Captain?"

"Please don't call me that."

He stepped close to me, his expression severe but kind. "I *will* call you Captain. You must get used to this kind of leadership. I know you'll be good at it. If you make your boundaries clear you will be an effective leader."

I shook my head. "Once again I'm a designer of fancy skywings and ships."

"I chose this assignment because I believe in you. If you start believing in yourself Bromin will have no chance of winning." He walked away.

I took a deep breath, my hand on the door handle. I did believe we could rescue my brother and more than believed in my ability to create new and useful machines. I was not so sure about the ideas of living machines and leadership. I steeled myself and entered the room. Hend and Drenth were talking excitedly. Senra was back to her tightlipped position, with her arms crossed, but she was nodding in agreement to things the men said.

Hend poked a thick finger at the map. "But how do we attack with only one ship? Bromin is bound to have a full regiment of soldiers aboard."

I glanced around the room thinking. How could I deal with Senra's hostility? My pair of stealth skywings were leaning in a corner by the window. Or floating, rather. I had infused Iridium into the frame. I chuckled to myself. The skywings also had chameleon skin so they blended with the wood wall behind them. An idea jumped into my head. I flipped the copper curls off my shoulder and a grin spread across my face.

"We don't attack," I said, my head held high.

Senra turned her narrowed gaze on me. "Then what do we do?"

I raised my brows and smirked. "We sneak on using skywings."

Drenth's mouth opened in a silent 'Oh.'

Hend grinned and nodded. "Yeeessss."

Senra's expression actually softened. She leaned forward

and pulled the map toward her. "Hmmmm. This ravine. The ship hides here—and we can be in the trees."

"Good." I sat down. "Keep talking. I like this plan."

She continued. "We get aboard Bromin's ship, then retrieve Gad as quietly as possible."

Drenth shook his head and slapped his hand down on the table. "There is no guarantee we can get in and out undetected. All it takes is one soldier to sound the alarm."

Senra pulled out a dagger. It's blade was black and the tip curved like a talon. "I can dispose of any obstacles."

"No." I looked at her, confidence now infusing me.

She gripped the dagger tightly and glared. "Why not?"

"Bromin may be willing to kill and maim, but I'm not."

We stared at each other. Her eyes burned, but I didn't back down. Venrick believed I could be a leader. The idea of using my skywings bolstered my confidence to do that. Hend and Drenth held still as we silently battled.

Senra relaxed her grip on the dagger. "Then what do you suggest?"

I had no answer.

Drenth grinned. "Renfor."

"What?" My brow scrunched with confusion.

Senra smiled. "Yes. That could work. And would be less messy."

"But what is it?"

Hend chuckled. "Renfor is a fluid. You put it on a cloth and cover their mouth. Knocks 'em out."

"It even erases short term memory," Senra said.

I nodded. "Like chloroform."

"Not sure what chlorifirm is, but this is the best stuff for the mission." Hend clasped his hands on the table looking smug.

"Uh…" Drenth pursed his lips. "Do we have any on board?"

Senra huffed and stood quickly. She strode out of the room. I looked at Drenth and Hend. What had we done? I stood to go check on her. Senra clearly didn't like me, but we needed to get along for Gad's sake. I was nearly to the door when Venrick entered, closely followed by Senra.

"Coming up with some useful plans I see," Venrick said as he walked over to a tall cabinet in the far corner of the room. Senra stayed at his elbow. He pulled a key from around his neck and unlocked it, then he pulled out a fat bottle of cloudy liquid.

Venrick held it up. "Senra said you needed Renfor?"

She took the bottle and came back to the table. "Renfor. We do have it on board."

"Actually." Venrick came over and took the bottle. "This is best kept locked up until you need it." He locked it up as Senra, Hend and Drenth continued talking out the plan. Everyone was more relaxed. As Venrick walked back to the door he winked at me and nodded.

The team worked well after that. Senra still had a tendency to be aloof, but very little direct hostility occurred again. They were thrilled to practice using the new stealth skywings I'd designed. My anxiety increased the closer we got to TwigWood. The Chase River was a massive blue ribbon of water cutting the forest in half.

Our scout air-skimmers reported that Bromin's transport

ship was sneaking through the lowlands. We didn't know if Bromin was on board, but all that really mattered was getting Gad off it.

The transport ship was covered in metal armor and drifted slowly through the trees. Long, sharp noses of mounted guns and cannons poked out like a prickly porcupine. It never heard the approach of our stealth ship which was hidden along a hill not far ahead. Hend, Senra, Drenth and I buckled on our skywings and hid in the trees like winged monkeys. Bromin couldn't possibly expect an attack by skywings.

Everyone was waiting for my signal. Months ago I had been a kid caring for an ailing grandmother. Now I was directing a small army. My hands shook. One mistake could cost lives, including Gad's. I fidgeted with my leather vest and the skywing straps, then wiped sweat off my palms.

The late afternoon forest light was working to hide us in the shadows. The prow of Bromin's transport ship edged into view around a clump of trees. I could hear the men whispering on the deck. Did they know what was about to happen?

Our ship was in place to attack if the extraction didn't work. Raising my hand, I prepared to give the signal to go. The minute my hand dropped, the team flew out of tree cover and onto the deck. I glided over and landed as Hend and Drenth knocked out the three deckhands. I pulled a cord and the wings collapsed snuggly against my back, then helped tuck the fallen soldiers behind a dinghy.

Senra led us through a small door and down a steep staircase.

"Stop," a soldier said as he came out of a room at the bottom of the stairs. Senra leapt, knocking him to the ground and covering his face with a Renfor soaked cloth. She stood and smirked at us.

Another soldier opened a door, his gun drawn. Drenth yanked him out by his arm and knocked the butt of a weapon on the man's head. He crumpled. We dragged them back into the rooms they came from. I strained to hear any evidence of more soldiers.

"The containment cells would be this way," Senra whispered. We snuck to the the end of the passage. I held my breath as Senra tested the door, and pulled it slowly open. I slipped through into the dark. Seconds felt like hours as I tiptoed to the metal bar cell in the corner. My breath stopped. It was empty.

A white cloth, marked with words caught my eye. I picked it up and pulled each side to make it taut enough to read.

'Nice try, my Copper Rose. Maybe next time. Bromin'

A swell of fear rose up in me. Gad wasn't here. Gad was never here. I dashed out of the room. "Quick. Get out." I jabbed my hand back the way we had come. My chest tightened, but I kept my breathing even. How could I have fallen for a trap?

The deck was still empty. I breathed a sigh of relief. Drenth and Senra opened their skywings and leapt off the ship rail. Hend turned to me, then took my hand to help me up. He jumped and looked back. His eyes widened as a yellow laser bolt seared through his chest. The skywings crumpled and he plummeted to the ground.

Chapter 25

Adrenaline raced through me. I jumped, but was yanked back. Hanging half off the rail, I flailed against the strong grip around my ankle. I kicked and tried to get a firm hold to get myself free to no avail.

Suddenly a hand reached out to grab my shirt front. The locket chain bit into my neck. I was pulled up and straight into Bromin's sneering face.

"Look what I caught! A little bird that needs her wings clipped," he said in a dangerous sing-song voice.

My eyes bulged and mind raced. This was *not* happening. I wasn't going to get free of his mechanical grip, but that didn't mean there was no way out. I wrapped my free hand around his neck and pulled him with me as I fell backwards over the rail. His soldiers were yelling, but we were falling fast.

Bromin didn't loosen his grip on my collar or the locket hidden beneath. I released his neck hoping he would let go, but had to pull the lever on the skywings to slow our fall. We collided into the ground, less than gently. Somehow, with that parasite attached, I managed to pull us into a roll by snapping the wings shut against my back. The forest floor was littered with dry leaves and a thick loam that softened the painful landing.

"Let go of me you rust bucket," I squealed as I tried to push him off me. His hand didn't give even a little. Even my vest was caught in his death grip keeping me from pulling away.

Bromin grunted and held tight. "Nice trick. They will be down here to retrieve us soon. You are not escaping from me again my little GearMaker. You left a task unfinished when you rudely excused yourself from my palace." His voice was a growl as he pushed his face close to mine. "Rumor is your nasty GearMade creature wasn't destroyed in that convenient explosion. What did happen to it?"

I gulped, sweat forming on my lip. How did he know?

He dragged me to my feet and started pulling in the direction the ship had gone. I dug my feet into the soil and pushed at his hands. "I—am—not—going—back." I pummeled his chest. Bromin slapped me across the face, stunning me into stillness. I rubbed my jaw as the sting subsided into an ache and my vision cleared.

"You are mine, GearMaker brat. You have eluded me long enough. I never expected such a fight from a whelp like you. Why resist me?" He shifted his grip on my shirt and looked at the fabric in his hand feeling the lump inside.

Not the locket! I had to distract him. "I'm supposed to serve a crazy machine that doesn't even know it isn't supposed to be alive?"

He ignored me and fingered the fabric till the locket popped out of my shirt. Bromin grabbed the chain so quickly I didn't have a chance to stop him.

"What could this be?" Bromin crooned pulling the locket, and my neck, close. "It looks...? I thought it only a bauble, a ladies ornament, yet now it sings it's own song like living gears.

291

So intelligent..." He looked up. Sparks flared inside his glass eyes. "I can hear the gears dancing to the beat of your heart."

He flipped it open.

"No." I pulled away, but not in time. Everything darkened and seemed to spin. My stomach heaved as the whirling grew chaotic. Where would it take us? The clacking pounded in my head. There was something tugging at my neck, tugging, tugging... biting the flesh. I kept spinning.

We dropped into bright daylight and down—wooden stairs? Tumbling into a heap on a stone walkway. I looked up. Could it really be Gramma's farm house steps? The familiar tree canopy shaded us. Bromin and my limbs were tangled up, but he had let go of the locket. I scooted quickly away from him into the grass. He rose slowly. I jumped to my feet and looked around. I didn't know when it was. Nothing seemed to have changed other than the amount of weeds and the length of the grass. Hadn't I been gone months? Wait...

"Where am I?" Bromin said much like I had when I landed in his world. He was looking around like he was dizzy. His legs wobbled nearly sending him to the ground. He stared at the soil confused. "What is this pl...?" He fell to his hands and knees.

Bromin looked straight at me, the sparks in his eyes flickering and fading. "Where is this—zz—z? The buildingz zzzo —so—sszzzmall. No hummm of machinezzz." His voice faltered like a dying computer. "Mmmetal? I demand y-y-y-you tell me where we arrrr."

The repercussions of the entire situation raced through my brain. The life seemed to be leaving Bromin. A GearMade couldn't survive on earth! All I had to do was stand there and watch him quit working like an old car puttering to a final stop. But what about Gad? With Bromin gone, maybe I could save him. I could live with my family in TreeCountry.

"Listen to me, Locket," I whispered, pulling it to my face. "We have to go back." Breathing to match the rhythm of the gears, my heart followed suit.

I put one finger on the lid, and flipped it open. Swirling darkness surrounded me. The clicking of the gears swelled louder, louder, louder. Elation ran through me. For once the locket did what I wanted.

Bromin stumbled at me and grabbed me around the neck. I was thrown backwards into the darkness, spinning—spinning—gasping, struggling for air.

The whirling darkness, twirling, clacking pounded in my senses then light filled the air around me. Bromin and I fell to the forest floor. I leaned over grabbing my neck, cool, fresh air filling my lungs. Bromin seemed to breathe in deeply, the lights growing stronger in his eyes as he looked up at me. The corner of his mouth raised into a smile.

And I ran. My arms pumped and legs burned with the strain. Glancing back, I saw Bromin push himself up from the ground and the light flared in his eyes.

I kept running till the sweat was running races down my back. I reached for the pack on my back and flipped the little lever on the side. The skywings slipped out gracefully. I grabbed onto the hand holds on the arm bone of the wings and they lifted me into the air, but my thoughts weighed down my mind.

I took the opportunity to look behind me again. There were

trees, endless trees. After another hour of rapid travel I latched onto a tree trunk and dropped to the thick branch exhausted. Leaves rustled around me as twilight covered the forest. Continuing in darkness would be too risky so I strapped myself to the trunk and pulled my knees up to my chest. Bromin could be anywhere, especially if his crew of soldiers found him. Hope's Wings was out there, but how would they find me?

I hung my head, sweat filling my eyes. Wiping it away, I found tears trickling.

What a maiden voyage! I'd fallen for faulty information. I should have never been put in command. Hend was dead. Dead—never coming back... This was my fault. There, on an uncomfortable tree branch in the dark, I knew I was done commanding. How did I ever end up in the chaos of such a scary world? I would never lead any GearMakers to their deaths again.

Who was I kidding trying to rescue my brother? Unless I could get Bromin back to earth and keep him there, I was fighting a villain with no weaknesses. I, a lowly college drop out? I didn't know anything about Seranova. It all seemed like a power struggle between the creators and a creation run amuck, but what was it really? Completely wrapped up in my sorrow about Gad, I'd ignored the greater implications of my actions and choices.

I fingered the locket, seriously considering what I should do. Maybe it would take me back to the farm house again. I would be able to leave that tree for a soft bed. Bromin would never be able to find me and would die if he tried to follow.

But I had my father. I needed to at least get back to TreeCountry so I could take him with me. That meant giving up

294

on Gad. It meant abandoning Alum—and Kricky. I was a coward, a weakling planning to run away. Calming myself I tried to hear the clicking of the gears, but the wind was growing stronger, blocking out small sounds.

"Take me to Dad. Take me to Dad."

I flipped the top and stared at the gears moving slowly in their casing. I might have to walk the length of Seranova to get to him. Then I could try every day until the locket obeyed and took us to Earth.

I slipped into a fitful sleep. Eery noises filtered into my restless dreams. Nightmares danced through my brain. Hend kept falling—falling, the life draining from him—just out of my reach. Electricity sparked down his body as he turned into Alum, who became Gad, then my father. The locket clacked and I was being pulled, pulled, pulled away from them, away...

A flash of light filtered through my closed eyes. The buzz of a ship echoing through the forest brought me fully awake. A search light swung toward me again. I cringed as it went past. Who was searching the wood? I couldn't risk Bromin finding me. The ship buzz came closer and the search light swayed my direction again. Hope's Wings wouldn't be so loud.

The ship silhouette approached, lingering above the trees. They were headed right at me. A full gust of air wafted across my skin, blowing my hair into my face. The leaves rustled and a branch near the ship cracked. The spot light jerked over to the falling limb.

If they kept going they would find me perched near the top of a tree like a bird.

Another strong wind swept by. My ears swelled with the

creak and shoosh of branches bending. I had to hide. There was only one option. I unstrapped myself from the tree, shook my cold hands and pulled open the wings. Leaning off the branch, I fell toward the next one veering into the gap between the trees. The ship loomed closer and closer, the spotlight dashing near me again. A gust pulled me back toward the tree. I yanked down on a wing and went into a stomach lurching dive. When the ground appeared a few yards away, I threw the skywings open to full wingspan and landed softly on my feet.

The buzz of the ship motors came closer. Limbs tingling, I pulled the wings closed and pressed against the tree, willing myself to vanish from sight. I wiped my hands on my breeches then grabbed the locket feeling the warmth coming from it. The ship slowly passed over me, the light never reaching into the deep shadow of the tree. The spotlight traveled back and forth through the trees further into the woods. I couldn't stay there. The ship might return. Scanning the forest, I found a silvery thread of a trail not far away. Leaves swirled down with the next gust of wind.

Pulling the leather coat around me, I shoved through the brush. My breath hissed in as thorns ripped at my legs, but I continued until I reached the path. I dashed down the trail.

The yellow moon was a sliver of light reaching for the forest floor. The waving branches cast shadows over the path. Something dark crossed by my feet and I fell. Thorns dug into my skin, tangling me in their grip. The creature leapt heavily on top of me.

"Get off." I shoved the creature away, and it squeaked, hopping over the bush.

Hands grabbed onto my arms, pulling me upward. "Let go

of me." I struggled. Getting one arm free, I hit at the man.

"Stop struggling." He pulled me upward again with a jerk that pulled the thorns across my skin and I yelped.

Once both my feet were on steady ground, I shoved at him. The creature jumped toward me and I stopped. It waggled big ears as it tilted it's head and squeaked.

"Kricky?" It was none other than my little living machine. "What are you doing here?" Kricky jumped into my arms. I looked at him, then at the man who had backed into the shadow of a windswept tree.

"Copper Rose." The man gasped as if out of breath. "I found you."

"Alum?" I gaped. Kricky jumped to the ground and over to Alum. "What are you—How did you—Alum." Was this another trap? I wanted to rush to him, but stepped back.

Kricky was doing excited laps around him.

"Copper Rose. It's safe. Bromin cannot follow me anymore." Alum stepped into the wane moonlight, pulling up the sleeve on his left arm. Dark scabs trailed across his skin like a bloody web, disfiguring the left side of his body and face. My jaw dropped and with a hand to my mouth, my heart skipped a beat.

Alum took another cautious step toward me. "Bromin messed up. He was so angry he continued to electra... He didn't realize when it failed. I was able to deactivate it for good." He pulled his sleeve down. "I couldn't stay there anymore. I couldn't ignore what was going on—or stay away—from you."

Kricky stopped, swiveling his huge ears. I scanned the

forest for the ship, but only saw the forest swaying with the extreme wind.

I stepped down the trail, eyes narrowed at Alum. "How did Kricky end up with you?"

A smile split his face. "He found me and we barely managed to escape from the palace before the shielding was active again."

"Did you actually deactivate the tracker?" I glared at him.

He shook his head. "Yes."

"Then how did Bromin's ship figure out I was in this part of the forest?"

Alum's jaw dropped and his eyes spread wide. "I was only following Kricky. The little beast seemed to think... He told me you would be here." He looked behind himself. "That ship is Bromin's? He's here?"

I fixed the GearMade creature with an assessing look. Could all this be true? Kricky would have needed to travel fast to get to Alum. Then they both had to travel to Twig Wood. How could Kricky know? How could he go so fast?

"We have to get you out of here, Copper Rose," Alum said, walking over to me.

I backed away.

He threw out his arms. "Copper, I am not going to betray you. Please. We have to find a place to hide."

Kricky sat in front of me and chittered. He wanted me to trust Alum. Could it be that simple? How could Kricky know who I should trust?

"Fine." I walked away from him with Kricky by my side. I glanced down at the beast and he seemed to grin at me. I grinned back. I had missed his constant presence.

Kricky looked behind us. "Screeeki chrip, chrip."

Alum came up behind me and I went faster. My mind was roiling. Instead of being overjoyed to see Alum, I was afraid. We'd grown close in the palace. I knew he served Bromin unwillingly, but there was always the possibility that Bromin would find him. I looked over my shoulder. The skin across his left cheek puckered from his soft smile.

Whirrrrrrr...

The shape of the ship appeared in the distance, quickly approaching. I shook my head and pushed myself faster along the trail. "We need to find—someplace to hide. If we could only find my ship..."

Kricky ran into a cluster of trees and started jabbering away. He poked his head back through the brush and vanished again.

"I think—I think he wants us to follow," I said, watching the spotlight veer our direction. Taking a deep breath I pushed into the brush. I stumbled when there was no resistance. Kricky appeared and led us into the copse of evergreens. The plants hugged a pile of large boulders. Kricky's eyes sparkled in the deep shadows. He dashed between two rocks to an overhang of stone.

"Perfect," Alum said and squeezed through the gap.

The wind swept through the trees, carrying the sound of the ship nearby. The spotlight appeared. I put my hand on the cool rock and shimmied between the smaller boulders. Other than Kricky's eyes the cave under the largest stone was dark. Alum moved at the back.

"Over here. The ceiling gets lower, but there is a nice spot back here where we can hide," he said.

I ran my hand along the stone ceiling, ducking as it got closer. Alum touched my knee. I kneeled and scooted until a rock wall hit my hand. "The ship is right above us. The light doesn't seem to reach inside the trees, but…"

Alum's moist breath blew across my cheek causing me to shiver.

He groaned. "But if they know we're here they might send troops to search the ground."

I leaned against the rock. "They never saw me." Cold seeped into my flesh and I started to shake. I pulled off the skywings, placing them to the side, then shoved my hands into the coat pockets. My stomach spasmed with hunger pains. My teeth chattered and I clamped down my jaw. It was too cold. Hunched against my knees in the dark, I ran through the events of the day. So much had happened. If we didn't find Hope's Wings we would have to get all the way to TreeCountry alone. I wanted to trust Alum. I wanted to believe Bromin couldn't track him. I wanted…

Warm arms wrapped around me. "Come here." Alum pulled me against his side.

I grunted and shifted closer to him. The shivering eased, but my heart raced. The tangy metallic smell of Alum dominated my senses. His warm breath swept over my scalp as he tucked my head under his chin. He seemed to relax as I adjusted my position so that I fit right under his arm.

"Alum… You don't need to…"

"Shhhh." He shook his head. "I only want to keep you safe.

Warmth is the least I can provide."

I sighed, cold still nipping at my feet. My eyes felt heavy. Pulling my feet under me, I gave up. I fell asleep with my head against Alum's chest.

***

"Shekriky."

Something heavy was pressing against my leg. I stirred, opening my eyes. Kricky looked from me to the opening in the rocks. Sunlight brushed the stone and the trees outside were still.

I looked at Alum, his face so peaceful in sleep. I gently caressed his injured cheek. The marred skin was hot to the touch. My throat constricted. What had he done to destroy the implant? I put my hand on his forehead. It was only warm.

"Alum?" I pulled his arm off my shoulder and stiffly walked to the opening. Birds flitted from branch to branch in the warm sunlight. "Alum? Wake up." I looked back at him. His silver eyes sparkled in the defused light.

"Is it...?" He rubbed his face then reached over to my skywings. Pulling them with him, Alum crawled towards the entrance. He stood once the stone ceiling was tall enough. He rubbed his shoulders with one hand then held up the wings, examining them. "They're so light and this fabric..." The chameleon surface had changed from the grey of stone to hold hints of green from the moss on the rocks.

"The fabric is treated to mimic whatever is near it."

"You did this?"

"Yes." I took the skywings from him. Holding them over my

head, I shimmied my way out of the stone shelter. "Hopefully Bromin has moved on." I sighed as Alum squeezed his way out of the rocks.

He put a hand on my shoulder and I looked up at him. "I found you. I thought I would never—see you again." He rubbed my cheek with his palm like I had done while he slept.

I leaned into his hand and closed my eyes. "I missed you, too."

"Skrittice. Squeey, Krick."

Kricky bounded back to us through the trees. He jumped up and down looking into the sky.

"Not Bromin," I mumbled and followed Kricky through the brush back to the trail. Kricky dashed down the path squeaking franticly. He believed we would be safe, but I slowed down and stopped on the edge of the clearing he was speeding through.

Alum came up behind me, gasping. "There's a ship. It's headed right for us."

I turned my head listening. There was only the sound of birds singing.

Alum took my hand and tugged. "We might be able to get back to the rocks. Please."

I cupped a hand around my ear straining to hear anything unusual. "Quiet. Do you hear anything?"

A shadow appeared in the clearing. Kricky was running in circles under it. The long sliver of a ship rose over the trees.

Chapter 26

Alum backed down the trail, tugging me with him. "No. No. I won't go back." His wide eyes darted, searching the sky.

"There." An airman was leaning over the prow pointing. Wings flared out from the sides of the ship and it sank closer. "Look near the trees!"

"What kind of ship is that?" Alum exclaimed.

I grinned at him. "That is Hope's Wings, a stealth ship."

He looked down on me, head tilted. "Stealth? It's so big— and there isn't a dirigible."

"Its the biggest Iridium frame ship ever." I stepped into the meadow still watching Alum's look of surprise. "This is our ride home."

His face went blank, but he took one step forward.

Activity erupted onboard. Alum stayed in the cover trees, staring wide eyed. The wounds across the side of his face stood out as dark lines against his pale skin. A air-skimmer descended quietly to the grassy meadow.

Venrick appeared at the rail, a broad smile splitting his normally serious features. "Captain Locke! You cannot imagine our relief. We'll have you back on board in minutes."

The air-skimmer stopped, hovering a foot from the ground, Kricky leapt in. The young pilot stared, his mouth slightly open. I grabbed Alum's hand, pulling him from the forest shadows to the air-skimmer.

"He called you captain," Alum said as he followed.

Dew soaked my pant hems chilling me, but I didn't care. I hoisted the skywings tighter under my arm and hurried forward, dragging the reluctant Alum behind me.

"Uh... Yes. I'm technically the captain." The image of Hend falling from the sky passed through my mind and I cringed. "But that was a mistake. I plan to... We need to get home."

The young man scrutinized Alum. "Who...?"

I climbed in. "This is Alum. He's a GearMaker."

Alum sat opposite me, his brow wrinkling as the pilot navigated up to the ship. The pilot watched Kricky who stood like a figurehead at the prow of the little boat. As the air-skimmer landed back on deck Kricky jumped off, landing with a thud.

"What is that?" the young man asked.

I looked at him, uncertain what to say. If he didn't know maybe I shouldn't tell him, but we would all be stuck on the ship together and lying wouldn't help. "It's—he's a one of a kind creature."

The youth shook his head. "That's for sure."

Suddenly two of the airmen, who worked as soldiers as well, pulled Alum from the air-skimmer.

I crawled out, stumbling in my haste. "Let go of him." I pushed one of them away from Alum and stood in front of him, glaring at the two men as they stepped back, hands on strange guns holstered on their hips. Daggers drawn, three other soldiers hurried over. I knew the tallest of the men as

Teran. He was a good squad leader, but rather suspicious.

Teran held his hands up and edged closer, eyeing Alum. "Captain. It's our responsibility to restrain prisoners. It's for your safety."

"This man isn't the enemy." I knew it was true. I looked over my shoulder at Alum. His surprised expression warmed me.

"Back off, all of you." I stepped back until I bumped into Alum. They all stepped back, relaxing slightly.

Another soldier came running over holding Kricky by the leg, struggling to maintain his grip.

I shook my head, teeth clenched. "Let Kricky go before you get hurt."

The GearMade beast squealed and thrashed. He sank his sharp metal teeth into the soldier's hand, and fell to the ground. He landed on his feet like a cat. The soldier yelled out, grasping his bleeding limb. Kricky swatted the man's leg then dashed over to me. He stood in front of us, legs apart and head turning back and forth as he emitted harsh hissing and growling sounds. I stepped around the irritated beast towards the bleeding man, but Teran pointed his lightning gun at Kricky and I froze. The other men followed his example.

Venrick and Drenth ran over.

"Teran, why are your soldiers pointing weapons at the Captain?" Venrick's voice was low and threatening.

"Sir." Teran pointed. "That creature. It attacked. We were commanded to protect Copper Rose. "

I put my fists on my hips and leaned forward. "Why would I bring them aboard if they were going to hurt me? What kind of soldiers are you?" Alum's hands covered my shoulders and he pulled me back against him. I breathed in deeply, to quell the anger.

Venrick stepped between the soldiers and me. "Since when is a captain's word not good enough?"

Teran's face went red. "The council directed my squad to keep her safe."

"She is still the captain." Venrick's voice was nearly a growl.

Teran stood, shoulders squared. "I was told that was just an honorary title, but that *you* were actually the…"

Venrick crossed his arms speaking with a voice like silk. "And who told you this?"

Teran looked down momentarily. "Kilain."

My heart dropped into my stomach like a hot coal. Would that man never stop plaguing me? Hope's Wings was only set to take a test cruise, but it was made to sneak into enemy territory. Why make me the captain in the first place?

"I will allow myself to be restrained if it will calm everyone," Alum said.

I turned around. "No. You haven't done anything wrong."

He touched my shoulders again and whispered. "I have spent my whole life with their enemy. Their reactions are what I would expect. I don't want to leave everyone feeling worried about me."

Venrick held up his hands again. "Alright. Everyone back up."

"Alum is not going to hurt anyone." I looked down at Kricky and shrugged. "Well, Kricky will, but only if they attempt to cage him up. Can we get this man some bandages?" I took a step toward the hurt soldier again.

Kricky chirped, then hissed. The soldier glared at him, still holding his hand, though the bleeding seemed to have slowed.

I patted Kricky. "Don't bite people. These are friends."

He sat and started preening himself. The soldiers all stepped back, this time putting away their weapons.

Venrick nodded. "Teran, take your men and secure the ship —from anyone not on the ship already. Drenth would you take Fath to the healer to tend to that bite and..." He looked at Alum his eyes narrowed. "And bring the healer back when she's done."

Drenth led the injured soldier down the stairs to the living quarters. Teran led his men away, leaving me and Alum alone with Venrick. Senra was leaning against the far rail, her expression disapproving. She noticed me watching her and pressed her lips into a line before she too walked away.

Venrick turned to us. "Captain. We're happy to have you back. Do you mind introducing me to our guest?"

Alum put out his hand. "I'm Alum."

Venrick shook his hand and nodded. "I see."

"I am willing to confine myself to a room if it would keep the peace on board."

"That won't be necessary." Venrick looked at me. "Can I assume that your creature won't do anyone else any harm?"

I sighed. "Kricky does what he wants." We all looked over at the creature as he sniffed his way along the deck, his ears turning at each sound.

The healer hurried over to us, a bag on her arm. She was a husky woman with her hair pulled up into a tight bun. "Drenth said I was needed? Oh young man! Those injuries... They appear to be getting infected."

"Would you please treat him right away?" Venrick asked.

"Of course, but..." She glanced at Kricky. "Fath has a strange set of punctures. He claims it was a bite."

Venrick put a hand on the lady's shoulder. "I'm fully aware of the situation and everything is calm now. If you would please help Alum..."

The woman looked Alum up and down, gasping. "Oh my, yes. What happened to you young man? Where can I take him?"

I pointed at the Captain's room. "Use my room." I cringed inside. How bad might the injuries be if the healer was shocked by the tangle of wounds?

"Rose?" Alum frowned.

"We'll talk later." I reached out to his left arm, but stopped. "Please go get help with those... With what happened to you."

We watched them enter the room and close the door.

Venrick cleared his throat. "Captain Locke, what are your orders?"

I shook my head. "No, Venrick. I'm giving up my position as captain. You're in charge for the trip back to TreeCountry. I..."

He leaned close, a hand on my shoulder. "You are the captain."

"You're wrong. It's my fault Hend is dead. Please take me home."

Venrick scowled, shaking his head. "I'll get you home, but this is your ship—One day you'll be ready to really lead." He walked to the bow of the ship, calling out orders. People hurried by, expressing relief that I was there, though everyone gave Kricky a wide berth.

The ship lifted above the trees as silently as a breeze. The side wings flared open and the ship sped forward toward home.

Walking to the opposite rail, realities sank into my mind. Venrick was not accepting my resignation as captain and Senra still didn't like me. Did she blame me for the trap—for Hend's death? I slammed a fist into the rail then rubbed the stinging skin. "It was my fault," I mumbled. My insides were a turmoil of feelings. Saving Gad seemed more hopeless than before.

Venrick came up next to me, looking out at the landscape speeding by. "We should be back to TreeCountry in two days, but we have to restrict transmitter communication in case the enemy ship is still close enough to overhear us. What happened yesterday?"

"Bromin happened. Always Bromin." I ran my finger along the wood grain. Two days. Two days until I returned to Dad—Two days to the council. If Kilain didn't banish me, the council might never let me leave TreeCountry again. Who would save Gad? "I made a complete mess of things. Please take over command of the ship."

"You need to understand the nature of leadership, Rose." He tapped the rail with his fingers. "You may like to hide behind your creations, but you have every skill for command. Everyone makes mistakes…"

"Mistakes that take lives?"

He tilted his head closer. "Yes. Mistakes that take lives."

I grunted.

"Who is the young man?"

My lips tightened. How much should I tell?

"And the creature?"

309

My throat constricted.

Venrick watched me, brow raised. "There was a rumor in TreeCountry of a GearMade creature. That beast is a living machine, isn't it."

I nodded.

"And Alum? I'm at a loss to guess."

Sighing, I turned around and leaned my back against the rail. I crossed my arms. "He has been Bromin's prisoner for nearly fifteen years."

Venrick gasped. "A GearMaker under Bromin's control for that long? Can he be trusted?"

I closed my eyes. "I believe so." I had two days to figure out how safe Alum was. If Bromin could still track him, he would notice how fast we were now traveling and follow. If not then Alum was actually free. I bounced on my toes. "Please take command Venrick. You really are better suited."

He grinned, shaking his head. "No, Captain." He patted my shoulder and walked back to the controls near the bow.

The healer exited my room and came over to me. "I sedated him. I don't know what happened to that poor young man, but it's a wonder his fever isn't worse."

My hand flew up to my mouth. Was it that bad? "Will he heal?" I bit my lip and took a step toward my room.

"He should—but the scarring may be extensive. Sleep will help him fight the infection that is setting in. I also gave him an immune booster." She smiled grimly and left. I turned back to the landscape. I'd only seen Alum's face and arm, but according to him the implant had spread across his entire left side. I buried my face in my hands, fatigue washing over me.

"You will be the death of us all," Senra said.

I turned on her. "You don't know what you're talking about."

"I heard. That man. He belongs to Bromin and Bromin wants you both."

I took a deep breath. "Senra. I…"

"Gad is the only good one among you, and he's dead just like Hend."

I gasped. "He can't be dead. I would save him—if…" I shook my head, pushing past her to the captain's room.

Alum lay on the bed in the attached sleeping chamber. The curtain nearly blocked him from view. But he was still asleep, his face flushed and sweaty. He had acted like he was fine while fighting the growing infection. Groaning, I stumbled to the table and sank into a chair. I bowed my head against my hands and let go, allowing the tears to flow.

Would the sorrow never end? I wiped my nose and buried my face in my palms as the tears ran. Senra was right. Bromin wouldn't stop until he captured me. I couldn't hide and hope he gave up. My body shook with quiet sobs until, weary, I slipped into sleep.

My next awareness was of a hand on my shoulder. There was comfort in the pressure. I looked up through raw eyes.

Alum stood over me. The angry red lines across his cheek and around his eye were coated in a shiny ointment, but his skin was less flushed. He traced a finger down the side of my cheek. "You miss Gad?"

I nodded.

"I know you still don't trust me completely—but I can

311

help."

Sitting up, I turned to face him. "How?"

"The CliffSide Fortress..." He sat in a chair and leaned toward me. "About eight years ago I helped build the prison cells. We needed to create air flow. Tunnels were drilled to the back of the rock. They are big enough for a person to walk through. If we prepare right we can get him out through those ventilation tunnels."

I sat up straight, holding my breath. Hope? Could we make this happen?

Alum picked up a pencil then rummaged through the maps on the table. He found a blank page and began drawing. "Here along the back is an opening big enough for someone to enter." He crisscrossed more lines along the drawing. They connected and combined as the map grew. Tapping the page, he continued. "Right here are the cells. We have to travel up two levels. The tunnels are tight, but we might be able to get in and out without anyone knowing."

I rubbed my eyes and shifted in my seat.

"What about early warning systems?" a voice from behind me said.

Drenth was standing in the doorway with Senra close behind. He walked over and sat, leaving Senra by the door. "I said, what about any early warning systems—or shielding?"

Alum pushed the map over to him. "There are electric shields blocking the ventilation from the halls. Like the dome at the palace, air can pass through even though physical bodies cannot, but I know where and how to counteract the defenses."

"Why would we trust you?" Senra took a few steps into the

312

room, tension radiating from her.

Alum stood up. "You don't have any reason to trust me, but I am telling the truth."

They stared at each other, tension filling the room. Drenth looked up from his scrutiny of the map. I was about to stand up when Senra scoffed.

"You've got to be kidding." She walked over to the table. "The four of us are going to sneak into a secret fortress and snatch a full grown man out of it? It's called a fortress for a reason."

Drenth pushed the map over to her. "There are plenty aboard who have the skills to join the extraction team."

She leaned her palms on the edge of the table and glared back and forth between me and Drenth. "You know this is a trap, right?" She narrowed her gaze on Alum. "You still work for that monster. Don't play at being trustworthy. I know what you are."

Alum looked at Senra with pursed lips. "I will never betray Copper Rose. I do this for her. Not Bromin."

I stood slowly. "We would appreciate your help."

She stepped back, rubbing a hand through her short hair. "Humph." Senra turned and walked out.

Silence blanketed the room. I sat down, staring at the map of CliffSide Fortress. Gad was there. I knew it. Bromin kept taking everything that was mine. That had to stop. "What do we need to do?"

Drenth pushed his chair back. "First of all I'm going to tell Venrick to turn this ship around!"

***

The next day I was sitting on a cot set up for me by the curved windows so Alum could use the sleeping room while he healed. I was mending a small tear in my stealth skywings. The team gathered around the table while Drenth went over the plans and Alum tinkered with a pile of wires and metal parts. Two additional soldiers had volunteered to help us.

Xiren was staring at the map of tunnels in the Fortress. "We have to remain undetected for hours?"

Pak, a stocky middle aged man, was standing over Xiren. "'Course kid." His gravelly voice seemed to vibrate the air. He looked at Alum, eyes thin. "Got a plan for that?"

Alum's eyebrow raised. The still red lines of scabbing puckered the left side of his face making him look menacing. He grabbed a pod with a flat side and held it up. "Electrical Shield disrupter." He put it down and picked up a small ball on a clip. "Personal body signal dampeners. And the one I've been working on is going to be infused with Copper Rose's blood code like a thither to help us track the exact location of Gad." Alum continued looking at Pak, his expression relaxed and blank of emotion. I leaned forward, my interest piqued.

Pak burst out laughing. "Very good young man. Very good. I think we are in for a dandy of an infiltration, young Xiren. This will be a good one."

I smothered a grin. The skill to create such machines was learned at great cost, but maybe Alum could win over his own people. Only one person was still against our plans. I sighed, setting the skywings down on the cot. The men talked about how to save Gad, though with less tension.

I pulled the door open to go out.

314

"Rose?" Alum was on the edge of the seat, ready to follow.

I waved him back down. "I'm fine. I need some fresh air."

He relaxed and went back to his machine, still glancing at me as I slowly left. A shiver ran up my spine. I lingered, part of me wishing he would follow. But that wouldn't help me get through to Senra. My intentions could only be carried out alone.

Chapter 27

Hands shaking slightly, I scanned the deck. Near the prow, Senra was sitting on a crate. Next to her, Kricky was curled up in the sun like a cat. She was scratching his head while he crooned.

I walked up behind her. "He loves that."

Senra pulled her hand away and stiffened. Kricky squawked. He swatted at her hand and she reached down to scratch his head again. She glared at me over her shoulder.

I sighed and sat on a crate beside Kricky. "Senra, I wish I knew how to earn your trust."

"You can't," she snapped. "If there wasn't a ban on communications I would be at the transmitter telling my uncle what's going on here."

Fidgeting with my vest, I tried to keep my voice calm. "Tenze would accept what we're doing."

"I'm talking about my other uncle, Kilain." She looked right at me, her lips pressed tight.

I gulped. Would she really do that? Kricky grunted, pulling both of us from our staring match. He rolled on his back and stretched. Senra chuckled and started scratching his exposed belly. I watched his movements, amazed that he had ever been a chunk of lifeless metal.

Why couldn't I get through to Senra? The men told me she was always willing to take on the impossible missions, yet something was stopping her this time.

"What are you looking at me for?"

I shrugged. "I want to understand you."

"What do you mean?" she said softly.

"When we first met you were willing to defy the council, but you thought Gad deserves to be Bromin's prisoner." I leaned down and started scratching Kricky's ears. "Now you want to report our actions. You claim Gad is dead, and you say he's a good person. I'm honestly not sure what you're actually thinking."

Senra grunted and focused on Kricky. "It isn't relevant if your brother is a scoundrel or not. He causes Bromin too many problems. Bromin wants GearMaker's who can create machines, not chaos. Gad's been a rod in his cogs since long before you came here." She shook her head. "There's no way he is keeping Gad alive after this long."

I paused, dropping my chin to my chest. Was Gad dead—like Hend? Was she upset about losing Hend? Maybe he was more than a fellow soldier to her. She might be blaming me for what happened. I looked out at the clouds, mulling over my thoughts.

"Would you be willing to do something for me?" I asked.

Senra stopped scratching Kricky's belly and turned her head slowly to look at me. "What would that be?"

"While we're gone will you take care of Kricky? He'll need to be locked up." I tapped Kricky on the head and he chirped then rolled over, nudging Senra's hand expectantly. "I don't want Bromin to capture him."

She put a hand to her chest. "You want me to look after him?"

"If you would."

"Yes. I'll do that much." She went back to giving Kricky attention.

The door of the captain's room opened and the men exited, laughing. Senra shook her head. I knew Senra had served with and trusted some of them for years, but nothing was changing her mind about the mission. I had to accept that.

Alum walked toward me, but Venrick stopped him. Both of them kept looking at me as they talked, their expressions serious. Alum took a strange copper tube from Venrick and held it down at his side. Drenth and Pak joined them. Several voices grew louder and Drenth was gesturing broadly. But I still couldn't hear.

"Captain Locke?" Venrick called out.

I jogged over to them. "What do you need?"

Venrick held out another of the strange, bulbous rods. It had a curved handle with a button, like a trigger pull. "It's a lightning gun—for you to use."

My heart dropped into my stomach. "A gun?"

Alum shook his head.

I stepped back, shaking my head. "I don't know how to fire a gun."

He held it out to me. "You pop in the charge and then fire. Pak can teach you how to use it."

"Uh." I pulled my hands away. "I—I don't want a gun."

Drenth took it from Venrick, and popped out the charge. He

smiled warmly, handing it toward me. "It's really easy to use. We can take an hour on the ground to teach you. It'll be fun and it's a useful skill you need to know."

I took the weapon and turned it over in my hands, examining the mechanics. The round chambers on the tube went from small to the size of a baseball where they reached the base. It was a completely unique design from anything I'd seen so far. "You don't understand. I create. I don't destroy." I had never used a weapon in my life. I wasn't about to try now on the eve of infiltrating a fortress. And I didn't want to be responsible for any more deaths.

I handed it to Venrick, but Pak took it instead.

"Everyone going on a mission this dangerous needs a weapon," Pak said, his voice harsher than usual. "You may never need to draw it, but at least you'll know how to use it if the need arises. We should stop now and give you some practice before dark."

I looked at Alum, silently pleading for help. He sighed and looked away. My breathing sped up, and my neck felt warm. Did he agree? They couldn't make me do this.

Venrick nodded as if reading my thoughts. "It is for the best —Captain."

I handed the gun back, slapping it into Pak's hand harder than intended. He winced. I looked back and forth between the men. Alum wouldn't make eye contact, his head bowed in the way I'd seen often at the palace. Venrick crossed his arms. I didn't seem to have a choice. Maybe we would be safer if I knew how to shoot the thing, but I didn't even know how they worked.

"Fine, but I need a few minutes to get my coat." I turned on my heels and strode to my room. Alum followed, but I closed the door before he got to it and started pacing the small room. I didn't want more people to die. I only wanted to get my brother home safe.

The door creaked slowly open.

"Copper?" Alum crept in, a lightning gun in the hand hanging by his side.

"Go away."

"I'm sorry." He rubbed a hand over his face. "I knew you wouldn't want to have a weapon, but you know how dangerous Bromin is."

I planted my feet, fists at my side. "So I should kill people like he does? Wouldn't that make me cruel like him? You never fought him."

Alum stepped back as if the words were a physical blow.

I went back to pacing. Lives would depend on my skill with the weapon. In only an hour I had to become far better than a reckless amateur. I stopped, deep in thought. "He gave you a lightning rod. You know how to fire it?"

He seemed to hold his breath then let it out in a gust. "I do."

I stepped toward him. "How?"

Alum pursed his lips and looked out the window, holding the lightning rod behind him. "I—I just do."

"I know so much about your life. Just tell me."

He moved the gun further from view and stared at me. Why wouldn't he tell me? There was far more to what Alum did for Bromin. Was trusting him a mistake?

"Leave me." I walked to the windows, breathing deep, desperate to remain calm.

"Please Copper Rose…"

I turned, my arms crossed. "I'll be there in a minute."

Alum nodded, his face returning to the passive, emotionless expression that had become normal for him, and he left. I felt like crumpling into a heap. Maybe Alum couldn't help his tendency to back down after a lifetime dominated by a frightening dictator. But I was on edge around him, never knowing what to expect or what I wanted. I grabbed my coat off a hook near the sleeping room and pulled it on, breathing in the comforting smell of leather.

The other members of the team were already in the long air-skimmer ready to go to the ground for a gun lesson. Hope's Wings was holding still in the air over a feeble forest of rocks and scraggly trees.

I climbed in and sat next to Venrick, determined to get this over quickly. Pak flipped a dial and the air-skimmer rose up a foot from the deck. Senra grabbed the edge, pushing it down before she leapt aboard. Kricky followed her and dashed over to me. He nuzzled under my arm and I grinned. The air-skimmer then lifted over the rail and down. I smiled at Senra, but she looked away.

Tall grey trees stood like weary sentinels. A light fog lingered near the ground like a thread-bare blanket. The overcast forest clearing looked like a painting drained of all color.

Once on the ground Pak walked to the nearby trees, stepping through the dry leaves. I tugged at the bottom of my vest while he inspected the bent spindly trunks that reached up toward the heavens. What was he looking for? There was cold sweat on my hands. I wiped them on my pants, anxious to have this over.

Pak mumbled to himself, his hands gripped behind his back. "Well. I prefer a big boulder, but one of these pathetic trees will have to do. It's damp enough to prevent a fire. Captain Locke, would you please step over here?"

Venrick handed me the lightning gun. "You'll do well. Focus and relax." He backed over to the air-skimmer, leaving me alone in the middle of the sad clearing.

I fingered the handle, cold and lifeless. The ridges bit into my palm, but I clasped it tightly. Kricky hurried over to me, sitting at my feet. Pak pointed at a tree then jogged back to me. My arm hung away from my body, the gun in my grip.

He took out his own gun. "Hold it like so." He gripped the handle, a finger resting over the brass button near the tube and lightning chambers. "You can use two hands to start, but the goal is a one-handed, quick action."

Kricky stood on his back legs. "Keric skeee."

"Does that nosy creature have to be here?" Pak snapped.

I rubbed my neck. "I can't help what he does."

"So be it." He waved dismissively and stood next to me. "Hold the rod steady. Aim at your target, then lift slightly higher."

Gripping with both hands, I focused on a weepy knot in the tree. The long barrel tipped downward and I lifted again.

"Now press the trigger firmly." Pak backed away.

Pointing slightly above the knot, I pressed. Lightning

sizzled from the smallest chamber, spreading out across the ground. Pak yelled out and danced away from the tendrils of light. The gun fell from my hands and bounced once, the lightning vanishing. Spots pocked my vision and my cheeks felt hot.

Pak was suddenly in front of me. "Aim above yer target."

"I tried to. It's too heavy in the barrel. I can't…" I slowly bent to pick it up, my knees quivering, barely holding me.

"Aim again." Pak backed away.

I let a breath out slowly. Again I steadied the gun, fighting the downward pull of the barrel. Once the tree knot was in my sight at the tip of the gun, I lifted up and squeezed the trigger. Electricity shot out like confetti strings, hitting a tree yards to the left of the target. The lightning chamber near my hand warmed up fast and it fell to the ground.

I blew on my hand. "Ouch." Blisters were forming where my hand had strayed from the handle. I growled, kicking the dirt in frustration. "I can't do this."

Kricky dashed back to the air-skimmer and stood on the prow chittering at me. I had to agree with him. This whole thing was turing into an embarrassing joke.

Pak picked up the gun, holding it between two fingers while smoke traveled up from the end. "How is it you never fired a weapon before?"

Clenching my jaw, I put my fists on my hips. "I never had a need before."

Venrick walked up, his hands in front of him. "Maybe we need a little break."

"It's the easiest weapon we have," Pak exclaimed.

I scoffed. "You call that easy? The thing is unbalanced and overheats!"

"Look, Miss Locke, I am the best trainer in all of TreeCountry. The fault here is not in the weapon."

I took a step toward him, seething. "You mean something is wrong with me?'"

Pak stared at me, his lips a white line. This was hopeless. If we ran into trouble in the fortress I would probably end up killing my own team.

Senra walked up to Pak and took the weapon from him. He scowled at her, but backed away. Venrick followed him. I relaxed my arms by my side, curiosity bubbling inside me. What was Senra planning to do?

Lifting the gun one handed, Senra fired at the tree. The bolt flared out like perfect veins of lightning, hugging the tree then vanishing once she released the trigger.

My shoulders drooped. Was she rubbing in how useless I was?

"Lightning guns aren't easy weapons. They are special. These were made specifically for true GearMaker's." She glanced over to Kricky then back at me. "You *are* a true GearMaker. The problems you perceive in the gun are actually to your advantage as you will discover." She handed the gun over to me.

I hesitated, then took it.

"Aim again, but this time think the way you do when you build the cogs and gears for a machine. Piece together the steps like the structure of a ship." She stepped back.

I wasn't sure what she meant, but instead of thinking about

how to keep the end of the barrel pointed up, I thought about how it was built. I slowed my pulse—slowed my breathing, and looked at the target with the eye of a mechanic. The locket felt warm against my chest, the barely perceptible tick of the gears slowing. "Not now," I mumbled to the locket.

How could the electrical charge get from the barrel to the knot in the tree? I lifted the gun until the arch I imagined was correct. Clarity pushed out my doubts. The shape of the trigger felt comfortable. I pressed lightly until it was stiff then I clenched my fingers over it. The buzz of the lightning filled the chambers. The charge seemed to pull from inside me, through my arm. Tendrils of blue light danced across the expanse in a single band of lightning and singed the knot. I released and the power ran back down the lightning bolt and into me. The locket's gears sped up and grew louder. Lowering the gun, I grabbed the locket with my other hand. It pulsed as if excited. I held it tightly, willing it to stay closed.

I realized people were clapping. Everyone wore satisfied smiles, even expressions of shock. Kricky was running in circles. He squealed and leaped off the air-skimmer.

Pak barked out a laugh. "I've never seen such precision in my life."

I suddenly felt cold, shaky. Where had that power come from? Kricky was staring up at me. I swayed slightly, feeling dizzy. Whatever this power was I couldn't control it. Was it coming from the locket? Or was it really something inside me?

"Prepare to fire again," Pak called out.

I stumbled toward the air-skimmer. "No." As I passed Senra, she smirked and took the gun. I nodded then lifted myself into the air-skimmer, ignoring the stricken look on

325

Alum's face.

Venrick touched my knee. "Are you alright?"

"I shot the weapon. Can we please get back to the ship and go save my brother?" My head throbbed, beating like a crescendo.

Venrick nodded. He waved the others over then sat near me. Kricky sat on my other side. I propped my head into my hand, and leaned over to get the dancing spots out of my eyes. My insides warmed as the locket continued to race.

The air-skimmer ascended like a helium balloon, lifting us back to the ship and the security of familiar surroundings. Ignoring everyone, I hurried to my room. I laid down on the cot and looked out the windows. The ship rose over the tree line, speeding forward. I stared at the clouds slipping past, hoping to ignore the tingling still tickling my gut.

I didn't want to feel that way ever again. And yet it was exhilarating. The two times that power coursed through me I felt clarity and euphoria. It was the let-down that left me shaking and queasy. The spicy smell of Alum suffused my senses, sending my heart racing again. He was standing a few feet away, his face blank.

I rubbed my face and stood up. "I didn't—I didn't hear you come in. If you need rest I can..." I walked past him.

Alum gripped my arm. "Down on the ground—what was that?"

I pulled away and grabbed my head. "I don't know. I really don't know." I tugged at my hair, then hugged my arms across my stomach. The floor seemed to sway. Alum's arms were suddenly around me, holding me up.

326

"Let me go," I said, breathing in deeply. "I'll be fine."

"Why won't you trust me?" His brows were drawn tightly together, a furrow between his eyes.

I pushed myself away, steady again. "Alum. I do trust you to help me save Gad. I can't think beyond that. I don't know what to believe about you sometimes. One minute you're a blank slate and the next you're strong and confident. Please. I'm going to go out on deck so you can rest. The healer said you still need..."

He pulled me to him, his lips meeting mine. Heat rose up my face—my neck. His breath swept across my cheek, his lips brushing ever so softly over my lips. I clutched his hair and pressed closer to him, feeling warmth spread as I kissed him back. All the fear and frustration melted—melted away. He caressed my cheek, his fingertips tickling across my skin.

"Ahem."

Panic rushed through me replacing passion like a cold waterfall. I pulled away, stumbling in my haste. "Venrick." I gasped and rubbed my flushed cheeks. My second in command was standing by the door, one eyebrow raised in surprise. Alum walked over to the table and sat down facing away from me.

Venrick glanced over to Alum then straightened his shoulders. "The scouts returned. We should be to HazeValley by morning."

Alum's head shot up, his face pale. "I'll—I'll be ready to lead you through the fog." He picked up a square metal box from the table and adjusted the dials, fumbling to keep a hold on a screwdriver.

"Thank you," I said. "Can you warn the others?"

Venrick watched us, then nodded and left. Alum put down the box and sat still. The light outside the window was fading. I touched my lips, my breathing returning to normal. I pulled the blanket from the cot and strode to the door.

"Copper, don't leave." Alum shoved his chair back and rushed after me.

I put a hand out to stop him. "No. I need—to be alone." Without looking him in the eye, I hurried out. I couldn't face the mix of emotions regarding him. Maybe after we saved Gad I could figure it out, but until then I had to focus. I couldn't imagine even being in the same room with him after that kiss. I wanted to rush back and let him hold me—keep me safe from all the fears ahead, but I couldn't.

Only the night watch and pilot were on deck settling into their evening routines. I sat on the deck out of sight from the captain's room, my back against the rail. The wind skipped over me, only ruffling my hair. The cool breeze felt good on my skin, clearing my mind. My thoughts ran through the events of the day. I pulled the blanket around my shoulders. Stars winked to life overhead, spreading their little lights across the heavens like a glittery blanket.

What was this power that reached out of me to give life to machines and deadly weapons? In all the months of living in Seranova, I had never stopped thinking of myself as an ordinary human. It would be easy to consider the locket the cause of these occurrences, but deep down I knew better. And it scared me.

"I'm a GearMaker."

The red moon hung above the horizon, the yellow moon fighting to catch up. "I am a GearMaker. Whatever that means."

What a strange world, and yet it was my home. It always had been my home.

Here my skills were not unique. Here I could learn more than I ever could on Earth. But relationships... how did one manage those. I'd never had a boyfriend or dated seriously. Now I didn't have time to even think about such things.

I pressed my cool hands over my warm cheeks. Heart hammering, I tried to force the memory of Alum's touch from my mind. I had never struggled with this attraction in the palace, but how could I when Bromin was breathing over our shoulders. Now Alum unsettled me.

"Rose?"

And there he was, his eyes sparkling in the dim light of the moons.

I pulled the blanket tighter, suppressing a shiver. "Please leave me be."

"Come back in the cabin." He leaned closer. "I can find other quarters. You need to sleep."

Cool wind ruffled my hair. I didn't want to go back in. I needed to watch the landscape zip by. I needed the breeze and the chill to distract me from my feelings—from my fears.

"Copper Rose?"

"I'm fine out here. I—I don't know what to do about you."

He sat next to me, leaning against the rail, and smiled. "Then lets talk. Maybe I will confuse you less if you know what I'm thinking. It's been a lifelong habit for me to hide who I really am."

I scoffed. "Anyone would do that to survive Bromin."

He scooted closer, wrapping a warm arm around my

shoulder. I tensed.

"I only want you to be warm—like in that cave—two nights ago." He squeezed me.

I relaxed into his arm. "Okay."

"Can you clarify something for me?" He tugged the blanket over my shoulder then rested his arm around me again.

"What?" I asked.

"Do you trust me?"

I paused, thinking. What if he didn't like what I had to say? "You don't seem to fight when you should. You back down. What if you back down at the wrong moment?"

He was quiet, staring across the deck.

I looked at him. "Maybe it's because you had to be this way to survive, but now that you're free, can you stand up for yourself consistently?"

"I don't know," he whispered. "But I will endeavor to. I don't want to put you at risk. I don't want to..."

I shook my head. "Alum, your actions can't be about me. The entire team is important. Besides I don't know what we are."

"Yes." He leaned back against the rail, putting his hands in his lap. "We can talk about us—another time."

"My mind is a mess. I don't know what I feel about you. I can't explain what happened with the lightning gun or how Kricky came to life. Can we just rest tonight?" I leaned back and lifted his arm around me. "Help me get my brother home and this trust issue will fix itself."

He pulled me close. "I can manage both."

Kricky's glowing eyes came toward us across the deck. He

330

squeaked in greeting. I rubbed his ears, and he curled up at my feet, closing his eyes. The more I observed the little beast, the more I knew how alive a machine could become. Snores rose from his still form. Alum and I both chuckled.

I laid my head on his chest and felt the rumble of his laughter. He sighed and wrapped his other arm around me. I was beginning to enjoy the peace I felt in his arms. If only I could make sense of what it all meant. Closing my eyes, I breathed in deeply. Sleep. I needed sleep first. Slowly my mind cleared of all my worries. Dreams slipped in to taunt and tease me. Alum's arms would tighten around me, and the eerie images would slip away.

Morning light peaked over the rail. I opened my eyes to the pink tinged sky and Alum watching me.

He stood and pulled me up, my joints aching slightly from the awkward sleep.

Alum stretched his arms. "Good morning." He continued to open and clench his left hand as if trying to regain feeling in it.

We watched each other, peace continuing to blanket us, then Alum's smile dropped, his gaze shifting into the distance. Alum pointed into the fog ahead of the ship.

In the hazy expanse, something large and black stood like a huge table. It was ominous in size, surrounded by a thick valley of mist.

Alum's hands closed around the rail, the ridges of his healing wounds becoming more pronounced. "The CliffSide Fortress. The main entrance is a massive stone lip jutting out from the cave opening. The roof is tall enough for full-sized ships to berth there." He paused. "Bromin's men can see anything coming for miles around. Our only chance of making it to the back of the plateau is through the fog."

I blinked rapidly hoping the view would change. "But can't he detect ships in the mist?"

"No."

I looked at Alum, curious.

He sighed. "It isn't a normal fog. It dampens electrical signals and can even shut down any machines that run on electricity."

"How?" This world never ceased to amaze me. "Is it naturally occurring or did Bromin..."

Alum grinned. "I don't know. Your curiosity is voracious."

I narrowed my eyes at him, and held back a smile. "I'll go tell Venrick we need to switch to steam." I started to walk away, but Alum put his hand over mine, pinning it to the rail.

"When we get through this—we talk." He squeezed my hand then released it.

I nodded, a tingle going up my spine. Then I walked to the front of the ship to find Venrick.

Chapter 28

Stealth was the key to this entire rescue. Stealth was the only thing going for us. HazeValley was less of a valley and more of a labyrinth of fog-glutted ravines between snaky stone plateaus. We were forced to wind slowly through the ravines to avoid detection by Bromin's patrols. The deeper we got, the thicker and higher the fog formed, until we were able to leave the stone passages and float through the misty air.

A buzz came from above us.

Venrick switched off his small light. "Douse the lights." A dark shape appeared above the fog, highlighted by sunlight. It was one of Bromin's scudders. I crouched, wrapping my arms around Kricky. He froze, almost lifeless. Everyone cringed, not moving as our ship drifted. Cold mist hugged us and a shiver ran through me. Moments passed like long, laborious steps. The patrol above us circled twice—three times then flew away. I exhaled and released Kricky. His sudden movement startled me. He flipped his tail and chirped as if to laugh.

The fog bank increased in height as we continued on. Most the lights were kept off, but some were still casting spectral shadows across the deck. The ship went deeper and deeper.

All the lights flickered, then vanished leaving us in a dim ghostly realm of endless grey.

"It's the fog." Xiren pulled out his small flashlight and

flicked the switch. The blue light wavered and fizzled. As the drear increased, all the electrical lights on the ship blinked off.

"Will our lights work in the fortress?" I mumbled to Alum.

He bent his head close to my ear. "They only fail in the mist. Don't worry."

I hurried to my quarters. Barely enough light touched the room. I gathered my gear into a pack and hoisted my stealth skywings over my shoulder. Back on deck I went to the prow where Drenth and Xiren waited, their gear piled along the rail.

Alum clipped one of the round metal body-signal defusers onto my collar. Then he walked back to the pilot and stared down at the black box in his hand. The little arm inside shifted and jumped as we moved onward. The sound of patrols became more and more distant until we could no longer hear any enemy ships skimming over the fog.

No one aboard made a sound. Even the ship seemed to know it had to be quiet as the ropes swung soundlessly. We crept along, time appearing to slow.

A black wall of stone appeared a few yards to the side of us. The ship's skin altered hue to match the rock. The wall curved and we followed, Hope's Wings gliding smoothly like a bird. Patches of hardy vines appeared at intervals, hanging like ragged curtains. They only added dingy green to the otherwise black and grey landscape.

Alum was leaning over the rail, scrutinizing each dip in the cliff and outcropping of vines. Around a deep bend in the rock he pointed, gesturing repeatedly at the wall where a black hole gaped. The ship slowed to a stop.

Without a word Alum, Pak, Xiren, and Drenth picked up

their skywings and packs. I tightened the straps of my skywings over my coat to prevent it from shifting. Several curls escaped my ponytail. I brushed them away with a huff. If only those curls would stay out of my way. I tightened a belt of pouches around my waist. The compartments were filled with power cartridges for the lightning gun, first aid items and water. I grasped the locket and tucked it into my shirt.

I was ready.

I leaned close to Venrick. "Don't let Kricky loose."

"Captain, I know what to do." Venrick nodded. "Drenth and Pak have signal chips. Just get back out as fast as you can."

Squeezing his lower arm, I smiled. When I reached the rail my stomach clenched. Pak and Drenth had already flown to the cave. Xiren followed them silently.

I waved for Alum to go, but he shook his head. Grasping my elbow, he helped me up to the small platform on the rail for skywing take-off. A quake rushed through me. I looked back at the crew. Senra was leaning against the far rail, barely visible in the mist. She was watching, her brow creased, until she caught my gaze. Kricky's muffled squeaks came from my room. Shaking her head Senra rushed away.

Sighing, I threw myself off the solidity of the ship. Weightless, my breath caught, my stomach dropped. The wings lifted on a gentle updraft of air, fresh with moisture and the smell of minerals and plants.

I reached the cave mouth, but my foot slipped on the rounded lip. Alum's skywings brushed the cave rim, his arms wrapping around me. He pushed us both into the tunnel.

"Careful there, sweet Copper Rose," Alum said, his warm

lips pressing into the hair near my ear. Fog drifted slowly across the opening as I stepped further down the tunnel.

Alum pulled out a small hand-held device. It looked like a compass without direction marks.

"Put your finger here." He indicated a small circle at the bottom. I pressed my finger onto the spot and felt a tingle of electricity. The arm spun in a circle, pointed at me then jumped in the other direction. "Now it will lead us to your brother."

The arm suddenly jumped to a different direction too fast for my brother to have moved. "What?" Alum fussed with the dial on the side. The arm jumped again back to the original direction. Back and forth it jumped.

"Try again." Alum held it out to me. I pressed my finger on again, holding it longer. Doubt crept into my mind. The arm balanced back to a single direction and remained steady. Alum touched my shoulder then slipped past me to the front, flipping on his small blue light. Like fireflies, other dim lights sparked to life. I fumbled with my flashlight. It flickered and dimmed until I stepped deeper into the cave, away from the unusual mist.

The tunnel wound and curved sometimes forcing us to duck, other times we slipped down damp declines. The dark was ever-present with the shuff, shuff, shuff of our feet on stone and the ominous echo of dripping water. Alum held up a hand. He gestured to the left. Other paths veered off, but Alum seemed to know where he was going. At first I thought my eyes were deceiving me. The walls seemed smoother. Then there was noise—or was that another echo off dead stone and water?

Our flashlights flickered off, one by one. Ahead, pink light colored the tunnel. Alum stuck a metal pod onto the stone by the ElectriShield. He scooted it forward until it reached the edge. The light flashed then fizzled and vanished. I suppressed a grin. Hope swelled in me. *Gad here we come to get you.* The first shield was down revealing a hallway on the other side. How many more to go?

Drenth waited by the shield disrupter until I passed. He cautiously slipped it off the rock. The pink curtain sizzled back into place. My hands were sweating as we continued. The walls, floor and ceiling were lined with metal. Light emanated from a groove along the top edge of the walls.

A look of confusion crossed Alum's face. He shook the blood code detector. Then pointed down the hall. What if the blood code device failed to get us to Gad? I shook off my worry.

At each switch from hallway to tunnel he deactivated shields and Drenth followed last to remove it. The tunnels were taking us up, up, up, until the backs of my legs ached from climbing. The folded-up skywings felt heavy and my mouth was pasty despite sips from my water bottle.

The lack of anyone from the fortress made me nervous. Where would this army of workers, inventors and soldiers be? This was too easy, too much like the first rescue attempt.

Alum stopped suddenly at a bend in the tunnel. Xiren stepped on my toe as he lurched back. I squelched a yelp, and rushed back quickly, freezing against the wall.

Clop, clop, clop, clop…

People were approaching quickly from the tunnel ahead. The pink glow of the shielding painted the ground and hid the hall from our view. I dared not move a muscle. The sound increased, stopping not far from us.

"Did you get anything on your monitor?" a man said. "I was

sure there was a blip." I held my breath. They were only feet away on the other side of the shield.

Alum was pressing a disk in his fingers, his eyes closed and sweat beading on his lip. I touched the round defuser clipped on my collar. *We're not here. We're not here.*

Something was tapping like a fingernail on glass. "No. It must have been a short in the shielding. That dreadful mist is still getting in through the south ventilation shafts," a gruff voice said.

One of them grunted and they walked away.

The moment the buzz of the shield was the only sounds, Alum hurried forward to disrupt it. We entered yet another metal-lined hall. This one was different, though. Catacombs of stone and metal surrounded us. Some doors were made of bars, but others were solid metal with only a slit at handle level.

"Where would he be?" I whispered. Drenth shrugged. We went a few more yards down the widening hall then stopped. Sweat trickled down my brow.

Alum and Drenth stepped around the corner. A strangled yell echoed through the winding prison. Alum and Drenth came back, each dragging an unconscious soldier. We helped carry them into an empty cell, pushing the door closed behind them.

The men spaced themselves along the corridor.

"Your brother will be in the back." Alum grabbed my hand and hurried me to the end of the cell block.

We stopped in front of a metal wall. A break in the metal shaped like a door caught my eye. This was the door? There was no slit or handle. It looked like solid wall. How would we get my brother out—if he was even in there? Alum stood there, flexing his left hand open and closed, staring at the smooth door. I rubbed my hands over the surface. My stomach tightened. I couldn't get in. Alum put a hand on my arm and I stepped back. He was calm.

He placed his palm flat on the door. At first nothing happened, but then there was a series of small clicks and it popped open an inch. I grabbed the lip and pulled. The thick metal fought my attempt to swing it open. Alum added his strength until we were able to open it enough to get through. The room was dark, but I could hear slow breathing.

"Gad?"

Switching on the blue light, I stepped in, holding it out in front of me, anxious, hoping. A metal slab, not unlike the one I had lain on at the palace, was sticking out from the barren wall. A curled-up figure lay on the slab with it's back to me. The person cringed away from the light. I reached out, my throat aching, but pulled my hand back.

"Gad?"

He jerked around. Dark hair fell in his eyes, but despite the split lip and swollen eyes, my brother's face was unmistakeable. One eye was so bruised Gad couldn't open it. The shirt he wore was dingy and torn. I rushed over, wrapping my arms around him. "Gad. Oh Gad. We found you. Can you get up? We have to get you out of here."

"Mmmm." He groaned, trying to stand. Alum helped him up from the other side. Gad looked at him warily, but nodded and tried to take a step. His breath hissed through his teeth and he pulled the foot back up. We helped him out of the cell, holding most of his weight off the injured foot. Gad pulled away from

Alum and me, limped forward. He grew steadier with each step.

"Can he do this?" Xiren shook his head, brows pulled together.

Drenth reached out to take Gad's arm.

"I—can." Gad pulled himself up straighter. Each halting step he took seemed to loosen up joints, stiff from injury and disuse. "Must—hurry. Must…"

Alum followed close to Gad, who exited the prison behind Pak and Drenth. I let my breath escape. Now to get Gad out. If our luck held we could get back to the ship unnoticed.

Drenth and Xiren pulled out their lightning rods, knocking the bottom of the handles to charge the power cell. A low crackling hum issued from the guns as the electrical current charged the chambers. Alum took the lead again while the other men surrounded me and Gad. Drenth took up a position behind me, his gun at the ready.

We managed to get back to the level we entered on, though we were going slower this time. No one crossed our path. Alum sighed in relief when he found the tunnel that led to where Hope's Wings was hiding in the mist. He deactivated the shield and slipped in, but Gad started mumbling and continued down the metal hall. I reached for him. "This way Gad."

"Stop him," Drenth whispered harshly.

I grabbed Gad's arm, but he shoved me away. "Gad? Gad. This is the way out. You have to follow Alum."

He shoved me again, still stumbling down the hall. "No, no —mu—have to get…" He dashed away with a burst of strength. Alum ran past me to head him off, but Gad managed to turn into another passage. We all chased after him.

Gad, no longer limping, slipped out of sight down yet another corridor.

"Must—must find..." he called out.

We sped around the corner into a large cavern of a room, lit from high above as if many skylights were somehow directing the sun into the deep recesses of rock. Gad was standing in the middle of the room looking at the dozens of hallways that sprouted off like spider legs.

I caught up to him right after Alum. Gad was pushing at Alum, mumbling incoherently again.

"Gad—you have to come back with..." I took his hand.

"What is this?" a familiar voice echoed across the room. I turned, my heart dropping. Bromin walked slowly toward us from a larger corridor, guards on either side of him. I winced at every click of his boots on the textured metal floor.

He stopped, a smile spreading across his smooth face. "Copper Rose! Have you come to be reunited with family? How touching."

Electricity arced from lightning guns, colliding into Bromin. Blinding light engulfed him. I squinted against the sizzling charges, but Bromin only smiled with ecstasy, his arms raised above him as the bolts seemed to absorb into him. The weapons fizzled, leaving the room quiet and dark. My vision cleared, my heart pounded as if we were still running down the corridors.

Bromin, unharmed, stood smirking at us. I pulled out my weapon, pointing it two-handed at him. My jaw clenched and quivered, but my arms were steady.

He threw back his head and laughed. "Mmmm. That was

nice of you to lend me some energy. With your weapons powered down, we can get to the business of putting you all into prison cells where you belong."

Chapter 29

My eyes were glued on Bromin. The malevolent GearMade was blocking us from going back the way we came, the way out of the fortress. I glanced at the many tunnels leading off of the room. Which would take us to safety?

Bromin took a step forward. "And Alum, my pet, I thought you were dead. That last treatment should have been enough. How did you escape? Maybe you are more skilled than you ever let on. Obviously I was too easy on you."

Alum gulped.

"Brom...in," Gad shouted. "He did it. He took her. He..." Gad seemed to falter, his shoulders sagging, his legs losing their strength. Alum caught Gad's arm over his shoulder as I did the same, leaving Gad crooked, but stable, between us. Alum's eyes dashed about, his lightning rod pointed directly at Bromin. I lifted up my weapon slowly, a slight tremor in my arm.

"How do we get out?" I mumbled to Alum. All of us kept our guns pointed at Bromin and the soldiers.

Bromin shook his head, his smile growing larger. "I am starting to think that the Steele and Locke family is a little more trouble than I need. Maybe we should dispose of the more useless of you in order to keep the talented ones in line." Bromin lunged forward. His soldiers pulled out laser guns and started shooting. A bolt seared through Pak's chest and he fell, smoke rising from the blackened circle on his chest. I winced, heartsick—another man down. A good man.

Xiren wheeled around, shooting at the soldiers recklessly, but hitting none of them. Alum pulled Gad away from me, threw him over his shoulder and ran to a tunnel on our left.

One of Bromin's soldiers had a squirming Drenth pinned around the neck. I lifted the gun one handed, held my breath and fired. The straight lightning bolt hit the arm holding Drenth, scorching it black. The soldier fell to the ground, writhing and screaming. I fired into the soldiers again with a spray of bolts.

Drenth ran after Alum. "Xiren, Rose, hurry."

The young man looked around, bewildered, then sprinted after Drenth.

"Run, Copper," Alum yelled from the tunnel.

I followed at a dead run, glancing back. Bromin was yards away, still unaffected by the lightning bolts we sent into the guards. I charged up the tunnel as Alum pulled Gad through a doorway several yards down the hall. Once we all sped through, Drenth shoved the double-door shut and flipped a latch in the middle. Xiren dropped to one knee and pointed his gun up at the small window in one of the doors. The room was all white with doors on every wall.

Alum was looking back and forth between the exits, his face scrunched at sharp angles. "Which…"

Bromin collided into the metal door, eyeing us through the window. "Copper Rose. There is no escape for you. I know my fortress better than anyone. If you do as I say your family will be safe. Open the door." He pounded and the hinges creaked.

Another pound and a dent appeared. For a moment I was frozen in fear. Gad was lying on the floor, possibly unconscious and Alum didn't seem to know where to lead us.

Stiffly I reached down to touch Gad's shoulder. His brown eyes flickered open. There was a pleading in his glassy gaze that wrenched at my insides. "Gad. We'll get out."

Boom!

Bromin stared at me through the still intact door window. "Copper Rose." He crooned in a sing-song voice causing a shiver up my spine.

"Alum, how do we escape?" I asked.

"Ahhhhhhh!"

We all jumped. A black-haired man in a long grey coat was standing in a door. He dropped a roll of papers. They fluttered across the floor around us. He ran back the way he'd come. The single door swung back and forth, blowing the papers over to Gad. He opened his eyes, blinking rapidly. Suddenly he focused on the papers, his mouth falling open.

Boom, boom. The hinges of the locked doors groaned against Bromin's fists. A crack traveled up it.

"Oh no." Xiren shifted away from the metal door. "We'll have company soon."

Drenth hauled Gad up and looked to me.

Alum opened the swinging door. "We have to go this way. Keep running. The only way out now is through the front."

"Papers." Gad pointed at the fallen items. "Get—papers." His voice was rough. He was acting so strangely. What did Bromin do to him?

Bending over, I answered, "I will." Gad allowed the men to

help him through the door. I glanced at the papers. They were a design for a machine, but why would Gad want them? Quickly I shoved them into a pocket then hurried along after the group. The pounding of Bromin's fists grew faint.

We entered a laboratory. Workers dressed similarly to the man were milling around their work tables in confusion. A crash of metal shook the walls behind us.

"Go, go, go go," I screamed, plowing through the crowd toward a door on the opposite side. I shoved a few of the workers aside to make room for Drenth and Gad. My brother's agitation increased while his eyes rolled around wildly. Pushing, shoving, we made it through the room.

Alum led us through another hall, leaving the chaos behind. We raced up a level, then down a wide long hallway, pushing past clueless workers. Passages spread out in dozens of directions, intersecting or splitting off unpredictably. We ran and ran, firing at soldiers. But each route only led to another passage or another squad we had to fight off. Any moment Bromin could appear.

"We can't keep on like this," I said while shooting around a corner at the last group of soldiers. My aim was getting weak. Gad lay on the floor behind us.

Alum's chest heaved with every breath, sweat trickling down his brow. "I—I can't find the way. We took a wrong turn— I think. It seems different."

Scooting over, I put a hand on Gad's forehead. His skin was hot to the touch and his breathing was growing erratic. He mumbled, shaking his head, delirious.

I sighed. "Can't we find the front entrance? Did someone

346

send the signal to Venrick?"

Drenth dropped a power cartridge to the floor and popped another into his gun. "Mine broke."

Xiren looked at me. "Pak had the other one."

Dread sank into my gut. What could we do? Even if we could get to the front entrance of the fortress, there would be no one there to pick us up. I bowed my head. Bromin was actively hunting us and we were nowhere near finding a way out. Before the end more people would be dead—or worse.

"In here," someone called out from behind us.

I spun around, my lightning rod aimed at the woman leaning out of a thin passage. Kricky jumped up and down by her side.

"Senra?"

A laser light shot over my shoulder from further down the hall. Senra spun around, crouched and fired her weapon, taking down several soldiers running up behind us.

I grabbed Alum's arm and dashed over, while Senra continued to send a crackling lightning arc into the oncoming soldiers. Drenth and Xiren shot a few times around the corner, lifted Gad up and hurried into the hallway. Darkness surrounded us as we approached a door at the end. Senra shot a last arc of electricity at the ceiling. Stone and wood crashed down to block us in.

"What was that for?" Xiren shouted, covering his head as the dust drifted toward us.

"A dead end?" I whispered.

Alum smiled, pulling the door open. We all slipped into a large, dimly-lit room. Senra and Kricky entered last.

Stacks of chairs stood near the door. The room was a maze of cabinets standing back to back. Some sat open, cleaning supplies or tools sitting on the shelves in orderly fashion. Others were chained shut. Alum led us to the back of the room where a few cabinets rested against the unfinished back wall.

Drenth gasped for breath "Senra, where did you come from?"

"It occurred to me that you louts might need some help." She cuffed Xiren on the shoulder and he ducked away. "There's an opening in the back, like the beginnings of a door. It leads to an unfinished part of this pit. Kricky found it—and you."

Alum looked behind a cabinet and grinned. "Yes, the unfinished cavern. Bromin intends to turn it into..." His expression dropped and he looked at me, nervous.

I watched him, narrowing my gaze. Yet more evidence he was unwilling or perhaps afraid to tell me everything. I shook my head, turning to Senra. "Can we use it to get out?"

"Yes," Alum said. Kricky, sniffing the ground, wandered over to the cabinet, then disappeared behind it.

Senra pursed her lips and stepped toward the cabinet. "Venrick may not exactly be aware that I am here." She tugged on her skywing straps.

I leaned closer. "What do you mean?"

She shrugged. "They're still expecting you behind the fortress. Maybe they'll figure out that we had a bit of a detour. We can always use skywings to fly over the top of this big black rock to get to them."

"Well." I sighed. "Alum, can you lead us?"

Alum pursed his lips. "Yes. We have to hurry though. This

isn't the only way into the cavern. They are going to find us before long." He rubbed his left arm, glancing toward the hall. I couldn't tell what he was thinking from the stricken expression on his face, but I could guess. He stood up, nodded and slipped behind the cabinet.

Drenth and Xiren hoisted Gad higher on their shoulders then, dragging his feet, followed. I scooted into the large gap in the wall. There was enough space for us to carefully pass Gad through. The dark stone room beyond seemed to go on and on. The outer wall of the building stretched into the distance opposite the cavern's rough stone. We had to watch our footing on the bumpy, rock-strewn ground. Black fell over us like a blanket of ink. I pulled out my light and switched on the blue glow. Lights appeared around me, casting an eerie gleam on each face.

Alum waved Drenth and Xiren forward with Gad. Senra took the lead and we walked as quickly as we could through the terrain. Spots of light blinked in the dark recesses of the cavern. Fireflies? They piqued my interest for a moment, yet I trudged on.

Alum was close beside me. I looked up at him as we hurried along. His silver eyes seemed to glitter.

"If we don't make it out…" I said.

He looked down at me with a soft smile, then his head shot up at the sudden sound of muffled voices behind the wall. "Hush."

Everyone froze. Holding a finger to his lips, Alum pointed for us to continue forward.

We tiptoed between the boulders, Alum looking behind us

nervously. He put his hand on the small of my back to guide me. The red lines of scabs puckered around his eye. "I think—I think they may have figured out where we are."

Drenth looked back, his eyes wide. He nodded, then hurried Xiren and Gad forward. Alum rushed to help them. Echoes started bouncing around the cavern, a dizzying cacophony.

"Keep moving!" Alum waved Senra on. "Douse the lights."

Twisting the flashlight, my sweaty palm slipped. I tried again and it blinked out, plunging me into complete black. I stepped cautiously forward on the uneven floor, my arms in front of me. "Alum?"

No one answered. I suppressed a groan and stepped—stepped... Still nothing. Edging sideways, my hands didn't connect with anything. The dark pressed in on me, oppressive, consuming. The noise bouncing off the chamber walls was growing more organized. The soldiers would find me soon.

"Keep moving, men—men—men."

Flickers of light ricocheted around only to disappear again, but it was enough for me to find the corner where the others must have gone. I went faster, but tripped. My knees throbbed and palms stung. I lifted myself up, shaking, and started forward again, shuffling with my arms out in front of me. Spots started dancing in my vision. I filled my lungs, holding the air, before slowly releasing it.

I could get there. I could do this. I would never again be a prisoner to Bromin. Time stretched, warped. Were the soldiers getting closer? I couldn't tell from the echoing noises.

Another shout echoed through the cavern. I spun around

and someone grabbed my hand. I yelped. Arms wrapped around me, a hand covering my mouth.

"Let me go," I demanded through the large palm. A warm smell of metal and spice filled my nose.

"It's just me," Alum said in my ear. "The others are near an opening at the front. We need to catch up." He slowly pulled his hand off my mouth, his fingers lingering momentarily.

Light again flared, reflecting off the wet cave ceiling. Alum pulled me around a corner.

"Krrrrr.... Tck, tck."

Alum jumped slightly then looked down. Two soft lights glowed near our feet. Large ears framed the eyes.

I put a hand up to my beating heart. "Oh, goodness. Kricky."

The little beast yanked on my leg.

"He wants us to follow him." I grabbed Alum's hand. "Show us."

Kricky scrambled forward. We ran along by the dim light of his eyes. He led us around another corner. Senra's gun was pointed at us. The men were close behind her.

Senra gasped, lowering her weapon. "It's you! Where have you two been?"

Xiren leaned forward, looking down at Kricky. "That creature is pretty smart." Kricky dashed past them, turning to chitter urgently.

"Follow him," Alum said. "He'll show us the way out."

Senra moved out immediately after Kricky. Drenth heaved Gad over his shoulder and ran at a lumbering pace, Xiren close behind. Alum didn't let go of my hand as we sprinted forward.

Stomp, stomp, stomp…

The soldiers were getting closer. We kept running toward a sliver of light in the stone. Kricky reached it and jumped through. I sprinted over and I peaked out.

We were a few ship lengths from the sunbathed lip of rock extending out into the misty valley. Ships large, small and covered in armor rested in cradles along each wall. The massive cave led back a mile to the opening of the fortress. Black rock loomed stories above casting a dark shadow over the shipyard in front of the entrance.

Few workers were in the shipyard, but a row of guards stood at the large metal gates. They were far enough away and seemed to be unconcerned with the tumult inside. The stretch to the rock edge would be a long run. I groaned. A very long run.

Xiren rubbed his neck. "But how do we get to Hope's Wings?"

I reached up to my shoulder strap and tapped the release cord on my skywings.

"Ah." Xiren turned back to the opening. I scratched my chin. How would we be able to fly carrying Gad? Would we survive the entire drop to the valley floor, flying blind and overweighted? I breathed out through my nose, my jaw clenched.

Senra pulled her head back in. "The patrol guards seem to be keeping people from exiting, but aren't paying attention to the shipyard." She fiddled with the release cord on her shoulder.

I scooted over to Drenth. "Can you manage?" I reached out to my brother.

Drenth adjusted Gad on his shoulder. "He'll be safe. I promise."

Senra cocked her head, looking at Gad's unconscious face. I caught a hint of worry and compassion in her eyes, but it was fleeting. She ducked through the opening with Kricky close behind.

"Now," she whispered back to us. Xiren scrambled through.

Drenth heaved Gad over his shoulder again and ducked out the crack. Alum clasped my hand, pulling it to his lips. He kissed it and, squeezing, let go. I slipped out, looking back only long enough to make sure Alum was with me.

The dark shadow masked us for a few minutes. My legs trembled as I ran, my breath a storm of gasps.

Not much further—not much further.

Senra and the men sped into the light, but still so far from the edge. Senra popped open her wings. They lifted her and she ran in long leaps. Kricky dashed along with her, his ears flat against his head. Drenth was lagging behind them under the weight of my brother. I wanted to help, but Alum and I were still in the shadow of the cave roof.

A man appeared around a large vessel near us. "Hey! Stop."

Noise erupted from the main entrance. Soldiers were leaping into air-skimmers or running after us. Laser fire bounced off the rock, singeing the wood ships.

Two small ships zoomed past the opening, drawing the soldier's laser fire. Had Hope's Wings come around the front or were Bromin's air patrols back to help?

I ran out from under the stone roof, no sign of Hope's Wings in the sky. Blinding light covered me. I shook my head, blinking fast until my vision cleared. Senra was leaping off the edge, her wings spread like an eagle's. Xiren skidded to a stop, and threw open his wings, but a laser bolt pierced through the fabric.

"Go!" I yelled at him. He looked at the hole, rubbed his burnt arm and followed Senra. Drenth was still yards from the edge, struggling to carry Gad.

More soldiers spilled into the light, firing indiscriminately. I ducked and wove, fumbling for my pull cord. Another air-skimmer buzzed over the soldiers. Yellow laser bolts rained down, nearly hitting me several times. Drenth laid Gad at the drop-off and sagged. He pulled out his weapon and aimed into the on-coming soldiers.

Gad screamed out, as a laser seared across his face.

"Gad!" I sprinted. "Gad!"

I crouched down next to my brother. He was writhing in pain, a bloody line stretching from his eye to his collar bone. The ragged edges of flesh were blackened. Drenth was shooting wide crackling beams of lightning across the stone expanse.

Alum also fired into the soldiers, taking out several each time. "Quickly—Drenth. We can overlap wings and..."

A beam of yellow seared across Alum's arm. He stumbled back—his foot slipping, slipping—and he was gone.

"Alum!" I leaned over the edge. Alum had fallen into the mist.

Drenth pulled Gad up. "He'll get his wings open. We have to go. Cover me."

I steadied myself and started firing a spray of lightning tendrils back and forth to keep the soldiers back.

Drenth wrapped a belt around Gad and him, threw open his wings and dove off the edge. I opened my wings, still firing. Bromin stood near the cave overhang, his eyes boring into my soul. He waved me toward him and smiled. I shook my head. "Never," I said, even though he wouldn't hear me. Why did he think I would go back to him when my father and brother were safe? I would never go back to Bromin.

"Kreeekish?"

Kricky yanked at my pant leg. I reached down, hugged Kricky around his middle and jumped off the ledge praying the dread would be washed away by the wind pelting past me.

Chapter 30

Open air...

I was falling—falling. My breath stuck in my throat. A breeze caught the skywings, lifting Kricky and me on the swell. My belly flopped and quivered. The locket seemed to click louder along with the beating of my heart. I scanned the foggy air for the figures that should be there. I couldn't see anyone in the thick mist. Where was Alum? Did Drenth manage to get Gad to safety?

The tumult of noise from the fortress vanished, leaving heavy, unnerving silence. I dipped into the fog, my head spinning from the void. Fat tendrils of mist drifted around me, clinging, grasping. I kicked at it. Kricky squeaked and I loosened my tight grip.

"I don't see them. Do you know where they are?"

Kricky looked into the haze, emitting another peep.

What if...?

Whirrrrrrrr...

Droning vibrated my head. I spun around, falling a few feet as my wings pulled close then spread back out. A dark shape rose toward me. Something big. Numbness overwhelmed me. I couldn't go back to that monstrous living machine. I tilted the skywings, catching a breeze that lifted us back out of the fog. I would not meet the enemy blinded and trapped by the noxious fog. The hum of the fortress sounds reached across the expanse to me.

Below, a mast poked out of the drifting mist. If I could just get around the ship then dive deep into the fog, maybe I could escape. I glided further from the cliff. A large dirigible lifted the ship out of the haze. Both Bromin and GearMaker's used that style. A large net hung from two long poles at the bow. Three writhing figures lay in it like flies caught in a web. My stomach clenched. I yanked a control cord on my wings, veering away. How could this be?

The buzz of Bromin's air-skimmers, like a swarm of hornets, jarred my senses. Kricky wiggled, lowering his ears. We had been so close, yet now Bromin had everyone.

"Rose!" A voice lifted on the wind. How could Bromin have reached a ship so quickly?

"Copper Rose."

I paused. It was a gentle voice. One I knew—a voice I could trust. Pulling on the opposite cord, I dropped closer to the ship. A man waved to me as he reached to get Gad out of the net.

My father.

A gasp escaped me. It was a GearMaker ship! I made my way lower and lower to the welcoming ship deck. Drenth and Alum were easing Gad over to Dad and a couple of airmen.

Taking Gad's feet, Dad called out to me once more. Kricky squealed and leaped to the mast as the deck loomed closer. He skittered down it, spiraling around the pole as he went. I laughed, my head raised to the sun.

357

Whop. I landed with bent knees. The ship lifted completely out of the fog, and sped away from the CliffSide Fortress. Three more GearMaker ships encircled us.

Like a murder of crows, more of Bromin's air-skimmers flew from the cave opening. Lightning sizzled from cannon tubes on our deck. The charges crashed into the pursuing air-skimmers. Lightning bolts lit up the fog and trailed across the opening of the fortress cave, sending soldiers scattering for cover. My heart drummed and I laughed.

Dad ran to me, hugging me awkwardly around the outspread wings. "If I had lost you both…"

"How did you get here?" I asked.

He pulled his vest straight. "When I got your note—I was beside myself. I went before the council and…" His eyes twinkled. "I convinced them that they should do the right thing by sending ships to help you. Tenze accused them of denying support to the only person actively fighting Bromin. We tracked you here."

"Oh, Dad." I unstrapped the wings, dropping them to the deck, then hugged my father properly. A mix of anxiety and relief twisted my heart.

He kissed my forehead, then hurried over to Gad.

Thump.

Alum had jumped out of the net leaving his broken skywings tangled in the rope. He scooped me into his arms. "Oh, Copper Rose. We got out. We did it."

I set my cheek on his shoulder, my arms around him. "Yes. We got away." Flutters caressed my insides.

Alum loosened his grip. The corner of his mouth twitched

upward. "This means we can have our talk—about us."

My cheeks warmed. "Uh…"

He kissed my cheek and chuckled.

Gad called out, his voice gravely and barely more than a whisper. "Fa—ther… Go back. Save…"

I let go of Alum, squeezing his arm, and turned. Gad's struggling form was being lifted onto a litter. In the bright light his face was a rainbow of bruises. The burnt skin across his neck puckered and cracked, blood oozing through. I crouched down, gently touching his arm, the only part of him uninjured.

Dad clasped Gad's hand. "Son, I'm here. You're safe. Rest."

"Go back—go—you must…" Gad tried to sit up, but we pushed him back down.

A thud sounded behind me. I spun around to see Senra straightening up from a landing crouch, her wings widespread. She snapped them shut and kneeled next to Gad, her face tense.

A healer dabbed ointment on the laser burn on Gad's neck while we tried to hold him still. The tingle of burnt flesh wrinkled my nose, but I held on until the she finished.

Air-skimmers buzzed. The crackle of lightning cannons continued around us. Airmen bustled across the deck working the cannons and pushing the steam engines for more power. A gust of air rustled my curls, and the shadow of a fourth ship crossed over us. It sped ahead, silent as a bird in flight, and leveled down to lead the group, its skin taking on the blue of sky. Hope's Wings!

"We did it," I whispered.

Worry and triumph jostled inside me. Bromin should have

been able to stop us. Why would he let me go? The look on his face before I jumped didn't make sense. He was self-satisfied, happy even.

Gad rolled over, scrambling away from us over the deck. He shoved the healer, trying to stand.

"Come back," Dad called out.

We ran after him. Gad had unreal strength, shoving airmen aside.

I grabbed his arm and he fell forward onto the deck. "Gad. Please, stop. You have to let us help you."

His skin was hot to the touch and the swollen eye could barely open to a slit.

"He..." Gad moaned, rolling over to face us. "Might kill... Pay—per." I leaned closer, hoping to understand. Was he delirious or...

Dad smoothed a hand across his son's brow, careful to avoid the laser burn. "Who? Who does Bromin have?"

We all waited as Gad writhed. Then he became still, staring past us. I touched his arm. Gad knew something. He had been trying to tell us since we left the prison cell.

"Who?" I frowned.

Gad made eye contact with me, his mouth opening. A soft croaking voice came out. "Pa—pers." Gad grabbed my arm, tugging weakly. He collapsed to the deck and lay still.

"No!" I reached out, shaking him lightly. My heart lurched. He couldn't leave me. I needed my brother.

The healer pressed fingers into his neck. "He's alive."

I bowed my head, breath whooshing out of me.

"What papers?" Dad said, putting his rolled-up coat under

360

Gad's head.

Alum caught my eyes and pointed at the pouch at my waist.

The papers the man had dropped. I wrested them out, tearing one edge. I smoothed them flat on the deck and quickly saw that it was designs for a large device. I flipped a page, then another. A wave of dizziness passed through me. This was a machine made to kill.

"It's a weapon?" Dad's eyes scrunched up, his lips pursed.

I looked over to Dad. "Yes. And from the look of it possibly an extremely destructive one."

"Oh no," Alum groaned, poking his finger at the bottom edge of a page. I ran my eyes down to the smudged letters.

"What does it say?" Dad leaned closer.

Alum face turned ashen, his lips quivering. "I—I never knew. I promise you. I really didn't know."

My eyes bulged, the neat, tight script seeming to magnify in my vision. "It can't be." The name of the designer: *Leatha Locke*.

I grabbed Alum's arm, then shifted away. How could this be? Mom couldn't be in Seranova. She couldn't be with Bromin. She vanished from earth. She could never work for such an evil being. Or did she choose this?

Dad clutched his head. "No—not my love, not my Leatha. No." He jumped up and dashed to the stern. A burning sensation bloomed in my chest. Such pain, such misery; all the results of Bromin's domination of the land.

How could Bromin have kept her for so long? She would never help someone destroy her family, her people. Would she? I hurried after my father, tears streaming down my face. "Dad?"

He stood at the rail, moaning, tears flowing freely. My

361

breath came in jumpy spurts. The dark fortress receded into the distance. The three support ships had fallen back to continue the battle against Bromin's ships. The lasers and lightening channels collided in the air.

"So long I have wondered, so long I've waited. We must go back. We have to save her." He pounded the rail with a fist. Dad turned, his eyes red. "How can I leave her?" His voice quavered. He wilted, leaning against the rail.

Mom was alive and in his control. My fingernails bit into my palms. I glared through the fireworks, wishing I was face to face with Bromin.

"We can't. We won't." I put my hand over Dad's.

"This is not over." I clasped the locket in my other hand, the pulse and click of the gears vibrating against my skin. Only one path was clear.

"Bromin is going to find out how big a mistake he made."

The End

About the Author

Shannon L Reagan was raised, always bare foot, in the fertile fields and the crimson forests of Northern California. By the glow of a night light she created puppets and stories to charm her sisters to sleep. As childhood turned to adolescence, like the turning of seasons, Shannon's family migrated north to the magic filled green of the Pacific Northwest. Her puppets and stories grew bigger and her imagination thrived in the lush countryside. Through the years Shannon followed a path to both coasts working with costumes, props and scripts for the stage then on to writing novels while caring for her unflagging children.

Shannon will continue to bring to life the stories in her mind and the characters that need a voice.

Acknowledgements

I could not have written this without the ever constant support of my husband, David, as I came and went to writers group and Grediaya.

Thank you Leanne for your wonderful costume ideas and your support. Without your steampunk locket there would be no GearMaker's Locket.

Sharon, Kathy, Jean and Kathleen. This book is alive because of your incredible insights into every aspect of my book. You are the best Writers Group ever.

My thanks to Abney Park, the steampunk band: the soundtrack in my ears and the inspiration for the story in the first place.

Made in the USA
Charleston, SC
28 November 2015